Jill Saudek was born in Oxford in 1946 and grew up in Marlow. She studied English Literature at Newnham College, Cambridge and became an English and drama teacher in various schools. She retired in 2009 and now lives in South London.

In memory of my father, who loved reading aloud to his children.

Jill Saudek

The Mind's Eye

Stories to be Read Aloud to Children

AUSTIN MACAULEY PUBLISHERS
LONDON * CAMBRIDGE * NEW YORK * SHARJAH

Copyright © Jill Saudek 2025

The right of Jill Saudek to be identified as author of this work has been asserted by the author in accordance with sections 77 and 78 of the Copyright, Designs and Patents Act 1988.

All rights reserved. No part of this publication may be reproduced, stored in a retrieval system, or transmitted in any form or by any means, electronic, mechanical, photocopying, recording, or otherwise, without the prior permission of the publishers.

Any person who commits any unauthorised act in relation to this publication may be liable to criminal prosecution and civil claims for damages.

This is a work of fiction. Names, characters, businesses, places, events, locales and incidents are either the products of the author's imagination or used in a fictitious manner. Any resemblance to actual persons, living or dead, or actual events is purely coincidental.

A CIP catalogue record for this title is available from the British Library.

ISBN 9781035803026 (Paperback)
ISBN 9781035803033 (ePub e-book)

www.austinmacauley.com

First Published 2025
Austin Macauley Publishers Ltd®
1 Canada Square
Canary Wharf
London
E14 5AA

With many thanks to all my small relatives who showed me the power of the mind's eye.

Table of Contents

Sam and the Moon Dog   15

  Chapter 1: The Little Dog!   17

  Chapter 2: The Jumping Cow   19

  Chapter 3: The Dish and the Spoon   22

  Chapter 4: Sleepus?   25

  Chapter 5: Wakus!   28

  Chapter 6: The Fiddling Cat   31

  Chapter 7: In the Car   34

  Chapter 8: Jemima the Cow   37

  Chapter 9: Suki the Cat   40

  Chapter 10: Home Again   43

  Chapter 11: Daddy's Coming Too!   45

  Chapter 12: Swimming   47

  Chapter 13: The Milky Way   49

  Chapter 14: Morning   51

  Chapter 15: The Violin   53

  Chapter 16: Stuck!   55

  Chapter 17: Rescued!   57

  Chapter 18: Sailing to School   59

  Chapter 19: Milkie   61

Chapter 20: Marmite and Toast	63
Chapter 21: Dandelions	65
Chapter 22: Hay	67
Chapter 23: Teddy	69
Chapter 24: Urs	71
Chapter 25: Ursula	73
Chapter 26: Breakfast	75
Chapter 27: In the Garden	77
Chapter 28: Granny Is Surprised	79
Chapter 29: What a Mess!	81
Chapter 30: Bathtime	83
Chapter 31: Urs Is Cross	85
Chapter 32: A Lovely Day for Sailing	87
Chapter 33: Where Can She Be?	89
Chapter 34: Who Pulled Her Out?	91
Chapter 35: Bye!	93
Chapter 36: Moon-Day	95
Chapter 37: Splash!	97
Chapter 38: Swimming Again	99
Chapter 39: The Birthday Tea	101
Chapter 40: The Dark of the Moon	103
Epilogue O Bother That Brother!	105
Charlotte and the Dandelion Fairy	**109**
Chapter 1: Dilly Dilly	111
Chapter 2: The Glass Bottle	114
Chapter 3: Very Small Indeed	117

Chapter 4: Back Again	120
Chapter 5: The Caterpillar	123
Chapter 6: Butterfly Wings	126
Chapter 7: The Two-Headed Bottle	129
Chapter 8: Flying	132
Chapter 9: The Sandpit	136
Chapter 10: Honey Bags	139
Chapter 11: Shopping	142
Chapter 12: The Frog	145
Chapter 13: Cross!	148
Chapter 14: Playing with Dilly	151
Chapter 15: Hiding	154
Chapter 16: Cross Again!	157
Chapter 17: Egg	160
Chapter 18: Nestling	163
Chapter 19: Fledgling	166
Chapter 20: Bird	169
Chapter 21: Talking to Ben	172
Chapter 22: The Dandelion House	176
Chapter 23: Goat	180
Chapter 24: Wet	183
Chapter 25: Night	185
Chapter 26: Breakfast	188
Chapter 27: The Last Day	192
Chapter 28: Sailing	195
Chapter 29: Goodbye	197

Hannah Goes to School — 201

- Chapter 1: The Rabbit — 203
- Chapter 2: The Schoolroom — 205
- Chapter 3: The Singing Lesson — 208
- Chapter 4: Bedtime — 211
- Chapter 5: Run, Rabbit, Run! — 214
- Chapter 6: Can You Dance? — 218
- Chapter 7: The Head — 222
- Chapter 8: Vegetables — 225
- Chapter 9: Digging — 230
- Chapter 10: The Listening Lesson — 234
- Chapter 11: The Yellow-Eyed Cat — 238
- Chapter 12: Friend or Foe? — 241
- Chapter 13: The Warnings — 243
- Chapter 14: Hide and Seek — 248
- Chapter 15: Friend? — 252
- Chapter 16: Turtle River — 255
- Chapter 17: Picnic Time — 258
- Chapter 18: Sunday — 261
- Chapter 19: Rain — 265
- Chapter 20: Flapjacks and Friends — 269
- Chapter 21: The Running Lesson — 273
- Chapter 22: Hunting — 277
- Chapter 23: The Exam — 280
- Chapter 24: Antlers — 285
- Chapter 25: Ben Goes to Animal School — 289
- Chapter 26: The Wild Boar — 292

Chapter 27: Hurtle Goes to Human School	*296*
Chapter 28: The Rabbit Lesson	*298*
Chapter 29: The Human Lesson	*303*
Chapter 30: Poems	*308*
Chapter 31: More Poems	*311*
Chapter 32: Sore Paw	*315*
Chapter 33: Goats and Jokes	*319*
Chapter 34: The Bull and the Bear	*322*
Chapter 35: Tails	*326*
Chapter 36: Cat Tails	*331*
Chapter 37: Chocolate Eggs	*333*
Chapter 38: The Treasure Hunt	*335*
Chapter 39: Late for School	*339*
Chapter 40: Last Day of School	*342*
Chapter 41: Spring Greens	*346*
Chapter 42: Always and Ever	*349*
Epilogue	*351*

Sam and the Moon Dog

Chapter 1
The Little Dog!

Sam woke up suddenly. He opened his eyes. Through the door, he could see a crack of light from the hall; everything else was dark. He listened: something had woken him up! But all seemed peaceful and quiet—just the gentle hum of a car driving down the road—and then silence.

And then, faint but clear in the night—there it was!

"Woof! Woof! Ha-ha; Woof! Woof! Ha-ha; Woof! Woof! Ha-ha!"

It sounded like a little dog…it sounded like a little dog laughing! And the noise was coming from somewhere up in the sky!

It was a warm night and Sam was lying on top of his best blue helicopter duvet. Mummy had left both of the top windows open to let in the air. Sam knelt up on the bed and carefully pulled back one of the curtains. At once, beautiful silver moonlight flooded the room. Sam looked out into the garden. All the trees and flowers and even the grass were shining silver in the moonlight. Sam looked up: yes, there in the sky was an enormous full moon.

It's lovely, thought Sam. I've never seen it so big.

And then, louder and clearer now, came the noise:

"Woof! Woof! Ha-ha." A little dog laughing! But where was it?

As Sam stared upwards at the beautiful silver moon, he saw another silvery circle, a very tiny, fuzzy one, moving fast through the night sky. And it was heading straight towards him! And as it came closer and closer, it seemed to grow bigger and bigger.

By now, Sam was standing on his bed, his little nose pressed against the cool glass of the window, his blue eyes staring. He watched intently as the little silver circle swooped down through the dark air, nearer and nearer. Now he could make out its shape: it was a sailing boat, sailing not on water, as you would expect, but through the night sky! And as it came nearer, he could hear the gentle swish of wind in its silver sails. It slowed, hovering in the air and came to a halt just outside his window. Steering the little boat and holding tight to the tiller with his two front paws, was a little dog, gleaming all over. He had a wagging silver tail, two floppy silver ears and two shining black eyes that were looking right through the window at Sam!

"Such fun," said the little dog quite distinctly. He wagged his silvery tail.

"Can I come in?" he asked in a cheerful voice. And without waiting for an answer, he stepped out of the boat, got his top two paws through one of the little open windows, then his nose and ears—and then, with a wriggle of his head, he came scrabbling through the opening and landed whumf on the bed, right in front of Sam!

"Such fun," he said again and laughed: "Woof! Woof! Ha-ha!"

Sam couldn't help laughing too; the little dog seemed so happy—and it was such a surprising thing to have happened.

"Did you see it?" asked the little dog.

"See what?" said Sam.

"The cow, of course! Jumping! You wouldn't think cows could jump, would you?" And he laughed again.

"No," said Sam. He meant: no, I didn't see it, I was asleep; and no, I didn't know cows could jump. It was all very puzzling. And then, out of nowhere, a tune came into his head and suddenly he remembered:

The cow jumped over the moon;
The little dog laughed to see such fun… .

"**You're the little dog**," he said, "the little dog in the moon!"

"Of course I am," said the little dog. "Who are you?"

"I'm Sam," said Sam. "That's my name."

"Oh," said the little dog, "that's a good name. My name's Loon. Hallo."

"Hallo," said Sam as he stared at the little dog in surprise. A Moon Dog! Whatever next?

Chapter 2
The Jumping Cow

"Come on," said Loon, "let's go and look! The cow will be jumping back again soon."

"Jumping back?" asked Sam. He was still feeling rather puzzled.

"Of course," said the little dog. "She's got to get back to her field by morning. And the quickest way is to jump back over the moon. She'll be off soon. Hurry up, or we'll miss her."

And before Sam could say anything, the little dog opened one of the big windows by Sam's bed. There was the silver sailing boat, hovering just outside – only one little step away.

"Come on," said Loon again; he stepped across the gap into the boat and held out his front paw for Sam.

"I'm coming," said Sam. He felt the warm night air on his face and then there he was, safe inside the silver sailing boat.

"Off we go!" Cried Loon with glee. "Hurrah!"

Sam held on tight as the sails filled with wind and the boat turned and sped through the dark sky, heading straight for the moon. He looked over the edge: there below him he could see the roof and chimney of his house and his road with the red brake lights of a car speeding up it; there was the High Street and the traffic lights, just turning from red to amber to green; he saw Granny's house, dark and still below him and all the sleeping streets of his little town. Sam wondered if he ought to be wearing his new life jacket; but there had been no time to put it on and anyway he felt very safe, snug inside the little boat, with the warm wind softly blowing.

I'm sailing, he thought. Hurrah!

Then he looked upwards—and there, right in front and getting bigger and bigger, was the great silver moon.

As they got nearer, Sam saw that it looked like a huge silvery sea, only made of rock not water, with hills and valleys like rising and falling waves.

"Here we go!" Cried Loon. "Hold on!"

With a gentle bump, the boat settled down on the bottom of a rocky silver valley.

Quickly, the little dog jumped out.

"Come on, Sam." He barked excitedly. "Follow me!"

So Sam did. He clambered out of the boat and ran as fast as he could after the little dog, up and up the steep slope of a silver hill, until, breathless, he scrambled up the last bit to the top.

"Now," said Loon, "the cow should be jumping any minute. Yes, look—there she goes. Such fun!"

He pointed upwards. There was a whoosh of warm wind and a bellowing Mooooo. Sam saw a big black-and-white cow leaping through the air right above his head! Her four legs were kicking, her tail was waving wildly and her black eyes were sparkling!

"Moooo-ooooo," she cried, "here I goooooo! Look at meeeee!" Loon laughed again as he waved his front paw at her in greeting. And indeed she did look rather silly—it was such a huge jump for such a fat cow! Sam laughed too and gave her a great cheer as she disappeared over the edge of the moon, crying, "I'm over the mooooooooooon."

"Hurrah," he said. "Well done, cow. Good jump!"

"She'll be back in her field soon," explained Loon. "She'll have a good sleep and tomorrow no one will know what she was up to."

Sam thought of the farmer, coming to milk her in the morning, with no idea of what his best cow had been doing. He laughed again.

But thinking of the morning made him think of his own little room. He had better get back, so that when Mummy came in with his mug of milkie, she would find him in his bed. And she would have no idea of what he had been up to, either! And nor would Harry, or even Daddy. He wondered if his milkie would have come from the same jumping cow!

"I want to go home now, please," he said.

"OK." Agreed Loon. "It won't take a minute. But it was fun, wasn't it?"

"It was." Agreed Sam.

They climbed back into the silver boat and set sail. Soon they could see the orange street lights of the High Street below them and Sam could make out the flashing green man by Sainsbury's as the boat sailed down and down. And there was his own garden, with the swing all silver in the moonlight…and there was his own little room. Loon landed the boat gently by the window, still open and so easy for Sam to scramble back inside his bedroom.

He knelt up on the bed.

"Thank you, Loon," he said happily. "That was fun!" He reached out a hand and gently stroked Loon's silvery coat. It felt smooth and soft and cool.

"I'll come again, if you like," said Loon.

"Yes please," said Sam, "that would be nice."

Loon carefully pushed the window shut, put his two front paws on the tiller and sailed off into the night sky. Soon, he was no more than a fuzzy silvery ball again—and then he had gone and only the moon was left.

Feeling sleepy all of a sudden, Sam snuggled down under his blue helicopter duvet. "It was such fun," he said to himself as he shut his eyes.

The next moment, he was fast asleep.

Chapter 3
The Dish and the Spoon

"O Harry," said Granny, "what have you done with your orange spoon? I can't find it anywhere!" Harry was Sam's baby brother.

"Hmmmmm," said Harry loudly. He wanted his breakfast and didn't like being kept waiting.

"And where's your Thomas bowl?" asked Granny. "That's gone missing too. Have you seen it, Sam?"

"Perhaps it's in the dishwasher," said Sam.

"No, it's not," said Granny crossly, "I already looked. Humph."

"Rmmmmmm," said Harry impatiently.

"Granny," said Sam, who had been wondering, "why is it called a dishwasher? What exactly is a dish?"

"It's just another word for a bowl or plate," said Granny, who liked explaining things.

"We always talk about washing up the dishes."

"O," said Sam. "I see."

"Grrrrrrrmmmmmmmm," said Harry, who was feeling hungry!

"Well, Harry, you'll just have to use an ordinary teaspoon," said Granny, "and one of Mummy's best yellow dishes. There aren't any others left. But don't drop it."

After breakfast, they all looked for the missing Thomas dish and orange spoon. Sam looked behind the radiator and in his animals' tin; Granny looked in the kitchen cupboards and on the window sills; Harry looked on the CD player and then decided to turn the music on while he was at it. But none of them found the missing things.

"O well," said Granny, "we'll just have to get another dish and spoon in Sainsbury's. And try not to lose them again."

So that is what they did. It was a lovely sunny day and Sam trotted happily beside the buggy, helping to push Harry along and thinking about last night's wonderful moon adventure. He wondered what the little Moon Dog was doing now that it was daytime. He looked up in the sky, but of course there was no sign of the moon now, just a few fluffy white clouds and a dazzling gold sun.

When they got to Sainsbury's, there were lots of people shopping. Granny pushed the buggy around the aisles looking for the baby section.

"I can't see any baby spoons and bowls," she said. "Bother! I'll have to ask the shop assistant."

And it was while Granny was busy talking to the shop lady, explaining exactly what she wanted, that the extraordinary thing happened!

Sam was just seeing whether he could stand up on the back bit of the buggy without tipping Harry over when he heard a familiar noise:

"Woof! Woof! Ha-ha! Woof! Woof! Ha-ha! Woof! Woof! Ha-ha!"

"It's Loon," he said excitedly. But when he looked around, he couldn't see anything. There was Harry, trying to pull his socks off and there was Granny, talking very loudly and fast to the shop lady and there were lots of other people with trolleys and baskets—but there was no sign of a silvery little dog with floppy ears and shiny black eyes.

"Loon," said Sam. "Where are you?"

"Shhhh," came a doggy voice, right next to his left foot. "I'm a secret! You can't see me in daytime, just like you can't see the moon—but we're both there, all right!"

"Wow," said Sam. "But where?"

"Here," said the doggy voice and Sam felt a lovely smooth, cool shiver of doggy hair on his left leg; and then a tickly, tingly warm feeling on his left knee, which must be Loon's little doggy tongue licking him.

"It tickles," said Sam happily and laughed.

"Shhhh," said Loon again. "Don't forget I'm a secret. I'll follow you home, but pretend you don't know I'm there."

"OK," said Sam. He looked up to see if Granny had noticed, but she was too busy looking at spoons to notice much at all.

"Can I tell Harry?" he whispered. "He can't talk properly yet, so he won't give away the secret."

"All right," said the invisible Loon. And he licked Harry's fat little hand, which was dangling over the edge of the buggy. Harry lifted up his chin, screwed up his nose and eyes and chortled with delight!

Sam quickly bent down to tell Harry to be quiet.

"It's a doggy," he said. "But don't tell Granny."

At last, Granny had decided on a red spoon and a blue dish to go with it.

"Come on then," she said. "Let's buy these and then go home. It's time for Harry's sleepus!"

So off they went, back down the High Street to home. Everyone could see Granny, pushing the buggy and Sam trotting beside her in his reins and Harry gurgling happily in the buggy; but no one could see a little silvery dog bounding along behind them and dodging all the people on the crowded pavement.

Chapter 4
Sleepus?

Granny opened the front door.

"Home again," she said, quite cheerfully, considering. "Come on, Harry! It's definitely time for bed."

"Waaaa," said Harry. He didn't want to go to sleep when there was a lovely doggy in the house, especially as he hadn't even seen it yet.

"It's all right, Harry," whispered Sam, "I'll go to bed too! Wait for me in your cot."

So Harry stopped complaining and let Granny carry him upstairs, change his nappy, put him in his blue sleeping bag and lay him gently down in his cot.

"You have a lovely sleepus," said Granny, "and we'll see you later."

When she came downstairs again, she was surprised to find Sam sitting on the bottom step.

"Please, Granny, can I go to bed too?" asked Sam. He almost laughed when he felt Loon's tongue tickling his knees, but he managed to turn it into a yawn instead.

"Well, I suppose so," said Granny, "if you really are tired. Didn't you sleep well last night?"

Of course, Sam had actually been too busy sailing to the moon to get much sleep last night, but he didn't say so. Instead, he said, "Well, it was a bit hot."

"Indeed it was," said Granny. "I didn't get to sleep for ages; it was so hot. And if you and Harry both go to sleep, I might just have a little snoozle on the sofa myself."

So while Granny was busy getting Sam his milkie, Sam whispered to Loon to creep upstairs and wait for him in his bedroom.

"Only not where she might trip over you," he said. "Hide under the bed; quick—behind the cushions, she won't see you there."

So up leapt the little dog into Sam's bedroom.

Granny got the milkie ready in Sam's purple cup. He drank it down quickly and was exceptionally good while Granny took off his shorts and shoes and snuggled him into bed.

"What story would you like?" she asked kindly.

"O, it's all right, Granny, I'm a bit tired. Just one song, please."

"All right." She agreed. She was a bit surprised, as usually Sam wanted lots of stories before he lay down, but she was quite happy to get a move on so she could have her snoozle before Harry woke up. "Which song would you like?" she asked.

"Hey, Diddle Diddle," said Sam at once. He heard a muffled doggy laugh coming from under the bed. But luckily, Granny didn't!

"Here we go then," she said and sang in her usual loud voice:

"Hey, Diddle Diddle,
The cat and the fiddle,
The cow jumped over the moon!
The little dog laughed…"

"What was that?" said Granny, breaking off in mid-song. "I thought I heard a sort of woofly noise under your bed!" And she got down on her hands and knees and peered into the gloom. Sam held his breath. Would she find him? O dear! But of course, Granny couldn't see anything behind the cushions, so she stood up, sat down on the chair and quickly finished the song:

"The little dog laughed to see such fun
And the dish ran away with spoon."

"Well," she went on, "I hope Harry's new dish and spoon don't run away; we don't want to buy anymore! Goodnight, darling Sam."

She gave him a kiss and went down the stairs quietly, so as not to wake Harry.

But Harry was not asleep!

"Waaaa," he began crossly. Sam had said there was a doggy; he had even felt the doggy licking his hand; but where was the doggy now? He wanted to see him. "Waaaa," he continued.

"Come on, Loon, quick," whispered Sam. He slithered out of bed—quietly, so as not to put Granny off her snoozle—and tiptoed over to Harry's room. He could feel Loon's warm doggy breath on his bare legs, although he couldn't see him.

"Shhhhh, Harry, we're coming." He hissed as he opened Harry's door. "Mmmmmmm," said Harry delightedly. And he sat up in his little cot.

Inside Harry's room, it was quite dark because of the green curtains being drawn.

"Sam! Harry! Look," said Loon. "It's dark enough to see me now!"

Sam and Harry looked. Yes, there on top of Harry's bedside table, they could just make out the faint silvery outline of a little moon dog. Hurrah!

Chapter 5
Wakus!

"I can see your shape," said Sam, "but not the middle bit."

"That's right," said Loon excitedly. "You need proper dark to see all of me, but when it's a bit dark, you can see my outline."

"Mmmmmmm," said Harry, standing up in his cot and pointing straight at Loon. Then, to everyone's surprise, he said, "Doggy."

"I thought you said he couldn't talk," said Loon.

"He can't usually," said Sam, "only mumumum noises and a bit of dadadada. And he did say brother once!"

Loon jumped up and down on top of the little table and Harry laughed at the bouncing silvery shape! Then Loon gave a great leap, landing right inside Harry's cot and knocking him down by mistake.

"Ha-ha!" Laughed Loon.

"Waaaa," said Harry.

"Shhhhh," said Sam. "Don't wake Granny."

They all listened, but there was no sound from downstairs. Granny must be asleep on the sofa.

"Now," said Loon, "shall we find Harry's dish and spoon?"

"Do you know where they are?" asked Sam. "Have they really run away together?"

"Yes, I expect so," said Loon. "They often do run off, especially spoons; that's why you can never find any."

"Where do you think they are?" asked Sam. He had already looked in the most likely places.

"Well," said Loon cheerfully, "they like warm, dry, snoozly sorts of places, especially the dishes."

"O," said Sam. He wondered which was the warmest and driest place for hiding. Not the fridge and not the washing machine and definitely not the dishwasher.

Then Harry pulled himself up again and rattled the bars of his cot. He pointed at the bottom drawer of his green cupboard.

"Spooooo," he said. "Di-di-di-di-di!"

"Harry," said Sam. "Do you know where they are? Did you see them hiding?"

"Let's look," said Loon. He loved finding things.

"OK," said Sam. "It will definitely be warm and dry in those drawers. They're full of Harry's clothes."

Sam was used to emptying drawers and got to work at once. Loon jumped out of the cot. He didn't know much about drawers or clothes and he was interested in finding out. Poor Harry couldn't get out of his cot, so he just stood up, rattling the bars and shouting "Spooooo" and "Di-di-d-di" encouragingly.

In no time, the floor was covered with t-shirts and shorts, blankets, towels, socks, sheets and nappies. Loon loved it! He used his teeth to get hold of the clothes and then threw them up as high as he could before they fluttered down and landed in a great pile.

Then: "Look! Look!" Cried Sam. "I've found them!"

Yes, there, huddled up together at the very bottom of the bottom drawer, lay an orange spoon and a blue dish.

"Hurrah," they all shouted happily. (Harry shouted too!)

And Loon barked with glee, "WOOF! WOOF! HA-HA!"

Then Sam remembered. "Shhhh," he whispered, "you'll wake Granny."

But it was too late.

The door swung open and there she was, glowering at them in the dim green light. "Sam," said Granny crossly, "what are you doing in here? You're supposed to be asleep, not awake! You too, Harry. And what was that horrible noise? And what is that mess all over the floor?"

Then suddenly, Granny caught sight of a strange, shining, silvery shape trying to hide underneath the cot.

"And what on earth is that?" she said, bending down to look. But quick as a flash, Sam drew open the green curtains and the room was flooded with daylight. And so, of course, the little dog disappeared from sight. None of them could see him at all (just as you can't see the moon in daylight).

"Doggy," explained Harry helpfully, but luckily, Granny wasn't listening properly.

"It's all right, Granny," said Sam. "We'll tidy it all up! And Harry found his spoon and bowl—look, here they are!"

"Good heavens! Well, I never did!" said Granny. She was so pleased that the dish and spoon had been found that she decided not to be cross about the mess. And she quite forgot about the unexpected silvery shape.

"Go on then," she said. "You and Harry tidy it all up nicely and then you can come downstairs and have some lunch."

She lifted Harry out of his cot and plonked him on the floor. Then off she went down the stairs, carrying the dish and spoon.

"I'll help," came a whispery doggy voice from under the cot. Out he came. And in no time at all, everything was back in its right place.

"Where's your boat?" asked Sam.

"On your roof," said Loon. "I tied it to the chimney. It's all right; no one can see it till it gets dark and everyone's asleep by then."

"Let's have another adventure," said Sam eagerly.

"OK," said Loon. "But I'm going to hide in the bottom drawer now. It looks lovely and warm and I could do with a sleep too. See you later."

Chapter 6
The Fiddling Cat

After lunch (beans on toast), Sam said he wanted to go to bed again.

"Again," said Granny, surprised. Then she remembered that he hadn't had any sleep the first time, so he probably was tired.

"Come on then," she said. "Harry, you'd better stay awake. It's gone half past two!"

Sam ran upstairs and snuggled down into bed all by himself.

"It's all right, Granny, I don't need a story," he said.

"Well, I never did," said Granny. "All right then; see you later."

And off she went downstairs to check that Harry wasn't eating anything.

Sam lay in bed, his little heart beating fast. Would Loon come and see him? Granny had drawn his curtains, so it was fairly dark in the room—enough to make out a silvery outline, he was sure. How excited he was when a few minutes later he heard the patter of tiny paws on the landing and a gentle "Woof! Woof! Ha-Ha!" at the door.

"Come in," whispered Sam and he sat up in bed.

In bounced the little dog; Sam could make out his silver shape quite clearly in the dim light.

"Hurrah," whispered Sam. "You came! What shall we do?"

"Well," said Loon cheerfully, "do you like fiddles? And do you like cats?"

"I do like cats," said Sam. Granny had a beautiful cat at her house and he was very fond of stroking her soft fur. "But what exactly is a fiddle?"

"Oh, a fiddle is just another word for a violin. Do you like violins?"

"I do," said Sam. He remembered listening to music with Granny on the radio; quite often she would shout out the different instruments in her excitement.

"Listen, Sam," she would say, "trumpets! Cello! Drums! Organ! Flutes! Violins!"

"Yes, I do," he said again. "Cats and fiddles!"

"OK then," said Loon. "You wait here and I'll go and get Suki. She's a cat! She plays the fiddle beautifully!"

"All right," said Sam. "Don't be long."

He watched as the little dog leaped up onto the bed, scrabbled up and through the top window and disappeared into the sunlight outside.

I wonder where he's gone, thought Sam. He opened the curtains a bit to peer out, but of course he couldn't see Loon; it was far too bright a day!

So he lay down again and after a bit, he did feel quite sleepy after all, so he just shut his eyes for a moment…Sam woke up with a start. The most beautiful music was playing very quietly! Where was it coming from? And who could be playing? He sat up in bed, blinking.

Of course—the cat and the fiddle! But where was she? And where was Loon?

"Loon?" he whispered. "Where are you?"

"Here I am," said Loon. His doggy voice came from somewhere up above! Yes, there was a silvery outline dog swinging round and round on the mobile, which was hanging down from the ceiling! "Such fun," he added, laughing with glee.

Then he jumped down and landed with a soft whumf on the bed. Sam reached out to stroke his beautiful smooth coat.

"Now," said Loon, "look outside your window."

Sam peeped through the curtain. There was his special garden and there was the swing and his best yellow digger and there was the apple tree—and there, perched high up on the topmost branches, was a dear little cat! And she was fiddling away like anything. She wasn't a silver cat at all; she was deep black with luminous green eyes. She was standing up on two paws and with her other two, she held her violin and bow.

"Isn't she a Moon Cat?" asked Sam. "I thought she'd be silvery like you."

"Oh, no," said Loon. "Suki lives on the farm with the jumping cow. She's just an ordinary animal, not like me."

"Oh," said Sam. He didn't think she was ordinary at all—not playing the fiddle like that! And he didn't think the jumping cow was ordinary either!

"Will she come up and see me?" he asked.

"She's too shy," said Loon. "She loves playing, but she goes all funny if you try to talk to her. It's much better just to listen quietly and not startle her."

So Sam and Loon lay snuggled up in bed together, looking down into the garden and listening to the beautiful music floating through the air.

But they weren't the only ones listening! As Sam lay there quietly, his arm tucked around Loon, he saw Granny and Harry come out into the garden! Granny was carrying Harry. "Listen, Harry," she was saying. "Can you hear that lovely music? I wonder where it's coming from!"

"Ca," said Harry excitedly, pointing at the apple tree! "Ca! Ca! Ca!"

But Granny didn't understand.

"I suppose it must be next door's CD player," she said. "Let's sit on the bench and listen. It's beautiful!"

And so little Suki the cat played her heart out, high up in the apple tree! And Sam and Loon listened from the bedroom and Granny and Harry listened from the garden bench. And when it was all over, everyone clapped. Suki, who was very shy, scrambled down the tree, holding her bow and fiddle carefully; then she scrambled up and over the garden fence – and disappeared.

"Good heavens," said Granny to Harry. "Whatever was that?"

"Ca! Ca," said Harry. But Granny didn't understand.

"Well, I suppose we'd better go and wake Sam," she said. "Mummy won't want him to sleep too long in the afternoon."

And she got up from the bench, carrying Harry and walked towards the house.

"I'd better be off," said Loon. "Goodbye." He gave Sam a lovely warm lick on his bare leg and disappeared out of the top window.

"Wait," said Sam. "Will you come back and see me again?"

But Loon had gone.

I suppose he's up on the chimney, untying his boat, thought Sam, but of course he couldn't see anything. He listened for the sound of doggy paws on the roof, but he couldn't hear any. What he did hear were Granny's heavy footsteps climbing the stairs.

I wonder if I'll ever see Loon again, thought Sam. And Suki the cat. And the jumping cow. I wonder if I'll ever go sailing to the moon again!

"Hello, Sam," said Granny. "You're awake! Did you have a nice sleep?"

"I did," said Sam. "Hello, Granny. Hello, Harry."

"Ca! Doggy! Brother," said Harry!

Chapter 7
In the Car

"Right," said Granny firmly. "Have we got everything? Sam, have you got your fleece? Just in case it gets cold later. Harry, where are your socks? I only put them on a minute ago."

"Mrrrrrrr," said Harry, who had carefully hidden his two stripy socks behind the television.

"He doesn't want to wear them," explained Sam.

"But it might get cold," said Granny again. "I'll get another pair. OK, keep still, Harry and don't fuss. Now, have we got everything?"

Granny had piled up all the important things in the hall. She counted them carefully: "Buggy; spare nappies; rice cakes; purse; keys; picnic; and rug. Right, let's go!"

They were going in Granny's car to Godstone Farm. Sam and Harry were very excited. Harry was looking forward to seeing the ducks and eating sand (there was an excellent sandpit at the farm); Sam was hoping that they might meet the jumping cow and the fiddling cat! After all, Loon, his Moon Dog friend, had told him that they were ordinary farm animals, not moon ones, so they might live there! He wondered where Loon was. He hadn't seen him for ages - at least three days. He did hope that the little dog would come back in his sailing boat to see him again. But meanwhile, it was very exciting to be off to the farm. Sam loved animals!

They all got into Granny's car and off they went. As soon as he was settled, Harry took off his socks, gave them to Sam and fell fast asleep, snoring gently. Sam kindly put the socks in his pocket. It was quite a long way to the farm and after a bit, he fell asleep too. Granny was wide awake, singing loudly as she drove the little car along:

Old MacDonald had a farm

EIEIO!

She didn't know that no-one was listening!

***

Sam woke up suddenly. He felt something soft and cool tickling his right leg! "What's that?" he exclaimed loudly and leaned down to look.

"Shhhhhhh," said a little doggy voice, "she doesn't know I'm here. Woof-woof! Ha-ha!"

"Loon," whispered Sam excitedly.

Luckily, Granny was making such a noise singing, with a miaow here and a miaow there; here a miaow, there a miaow, everywhere a miaow, that she didn't hear anything, but she did notice Sam leaning down in his seat.

"Sit still, Sam," she said. "We're not there yet. And on that farm he had a donkey…" On the darkness of the car floor, Sam could just make out the silvery outline of the little dog. He clapped his hands with glee! Granny thought he was clapping for her singing and was so pleased that she decided to launch into a new song:

"O, the animals went in two by two, the hairy gorilla and the gnu," she sang happily.

"How did you get here?" Sam asked Loon, under cover of the song. "Where's your boat?"

"I tied it to the car roof," explained Loon. "But it's OK, no one can see it while it's daytime and I don't expect there'll be any low bridges."

He gave Sam a lovely warm lick on his legs. It tickled. Sam started to laugh. Granny was very pleased.

"Do you like my song?" she asked. "It's good, isn't it? O the animals went in six by six," she continued, "the crocodile ate the weetabix…"

Then Sam felt a lovely, heavy whumph on his lap. He couldn't see Loon at all, as the bright light came streaming through the car window, but there he was, all right, sitting snugly on Sam's lap. Sam could feel Loon's doggy heart beating quickly and his soft breath on his face.

"Does Suki live on the farm?" he whispered excitedly. "And the jumping cow? Can we see them?"

"Yes, they do—and yes, we can," said Loon. "You can give me a piggy-back and I'll tell you where to find them. Such fun!"

"Not a piggy-back, a doggy-back," whispered Sam. And he laughed aloud!

"I'm glad you like my song," said Granny from the front seat of the car. "O the animals went in eight by eight, the old rhinoceros broke the plate…"

The car slowed down and stopped. They had arrived!

Chapter 8
Jemima the Cow

"Harry," said Granny. "Don't eat the sand!"

She lifted him up and peered into his mouth.

"Waaaaaaaa," said Harry.

"Come on, Sam," said Granny, "we'd better go and look at the animals, or Harry won't have any room left for lunch!"

She plonked Harry in the buggy and strapped him in.

"What would you like to see?" she asked Sam.

"The cows, please," said Sam at once. He heard a soft "Woof! Woof! Ha-ha!" in his left ear. Loon was having a lovely doggy-back and he wasn't at all heavy; only sometimes he tickled!

"All right." Agreed Granny. "I think they're up on the hill."

Some of the cows were peacefully grazing on the green grass, their great mouths munching away noisily: Myum, myum, myum.

Sam looked at them carefully, but he couldn't see his jumping cow anywhere!

"She'll be in the barn," whispered Loon in his left ear. "She stays inside most of the time. She likes the hay."

Of course! Hey, diddle diddle! thought Sam and his heart beat fast with excitement! "Granny," he said in a loud voice, "please can we go and look in the barn, please, Granny?"

"Come on then." Agreed Granny and she turned Harry's buggy round.

"Moooooooo," said Harry.

"Well, I never did; what a clever boy! Did you hear that, Sam? Harry said moo!"

Inside the barn, it was much darker. Loon's silvery outline could be clearly seen now.

Quick as a flash, he leaped down from Sam's back and hid under the buggy. He definitely didn't want Granny to see him.

"Doggy," shrieked Harry in delight. His eyes were sharper than Granny's!

"No, Harry, these are cows, not dogs," explained Granny kindly. "Dogs say woof."

She was too busy reading the notices to notice the silvery gleam from under the buggy.

"O look, Sam," she said, "all the cows have got names. How funny. This one's called Jessica. Hallo, Jessica."

Jessica was a big brown cow.

"Mooooo," she said politely, "Halloooo."

But the jumping cow had been black, not brown with white splodges! There were three black and white cows in the barn and they all looked much the same. Sam felt sure that Loon would know which was which. But how to ask him without Granny noticing? Then he had a good idea.

"O look, Granny, I've found a sock in my pocket; it must be Harry's," said Sam. "I'll put it on for him, shall I?"

He got down on the floor. Yes, there was the silvery shape, under the buggy and just in front of his nose.

"Don't wriggle, Harry," he said loudly. Then, "What's her name, Loon?" He hissed, "the jumping cow?"

"Jemima," said Loon and laughed happily. "Such fun!"

"Doggy," shrieked Harry.

"Not dogs, cows," said Granny. "I wonder where the other sock's gone."

"Granny," said Sam, "please could you read the names of the black and white cows for me?"

"Of course I can, darling Sam," said Granny, who liked reading things. "Let me see. This one's called Jennifer and this one's Jill and this one at the far end is called…Jemima! What a nice name."

Sam stared at the big black and white cow. You would never imagine she could jump over the moon!

"Hallo, Jemima," he said shyly.

"Mooooooooon," said Jemima. She stared at Sam with her two great black eyes; and then—**she winked!**

"Moooooon," she said again and did a little tap dance on the stone barn floor with her four little hooves.

Harry chortled with glee; Sam clapped his hands.

"Good dancing, Jemima," he said.

Granny had already started to sing in a loud voice:

"And on that farm he had a cow; EIEIO…"

Loon ran out from under the buggy, gave a great leap—and there he was, a faint silvery gleam on the cow's back!

"Woof-Woof! Ha-Ha!" He cried. "Jemima the jumping, dancing cow. Such fun!"

Luckily, Granny was too busy singing to hear:

"O the animals went in nine by nine, the black and white cow on the washing line!"

"Moooooon," said Jemima again and twirled right round!

"Good heavens," said Granny, "what an interesting cow. I didn't know they could dance!"

"They can do lots of things," said Sam, happily.

"Moooooon," explained Harry. But Granny didn't understand.

Chapter 9
Suki the Cat

"Come on, then," said Granny, "it's time for our picnic."

She pushed the buggy out of the barn and onto the sunny hillside.

Sam followed her and Loon leaped down from Jemima's back and followed Sam. As soon as he got into the bright sunlight, his silvery outline disappeared, but Sam knew he was there, trotting just behind him; he could feel Loon's doggy breath warm on the back of his legs!

"This looks like a good place," said Granny, stopping under an old apple tree. "It's nice and shady."

She took out the rug from the buggy pocket and spread it carefully in the shade. "Out you get, Harry."

Then she bent down to unpack the rucksack.

Yum, thought Sam as he watched Granny putting his lunch out on the rug. There were ham sandwiches, honey sandwiches, sausage rolls, bananas, satmoomas and chocolate biscuits! There was also a big bottle of water and three yellow plastic cups, two of them with drinking spouts and one without.

"What do you like eating?" he whispered to Loon.

"Oh, I only have milk," whispered Loon. "I usually get it from the Milky Way. I know, I'll go and ask Jemima for some milkie while you have your lunch. See you later!" And off he trotted back to the barn.

Sam sat down nicely on the rug, but Harry crawled speedily off towards the cows and Granny had to get up hastily to rescue him from some cow poo. But eventually, he too settled down happily and they all had a lovely picnic.

"I think it's time for Harry's sleepus," said Granny. Harry had eaten masses and he was now lying down on his tummy, grizzling gently.

"Come on, Harry, in you go." She strapped him carefully in the buggy.

"I'll push him round and round the tree; he'll be off in a minute," she said. And off they went, Granny happily singing: *Here we go round the apple tree, the apple tree, the apple tree…*

Sam peered up into the branches of the tree: the sunlight was all dappled as the leaves rustled in the warm wind. It was lovely. And then, faintly and sweetly, from somewhere high up in the tree, he heard the sound of a violin!

Suki, he thought and he flapped his arms with excitement. Yes, there she was, right up on the topmost branches, with her bow and fiddle. She was playing the tune of *Here we go round the mulberry bush*, keeping perfectly in time with Granny's singing. It was lovely!

"Hurrah," shouted Sam and he clapped his hands. "What beautiful music!"

"Thank you, Sam," said Granny, a bit surprised but very pleased, as she finished her second circle around the tree. "Harry's nearly asleep; I won't be long."

She changed her singing to: *Rock a bye baby, on the tree top* and, perfectly in time, Suki changed her playing to match! When they got to the *Down will come baby* bit, Sam heard a scrabbling of paws on the apple tree trunk and there, on the grass just in front of him, was Suki! Her black fur was gleaming in the sunlight and her green eyes were shining. She must have left her fiddle and bow up in the branches because she was standing on all four paws.

"Hello, Suki," whispered Sam and he bent down to stroke her soft fur.

Suki didn't say anything (she was very shy) but she purred and purred, arching her back with pleasure.

Then, round came Granny again.

"Harry's finally sleepus," she announced proudly. "Good heavens! What a lovely cat. Wherever did she come from?"

Granny bent forward to stroke her, but Suki took one look at Granny's outstretched hand, gave a startled miaow and disappeared up the apple tree. After all, she was very shy!

"Oh dear," said Granny. "Never mind. Well, I suppose we'd better be making our way back. We've got to be home in time for Mummy and it's quite a long drive."

She set off downhill, pushing the sleeping Harry, with little Sam trotting beside her. As they went, she sang (not too loudly so as not to wake Harry) *"He marched them up to the top of the hill and he marched them down again!"*

And as he marched down again, Sam could hear, faintly but sweetly, Suki playing the tune from her apple tree!

Chapter 10
Home Again

Sam was very pleased when he heard the patter of paws behind him on the gravel path and felt warm doggy breath on his bare leg.

"O, there you are, Loon," he whispered. "Goody!"
"Woof! Woof! Ha-Ha," said Loon.

"And when they were only halfway up…" sang Granny loudly.
"Knknrrrrr." Snored Harry.
They got to the car park and finally managed to find Granny's small blue car in the middle of all the big silver ones.
"Are you coming home with us?" whispered Sam, as Granny heaved Harry out of his buggy and into his car seat.
"I am," said the little Moon Dog—and he jumped up and hid under Granny's driving seat.
"Waaaaa," said Harry. He didn't like being woken up and plonked.
"It's all right, Harry," said Granny. "Come on, Sam, in you get. I'll count up to ten…" Sam knew exactly how long to wait annoyingly (Loon was happily licking his bare toes) before scrambling into his seat just in time! Granny strapped him in, gave both boys a rice cake and started the engine. Off they went. In no time at all, Harry was fast asleep—again!
This time, Sam didn't feel sleepy. He was thinking about what a lovely day at the farm he had had! He'd seen Jemima and actually stroked Suki and it had all been such fun! Then he wondered about what would happen when they got home again. Would Loon stay the night with him? Or would he want to get back home again to the Moon? He bent down to look at the little dog, but to his

surprise, he saw that Loon was fast asleep, curled in a little silvery outline under Granny's seat.

"Sit still, Sam," said Granny, peering crossly at him through the mirror.

So Sam did. He looked out of the window as the car sped home, feeling very happy!

When they got back, there was the usual kerfuffle of opening the boot, unlocking the front door, unpacking the bags and unstrapping the boys. Granny carried Harry inside first, still asleep in his car seat and while she was doing this, Sam and Loon had a quick talk.

"Will you stay the night with me?" asked Sam eagerly.

"No, thank you, I've got to get back," said Loon, "but I will come again and see you soon, I promise."

"O," said Sam, "all right."

"Come on, Sam," said Granny, returning from the house, "it's your turn." She lifted him up and carried him into the hallway before dashing back to lock the car doors.

Sam stayed in the porch to watch! He saw a dim silvery dog shape jump down from the car floor and then scramble up onto the roof, where he disappeared in the bright sunlight. "Are you coming in, Sam?" asked Granny. "I want to shut the door."

"In a minute, Granny," said Sam. Luckily, Harry woke up with a startled Waaaa and Granny was too busy dealing with him to notice what happened next.

A dark black rain cloud had been blown over the bright sun and in the shadow, Sam could just make out the silver outline of the sailing boat, gently slipping away from the car roof. He waved and waved and the little silvery dog waved back as the boat sailed high into the sky. Sam could just hear a faint, "Woof! Woof! Ha-Ha!" before the boat disappeared behind the black cloud. Then it started to rain.

"Come on, Sam," said Granny, "if we don't shut the door, we'll get all wet." So they did—and they didn't.

Lying in bed that night, Sam thought about his lovely day on the farm.

"I wonder when Loon will come back," he said to himself. "He did promise!" Then he fell fast asleep.

Chapter 11
Daddy's Coming Too!

Daddy woke up suddenly. What was that funny noise? He turned over in bed and listened. Beside him, Mummy lay fast asleep, breathing gently; there was no sound from Harry's room, except the usual gentle snoring; but what was that noise coming from Sam's room? It sounded like laughing!

"Golly," said Daddy to himself. "Sam doesn't usually laugh in the middle of the night.

"Perhaps he's having a funny dream. I'll just go and see."

Daddy got out of bed—very quietly so as not to wake Mummy—put a t-shirt on over his shorts and crept into the hall. There he stopped and listened. Whatever was going on?

"Woof! Woof! Ha-Ha!" It sounded like a dog!

And then came the happy sound of little Sam laughing. Then Daddy could hear the bed creaking. Was Sam bouncing up and down? At this time of night?

Daddy opened Sam's door and strode in. The noise stopped suddenly:

"Woof! Woof! H…umph!"

"Sam!" Cried Daddy. "What are you doing? And who is that?"

There on Sam's blue helicopter duvet, shining silver in the darkness, was…a little dog! "Golly," said Daddy.

"Hallo, Daddy," said Sam. "This is Loon; he's a Moon Dog."

"Woof," said Loon. He jumped down off the bed and ran over to Daddy's bare feet, which he started to lick happily.

"We're going to the Moon," explained Sam. "Would you like to come too? Loon's got a beautiful sailing boat!"

Well, Daddy had been about to say, "Going to the Moon? You can't go to the Moon! It's much too far away. And you should be asleep." But when he heard the magical words sailing boat, he stopped. You see, Daddy just loved sailing!

"O," he said instead. "A sailing boat! Where is it?"

"Look," said Sam, proudly. He drew back the curtains and pointed outside the window. There, gently rocking on the warm night air, was a shining, silvery sailing boat! "O," said Daddy again. "Well, I'd better ask Mummy. You wait here—and don't go without me!"

Very excited, Daddy crept back into his bedroom—quietly, so as not to wake Harry. "Mummy," he said in a whisper, "Sam and I are just off to the Moon; I expect we'll be back for breakfast."

But Mummy was fast asleep!

"O," said Daddy, "bother." He didn't want to wake her up, as she was always so tired, so he decided to write a letter explaining. Then she wouldn't be worried, just in case he and Sam were a bit late for breakfast. So he found a pencil and a scrap of paper. This is what he wrote:

Dear Mummy,

I'm just off to see the moon. Sam's coming too. He's found a little dog who knows the way. See you for breakfast.

Love, Daddy.
P.S. Harry's not coming.

Daddy carefully put the note on Mummy's tummy, where she would be sure to see it when she woke up. Then he quickly put on his sandals (just in case the Moon was a bit hard underfoot) and crept back to Sam's room (very quietly, so as not to wake Harry).

Meanwhile, Sam had been busy. He had found his slippers and Loon had helped him put them on. He had also put on his fleece (just in case it got cold on the Moon). Yes, he was ready!

"Such fun!" Cried Loon. "Come on!"

He opened the big window and jumped into the boat. Sam went next, holding on to Loon's front paw so as not to wobble.

"Here you are, Daddy," said Sam, reaching out his hand. "In you get!" And in got Daddy, very excited. He was definitely coming too!

Chapter 12
Swimming

Have you ever sailed through the night sky in a beautiful silver boat? It's just lovely! Loon steered, holding tight to the tiller with his two front paws, while Daddy and Sam sat side by side at the front of the boat, peering over the side and watching the roofs and chimneys of their little town fade into the distance. Up above them, the great Moon shone and the stars twinkled.

Twinkle, twinkle, little star, sang Sam quietly to himself. He felt very happy!

"O look," said Daddy, pointing as a great white bird swooshed past them through the dark sky. "It's an owl!"

Wow, thought Sam. An owl! He remembered the song about the owl and the pussycat, and he thought of little Suki and wondered what she was doing. Perhaps the owl was going to see her? In the song, the owl and the pussycat went to sea in a beautiful pea-green boat. Well, here he was, going to the sky in a beautiful silvery boat!

"Woof! Woof!" Cried Loon. "We're nearly there!"

He turned the little boat into the wind; the silver sails swooshed and fluttered—and then, there they were, on the surface of the Moon. Everyone climbed out and Loon tied the boat to a thorn bush that was growing nearby.

"Hurrah!" Cried Sam; "Golly," said Daddy; "Such fun!" Barked Loon.

Together they climbed up a little hill. There before them lay the silver land of the Moon. There were little hills and valleys, all gleaming silver and a great silver sea.

"I didn't know there was any water on the Moon," said Daddy.

"O yes," explained Loon. "That's called The Sea of Tranquility. Shall we go swimming?"

"Yes, please!" Cried Sam. He was a very good swimmer, although so far only in swimming pools. He thought it would be brilliant to swim in a silvery sea beneath the shining stars.

"Yes, let's!" Agreed Daddy. He was a very good swimmer too, especially at sea.

So Sam and Daddy took off their tops and shoes and put them in a straggly pile on a rock. Loon bounded ahead, shouting, "Woof! Woof! Ha-ha!" He loved swimming too. "Come on," he barked. And they came!

The Sea of Tranquility was surprisingly warm. The water felt lovely and smooth on their bare skin and it gleamed in silver sparkles whenever they splashed. Sam held on to Daddy's back and kicked like anything! Even so, Loon was much faster, swimming doggy paddle, round and round them, laughing with glee, his little tail wagging wildly. Then Sam and Daddy took a deep breath and went underwater! Sam could see little silver fishes dancing and beautiful silvery seaweed waving on the shining silver sand. It was brilliant.

After a bit, they all clambered out of the sea. Loon shook himself, the way dogs do and the sparkling watery drops flew everywhere! Daddy helped Sam get nice and dry, using his fleece as a sort of towel; then they both put their shoes and tops back on. They weren't at all cold. But they were hungry—especially Daddy.

"Is there anything to eat on the Moon?" he asked. "Do you have any apple trees?"

"No," said Loon. "Only thorn bushes and they're a bit prickly for eating. I just have milk. And I get that from the Milky Way. Shall we go and get some?"

"Yes, please," said Sam, who loved his milk. And even Daddy, who didn't particularly, thought it would be an exciting thing to do.

"OK," said Loon. "I'll just get my milk pail."

He scampered off into the bushes and came back with a big silver bucket tied to a long rope. Inside the bucket were a big silver spoon and a little silver dish.

"Come on then," he said. "Let's go. We've got to get back into the boat." So they did!

Chapter 13
The Milky Way

"Daddy," said Sam as the little boat sailed onward, the wind swishing in its sails. "Where exactly is the Milky Way?"

"It's up there," explained Daddy, pointing high above them. Sam looked. He could see a great swirling stream of silvery stars. Yes, it did look a bit like milk—spilt milk.

It's no good crying over spilt milk, he thought, remembering the time when Granny had spilled some in the car. But Loon definitely wasn't crying; he was laughing with glee!

As they got higher and higher, the stars shone brighter and brighter. Then Sam saw that they were sailing along a brilliant foaming silver river—the Milky Way! Loon turned the little boat into the wind so that it stopped sailing but just gently rocked up and down. He reached for the milk pail and took out the dish and spoon; then he gently lowered them over the edge.

"You hold the end of the rope," he said to Sam. Sam clutched it tightly in both hands. "What are you doing?" asked Daddy.

"I'm fishing for stars," explained Loon. "Sometimes they're quite hard to catch; they're a bit slippery!"

Loon leaned over the side of his boat and Daddy and Sam watched as Loon gently swished the milk pail through the stream of stars.

"Got one," he barked excitedly. "Now, pull," he told Sam.

So Sam pulled hard on the rope and up came the pail. Daddy helped Loon haul it over the side and into the boat. Yes, there at the bottom was a silver star! Loon tipped it onto the floor of the boat, where it gleamed in the darkness.

"Again!" Cried the little dog.

They managed to catch three stars—one each. Loon stirred them round and round in the pail with his silver spoon and Daddy and Sam watched as the stars slowly crumbled and turned into milk!

"Now, you hold the dish," Loon told Daddy. Carefully he poured the milk into the dish and they all took turns to drink.

"It's nice," said Sam. The milk was warm and sweet, just the way he liked it. Even Daddy licked his lips and asked for some more. You can get quite a lot of milk from three stars, so they all had plenty.

"Now what?" asked Daddy.

"Let's go back and look for Jemima," said Loon. "It's nearly time for her jump."

"Can I steer the boat?" asked Daddy. "I know how to sail." He loved holding the tiller and feeling important!

"All right," said Loon. The little dog showed Daddy exactly what to do and soon they were heading back down again to the Moon.

"What's that thing?" asked Sam, pointing to a little blue shining ball far away in the night sky.

"That's the Earth," said Loon. "That's where you live!"

Sam was surprised. Then he remembered a picture that Mummy had drawn for him, of the world looking just like a big round blue ball.

"Well, I never did," he said.

Meanwhile, Daddy had cleverly sailed the little boat right back to the shores of the Moon; they landed with a gentle bump and scrambled out.

"This way!" Cried Loon, pointing to the little hill. "Hurry up, or we'll miss her."

Chapter 14
Morning

"Look, Daddy! There she is!" Cried Sam, flapping his arms with excitement. "Hurrah!" They all gazed upwards. And there she was—her four legs kicking madly, her tail streaming behind her, her black eyes gleaming with joy. As she passed just above their heads, Sam was sure that she winked at him.

"Halloooooooo!" Cried Jemima. "I'm over the Mooooooon!"

"Halloooooo, Jemimaaaaaaa!" Cried Sam, Daddy, and Loon, waving furiously as she disappeared over the rim.

"She'll be back in her field soon," said Loon. "It's nearly morning now. Look!"

He pointed to the east, where they could just make out a rosy pink flush in the black sky. "Good heavens," said Daddy, "he's right. That's the sun rising. I wonder what the time is."

Suddenly, Daddy remembered Harry. He always woke up just after sunrise, at 5:45 exactly. He felt a bit guilty.

"I think we'd better be going," he said. "Mummy and Harry will be awake soon."

So, back they went, down the hill to the little sailing boat. Loon jumped in last and pushed off. Soon they were sailing down and down. And as they did, the little blue ball, which was their world, grew bigger and bigger; the rosy pink light in the east turned into a great fiery red ball, which was the rising sun; and soon all they could see of Loon was his little silver outline, while the boat grew fainter and dimmer in the morning light.

Then, there they were, home again. There was the apple tree and the swing and Sam's special garden, shining in the morning sunlight. Loon moored the boat outside Sam's window and Daddy and Sam stepped back into the room.

"Goodbye, Loon," they said, not too loudly, just in case. "Thank you very much!"

"Woof! Woof! Ha-Ha!" Cried Loon. "Such fun! Goodbye."

And off he went, the little boat soon disappearing in the morning sky.

"Right," said Daddy, a bit nervously. "Let's see if Mummy and Harry are still asleep." Hand in hand, Daddy and Sam walked out into the hall. First, they peered into Harry's room and then they looked into Mummy and Daddy's room. But there was no one there!

"I expect they're having breakfast," said Sam cheerfully. "Come on, Daddy." And he bounded downstairs. He wanted to tell them all about their lovely Moon adventure. Daddy followed slowly.

There they were, in the back room. Harry was sitting in his chair, happily dropping bits of toast on the floor.

"Dadada," he said. "Brother!"

Mummy was sitting in her chair. She looked cross.

"Where on earth have you been?" she demanded.

Daddy looked a bit sheepish.

"Actually," he said, "we haven't been on earth at all!"

And together he and Sam explained.

Harry soon understood: "Mooooon!" He cried excitedly. "Doggy! Did-di-di-di."

"Spooooo!" And he threw his orange spoon right across the room, where it landed with a bump in the Thomas dish.

It took Mummy quite a bit longer before she understood properly. She was still a bit cross, but when Daddy explained what fun they had had and how very carefully he had looked after Sam, making quite sure he was safe, she decided to forgive him.

They finished off the toast and Marmite together and then it was time to clear up. "You can help me put the things in the dishwasher," she said.

But when they looked for Harry's Thomas dish and orange spoon, they couldn't find them anywhere!

Chapter 15
The Violin

"Sam," said Granny, "what are you doing with those clothes pegs?"

"I'm sorting them into colors," explained Sam. He had dumped all the pegs in a big heap on the grass. It made it rather difficult for Granny, who was in the middle of hanging up the clothes on the line.

"Well," said Granny, "I need them."

"O," said Sam. "Bother."

But at that moment, they both heard a loud Waaaaa coming from inside.

"Bother," said Granny. "Harry's woken up. Already!"

She left Daddy's red top dangling from the line by one of its arms and hurried into the house. Harry didn't like to be kept waiting!

Sam got on with his sorting. He finished the blue pile and started on the green one. But then, he stopped. What was that strange sound coming from the top of the apple tree? It was a violin! Someone was playing the tune of *Pussycat, Pussycat, where have you been?*

"Suki!" Cried Sam and he clapped his hands in glee! Leaving his pile of pegs, he ran over to the tree and peered upwards. Yes, there, on the topmost branches, was a beautiful black cat with luminous green eyes. And she was playing the fiddle!

"Hurrah," said Sam. "I was hoping I would see you again."

Suki didn't say anything (she was very shy); she just went on playing. But when she had finished the last line of the song, she carefully balanced her little violin on one of the branches and, with her bow tucked under one paw, she scrabbled down the tree and landed elegantly at Sam's bare feet.

"Suki," said Sam again; and he leaned forward to stroke her soft black fur. He did love that cat! And she loved him too! She arched her back and rubbed against his bare legs, purring happily and staring up at Sam with her luminous green eyes.

Sam softly started to sing:

"I love little pussy, her coat is so warm, and if I don't hurt her, she'll…bother!"

For there was Granny, carrying Harry and striding purposefully into the garden. Suki took one look at her, dropped the bow in her alarm and scrambled back up the tree. She was very shy!

"O, Granny," said Sam crossly.

"Ca-ca-ca," said Harry excitedly, pointing upwards.

"What's the matter?" asked Granny.

"You've frightened her away," explained Sam.

"Who?" asked Granny. "Little Miss Muffet?" And she laughed.

"NO," said Sam. "Suki the cat."

"O, is there a cat up there?" asked Granny. She liked cats. Still carrying Harry in one arm, she marched over to the tree and peered upwards. But Suki was sitting absolutely still and it wasn't easy to spot her, as her black fur looked like leaf shadows and her green eyes like baby apples!

"I can't see a cat," said Granny. "But there is something up there. Good heavens! It looks like a violin. Well, I never did!"

"Ca-ca-ca," shrieked Harry, squirming forcefully. (His eyes were sharper than Granny's.) He was quite hard to hold when he squirmed, so Granny plonked him down on the grass to get a better look.

"Waaaaa," said Harry.

"It is a violin!" Exclaimed Granny. "How extraordinary. Well, I'd better rescue it. It can't stay up a tree. Violins are very delicate and they have to be looked after."

"No, Granny…" began Sam. But it was too late.

With a determined gleam in her eyes, Granny grabbed hold of the lowest branch and started to heave herself upwards. Poor Suki took one look at her, gave a startled miaow and leaped off the top branch and down onto the washing line; then she jumped down, hurtled across the grass, clawed her way up the garage wall and disappeared onto the garage roof. There she hid behind the clematis, her little heart beating wildly!

"O, Granny," said Sam sadly, "now look what you've done!"

Chapter 16
Stuck!

It was hard work climbing that tree! Granny wasn't quite as young as she used to be and the branches were sharp and unwelcoming. Still, she was determined to get that violin and bring it down safely. She loved violins and she knew that apple trees were not suitable places to keep them. Up she went, slowly and painfully, until she reached the middle branches. Then, with one hand, she reached out and just managed to grab the violin by its neck.

"Well done, Granny!" Cried Sam. He was impressed—he didn't think that grannies could climb trees!

Meanwhile, Harry had spotted Suki's bow, lying conveniently nearby on the grass. He crawled quickly over and started to bite it!

"No, Harry," shouted Sam. He snatched it away from his little brother. Suki definitely wouldn't want Harry's dribble all over her nice bow.

"Waaaa," said Harry. He decided to go over and eat the earth from Sam's special garden instead; that was always nice and crumbly and sometimes you found worms too!

"Harry! Don't eat that earth!" Cried Granny, who had spotted him from her tree. "Stop it! O dear, I'd better get down quick!"

But that was easier said than done!

"Um," said Granny. "I can't quite turn around."

"Bother," said Granny. "It's not easy when you have to hold onto a violin!"

"Humph," said Granny. "I can't see where I'm going when I go backward."

"Help," said Granny. "I'm stuck!"

And stuck she was! Poor Granny. One foot was holding her nice and safe on a big branch, but the other foot just seemed to dangle into empty space. She just couldn't move at all.

"Hold on, Granny," shouted Sam. "I'll help you."

But Sam wasn't tall enough; you really needed Daddy for a job like that. But Daddy was at work and so was Mummy. And it was only 10 o'clockish and neither of them would be back for ages.

"O dear," said Sam. And he wondered what to do next.

O no, thought Suki, hidden behind the clematis on the garage roof. My poor violin! But she didn't say anything out loud and she kept quite still in case anyone saw her.

"Yum," said Harry. He did like earth and it always tasted especially good from Sam's garden.

"Bother, bother, bother," said Granny.

But at that moment, there was a strange whooshing noise coming from the sky and a strange silvery gleam in the shade of the tree—and there, right in front of her nose, she saw the most extraordinary shape floating in the air! It seemed to be a silver sailing boat!

Chapter 17
Rescued!

"Hurrah!" Cried Sam. "It's Loon!" And he waved Suki's bow excitedly in the air.

"Woof! Woof! Ha-ha," barked the little dog happily. "Hallo, Sam!"

Then he leaned over the side of his boat and reached out a paw to Granny.

"In you get," he said helpfully.

Granny was surprised. No one had told her about Sam and Daddy's Moon trip and she had no idea who the little dog could be. She could see his silver outline quite clearly in the shade of the tree. But she didn't know that dogs could talk and she certainly didn't know that boats could fly. "Um," she said doubtfully.

But little Sam shouted up

encouragingly, "Go on, Granny; it's all right—he's my friend. And it's a lovely boat—Daddy's been in it and Mummy said it was OK."

"Well, I never did!" exclaimed Granny. But she needed to get down, especially as she could see that Harry's face was now covered in earth and there was a pink wriggly worm in his chubby little hand and there seemed to be no other way. Still holding the precious violin in one hand, she grabbed the little dog's paw with the other and stepped heavily into the boat. In no time at all, Loon had sailed the boat away from the outstretched branches, steered a quick circle around the garden and then swooped down and landed elegantly on the lawn.

Shakily, Granny clambered out. She was just about to launch into a stream of questions when the phone rang, loud and clear from the front room.

"Bother," said Granny. Scooping Harry up with one hand and clutching the violin in the other, she disappeared into the house.

"Loon," said Sam. "How nice to see you! Thank you for rescuing Granny."

"That's all right," said Loon cheerfully. "Have you seen Suki anywhere? I gave her a lift here, but then I went off to chase some pigeons and now I can't find her."

"Well," said Sam. "She definitely was here. Granny's got her violin. But I didn't see where she went."

The little boy and the little dog stood together on the grass, calling loudly, "Suki," they shouted. "Where are you? Suki!"

Perched on top of the garage, Suki heard them. Thank goodness! That was definitely Loon's voice. He must have come back to rescue her from that strange woman! And she knew she could trust Sam. She didn't say anything, but she scrambled down from her hiding place, leaping elegantly onto the grass beside them.

"Hurrah!" Cried Sam.

"Woof! Woof! Ha-ha!" Laughed the little dog. "Such fun!"

Gently and lovingly, Sam stroked Suki's soft fur. Then he knelt down and gave her back the bow.

"Here you are, Suki," he said. "I rescued it from Harry's dribble!"

"Pnrmrrrr," said Suki lovingly. She was so pleased to have it back again.

But where was the violin?

Chapter 18
Sailing to School

Just then, Granny came striding excitedly back into the garden. She was still carrying Suki's violin under one arm and Harry under the other.

"Ca-ca-ca! Doggy," shrieked Harry in excitement—and he squirmed so hard that Granny had to put him down quickly on the grass. (Otherwise, she might have dropped him). Harry crawled straight over to Suki and stared right into her luminous green eyes. They were about the same height.

"Ca-ca-ca," he said again, putting out one of his fat little fingers to touch her nose. He was so sweet that Suki immediately decided she loved him too.

"Prrrrrr," she said.

"Well," said Granny loudly, "that was Daddy on the phone. He's forgotten his laptop and he wants us to take it to school. He says he knows all about the sailing boat and the dog; in fact, he thought it would be a good idea if we sailed there. He says he needs it for his next lesson and the boat's much quicker than my car."

"Hurrah," shouted Sam. "You will take us, won't you, Loon?"

"Da-da-da-da." Cried Harry excitedly. "Doggy!"

"Woof! Woof! Ha-ha!" Barked Loon. He had only met Daddy once, but he thought he was interesting and it would be such fun going to school.

"Well, I don't know," said Granny. "I suppose Mummy wouldn't mind."

"Of course she wouldn't," said Sam. "She always gets things for Daddy when he asks.

"I'm sure she would like us to help."

"Well, I suppose it's all right," said Granny. Actually, she really wanted to go for a sail—she loved sailing—and a ride in the sky would be very exciting. Granny liked excitement.

So in they climbed. Granny sat at the front, holding Harry tightly with both hands in case he wriggled. This meant that she had to let go of the violin.

"Is it really yours?" she asked the black cat.

Suki didn't answer, but she purred like anything! Perhaps the strange Granny person wasn't so bad after all. She climbed in next to Harry, holding her precious bow and fiddle tightly with both front paws.

"Ca," said Harry and reached out to poke her nose.

Sam climbed in next and then Loon scrambled in last. He took the tiller and steered the little boat up and up into the bright sky. As soon as they left the shade of the garden, no one could actually see him, but they could hear his happy voice woofing away and Sam could feel his lovely cool hair tickling his bare feet!

Up and up that little boat climbed and then it circled once around the streets of their little town. Then off they went, sailing swiftly through the cool blue air. Loon seemed to know exactly how to get there and he didn't need directions.

Everyone felt very happy. And after a bit, little Suki put her fiddle under her chin and started to play:

O the big ship sails on the Alley Alley O…

And even though it was really only a little boat, not a big ship, they all joined in the singing!

It was just lovely!

Chapter 19
Milkie

"O goodness me," said Mummy, "where's all the milk gone?"

She peered anxiously into the fridge, but she couldn't see any milk: no Harry milk, no blue milk, no green milk, or even Granny's red milk!

"Waaaaa! Grrrrmmmmm," said Harry from the back room. He was sitting in his high chair and feeling particularly hungry! He wanted his cereal!

Little Sam came trotting into the kitchen to help Mummy look. But it was no good—there just wasn't any milkie at all.

"Where's it all gone?" asked Mummy. "I know we had lots yesterday."

Sam thought hard. Then he remembered. O dear! Yesterday, they had all sailed to Daddy's school with the laptop computer and when they got back, they were all very thirsty! Granny had put red milk in her tea; Harry had been given Harry milk in his bottle; Sam had blue milk in his purple cup; Loon had had green milk in a china dish—and little Suki had had green milk too, out of a saucer. No wonder it was all gone.

"Well," said Mummy, "we'll just have to manage with toast and Marmite for breakfast. And then we'll have to go shopping to Sainsbury's."

Mummy didn't really want to go shopping on her day off work, especially as Daddy had taken the car, as usual. But there it was: you had to have milk in the house!

Sam didn't mind too much about not having his Weetabix and Mummy gave him some nice pink cranberry juice to go with his toast. Granny would definitely have minded about not having any tea, but luckily it was Friday and she was at work. Mummy was always quite happy with toast and Marmite. But it was Harry who was the problem. He did make a fuss!

He threw his bits of toast all over the carpet in protest. Then he threw his cup. Poor Mummy had to get down on her hands and knees to tidy up.

Harry was just wondering what else he could throw when he happened to look outside. There, standing in the garden and looking straight at him, was an enormous cow!

"Moooooooo!" Cried Harry excitedly and pointed. Sam looked out of the window. What a lovely black-and-white cow! Then, slowly, she lifted up her great head and winked!

"Wow!" He cried. "It's Jemima! Hurrah! However did she get here?"

The whole family watched in wonder as Jemima bent her four knees, took a huge breath and jumped! Up, up she went, over the apple tree, over the washing line, over the house, higher and higher up in the air. Then she disappeared from sight.

"Wow," said Sam. "Good jumping, Jemima!"

And indeed it was!

Chapter 20
Marmite and Toast

"Mummy! Look!" Cried Sam excitedly!

"What?" asked Mummy. "Where? Wait a minute."

She was still down on her hands and knees, trying to find all the toast bits. As she was now under the table, it was hard to look up without bumping her head.

Meanwhile, Jemima had seen Harry and Sam through the window. She climbed up the patio steps, stepped over the sandpit and started licking the glass with her great pink tongue.

"Mooooo!" She cried. "Halloooooo."

Harry shouted back, "Looooooo!"

And Sam said, "Hallo, Jemima!"

"Now," said Mummy, finally crawling out from under the table. "What's all the fuss about?"

She stood up and looked around. There, standing on the patio and staring straight at her, was a cow! An enormous black and white cow!

"Mooooooo," said the cow.

"Good heavens," said Mummy. **"What on earth is a cow doing on my patio?"**

"It's all right, Mummy," explained Sam. "It's Jemima! She's my friend."

And quick as a flash, he scrambled down from his chair, ran through the kitchen and into the garden.

"Jemima!" He cried. "Would you like some breakfast?"

"Mooooo," said Jemima. She was very hungry. She had come a long way to see Sam—all the way from Godstone Farm.

"Come on then," said Sam, "this way!"

He opened the patio doors and Jemima waddled into the kitchen.

"Sam!" Cried Mummy. **"Why have you brought that cow into the house?"**

Mummy was a bit upset. She hadn't met Jemima before and she didn't understand. And Jemima was an exceptionally big cow. She filled up most of the kitchen and there was hardly any room left to stand. So Mummy sat down instead. She felt very surprised.

But Harry was **delighted!** He wriggled and squirmed furiously in his high chair, reaching out his chubby little hand and pointing.

"Mooo! Mooo! Mooo," he cried happily.

Then he said, "Maaaaaa," which was his way of saying Jemima.

"Would you like some marmite and toast, Jemima?" asked Sam politely.

He picked up one of his soldiers and put out his hand, holding the fingers nice and flat because of Jemima's big yellow teeth. Jemima took a great lick with her pink tongue. It felt rough and tickly on Sam's hand! But do you know what happened next? O dear! She spat it all out! On the floor! You see, Jemima didn't like marmite and toast at all.

Harry thought it was very funny! He laughed with delight and then he pointed at Jemima and said, "Mooooo! Pooooo!"

Mummy stood up in alarm. "O, no," she said. "Not in here. Sam! Take that cow out into the garden. **Now!**"

So Sam did. Just in time! Jemima did a great big poo all over the pile of weeds at the bottom of the garden.

Then he remembered that cows liked to eat grass; he had seen them grazing on the farm.

"Here you are, Jemima," he said kindly. "You can have some grass."

Well, Jemima did like grass, but there wasn't much in the garden. Daddy had mown the lawn only yesterday and it was all a bit brown and dusty.

"Noooo!" Cried Jemima sadly. She decided to try the flowers instead.

Sam watched in dismay as Jemima ate up a clump of purple pansies in his special garden. *O no!*

Then suddenly he remembered: **Hey** *diddle diddle!*

Of course! Jemima liked hay!

"Mummy," he shouted as loud as he could. "Have we got any hay?"

Chapter 21
Dandelions

By this time, Mummy was feeling calmer. She lifted the squawking Harry out of his high chair, stepped carefully over the bits of Marmite and toast and made her way to the kitchen door.

"Hay?" she said. "No, we haven't got any. And I don't think Sainsbury's sells it. But I suppose we could ask Daddy to get some."

"Yes please, Mummy," said Sam. "Jemima's really hungry. And she's eating all the flowers."

So Mummy called Daddy on his mobile phone and Sam took the phone and explained everything. Daddy understood at once.

"OK," he said. "I'm sure I could find some hay somewhere. I know, I'll ask the farmer at the bottom of the school field. I'll be back as soon as I can!"

"Thank goodness," said Mummy when Sam had explained. "But please can you stop Jemima from eating up all the flowers?"

So, while Mummy tidied up the floor (again), Sam and Harry went into the garden to talk to Jemima. Sam was thinking hard. How did you stop cows from eating what they weren't supposed to? Just then he noticed that Harry was busy copying Jemima. He had started to eat the flowers too!

"No, Harry," said Sam. "Come and play ball instead."

If you wanted to stop Harry from doing things, you had to give him something to play with. It was the only way. Perhaps it would work with Jemima too?

"Come on, Jemima," said Sam. "You can play ball too."

He kicked the white ball hard, straight at Jemima's two front hooves. And do you know what? She kicked it straight back! She was brilliant at kicking! Of course, having four legs helped. So Sam and Jemima played football there in the garden and Harry crawled furiously about trying to get hold of the ball, sometimes managing it! And, for the moment at least, the flowers were safe!

Mummy finished tidying up the back room and came out to watch. She saw Jemima dribbling the ball neatly up the garden and pass it to Harry; she saw Harry dribble the ball and try to bite it; she saw Sam tackle Harry and then score an excellent goal right through Jemima's four legs.

"Hurrah! Goal," he shouted happily.

"Well done, Sam," said Mummy proudly and went back into the kitchen to get on with the washing up.

But then, Harry decided to climb the patio steps; he was quite good at this and didn't always fall down backwards. Jemima decided to follow him. And when Sam turned round again, he saw that Jemima was back on the patio, eating Granny's geraniums. Oh no!

Then Sam had another brilliant idea.

I know, he thought to himself. Jemima likes flowers, so she should like dandelions. And Daddy wants us to dig up the dandelions!

"Come here, Jemima," he said firmly. "This is a dandelion. You can eat that up. And there are loads more for you."

Jemima was very good at digging up the dandelion roots with her sharp hooves. And she did like munching the sweet yellow flowers! Hurrah!

Chapter 22
Hay

Then the front doorbell rang and there was Daddy, proudly holding a huge bundle of yellow hay.

"The farmer said I could have some," he said proudly. "And it just fitted into the boot. Now, where is that cow?"

"In the garden," explained Sam.

"Please take it round the side," said Mummy firmly. "I've only just finished sweeping up!"

So Daddy and Sam carefully carried the big bundle of yellow hay round the side, past the garage and through the little door into the garden. Harry wanted to help too, but he was too little.

"Here she is," said Sam. "Look, Daddy, she's eaten up all the dandelions!"

"Well done, Sam," said Daddy. "Good thinking!"

Well, Jemima just loved her hay. She ate it all up with great myummm, myummm noises. And, just in case she was thirsty, Daddy pumped up the paddling pool and filled it all up with water from the hosepipe. She was very pleased. She drank it all up, every last bit. "Mooooo," she said. "Thank youououououou."

"Well," said Mummy, "at least she's had a good breakfast. We couldn't have our cereal because there wasn't any milk."

Then Mummy had a brilliant idea. Of course: milk! You can milk cows!

"Jemima," said Mummy politely, "please could you give us some of your milk? We've run out, you see and it's definitely time for Harry's bottle."

"And for my purple cup," said Sam.

"And for my chocolate milkshake," added Daddy anxiously.

Jemima looked at them. Of course she would give them some milk. She had had a lovely morning, playing football and eating dandelions and hay and she wanted to say thank you. So she filled the paddling pool right up with beautiful warm creamy milk—plenty for everyone.

And then, she thought, she really should be getting back to Godstone Farm.

"Can we take her in the car, please, Daddy?" asked Sam. He would love to visit the farm again. It was one of his favourite places.

Daddy eyed Jemima; no, there was no way she would fit—not even in his nice new car! She was just too big and wobbly.

But it didn't matter. After all, Jemima was a jumping cow. She had jumped her way here and now she would jump back again.

The whole family watched in wonder as Jemima bent her four knees, took a huge breath and…jumped! Up, up she went, over the apple tree, over the washing line, over the house, higher and higher up in the air. Then she disappeared from sight.

"Wow," said Sam. "Good jumping, Jemima!"

And indeed it was!

Chapter 23
Teddy

Sam stared out of his bedroom window: yes, he was sure he could see a fuzzy silver circle moving fast across the night sky. As it came nearer and nearer, it got bigger and bigger.

"Look, Teddy," said Sam, holding his little brown bear up to the window. "It's Loon, coming to see us!"

And so it was! There was the silver sailing boat, floating on the dark air just outside Sam's room; and there was the little Moon Dog, scrabbling through the top window and landing with a soft wumph on Sam's bed.

"Woof! Woof! Ha-ha!" Cried Loon happily. "Such fun!"

"This is Teddy," explained Sam. "He's my bear."

"Do you like bears?" asked Loon. "Because tonight's the night the Great Bear goes fishing on the moon! Shall we go and see?"

"Yes, please," said Sam excitedly. "Can Teddy come too? And Daddy?" he added. He wasn't quite sure about bears and he thought it would be nice to have Daddy with him. "He can!" Agreed Loon. So Sam tiptoed next door (very quietly so as not to wake Harry—or Mummy, either).

"Daddy," whispered Sam in Daddy's left ear. "Wake up! Loon's here and he says we can see a Great Bear. And Teddy's coming too."

Well, you wouldn't believe how hard it was waking Daddy up! Sam had to climb up on the big bed and pull his hair and even tickle his toes, before finally he opened his eyes and grunted.

"What's the matter, Sam?" he asked sleepily. "It's the middle of the night!"

"Don't you want to see the Great Bear?" asked Sam. "And watch him fishing?" Suddenly, Daddy was wide awake and very excited.

"I do," he said, only quietly so as not to wake Mummy (or Harry, either).

He slithered out of bed, quickly put on his tracksuit, trainers and a fleece, in case it got cold, wrote a letter to Mummy to explain and followed Sam into his bedroom. There was Loon, happily bouncing up and down on Sam's bed.

"Come on," said Loon. "I've got to help with the catch."

Daddy said that Sam should get dressed properly, so he put on his trousers and fleece. He couldn't find any socks, so he had to creep into Harry's room to get some; Harry always had loads of socks that he didn't like wearing. He was snoring peacefully in his cot; he rolled over and gave a little grunt when Sam opened the sock drawer, but luckily he didn't wake up.

Then Sam found his blue shoes under his bed, Daddy helped him put them on—and they were ready! Loon opened the big window and they carefully stepped into the little silver boat. The sails were shining beautifully in the dark sky. Sam sat next to Daddy, holding Teddy tightly in his arms. Loon grabbed the tiller firmly in his two front paws—and off they went.

Off to see the Great Bear fishing on the Moon!

Chapter 24
Urs

Loon landed his boat on the silvery shore; out got Daddy and Sam. Then they watched, hand in hand on the edge of the sand, as Loon sailed his boat out on the waves of the Sea of Tranquility. What was he doing? And where was the Great Bear?

Suddenly, there was a great splash and out of the whirling water came the huge head of the Great Bear. He was a beautiful polar bear, with silky white fur and gleaming dark eyes. In his mouth, he had a silver fish! With a twist of his enormous neck, he opened his mouth and threw the fish, over the waves, towards the boat. Loon jumped up and caught it in his two front paws.

"Well done, Loon. Good catch!" Cried Daddy and Sam clapped his hands.

Loon put the fish in the bottom of the boat and got ready for the next catch.

And so it went on; the Great Bear dived smoothly down into the silver water and came foaming up with a fish gleaming in his mouth; he threw it to Loon, who was brilliant at catching! He only missed once.

Then the Great Bear paddled out of the sea and shook himself all over. Sam and Daddy stood well back as the water drops flew everywhere. Meanwhile, Loon sailed his boat to land and jumped out.

"This is the Great Bear," he told Sam and Daddy. "He's called Urs."

Sam looked up at the huge white animal.

"Hallo," he said timidly. "I'm Sam. This is my Daddy and this is Teddy."

The Great Bear peered down at him. When he spoke, his voice was growly and deep, but kind.

"Do you like fish?" he asked.

"Um," said Sam. He did quite like tuna and sardines out of a tin; and he definitely liked fish cakes; but he wasn't at all sure about raw moon fish! Nor was Daddy.

"Well…" began Daddy, who usually liked his fish cooked.

"Or ice cream?" asked Urs. "Do you like ice cream?"

"Yes," said Daddy and Sam together. They did like ice cream.

"Would you like to come to tea?" asked Urs.

"Yes, please," said Daddy and Sam together.

"Then up you get!"

Sam and Daddy looked at each other. Get up? Where? What did he mean?

"Woof! Woof!" Barked Loon. "It's all right. He's going to give you a Bear-Back ride! Such fun! You can't come in my boat because it's full of fish."

Sam and Daddy looked at each other again. A Bear-Back ride! Whatever next?

I'm glad I put my fleece and socks on, thought Sam. The Great Bear knelt down on the silver sand and Sam grabbed hold of the soft fur as he scrambled up the Bear's massive white back.

I wonder what Mummy would say, thought Daddy as he followed.

With a mighty roar, Urs leaped upwards! Of course, bears don't have wings, so they can't exactly fly; it felt more like swimming through the dark, cold sky. With one hand, Sam held on tight to the bear's fur and with the other, he clutched Teddy. Daddy held on tight to Sam's middle with both hands! Behind them came Loon in his silver sailing boat. They were on their way!

Chapter 25
Ursula

The Great Bear carried them up through the stars; soon the Moon was just a silvery ball far below. Sam felt a bit cold but very excited.

"Look, Teddy," he said. "Here's the Milky Way."

But they didn't stop there. They went up and up until at last the Great Bear slowed down and landed. He knelt down on a great sheet of ice and Sam and Daddy scrambled off his back and looked around.

"Here comes Loon with the fish catch," said Daddy as Loon landed his boat on the ice. "I wonder where we are."

The Great Bear led the way.

"This is my house," he said in his deep, growly voice. "Come inside."

It was a strange house, made of ice bricks—a bit like Sam's building bricks, only much bigger and all white and gleaming with starlight.

"First, we must unload the catch," said Urs, the Great Bear, "and then we can have tea." So Loon and Urs started to unload the fish and put them neatly inside a great ice box (a bit like a fridge). Daddy thought it would be only polite to help, so he did.

While they were busy with the fish, Sam noticed a ladder in the corner of the room. It was made of icicles. He stuffed Teddy down his fleece, with just his little head poking out and he started to climb. The ladder was cold and a bit slippery, but Sam was good at climbing. Up, up he went. At the top of the ladder was a little round ice room, with curving walls and ceiling; and there, curled up on the floor, was a Little Bear, fast asleep and growling gently.

A bit like Harry snoring, thought Sam.

He tiptoed closer. Little Bear was white and furry, with a funny little black nose. Sam was just wondering what color the bear's eyes were when they opened wide. They were black like Urs's. Little Bear gave a startled squeak and sat up.

"Who are you?" said the Little Bear.

"Sam," explained Sam.

"I'm Ursula. My Daddy's the Great Bear," said the Little Bear.

"My Daddy's downstairs helping with the fish," said Sam. "And this is my Teddy."

"O look!" cried the Little Bear excitedly. "Isn't he sweet? Can I hold him?" So Sam let Ursula hold Teddy in her soft white paws.

"Do you like slides?" said Ursula.

"Yes, I do," said Sam.

"Come on then," said Ursula. "Let's go sliding."

And she padded over to a small hole in the wall. She lay down on her tummy and wriggled through the hole. Sam lay down too and followed her. He found himself outside on an ice platform, with a great ice slide curving down below.

"My turn first!" Cried Ursula. Still holding Teddy, she sat down and pushed. Sam could hear her laughing with glee as she hurtled down the slide. Then he heard her squeaky voice calling up.

"Come on, Sam. Your turn!"

Carefully, Sam sat down. The ice felt cold and slippery. He took a deep breath and pushed off! Wheeeeee—he was zooming down the smooth slide. It was brilliant! All around, he could see the dark sky and the glittering stars. He landed with a soft whumph on a snow pile next to Little Bear.

"Again!" She cried and Sam followed her back into the ice house.

"Have you got a slide in your house?" she asked.

"No, I haven't," said Sam, "only stairs. But I have got a swing and a sandpit," he explained.

After two more slides, the others had finished unpacking the moon fish. It was time for tea.

Great Bear got five little frozen stars out of the ice box. They all sat down on a great white rug and ate starfish ice cream, caught from the Milky Way. You held one of the points and nibbled your way through the others. Then you ate up the middle bit. And they tasted delicious!

Chapter 26
Breakfast

That was a very strange bear picnic. There they were, in the middle of the night, sitting in a circle on the floor of a huge ice house and eating starfish ice cream: Sam and Daddy and Urs and Ursula and Loon.

"I wish Mummy and Harry were here too," said Sam. "They love ice cream."

"I suppose we ought to be going home soon," said Daddy. "It must be nearly time for breakfast."

So they finished their ice creams and climbed into Loon's boat, ready to sail back home. The Great Bear kindly put some raw moon fish and some starfish ice cream in an ice bucket so they could take them home for Mummy and Harry to try.

"Can I come too?" asked Ursula. She would love to go exploring and see Sam's house and the swing in his garden and the sandpit.

"Not this time," said Urs firmly.

"Goodbye, goodbye," shouted Sam. "Thank you!"

And then, just as the little boat lifted up into the sky, Sam remembered.

"Teddy!" He cried. "Ursula, you've still got my Teddy!"

"Catch!" she shouted up. And she threw little Teddy high up and Sam leaned over the side of the boat and caught him!

"Well done, Sam, good catching," said Daddy.

And then they were on their way home, with the red sun below them just beginning to light up the dark sky.

When they got back, Mummy and Harry were, amazingly, still asleep!

"Come on, Sam," whispered Daddy as they tiptoed out of the bedroom. "Let's cook a surprise breakfast!"

So Daddy got out a frying pan and some olive oil and garlic and cooked the moon fish! They smelled brilliant—much better than raw. Meanwhile, Sam managed to find enough dishes and spoons: one for Sam and one for Harry and one for Mummy and one for Daddy, which made four altogether! There were six starfish ice creams, so he put one in each dish and the two extra ones in the freezer.

When everything was ready in the back room, Sam and Daddy went upstairs. As he was climbing the stairs, Sam wished he had an ice ladder and a slide instead! First, they went into Harry's room. He had heard them coming and was already standing up in his cot, smiling his happy smile!

"Mmmmmmm," he said as Daddy lifted him up. And do you know what? Harry was holding his teddy bear, almost as if he knew what had happened!

It was much harder waking Mummy. In the end, Sam had to climb up on the bed and tickle her nose. Then, at last, she sneezed and opened her eyes.

"Hallo, darling Sam," she said. "You're up early."

"I haven't been asleep yet," said Sam proudly. "We've made breakfast. Come and see."

When Mummy saw the table all beautifully laid out with plates of fried fish and dishes of ice cream, she was very impressed.

"Goodness," she said. "Wherever did this come from?"

So they told her all about it.

Chapter 27
In the Garden

It was another sunny day. Sam and Harry were weeding Sam's special garden and Granny was having a quiet snooze on the patio.

Then Sam heard a strange noise: wheee-oooo-shshsh; it seemed to be coming from the sky!

"Shshsh, Harry," said Sam. "Stop squawking, I can't hear properly."

Harry stopped; sometimes he did just what his big brother told him!

"Wooooo!" Cried Harry, pointing excitedly up to the sky. He could hear something *too: wheee-oooo-shshsh.*

It's not Loon, thought Sam, or Jemima. Their noises are quite different. I wonder who it can be.

He stood up, listening and looking as hard as he could. Harry stood up too, but then he sat down unexpectedly! The noise was definitely getting louder now. And then Sam saw it: a great, shiny, ice slide coming down from the sky and getting nearer and nearer. "Wow!" Cried Sam excitedly. "It's Urs, the Great Bear! It must be!" But it wasn't…

With a great wheee-ooo-shshsh-whump, the slide reached the grass, just beside the boys' four bare feet. Then, down the slide came a white furry creature, head first and very fast. It landed with a whumph on the grass.

"Ursula," shouted Sam joyfully! "It's you!"

"Did you see me sliding?" Cried Ursula squeakily. "I came all by myself. I'm so clever." She picked herself up off the grass and looked around.

"Harry," she squeaked excitedly. She thought Harry was sweet! She bounded over to him and started licking his bare toes.

Harry chortled with glee!

"Is your Daddy coming too?" asked Sam.

"Oh, no," said Ursula. "He doesn't even know I'm here. He went to the Moon to catch some more fish. He told me to go to sleep in my room. But I wanted to come and see you instead."

"But how did you build the slide?" asked Sam.

"I didn't," said Ursula. "My Daddy built it. He said we could both come later, after the catch and give you some fish and starfish ice cream. But I didn't want to wait, so I came all by myself."

"Oh," said Sam. He wondered if Urs would be cross when he found out. He thought a cross Great Bear would probably be quite fierce! He knew his Mummy and Daddy would be cross if he didn't wait for them. But Ursula didn't seem at all worried.

Just then, Granny woke up from her snooze.

"Sam? Harry?" she asked. "Are you having a nice time?" She got up and started walking over the grass towards them.

O dear! What would she say if she saw a little white bear in the garden? Would she be cross too?

Chapter 28
Granny Is Surprised

"Good heavens!" said Granny. "There's a bear in the garden!"

She hadn't met Ursula before, as she had missed the picnic party, so she was very surprised.

"Well, I never did," she said. "Sam, Harry, why is there a bear in the garden?"

"Baaaa," said Harry. "Grrrrrr!"

"Well," said Sam, "she didn't want to wait for her Daddy. So she came."

"I'm Ursula the Little Bear," explained Ursula proudly. "My Daddy's Urs the Great Bear. And Sam is my friend and Harry is sweet!"

Granny was still surprised, but as they all three really did look friendly, she decided not to be too cross.

"But where is your Daddy?" she asked. "And why didn't you wait for him? You should always wait for Daddies, even if they are slow!"

"He was fishing," explained Sam. "So Ursula came down the slide by herself. Look, Granny!"

So Granny looked. When she saw a massive ice slide in the garden, she felt even more surprised.

"I think Ursula should go back and tell her Daddy where she is," said Granny, "or he'll be worried."

"Don't be silly, Granny," said Sam. "You can't go up slides," he explained kindly.

"Ni," shouted Harry excitedly. He was very good at climbing and wanted to try. But even Harry couldn't manage the ice slide, as it was so steep and slithery—and cold!

"It's no good, Granny," said Sam. "Ursula will have to stay here until her Daddy comes to get her."

"Well, I suppose so." Agreed Granny.

"Hurrah," squeaked Ursula excitedly. "I can stay! I want to look inside your house! Come on!"

And she bounded happily on all four paws across the grass, up the patio steps and into the kitchen. Harry followed as fast as he could on his four paws.

"It will be OK, Granny," said Sam. "Come on."

So Sam and Granny went hand in hand into the house to see what the others were up to!

Chapter 29
What a Mess!

Ursula had never been inside a human's house before. She was very excited! The trouble was, having a polar bear inside your house, even a little one, can make a lot of mess!

"O look!" Cried Ursula as the boys showed her the back room. "What's that for?"

"It's Harry's high chair," explained Sam. "It's where he has breakfast."

"Ni!" Cried Harry. He had heard the word breakfast and, even though he had had his already, he didn't want to be left out!

Ursula didn't know what breakfast meant, but she thought the chair was sweet and wanted to sit in it. She scrabbled up the sides with her sharp claws scratching the wood and landed headfirst on the seat. Her two front paws went through the holes where Harry's feet were supposed to go and her two back paws were left waving in the air. "I'm stuck!" She cried. "Help."

Then she wriggled so much that the chair fell over. Ursula landed with a whump on the tiled floor. Luckily, she had lots of soft white fur, so it didn't hurt. But the remains of Harry's milky-and-oats went all over the floor. Never mind— that was nothing new!

"Wow," said Ursula, picking herself up. "What's that?" She was looking at a strange green thing with lots of round shapes on it.

"It's Harry's present," explained Sam. "It goes round and round and plays music. Look, I'll show you."

"Ni," said Harry quickly—but he was too late! Sam pressed the switch and the little cogs whirred around and music played.

"It's brilliant," said Ursula. "I want a go." But when she put her big front paw on the switch, it was so unexpectedly heavy that the music suddenly stopped playing and the green cogs stopped spinning.

"Bother," said Sam. "Never mind, I expect Granny can fix it."

Well, Granny did try, but she wasn't much good at fixing. While she was busy trying, the others went into the front room.

Sam showed Ursula how to climb up the sofa and then jump off onto the cushions and the bean bag. He liked doing this—and so did Ursula! She was an excellent jumper. Once, Harry had to crawl quickly out of the way before getting squashed, but he was usually OK. Sam had a great time, racing the little bear up and down and around again.

But then:

"Look out! Here I come," shouted Ursula. She gave a spectacular leap onto the bean bag. But she was much heavier than Sam (bears usually are, even little ones) and the poor bean bag had had enough. Ursula's paws tore a big hole in its green side and out came the beans, rolling all over the carpet in a massive mess.

"Bother," said Ursula.

"Ni!" cried Harry excitedly.

"No, Harry," said Sam, quickly taking a handful of beans out of his little brother's mouth. "What a terrible mess!" said Granny, coming into the front room to see what all the noise was about.

"Can you mend it?" asked Sam anxiously. He was very fond of his bean bag.

"Well, I suppose I can try," said poor Granny with a sigh. "I wonder when your Daddy will come and get you," she said quite crossly to Ursula. "I know. Sam, take Ursula and Harry upstairs and have a quiet look at some books while I tidy up."

"Stairs!" Cried Ursula. At her house, she didn't have stairs, only ladders and slides, so she was very excited. Harry was excited too. He loved climbing stairs and didn't often get a chance. So Granny kindly opened the stair gate and saw them safely up before getting down on her hands and knees to start picking up the beans.

Chapter 30
Bathtime

Ursula quite liked the books, only they were a bit too peaceful for her taste. She was an adventurous sort of bear. So after Sam had showed her Monkey Puzzle and some of Aesop's Fables, she got a bit restless.

"What's in here?" she asked, padding out of the bedroom door and around the corner into the bathroom.

"It's a bath," explained Sam.

"What's a bath?" asked Ursula. They didn't have baths in her star house; her Daddy just licked her clean with his great pink tongue whenever she needed it.

"Where you get washed all over," said Sam. "It's nice. There's lots of water, not too hot and you can have a splash."

"I love splashing," said the Little Bear. "Can we have one now?"

"We'll have to ask Granny first," said Sam. "And she might say we aren't dirty enough yet. You are supposed to have a bath when you get dirty."

"That's easy," said Ursula. "Come on, let's all get nice and dirty!"

And it was easy! Harry found a tube of toothpaste on the bathroom floor and in no time at all he had squeezed loads of toothpaste all over his face, hands and knees. Ursula padded into the back bedroom and soon discovered Mummy's make-up bag with some beautiful pink lipstick.

"This is perfect!" She cried. "Come here, Harry." She drew some lovely pink lipstick patterns all over the bits where the toothpaste hadn't reached. Then she got Harry to draw some on her and he was surprisingly good at it!

Sam wasn't quite sure what Granny would say, so he went downstairs to ask.

"Please, Granny," he said politely, "can we have a bath?"

"Hang on," said Granny. She crawled out from behind the sofa, where she had been chasing beans. "It's not nearly bath time yet. Why do you want a bath?"

"Come and see," explained Sam.

So Granny followed him up the stairs. When she saw Ursula and Harry, just covered in pink and white scrawls, she was quite cross!

"What are you doing?" she cried. "Is that toothpaste? And is that Mummy's lipstick? Oh, Harry! And you," she went on to Ursula, "are a very naughty bear! What a mess!"

"We're nice and dirty now," said Ursula happily, "so we want a bath!"

She wasn't at all afraid of Granny. When her Daddy got cross, he was very growly and you really had to be good, but Sam's Granny seemed much easier to manage.

"I suppose you will have to." Agreed Granny. "Oh dear, what a nuisance. Bother, bother!"

She went into the bathroom and turned on the taps. Soon the bath was filled with lovely warm water.

Granny plonked Harry in and helped Sam scramble over the edge. But Ursula didn't need any help. She gave a massive leap and landed in the water with a mighty splash. Poor Granny got very wet and so did the bathroom floor.

"Right," said Granny firmly. "Shampoo!" She squirted baby shampoo all over Ursula's fur and scrubbed hard. Slowly, the pink lipstick disappeared into the bath water. Then it was Harry's turn. Sam didn't need much scrubbing as he hadn't really got dirty at all, so he and Ursula had a gentle splashing game while they were waiting.

Granny had just finished Harry, when they were all startled by a strange growly noise, coming from the garden. It sounded like this:

"Grrrrrrr. Urrrrrsula? Wherrre arrre you?"

"It's my daddy!" Cried Ursula. "And he sounds very cross!"

Chapter 31
Urs Is Cross

Well, it was difficult to know what to do next. Granny wasn't at all used to Great Bears, especially cross ones and didn't really want to meet one on her own. In any case, she couldn't leave Harry in the bath. Baths are quite slippery places and sometimes you wobble. And everyone was wet.

"**Urrrsula! Come out** herrrre! **Now,**" came the mighty growling voice from the garden.

"I'll have to go," said Ursula. "He does sound cross!"

She stood up in the bath and shook herself. Water flew everywhere, all over the room (and all over Granny too).

Then she scrabbled out of the bath and slithered down the stairs on her bottom. (Like Harry, she hadn't yet got the hang of walking downstairs.) The others heard her padding across the kitchen floor and out into the garden.

"Come on," said Sam. "Let's go and see."

As quickly as she could, Granny helped Harry and Sam get dried and dressed. Then Granny picked Harry up and carried him downstairs and Sam followed. He was excited about seeing Urs again, but a bit worried in case he really was cross.

And he was! Very cross! But not with Sam or Harry, or even Granny, but with Ursula. "Why did you come without me?" he roared. "You were told to wait. You are too little to go out by yourself."

"Sorry, Daddy," said Ursula.

"We did try to send her back," explained Granny. "But we couldn't climb up the slide."

"None of us could—not even Harry."

"You can't go up slides." Agreed the Great Bear. "But Ursula shouldn't have gone down it in the first place. She should have waited for me."

"Sorry, Daddy," said Ursula again. Then she said, "Did you bring the starfish ice cream?"

"No, I did not!" Growled Urs. "Naughty bears do not deserve ice cream."

"But I'm hungry," squealed Ursula. She started to cry. Sam and Harry were hungry too. No one had had anything to eat since Ursula's arrival—and that seemed a long time ago. "NI," said Harry loudly. And then he started to cry.

It was Granny who came to the rescue.

"I could make us all some sandwiches," she said. "And then we'll feel much better. Do you like sandwiches?" she asked Urs.

"I do," said the Great Bear. "Thank you very much."

So Granny made some ham and cheese sandwiches, which were good for you as well as tasting nice. They all sat down on the grass to eat them. By the time they had finished, Urs had stopped being cross and Granny had decided that she really liked bears, after all. Urs was very polite and they had an interesting talk about how to teach children manners!

And then it was time for them to go home. Urs knelt down on the grass and Ursula scrambled up on his back for her bear-back ride home.

"Goodbye, goodbye," they all shouted and waved like anything.

"Come and see me soon," squeaked Ursula as they swam up into the sky. "Loon will take you in his boat!" And then they disappeared from view.

Harry wanted to try the ice slide again to see if he could manage it this time, but when they went to the bottom of the garden to have a look, it had melted away.

Chapter 32
A Lovely Day for Sailing

Harry was asleep in his cot, probably dreaming about walking, which he was beginning to be quite good at! Sam was helping Mummy hang up the washing in the garden.

"Daddy's red t-shirt," he said helpfully, as he passed it up to Mummy. "Harry's stripy socks. Mummy's pink top…what's that?"

He peered up into the sky. He couldn't see anything unusual—just pigeons and an aeroplane—but he could hear something: whoosh, flutter, woosh.

"Something's coming." He cried excitedly. "Listen, Mummy. Oh, look!"

For now he could see a faint silvery gleam high up in the blue sky.

"Hurrah! It's Loon in his boat!" Cried Sam, jumping up and down for joy.

And so it was. With a final whoosh and flutter, Loon landed his silver boat on the grass just beside the washing line and climbed out.

"Woof! Woof! Ha-ha," he barked. "Such fun!"

Sam couldn't really see him properly, as it was such a sunny day, but he could definitely feel Loon's soft fur rubbing against his bare legs.

"Hello, Loon," said Sam happily. He bent down to look closer. Yes, now he could just make out his faint silvery shape. "I thought it was you."

"So did I," said Loon. "Do you want to come sailing?"

"Yes, please," said Sam. It was a perfect day for sailing, with a lovely warm wind chasing just a few white clouds across the sky.

"Would you like to come too?" Loon asked Mummy politely.

"Oh, no thank you, I really can't," explained Mummy. "I've got to go to Sainsbury's when Harry wakes up. We haven't got anything for supper."

"But I can go, can't I, Mummy?" asked Sam anxiously. He really did want to—only you never knew with Mummies.

"Well, yes, I suppose you can." Agreed Mummy. "Only be sure to hold on tight so you don't fall out. Where are you going?"

"Godstone Farm," shouted Sam. It was one of his favourite places.

"OK," said Loon. "Then we can say hello to Jemima and Suki."

"Would you like to take a picnic?" asked Mummy kindly. "It's quite a long way."

Yes, they would! Definitely!

"Please will you pack it in my Thomas bag?" asked Sam. "Loon hasn't seen it yet." Sam was very proud of his Thomas bag and he wanted everyone to admire it.

"All right." Agreed Mummy. "Wait here, I won't be a minute."

So off she went into the kitchen to make some cheese and honey sandwiches. Meanwhile, Sam and Loon kindly finished hanging up the washing. This was how they did it. Sam climbed up on the front seat of the sailing boat, so he could reach up to the washing line and Loon passed up the clothes.

Soon, they had finished—and so had Mummy!

"Here you are," she said, giving Sam his bag. "Have a lovely time!"

"Thank you! Goodbye, Mummy, goodbye," shouted Sam.

He held tight to his Thomas bag with one hand and tight to the edge of the boat with his other. Loon jumped in, took the tiller in his two front paws—and they were off!

Off to Godstone Farm—hurrah!

Chapter 33
Where Can She Be?

It was quite a long way to the farm, but it didn't take that long in Loon's little sailing boat. And it was lovely, feeling the warm wind on your face and looking down at the tops of the houses and shops as you sailed over them.

"There's Sainsbury's," Sam explained to Loon—and he wondered when Harry would wake up to go shopping. Soon they were out in the countryside and now Sam could see the tops of great trees just beneath him, waving gently in the wind.

"That's a silver birch," he told Loon. "And that's a chestnut tree—look, can you see the chestnuts? And I think that one's a sycamore tree."

Loon was interested; you didn't get any trees on the Moon—just a few prickly thorn bushes. Then they zoomed over the tall steeple of a little church; Sam could see the golden face of the steeple-cock looking up at him. It was lovely sailing through the sky and seeing everything from on high! And of course, no one on the ground could see the boat in the bright light—although if anyone had bothered to look up, they might have caught a glimpse of Sam's little face peering over the side. But no one did.

Soon, the green fields and wooden barns of Godstone Farm came into view and Loon steered the little boat down and down—until they landed with a gentle whumph on the grass beside Suki's old oak tree.

"Here we are," he woofed happily as he and Sam scrambled out of the boat. "Now, where's that cat?"

"Suki!" Cried Sam. "Where are you? We've come to see you!"

But she didn't seem to be there! He peered up into the branches of the tree, but he couldn't see any sign of a little black cat.

He tried singing, *Pussycat, Pussycat, where are you?* But there was no answer; only the gentle rustling of leaves in the wind.

"Bother," he said. "Where, oh where, can she be?"

"I don't know," said Loon. "Let's ask Jemima."

Jemima was eating grass in a field on top of a little hill. She was very pleased to see them.

"Moooooo," she said, winking her big black eye. "How are youououououu?"

"We're fine," said Sam. "Only we can't find Suki. Have you seen her?" Jemima hadn't, not recently. Her voice was much louder than Sam's or Loon's, so she tried calling her. She lifted up her great head and bellowed:

"Mooooo!" She cried. "Sooooooooki! Where are youououououu?"

Everyone listened. They could hear the rustling of the wind across the tall grass and the calling of a robin from the top of the hedge. But no Suki.

"Try again," suggested Sam. So Jemima did.

"Soooooooki," she bellowed, even louder. "Where are youououououu?"

And then, very faint and far away, they heard the sound of a violin! It was playing the tune of Ding, Dong, Bell.

He remembered Granny singing the old song to him:
Ding dong bell
Pussy's in the well
Who put her in?
Little Johnny Flynn.
Who pulled her out?
Little Tommy Flout.
What a naughty boy was that
To soak a pussycat
Who never did any harm
But chased all the rats
In his father's farm.

"It's Suki," said Sam. "She must be stuck in a well! I expect she can't get out." He wondered if a naughty boy had really put her in the well. O dear!

"We must pull her out." He cried. "Jemima, do you know where the well is?"

"I doooooo," said Jemima. "Follooooooooow meeeee!"

Chapter 34
Who Pulled Her Out?

Cows can move very fast when they want to! She didn't wait to swallow her mouthful of grass before she was off. She hurtled up to the top of the field and jumped neatly over the hedge. Then she pounded up a little lane and disappeared around a bend.

"Come on, Sam." Cried Loon. "Get into the boat. Quick! We must follow her!"

So Sam and Loon ran back down the hill and scrambled into the boat. Soon they were up in the sky again.

"There she is!" Cried Sam, pointing below. He could easily make out Jemima, zooming along the lane as fast as her four hooves would go.

Loon steered the little boat while Sam pointed out the way to go. He saw Jemima jump over a big white gate. Then she stopped suddenly. And yes! Sam could just make out the round shape of a little well beside the gate.

"There it is," he shouted. "Stop the boat, Loon."

"Woof! Woof! Ha-ha!" Barked the little dog. "Such fun!"

He landed the boat just beside the well and in no time at all the three friends were standing at the edge of the well, peering down into the darkness.

It was difficult to see clearly, so Sam tried singing:

Pussycat, Pussycat, where are you?

And this time, they heard it! Loud and clear came the sound of the fiddle playing the tune:

Here I am! Here Iam! How do you do!

"Hurrah, we've found her," said Sam. He peered down into the darkness of the well again. He could just make out the two green eyes of the little cat, curled up on a ledge far below him.

"There she is!" He cried excitedly. "But how can we pull her out?"

It was definitely too far for him to reach and the well was too small for Loon's boat to go to the rescue—and far too small for a wobbly cow to get in. Then Sam had a brilliant idea.

"I know." He cried, "The Milky Way bucket! Is it still in the boat?"

"Woof! Woof! It is!" Barked Loon. He did think Sam was clever! "Here it is."

Loon had a beautiful silver bucket with a long chain, which he usually used for catching milk. It would be just perfect for rescuing a pussycat!

Together, Sam, Loon and Jemima carefully lowered the bucket down into the well, holding tight to the chain so it wouldn't slip.

"Can you reach it, Suki?" Cried Sam. "Can you get in?"

They all heard a miaow and a soft wumph—and then suddenly the bucket felt much heavier.

"She's in," said Sam. "Pull!"

Gently and carefully, they pulled on the chain. They could hear the bump, bump of the bucket against the side of the well. Up it came, up and up—and then, there it was, gleaming silver in the daylight—and there was little Suki, curled up inside it, holding tight to her violin! In no time at all, the bucket was safely on the grass.

"Suki," said Sam gently. "Are you all right?" He leaned down and, very gently, picked up the little cat and gave her a big cuddle.

Suki didn't say anything (she was very shy) she just purred and purred! She loved Sam!

Chapter 35
Bye!

After all the excitement, everyone felt very hungry. It was definitely time for the picnic. They all sat down on the grass by the well and Sam unpacked his Thomas bag. Clever Mummy! There were honey and ham sandwiches, chocolate biscuits in a plastic box, an apple and some cranberry juice in a little bottle. Yum!

Jemima helped Sam eat the sandwiches and apple, but Loon and Suki only liked milk and Mummy hadn't packed Sam's purple cup, as it wasn't time for milk yet. But it was all right. With Sam's help, Jemima kindly squirted some lovely warm milk into the empty sandwich box and the little dog and cat took turns lapping it up.

Then Jemima said she was thirsty, so Sam helped her lower the bucket down the well—right down to the bottom where the water was—and then pull it up again. Jemima had a lovely cool drink of water, which she really needed after all that running and jumping!

"How did you get in the well?" Sam asked Suki when they had all had enough. "Did someone put you in, or did you fall in by mistake?"

Suki didn't say anything. She just looked at Sam with her shining green eyes. Then she picked up her fiddle and played. It was the tune of *London Bridge Is Falling Down*.

"She must have fallen down by mistake," Sam explained to the others. "Poor Suki!" He was glad it hadn't been a naughty boy after all. But you do have to be careful with wells!

After tea, Jemima ambled back to her field and Loon and Sam gave Suki a lift back to her old oak tree. She was very pleased to be safely home again. Suki came and sat on Sam's lap, purring like anything while Sam stroked her lovely soft black fur.

And then it was time to go home again.

"Bye, Suki; bye, Jemima," Sam shouted as the little boat rose up into the blue sky. "See you soon."

"Moooooooo!" Bellowed Jemima. "See youououououou!"

Suki didn't say anything, but she climbed to the very top of her tree and waved her tail.

Then she lifted up her violin and played her goodbye tune:

Rock-a-Bye, Sam-Sam, from the treetop.

Sam sang the words until the sound of the violin faded away. And then there was just the noise of the wind rustling the leaves below him.

"There you are!" cried Mummy. The little boat had just landed in the garden. "Did you have a lovely time?"

"Ni," said Harry. He wished he could have gone too! He had been quite cross when he woke up and Mummy had explained that Sam had gone sailing without him. That was the trouble with going to sleep in the daytime—you never knew what you might miss!

Going to Sainsbury's was fun, but definitely not as exciting as sailing.

But now it was Sam's turn to feel sleepy after his very exciting day. He couldn't help yawning as he waved goodbye to Loon. Then he went into the house.

And there was Daddy, back home from work and ready to hear all about his adventures!

Chapter 36
Moon-Day

"Sam," said Loon, "would you like to come to a picnic party on the Moon?"

"I would," said Sam. He stroked the little dog's back. As it was nighttime, he could see Loon clearly. He loved the feel of his soft, silvery hair.

"Can Daddy come too?" he asked.

"He can," said Loon.

"And can Mummy come too? She hasn't been to the Moon yet," said Sam. "And what about Harry?"

"They can," said Loon. "And Urs and Ursula and Jemima and Suki. It will be a huge party!" Loon bounced excitedly up and down on Sam's bed.

"Let's go and wake them up!" Cried Sam, pushing back his blue helicopter duvet.

"But the party isn't now," explained Loon. "It's tomorrow."

"Oh," said Sam, a bit disappointed. "Why?"

"Because it's my birthday tomorrow," said Loon. "And tomorrow is Monday and Monday is a Moon-day. Today's Sunday; you can't go to the Moon on Sun-Day."

"Oh," said Sam. "But won't it be Moon-night?"

"It will," said Loon. "Such fun!"

And so it was agreed. Loon said goodbye and see you tomorrow. He would pick them all up in his sailing boat as soon as it got properly dark.

"And don't forget your swimming things," he shouted, as he scrambled out of the little window and jumped onto his boat.

Daddy and Harry were very excited about the party when Sam told them the next morning at breakfast. Mummy wasn't quite so sure.

"How can we go swimming on the Moon?" she asked.

"There's a sea," explained Sam. "It's called the Sea of Tranquility." "Isn't it a bit cold on the Moon?" she asked.

"No, it's not," said Sam. "It's all silvery and beautiful."

"Perhaps we should take some food," suggested Daddy. "Last time, there was only raw fish to eat."

"And starfish ice cream," said Sam.

"Ni," said Harry, who had heard the word ice cream.

"I know," said Mummy, "I'll make Loon a special surprise birthday cake, shall I?"

"Yeah!" Cried Sam and Harry together. They loved cake.

So that is what Mummy did. She took the boys on a quick trip in the buggy to Sainsbury's to get the ingredients. Then, while she was busy in the kitchen, Sam made Loon's card. He drew a picture of Loon in his sailing boat and wrote a big S for Sam under it. Meanwhile, Harry went upstairs (he was getting very good at this now!) to look in his bottom drawer. Yes, there was a silver spoon and a little white dish. One early morning, when only he was awake, Harry had seen them run into the room and hide in the drawer under his spare sleeping bag! He thought they would be very useful for eating ice cream.

Then Daddy came back from school and they all went into the kitchen to look at the cake. Mummy was just finishing the lemon icing on top.

"How many candles shall I put on, Sam?" she asked. "How old is Loon going to be?"

"I don't know," said Sam. He thought hard. "Perhaps he's going to be three, like me!"

"That sounds about right," said Mummy. "Here we are then." And she put three lovely blue candles on top of the cake.

"Now, let's all pack our swimming things and fleeces, just in case," she said. "It's getting dark already. Loon will be here soon!"

Chapter 37
Splash!

Everyone enjoyed sailing to the Moon. Daddy was allowed a turn at the tiller, which made him feel important and Mummy sat Harry firmly on her lap and held him tight when he wriggled. Sam was very pleased to find little Suki already curled up inside the boat. She purred like anything when she saw Sam. She loved Sam. As they sailed over the sleeping streets of their town and up into the night sky, Suki took out her fiddle and played and they all sang the words:

Twinkle, twinkle, little Loon
Sailing up towards the Moon;
Up above the world so high
Like a football in the sky;
Twinkle twinkle, little Loon,
With a dish and silver spoon.

The Moon grew bigger and bigger as they got closer and closer. Then they were there; Loon took the tiller from Daddy and steered the boat down. They landed on the silver sand right beside the Sea of Tranquility.

As they all scrambled out of the boat, they heard an excited squeaking sound coming from the water!

"Look, Daddy, it's Sam! And Harry! Isn't he sweet! Sam, Sam, look at me swimming. I'm brilliant! Look, Harry!"

It was Ursula. Urs had given her a bareback ride down to the Moon earlier that night. He was giving Ursula a swimming lesson while they were waiting. When they saw the others, they paddled out of the silvery waves and shook themselves dry on the sand. But where was Jemima?

"She said she would jump," said Loon. "But I don't know where she is. Have you seen her?" he asked Urs.

"No. She's not here yet," said Urs in his deep growly voice.

"I hope she hasn't got lost," said Loon. "She's very good at jumping over the Moon, but she's never landed on it before."

Sam ran up to the top of the little hill to look. He stared up into the dark sky. He could see lots of stars and the Milky Way, but no Jemima. But then he heard a familiar noise: "Hellooooooo," it went. "Here I am! Where are youououououou?"

And now he could just see the great wobbly shape of the cow high up above him. He could see her four legs kicking madly and her tail streaming out behind her.

"Jemima," he shouted as loud as he could. "This way!"

Down came Jemima, down and down. Now Sam could see her big black eyes gleaming in the moonlight.

"Look out, Jemima," he shouted. "This way. That's the sea over there."

But it was too late!

There was a massive splash—and Jemima disappeared under the water!

Chapter 38:
Swimming Again

"Help!" Cried Sam, running as fast as he could down the hill. "Jemima's come. But she landed in the water. Over there. Can cows swim?"

No one knew. Urs, who was an excellent swimmer, ran across the sand and into the sea. He swam as fast as he could over to where Sam was pointing. Then he took a deep breath and dived underwater. Everyone watched anxiously. Would Jemima be all right? Would Urs find her?

And then, up came the great white head of the polar bear. And, right beside him, up came the big black and white head of the jumping cow!

"Moooooo," bellowed Jemima. "Looook at me! I can swiiiiimmmm!"

And so she could. Clever Jemima. She had meant to land on land, but when she found herself underwater, she had just kicked her four legs and waggled her tail. She was a very resourceful cow!

"Hurrah," they all cried.

"I'm going in too," squeaked Ursula. And with a squeal of excitement, she rushed into the waves.

"Come on, Mummy. Come on, Daddy." Cried Sam. "Let's all go!"

"Ni," said Harry. He definitely wanted to swim. Sam and Harry had both had lots of swimming lessons and they were pretty good at it.

So, as quickly as they could, they got into their swimming things and ran into the sea. It was lovely! The waves were all silvery and surprisingly warm. Daddy held tight onto Sam and Mummy held tight onto Harry. Ursula swam round and round in circles, squealing with delight and making lots of splashes. Urs showed Jemima how to kick properly and Loon did a brilliant doggy paddle. It was such fun!

But little Suki didn't go in. She didn't like water; cats don't really like swimming as it makes their fur go all soggy. Instead, she lifted up her violin and played. The tune of *The Owl and the Pussycat* came floating over the waves and all the swimmers tried to sing the words. Only sometimes, if they opened their mouths too wide, the water came in instead of the song coming out.

After a bit, everyone had swum enough, so they paddled out of the sea.

"Let's dance!" Cried Sam. He loved dancing and he thought it would be a nice way to get dry. So they all joined hands and danced to the music of Suki's violin.

Then hand in hand, on the edge of the sand
They danced by the light of the Moon!
They danced by the light of the Moon!

They got dry in no time.

As soon as he was dressed again, Harry found his silver spoon and waved it proudly. "Ni," he said loudly. He was feeling hungry.

"Come on, everyone." Cried Loon. "Follow me. This way to the picnic!"

Chapter 39
The Birthday Tea

Loon didn't live in a kennel like most dogs. There aren't any trees on the Moon, you see, only thorn bushes, so you can't find enough wood to make one. Instead, he lived in a cave inside a white rocky hillside.

He led the way, woofing happily. When they got there, they saw that he had made a little bonfire out of thorn branches and twigs. It was crackling and burning happily just outside the cave entrance. And there was a most delicious smell!

"Fish!" Cried Daddy, who was also feeling hungry. "Someone's been cooking fish!"

"I have," said Urs, the Great Bear. "That's why we got here early. I remembered that people don't like raw fish."

"I helped too," squeaked Ursula. "But I don't like cooked fish! So we've got both sorts."

Everyone sat down on the ground by the fire. Mummy, Daddy, Sam and Harry all had cooked fish, which tasted lovely, even though it had got a tiny bit burned on top when Ursula had forgotten to turn it over. And Urs, Ursula, and Suki all had raw fish. Jemima tried some, but she didn't like it at all (A bit like marmite and toast, she thought as she spat it out). She decided to wait for pudding instead. Loon only had milk, which he drank from his Milky Way bucket.

For pudding, there was star-fish ice cream! Delicious! Harry got out his dish and spoon and had an extra-large helping. And then came Mummy's surprise Birthday Cake. "Here you are, Loon," she said proudly. "Happy Birthday!"

Daddy lit the candles with some matches that he had cleverly remembered to bring and everyone sang, *Happy Birthday, Dear Loo-oon, Happy Birthday to you*, while Suki played the tune on her fiddle.

What a lovely tea it was.

"Are you three?" Sam asked Loon anxiously when they had finished eating. "Are there enough candles for you?"

"Well," said Loon, "actually, I don't know how old I am. I'm not very good at counting. But three is a nice number to be."

"It is, isn't it?" Agreed Sam.

"Anyway," said Loon, "this is my best birthday ever!"

And then it really was time to be getting home. Next day was Tuesday and Sam and Daddy would have to go to school early; Mummy would have to go to work; and Harry would have to look after Granny. So they all needed a bit of sleeping time.

First of all, they waved goodbye to Jemima, who did a massive jump up into the sky. "Look at meeeee," she cried. "I'm over the Moooooon!" Then she disappeared into the darkness.

Then Ursula gave Sam a big bear hug and Harry a big wet kiss. She scrambled up onto her Daddy's back—and they were off, back to their ice house among the stars.

The others all climbed back into the boat. Loon took the tiller in his two front paws and set sail for Earth.

Suki was too tired to play her violin, so she sat on Sam's lap and they listened to the whooshing and fluttering of the wind in the sails. When they were nearly home, Sam could hear the twit-twoo of a barn owl flying in the dark air; and then he saw it swoop down and give Suki a kiss on her nose! Off it flew again. Now Sam could hear the faint hum of traffic on his road. But Harry didn't hear anything, as he was fast asleep—and so were Daddy and Mummy!

"Daddy, Mummy, we're here," Sam whispered, so as not to wake Harry. Loon had kindly landed on the patio to make it easier for the grown-ups. Out they got.

Sam was the last to scramble down from the little boat. "Goodbye, Suki," he said. But she was fast asleep too!

"Goodbye, Loon," he said, giving the little dog one last stroke on his silvery back. "Thank you for a lovely party!"

"Woof-Woof! Ha! Ha," barked the little dog. "Such fun!"

Chapter 40
The Dark of the Moon

It had been quite cloudy for the last few days and when Sam climbed onto his bed to look up into the night sky, he hadn't been able to see the moon at all. But tonight was clear again—hurray!—except…where was the moon? He couldn't see it anywhere, even though all the stars were shining as brightly as ever. He had noticed that for some time the moon seemed to be getting thinner and thinner, until it looked more like a silver bow than a round football. But that night it hadn't been there at all. Oh no! He wondered if Loon had disappeared too. Would he still come down in his boat? Sam opened his window wide and listened. And there it was! The swish of sails in the wind and a gentle bump, along with a familiar voice saying, "Woof Woof! Ha Ha! Such Fun!"

But why couldn't he see anything?

"Loon!" He cried. "Are you there? Have you come to see me?" Then he thought that if he couldn't see Loon, perhaps Loon couldn't see him either. It was a strange thought. But now he could feel the soft weight of the little dog on his lap, the lick of a doggy tongue on his hand and the touch of warm breath on his face. He was there all right! Thank goodness.

"Why can't I see you?" he asked. Surely on such a dark night, the silver dog should be shining more brightly than ever?

"It's the Dark of the Moon," explained Loon. "It's time for the Moon to have a long rest, so she turns her back on the sun. Seven whole days to sleep—and then she will wake up again."

"Oh," said Sam. That would be a very long sleep. He always woke up when the birds started singing in the first light of dawn. Sometimes he thought it was the birds who woke him up with their song and sometimes he thought it was the sun peeping through the gaps in the curtain. But if you lived on the moon, there wouldn't be any songbirds—and if there wasn't any light either, he supposed you would just sleep and sleep…

"Where do you go to sleep?" he asked.

"Oh, I curl up in my rocky cave; it's quite comfortable."

"Don't you get hungry?"

"Only when I wake up after seven days. I always sail straight down to Godstone Farm to find Jemima. She fills my pail with lovely warm milk. And when I get back, Urs brings me some starfish ice cream."

"I see," said Sam, a bit doubtfully. He knew he could never manage a whole week without any food. Harry couldn't even manage a whole morning!

"And I do like all the dreams," said Loon. "They are just as exciting as real life, don't you think?"

"I suppose so," said Sam thoughtfully. It was true—dreams could be exciting; he liked the ones about playing football and scoring lots of goals. But he had never had a dream quite as exciting as meeting Loon in real life and sailing to the moon.

"Will you come and see me when you wake up?" he asked. It would be really sad if Loon forgot about him. He would never forget about Loon!

"I will!" exclaimed Loon. "Of course I will!"

Then he gave a great yawn and Sam could see two rows of milky-white teeth inside his mouth. He wondered if that was why Mummy talked about Harry's milk teeth coming through.

"Well, sleep well," he said to his dear doggy friend. It was what his Mummy always said to him when she tucked him up in his snug bed under the blue helicopter duvet.

"Sweet dreams," he added…

Epilogue
O Bother That Brother!

O, bother that brother,
Said Sam, said Sam,
O bother that brother!
Said he.

Why is Sam's car seat
All covered in biscuit?
O what a palaver!
No, don't kick the driver…
O, bother that brother,
Said Sam.

There is mud from the buggy
All over the hallway,
And a hairy toy spider
On top of the sofa!
O bother that brother,
Said Sam.

In the garden together:
What horrible weather!
No, don't fall over;
Now, where's my umbrella?
O, bother that brother,
Said Sam.

Harry, that's not a weed;
And don't eat the birdseed;
You should wait till you're bigger
Before climbing the ladder.
O, bother that brother,
Said Sam.

Now, what's for supper?
It's tuna and pizza.
Harry, don't throw your water
All over Sam's dinner.
O, bother that brother,
Said Sam.

Two boys in the bath!
And they're having a laugh.
Harry's thinking - how can he
Splish-splash that Granny?
O bother that Harry,
Said Gran.

How can Sam get undressed
When it's all in a mess?
There's one bit of pyjama,
But where is the other?
O, bother that brother,
Said Sam.

Teddy's sticky with honey,
And it is not funny;
Harry's rolling all over
Sam's blue duvet cover –
O, bother that brother,
Said Sam.

There's the other pyjama
On top of the banister!
There's a green caterpillar
Under Sam's pillow;
O, bother that brother,
Said Sam.

Goodnight, darling Mama,
And good night, dear Dada.
Harry, don't be so noisy –
Why aren't you sleepy?
O, bother that brother,
Said Sam.

Charlotte and the Dandelion Fairy

Chapter 1
Dilly Dilly

Charlotte was sitting at the edge of Flower Meadow, singing to herself. Or at least she thought she was! Anyway, David, her older brother, wasn't listening because he was too busy throwing stones into the trickle of water, which was all that was left of the little stream on that hot May day. No one else was in sight. Mummy and Ben were back in the garden weeding and Daddy had gone to get some petrol for the strimmer.

Charlotte was singing flower songs. She loved singing and was very good at it, keeping beautifully in tune with her high, clear voice. She decided to sing all the flower songs she knew because she was in Flower Meadow. So first of all, she sang *Daisy, Daisy* and all the little white daisies beamed at her with their single golden eyes (did you know that **daisy** means **the day's eye**?); then she sang *With silver bells and cockle shells*, only she couldn't see any of those; and then she sang *Lavender's Blue* because there were lots of blue and green lavender bushes around and she liked the *dilly dilly* bit.

Lavender's blue, dilly, dilly
Lavend...O what's that!

The song wobbled and was silent. Charlotte had seen a quite unexpected **something**. On the green grass beside her was a clump of golden dandelions and sitting on top of the biggest one was a little creature! It definitely wasn't a dandelion, though it looked very much like one. Charlotte leaned right forward until her long hair touched the grass and stared with her eyes and mouth wide open in surprise.

"Go on," said the creature. "What were you going to say?"
"I wasn't," said Charlotte. "I was singing, not saying."

"I heard you calling," said the creature. "What do you want?"

"But I wasn't," said Charlotte, "and I don't want anything."

"Don't you?" said the creature. "I want masses of things. But why did you call me then?"

"But I didn't," said Charlotte. "I just sang the dilly dilly bit. I wasn't calling."

"But I'm called Dilly," said the creature. "It's my name. So when I heard you, I thought you wanted me. So I grew."

"You grew?" said Charlotte. "I don't understand. I don't understand anything!"

"Don't you?" replied the creature. "I understand loads of things."

Charlotte didn't know what to say. Being three and a lot, she understood loads of things too, but the last few minutes had been very puzzling. So she didn't say anything but just stared in wonderment. This is what she saw:

A little creature, about as big as her hand, with a mass of fluffy silvery curls, two shining green eyes, a beautiful yellow petal dress and two long, pointed green wings folded neatly down each side. Very gently, Charlotte reached out to touch the little thing; it quivered and lifted its green wings, but it didn't fly away. Perhaps it was too interested in Charlotte, or perhaps it just liked the singing.

"What's your name?" asked the creature.

"Charlotte."

"Why?"

"I don't know why. It just is. Sometimes I'm called Tot though, or Tottle. But I don't know why."

"Don't you? I know why my name's Dilly," said Dilly. "It's because of being a dandelion fairy. Listen: dan-*deli*-on: Dilly!"

"O," gasped Charlotte. "Are you a fairy?" She loved fairies; she had seen lots of pictures of them and she even had some fairies sewn on her blue denim dress, but she had never seen a real live one before. How exciting!

"I've never seen a real fairy before," she said.

"Haven't you? I've seen loads of humans. But they don't call me, like you did. And they don't usually sing either. Will you sing some more?"

"I will," said Charlotte. And she did. She sang the whole of Lavender's Blue, making sure that the dilly dilly bits were particularly beautiful. And then she sang:

Have you seen the Dandelion, the Dandelion, the Dandelion?

Have you seen the Dandelion that lives down my Flower Meadow? (Charlotte was always particularly good at making up words to fit.)

The little fairy sat very still on the palm of Charlotte's hand, just gently swinging her legs over Charlotte's thumb, her long green wings quivering softly and her silvery curls gleaming in the hot sunlight. She had closed her two green eyes because that way she could listen better and so it was that she didn't notice David until almost too late. David had finished his stone-throwing and was clambering back up the bank to see what his little sister was doing.

"That's not the right words," he said in a loud voice. "It's Muffin Man, silly."

Quick as a flash, the fairy opened her eyes, lifted her wings, stood up on her two little feet—and disappeared.

"David!" Cried Tot. "Look what you've done!"

But he couldn't look, for there was nothing to see: just a clump of golden dandelions, some green grass and a cross Tot.

"Come on," said David. "I'm hungry. Maybe there'll be muffins for tea." And off he ran.

Tot followed slowly. The fairy had gone and the afternoon was spoiled. And there weren't even any muffins, just toast and peanut butter as usual.

"Did you have a nice time?" asked Mummy.

"It was OK," said David.

But Charlotte didn't say anything.

Chapter 2
The Glass Bottle

Next morning, Charlotte got up early, quickly drank her milk and set off down the little path to Flower Meadow. All the others, except for baby Ben, were fast asleep; Ben was just thinking it was about time to start demanding *his* milk, but Tot told him to be quiet and so he was. Everything was cool and fresh in the early morning mist and all the long grasses were covered in silvery dew. Charlotte liked the swishing sound on her bare legs and the damp feel on her toes. She had put on her blue denim fairy dress and her pink sandals to be ready for Dilly.

But would Dilly be there? When she reached the dandelion clump in the misty meadow, Charlotte saw that the flowers were still closed tight in a little ball. And there was no sign of the fairy. Perhaps she hadn't gotten up yet either. Oh dear. Charlotte settled down to wait: it was a bit wet on the green grass, but she could see the rays from the golden sun making their way up over the hill and she knew that soon it would be lovely and warm.

As soon as the sunlight reached the clump of dandelions, the mist began to melt away and Charlotte decided it was time to start singing. She had been wondering about the words of her calling song and thought that they needed changing a bit. So this is what she sang:

Dandelion green, Dilly, Dilly,
Dandelion gold;
Come and see me, Dilly, Dilly,
Do as you're told.

Charlotte sang her new words three times, watching the clump most carefully. But nothing stirred. Now the golden sunlight was pouring through the last swirls of mist, but still, the flower was closed.

"O dear," said Charlotte to herself. "Perhaps Dilly didn't like the words. Perhaps she's cross."

So Charlotte tried again. And this time she sang:

Dandelion gold, Dilly, Dilly,
Dandelion green;
I'm just a child, Dilly, Dilly,
But you are a queen.

Surely Dilly would like being called a queen? After all, her lovely silvery curls did look a bit like a crown and her petal dress really was like gold!

"Come on, Dilly, please," said Tot. "I'm all by myself and I do so want to see you."

She sang the new words again, but still there was no movement.

"I know," said Tot. "Perhaps she'll like this."

And this time she sang:

Dandelion gold, Dilly Dilly,
Dandelion silver,
It isn't cold, Dilly, Dilly,
So you needn't shiver.

And then, as Charlotte gazed and gazed at the tight little dandelion ball, this is what she saw: the petals began to quiver and slowly unfurl; the round green ball became a beautiful sun, with wonderful shafts of golden petals like rays of light.

"Come on, Dilly," said Charlotte. "I'm calling you. Out you come."

And as she looked, she saw that the petal right in the middle of the flower was growing! It grew in a swirly way, like a dancing mist and the sunlight made it all sparkly and beautiful. Charlotte blinked and then when she opened her eyes again, there was Dilly, sitting on the flower and swinging her legs, her long green wings tightly furled.

"Hurrah," said Charlotte. "There you are!"

"I liked the second bit best," said Dilly. "I'm not really a queen, though; and you're very big for a child."

"Am I?" said Tot. "O." She thought about it. David was much taller than she was and although she had definitely grown bigger each year (she was well over three now), she sometimes still felt quite small!

"Would you like to grow smaller?" asked Dilly.

Charlotte was puzzled: how could you grow smaller? It didn't seem to make sense.

"I'm not sure," she said. "Can you grow smaller?"

"I can," said Dilly. "I can grow bigger and smaller whenever I want. Look!"

Dilly stood up. She reached into a little pocket in her golden petal dress and brought out a tiny glass bottle. The bottle was divided down the middle and had two tops, each with a little glass stopper on it. Inside one half, the juice was a bubbly green and inside the other half, it was pure yellow. Dilly took out one little glass stopper and sniffed.

"Dandelion wine," she said proudly. "Watch."

She lifted the bottle to her lips, drank one mouthful of the green juice—and started to disappear!

"O, no, come back." Cried Charlotte—but it was too late. The fairy had melted away back into the petals of the flower. Charlotte got on her knees, leaned right down and stared—and then she saw! The very middle petal wasn't a petal at all but a tiny, tiny fairy, even smaller than the fingernail on Tot's little finger.

"Watch me," whispered a tiny, tiny voice. And as Charlotte watched, she saw the fairy grow and grow until she was as big as her hand again!

"There you are," said Dilly triumphantly. "Now it's your turn. Green for small and yellow for big. Which do you want?"

"O," said Charlotte. She considered. Although she had often wanted to be as big as her older brother David, just now she thought that being small like Dilly would be more exciting.

"Green, please," she said politely and held out her hand…

Chapter 3
Very Small Indeed

Charlotte took the tiny bottle and held it carefully; then she lifted it up to her lips, making quite sure that the stopper had come off the *green* side. Then she took a small sip and swallowed. The juice tasted sweet and fizzy. Charlotte sat quite still and waited. Then there was a swirly, slithery sort of feeling in her tummy, as if she were falling down a long slide (much bigger than the slide in her garden) and a whooshy sort of sound. She felt a bit dizzy, so she shut her eyes, just for a moment. When she opened them again, everything had changed!

One moment ago, Charlotte had been sitting on damp green grass with golden sunlight all around her. Now she was in shadow. Great grass stalks stretched high above her, cutting out much of the light, although here and there brilliant dewdrop rainbows glittered in the gloom. Looking down, Charlotte could see ten tiny pink toes peeping out of two extremely small pink sandals.

"Goodness," she said. "I am very small indeed."

She was excited but just a little bit scared too, especially as she couldn't see any sign of the dandelion fairy.

"Dilly, Dilly," she sang urgently in her high clear voice—but the sound was much thinner and squeakier than usual. "Where are you, Dilly?"

Looking around, she noticed a clump of enormous, thick and rather hairy green trees stretching upwards; except they weren't trees at all but the stems of the dandelion cluster! And then, to her excitement, she saw Dilly come slithering down one of the stems, landing gracefully on her little bare feet right next to Charlotte.

"O Dilly," said Tot, "I am glad you're here; I was just…aaaah!"

Charlotte leaped backward as a massive, shiny black monster with two horns, a fierce scaly back and six huge legs came lumbering past, making a sound like thunder with each earth-shaking step.

"It's all right," said Dilly, "it's only a black beetle; he won't hurt you."

"A beetle!" exclaimed Tot. She remembered watching black beetles scurrying around the patio stones by her house. Then they had seemed tiny—but now…

"It's ants you want to watch out for," Dilly went on, "because sometimes they bite."

O, no, thought Charlotte. What would a massive ant bite feel like? Even small ant bites were itchy enough.

"Ants don't bite, though, unless you bother them," Dilly continued. "So if you don't get in their way, you'll be fine."

"**I definitely won't**," said Tot as loudly as she could, in case a passing ant happened to be listening.

"Anyway, you look much nicer now," said Dilly encouragingly. "I can talk to you properly. And I can see all your face at once. You're a lovely girl!"

"Yes," said Charlotte, "I am. And it is easier to talk to you, too." She was beginning to feel much better and ready for an adventure.

"Come on," said Dilly, "you can hold my hand now. This way."

"Where are we going?" asked Tot. But Dilly was already running and Charlotte needed all her concentration to keep up with her. The two friends were weaving around great stalks, clambering across huge slithery rocks *(Little pebbles really, I expect*, thought Tot) and dodging massive dewdrops that fell from a great height and splashed in a glitter of color on the bumpy ground.

"Here we are," said Dilly at last. Charlotte was quite tired by now and very glad to have a rest.

"Where are we?" she asked once she had gotten her breath back. Now that she had stopped panting, she could hear a strange roaring noise and she noticed that her little blue dress was quite soaked with glittering spray.

"By the stream," said Dilly excitedly. "I want to go sailing! It's fun: you wait until a leaf or a stick comes floating by and then you jump on it and go whizzing down the stream. And if you spread your wings, the wind takes you sailing—it's brilliant. Only you have to be careful not to fall in and get your wings wet. Otherwise, you couldn't fly away when the leaf starts sinking. They always do, after a bit. Here comes one!"

And with that, she jumped neatly onto a great green leaf that was whirling past, spread her wings and balanced beautifully as the stream swirled and whirled and roared past huge grey rocks.

"But I haven't got any wings!" Cried poor Tot, as the fairy disappeared downstream. "O, no," she went on, "now what am I to do? Dilly, come back!"

But Dilly had vanished from sight. Just then there was a great whump, which almost deafened her and a huge green wave rose up and swept toward her. Charlotte turned and ran, just out of reach of the seething water.

And there, right in front of her and completely blocking her way, was a massive browny-pink shape! It seemed to have come from nowhere. It had five great, knobbly mounds, all joined together at one end and each mound had a shiny white top. Then there was a crashing sound as several grass stems tottered around her and there was another knobbly shape, seemingly dropped from the sky above.

"O goodness!" Cried Charlotte, peering upwards. "It's a foot! It's David's toes!"

Chapter 4
Back Again

"David!" cried Charlotte joyfully. Her big brother would surely be able to help. But the trouble was, she couldn't see him properly, except, of course, his enormous feet. And although she shouted *David* as loud as she could, she realised that he probably couldn't hear her squeaky little voice. O dear! What should she do?

Then she had an idea; it would be difficult but it might work. She took her two tiny pink sandals off to get a better grip. Then she started to climb. Up the slithery black ridge of David's right sandal she went, clinging on with her two little hands. If only she could reach his toes! Slowly and carefully Charlotte moved onwards and upwards.

When she finally got to the top of the sandal, she paused for breath. Then she scrambled across the big black strap (taking care not to get tangled up in the scary Velcro bit) to where the five great toes stretched out before her. She knelt down on the biggest toe—and started to scratch, as hard as she could.

David had been standing quite still, looking across Flower Meadow. Mummy had told him to find Charlotte and he thought she would have probably gone to Flower Meadow as this was her favourite place. He looked carefully under the hazel trees in all the shadowy places, in case she was hiding.

"Charlotte!" he called—but there was no answer.

Then he felt a tickle on his right-hand (or rather his right-foot) big toe. Something seemed to be crawling up it: perhaps an ant or a beetle or a bothersome fly.

"Bother!" said David and he bent down to scratch the place…

Imagine his amazement when he saw, in front of his nose, not a bothersome insect but a tiny, tiny Charlotty!

"David," shouted Charlotte again, as she saw two huge brown eyes staring at her. "Help!"

Well, David was a clever and resourceful boy and once he had got over his first shock, he picked his tiny sister up very gently in his left hand, holding her carefully round her tiny waist. Then he stood upright and lifted her up, up, up, until she was on a level with his face and he could talk to her properly.

"O David," said Charlotte, "I'm so glad to see you."

And she explained everything that had happened. David was most impressed. At first, he wanted to be tiny too—it did look exciting—but then he thought that the important thing was to get Tot back to her normal size again so she could have her breakfast.

"Are you hungry?" he asked.

Charlotte was exceedingly hungry. But she couldn't possibly go back to the house as she was. What would Mummy and Daddy say when they saw her? What would baby Ben think about having a smaller instead of a bigger sister? And how would she manage to eat her cereal? Why, she wouldn't be able to lift the spoon up, let alone get a great chunk of Weetabix into her mouth.

"We'll have to wait for Dilly," she said. "I do hope she comes back soon. She went sailing, you see, but I couldn't go because of not having wings."

The two children decided the best thing would be to go back and wait by the dandelion clump; David would carry his sister there to save time. Charlotte thought that Dilly might be frightened if she saw a Huge Boy, as she didn't know him at all and might think he was fierce. So David obligingly climbed up a nearby hazel tree where he could hide among the branches. He took off his sandals first so as to get a better grip on the bark. Little Charlotte sat down on a dandelion leaf and waited; the leaf felt cool and slithery and she held on tight with both tiny hands. Then she sang her dandelion calling song, making the Dilly Dilly bits as loud as she could. She had just got to *But you are a Queen,* when there was a flutter and a whirr of wings—and there was Dilly, coming to land on top of her flower.

"O Dilly," cried Charlotte, "I am glad to see you." And she explained about not having wings for sailing and how David had rescued her and how she wanted to be big again so she could have breakfast.

Dilly wanted to see David for herself, so she flew up to the hazel tree branch and perched on his right shoulder while she inspected him. She wasn't at all frightened! She thought he was quite interesting, but she liked Charlotte's fairy dress better than his t-shirt and shorts. Then she flew down again and got out her two-headed glass bottle.

"Right," she said. "This time you must drink from the yellow side."

"I will," said Charlotte. She certainly didn't want to be even smaller and she made quite sure to take off the yellow not the green stopper.

"Here I go," she said. "Goodbye, Dilly and thank you for having me."

The yellow drink tasted sweet and fizzy too and soon Charlotte felt the strange swirly feeling inside her tummy. This time, she kept her eyes wide open and watched excitedly as her bare toes grew bigger and bigger and further and further away. Then there was a little jolt and everything was still. She was her normal three-year-old self again.

Charlotte remembered to reach down and gently lay the little glass bottle on the green grass. Dilly would certainly need it again and—who knows?—perhaps she and even David might too. David slithered down from the hazel tree and the two children set off hand in hand back again.

"You have been a long time," said Mummy. "O dear, where are your sandals?"

Both children looked down at their bare toes.

"In Flower Meadow; we'll get them after breakfast," said Charlotte.

Well, David easily found his two black sandals lying side by side under the almond tree. But Charlotte remembered that she hadn't been wearing hers when she grew bigger and even though both children went down on their hands and knees to look, they were nowhere to be seen.

"I wonder if Dilly took them," said Charlotte. "They would fit her beautifully."

Chapter 5
The Caterpillar

Charlotte thought that it would be fun to find Dilly again. She hadn't been to Flower Meadow for almost a week now. They never could find her little pink sandals and Mummy had had to get her some new ones. They were bright orange and she wanted to show them to Dilly. And perhaps, if she was feeling *very* brave, she might try being very small again! David was still asleep, as it was very early in the morning; Mummy and Daddy were asleep too, of course and Ben was sitting up in his cot playing with a red bucket and a spoon.

"Goodbye, Ben," whispered Charlotte and gave him a kiss on his nose. Ben laughed and waved his spoon and he didn't cry at all! So Charlotte tiptoed out of the house and ran down the little path to flower meadow. It was quite cold but she had put her stripy jersey over her pyjamas and some stripy socks under her new sandals. So that was all right.

As soon as she got to the dandelion patch, she sat down and started to sing. She sang Dilly's favourite verse about being a Queen—and she had only just finished it when she saw the swirly yellow mist dancing before her eyes. Yes, there was Dilly, sitting on the edge of her dandelion flower and dangling her legs! And—yes!—she was wearing Tot's tiny pink sandals!

"Hallo," said Charlotte, bending right down to talk to the little fairy. Suddenly, she felt very excited and brave! "Can I be small again, please?" she asked.

"Yes!" said the fairy. "Here you are." And she held out the little glass bottle with its two heads. Carefully, Charlotte took a little sip of the green wine! She felt the slithery feeling in her tummy and she watched her legs and feet getting smaller and smaller and nearer and nearer—and then there she was, sitting next to Dilly on top of the flower.

"Now," said the fairy. "What do you want to do?"

"O," said Charlotte. She hadn't really thought about it. What would she like to do? Certainly not go sailing again, because of not having wings. But O, wouldn't it be lovely to have wings like Dilly and go flying?

"Go flying with you," said Charlotte. "Only, I can't. O dear."

"Well," said Dilly. "You could grow some butterfly wings, if you like. But you would have to be a caterpillar first. And then a chrysalis. Would you like to?"

"No," said Charlotte quickly. Just think of being a horrible hairy caterpillar with hundreds of legs! She wasn't quite sure what a chrysalis was, but it didn't sound encouraging. And anyway, she had to get home in time for breakfast and it would probably take far too long.

"No," she said again. "I can't." And then she said, rather wistfully, "Although it would be just lovely to have butterfly wings!"

"Well," said Dilly, "you can't. Not unless you grow them. Why don't you? It would be fun!"

"I know," said Charlotte. "But I have to get back in time for breakfast. Otherwise they won't know where I am, you see. How long does the growing bit take?"

"It doesn't take long at all!" said Dilly. "How long does your growing take?"

"Ages!" said Charlotte. She thought of all the time she had spent growing till now. "Three whole years! And quite a lot more, too." She wondered how many breakfasts that would mean, but she couldn't count as far as that. Not even David could count that far!

"Goodness!" said Dilly. "I could never wait three years. But it's different with fairies. It didn't take long for you to grow small, did it?"

No, it didn't! thought Tot.

"Three whole minutes, more like," Dilly went on. "One minute to be a caterpillar; one minute to be a chrysalis; and one minute for your butterfly wings to dry properly. Then you'll be a tiny girl again, only with wings!"

Charlotte thought about it. She loved butterflies and thought that having wings would be brilliant. But what about the caterpillar bit? And she didn't even know what a chrysalis looked like. Still, three minutes wasn't much at all…

"Hurry up," said Dilly. "Make up your mind! Yes or no?"

"Um…Yes!" said Charlotte bravely. "As long as it really isn't long!"

"As long as it isn't long?" exclaimed Dilly. "What *are* you talking about? Come on!"

With that, she slithered down the dandelion stem onto the thick, soft grass. Charlotte followed and landed with a bump.

"Lie down—on your tummy!" said Dilly.

"O dear," said Charlotte. But she did as she was told. The earth felt bumpy and prickly beneath her stripy jersey and pyjama bottoms.

"Shut your eyes!" commanded Dilly. "I'm going to do some fairy magic. You can't open them until I've counted three. Ready?"

Charlotte shut her eyes and listened intently.

"One—two—three—open!" cried her fairy friend.

Charlotte opened her eyes. It was like looking through shiny green water—everything around her was green and wavy and fuzzy. She tried to get up—then to her horror saw that her little pink hands had disappeared. Instead, she had lumpy, hairy green things. They slithered along underneath her. It felt like crawling through slimy rice pudding. As for her new orange sandals—they were nowhere to be seen! She wanted to shout for help, but no sound came out. Her mouth, too, felt all slippery and soft—and her tongue and teeth seemed to have disappeared. One minute to be a caterpillar. She wondered how long a minute would take. She remembered Daddy saying once that each minute had sixty seconds in it. Some of those seconds must have gone already. She started counting from twenty—that seemed about right.

"Twenty caterpillars; twenty-one caterpillars; twenty-two..." It seemed to take forever. And she wasn't quite sure what came next, after twenty-nine. O dear! Usually, Charlotte would sing if she needed cheering up, but when she tried, she could only hear a soft whispery sound and no musical notes at all! But it was no good crying—she couldn't cry, even if she wanted to—and she was determined to be brave. So she slithered along a bit more—until...

"Shut your eyes!" came Dilly's loud voice just above her. "Then count three and open them!"

Chapter 6
Butterfly Wings

Charlotte opened her eyes.

"O no!" she gasped. She couldn't see *anything*. It was like being inside a deep, dark cave. It felt cold and damp and it was hard even to breathe properly. When she tried to wriggle around, she found that she couldn't move her arms and legs. Did she even *have* any arms and legs? Was this what being a chrysalis was like? Horrible! And very lonely.

I wish David was here, she thought, *or even Ben!*

She wanted to cry, but she wasn't sure if she had any eyes to cry with! And her mouth seemed to be covered with soft stickiness so she couldn't even open it.

All gluey, she thought. And everything was so quiet…did she have any ears to hear with? She wasn't sure.

I'll just have to pretend I'm asleep, she thought bravely. "Fast asleep in my own bed. Mummy's put the light out and everyone's fast asleep. And I'm breathing very gently."

Well, that was the best thing Charlotte could have done. Clever girl. Being fast asleep isn't at all frightening and you *want* to shut your eyes and be peaceful and quiet and not hear anything. Soon she felt much better…

And it wasn't that long before she felt a lovely warm wind blowing on her head and she opened her eyes again and saw bright light in front of her. She wriggled and stretched and found she could move again! Very carefully she crawled towards the beautiful light—and she felt warmer and warmer—and then she was out of the dark cave and all around was a lovely sweet smell! She was on top of a great green and purple flower—and it was swaying very gently in the breeze. And on each side of her she could see a beautiful, shiny, trembly wing!

The wings were soft pink with white spots and orange patterns—and they were just lovely!

Then she felt the flower shake and judder—and there was Dilly, right beside her!

"I love lavender!" said Dilly. "Do you? Now just keep very still until your wings are dry. You've got about ten more seconds to go!"

That's easy! thought Charlotte happily. And she counted quietly, inside her head: "One butterfly; two butterflies; three butterflies…" When she got to ten, she felt her beautiful wings opening wide in the soft wind. She saw that her little feet in her orange sandals had come back again. And there were her little pink hands, just as they should be. So, without even thinking about it, she stood up on tip-toes, stretched out her arms, flapped her new butterfly wings…and flew!

It was amazing! Below her, was a mass of flowers and she could see their bright, colourful faces smiling up at her.

"Come and taste us!" they seemed to be saying. So Charlotte fluttered and hovered and put out her little pink tongue and licked the petals, which tasted of the sweetest honey you could ever find. Then she felt thirsty. On the green leaves, she saw some sparkling dew drops, so she landed on a trembling leaf, put out her tongue and drank up the sweet water.

"O Dilly," she said. "I love having butterfly wings! Thank you."

The two friends raced round the meadow, flying through the bright warm air and stopping every now and again for a rest and a drink or a taste of nectar. Once, a great buzzy bumble bee flew past and Charlotte felt a bit frightened as it sounded as loud as a helicopter and had great glittering dark eyes that looked fiercely at her. But with her butterfly wings she twisted and turned and fluttered and soon the bee was left far behind. Once, she saw, only just in time, the sparkling silk strands of a huge cobweb, woven between two bushes and glimpsed a great hairy spider waving its eight legs at her and looking hungry! But she just fluttered her butterfly wings and flew up and away.

"You can't catch me!" she cried. "You'll have to have someone else for your breakfast today!"

And then she remembered! Breakfast!

"Dilly!" she shouted. "Stop!" She landed on top of a great lavender bush, folding her wings neatly behind her. Dilly flew down and landed beside her.

"I have to get back," said Charlotte. "They must have woken up by now. It's time for my breakfast. I must go!"

"But you've had loads to eat!" said Dilly. "And we were having such fun!"

"Yes," said Charlotte, "but they'll wonder where I am. Please, Dilly"

"O, all right then," said Dilly. And she felt inside the pocket of her yellow petal dress for the little glass bottle. Then she frowned.

"It's not there!" she said.

"O no!" cried Charlotte. "But I need it. I have to grow big again. Where can it be?"

"I don't know," said the fairy. She thought hard. "I definitely had it to make you grow small. But I must have put it down when I magicked you into a caterpillar. Bother!"

"O dear," cried Charlotte. She loved having butterfly wings, but not for ever! She was really a girl and she wanted to be one again. She didn't mind about not eating breakfast, because she wasn't at all hungry, but she did mind about her family being worried.

"Can't you find it?" she asked anxiously.

"I don't know," said Dilly. "But if not, I can always get some more from the shops."

"What shops?" asked Charlotte, puzzled. "How long will it take?"

"I don't know," said Dilly carelessly. "You always want to know how long things are! About three hours, I suppose."

"But I want to go home now," said Charlotte. She was being very brave, but even so her bottom lip wobbled a bit.

"See you," cried Dilly as she lifted her long green wings. "Goodbye!"

"But Dilly…come back!" cried Charlotte. "Help!"

But Dilly had disappeared.

"O dear," said Charlotte again. She really couldn't wait three hours. She had to get back home. But whatever would they say when they saw her? A tiny little Charlotte with butterfly wings!

Chapter 7
The Two-Headed Bottle

"David, wake up," came a soft whispery voice. It was Mummy and she was gently tickling his ears.

"What?" said David crossly. "I'm asleep."

"No you're not!" laughed Mummy in a whisper. (*Can* you laugh in a whisper?) "Don't make a fuss, I don't want to wake Charlotte up. Now listen. Daddy and Ben and me are going down to the pontoon. Daddy wants me to help him mend the wobbly bit. So I want you and Charlotte to get your own breakfast, OK? We'll be back by lunch time."

"OK," said David, yawning. He was still half asleep. "Bye, Mummy."

Off they went. David lay in his nice warm bed a bit longer, thinking about sharks and whales. Then he thought it was time to wake Charlotte up. He pushed back the duvet and stood up. He couldn't see his little sister at all. However, this was quite normal—she liked sleeping in a tight bundle, with the duvet covering her nose and hair. She was a very good sleeper and David knew that she wouldn't wake up unless he did something dramatic. Bouncing was usually effective—a good bounce on the end of the bed would set Charlotte up for the day. But not this time! Nothing stirred under the soft white duvet.

"Come on, Charlotte!" said David. No answer. He bounced again.

"Get up, Tot," he said. Nothing.

"OK," he said cheerfully. "If you don't get up after three, I'll throw the duvet downstairs. Ready? One…two…three…Right!"

With a mighty swoop, David heaved the duvet off the bed and tumbled it down the stairs. Imagine his surprise when he found nothing there! Just an empty white sheet. Not even any pyjamas.

"Goodness!" said David to himself. Then he thought that she must have got up early and gone down to Flower Meadow by herself. Well, after breakfast (he was very hungry) he would go down there himself and see. He got dressed quickly, bounded down the stairs and inspected the table. Mummy had put everything ready. He liked having the whole house to himself; it felt peaceful and he liked being able to do what he wanted, without any quarrelling. As today was a Saturday, there was no school to worry about.

David kicked his ball about a bit (carefully, so as not to break anything); he played This Old Man on the piano a few times; he removed his best green frog from Ben's cot and put it by the sink; he spent some time leaping across the gap between the sofa and the big armchair; he helped himself to a flapjack, which someone (Daddy, probably) had carelessly left out of the tin; and finally he sat down at the table to eat his Weetabix.

He had only just started when he heard a tapping noise at the window.

Surprised, David got up and went across to the window to have a closer look. Good heavens! There was a rather pretty butterfly fluttering and skittering just outside! Except it wasn't exactly a butterfly—it had little arms and legs and long curly hair and a stripy jersey over its pyjamas.

"Charlotte!" cried David excitedly. "What are you doing?"

"Let me in, let me in quick," said the almost-butterfly.

David opened the window and in she flew. She landed on top of the p-but jar and stood there fluttering her lovely bright wings.

"O dear," said poor little Tot. "Do sit down, David; you look so big standing there and I can't see you properly, only your t-shirt."

"OK," said David and he sat down.

"That's better!" said Charlotte. She folded her wings and explained everything that had happened. David listened open-mouthed. After a bit, he remembered to swallow his Weetabix. He listened some more. Soon he understood everything. His sister had grown small, with tiny butterfly wings, but now the glass bottle was lost and Dilly had disappeared. Without the yellow drink, there was no way Charlotte could grow back again.

"I wish *I* had wings," said David. "Can you really fly?"

"Of course I can, stupid!" said Tot and to show him she did a circle round the room, perching briefly on the lampshade and avoiding the sticky cobwebs in the top left hand corner. Then she settled down again on the p-but jar and folded her wings.

"But I want to be my own size again. What would Mummy and Daddy and Ben say if they saw me like this? Where are they, anyway?"

David explained. Then he said, "OK. I know. We'll zoom down to Flower Meadow and look for the bottle. It must be somewhere. Come on, I'll race you."

"Thank you, David," said the tiny girl. And off they went!

Well, usually, David would easily beat Charlotte in a race, but this time the fluttering butterfly reached Flower Meadow well before her brother came running down the path to the stream. You see, with wings you can take shortcuts and not have to keep to the up and down path. As soon as they arrived they started searching. Dilly had said that the bottle must have fallen out of her pocket when she was doing her magic caterpillar bit. So where was that?

"I know," said Charlotte. "Let's look over here."

They made their way to the dandelion clump and then a tiny bit further on, where Charlotte had lain down on her tummy.

"Somewhere round here, I think," she said.

David got down on his hands and knees to look, while Tot fluttered from one grass stalk to another, peering anxiously down. And it wasn't too long before...

"I've got it!" shouted a triumphant David. "At least, I think so. Is this it?"

"Yes it is!" cried Charlotte. "Hurray!"

The bottle was so tiny that you could have mistaken it for a dew drop, but it really was the right one. And luckily, neither of the two glass stoppers had fallen out so there was still plenty of green and yellow dandelion wine inside.

Tot picked it up carefully in her little hands. She opened the left-side stopper and took a long drink of the fizzy yellow juice. Almost at once, she could feel herself growing. Thank goodness, she was her nice girl size again! She could go home and have her breakfast!

"But Charlotte," said David. "Look behind you."

Charlotte peered over her shoulder. There, growing out of her shoulder blades were two huge pink and orange wings!

Chapter 8
Flying

"O, no!" said Charlotte. She wasn't really her proper self after all. She hadn't realised that her wings would grow big with the rest of her! There they were, huge and lovely, gleaming in the bright sunlight.

"Wow!" said David. "Do they still work? Can you still fly?"

"I don't know," said Charlotte miserably. "I wish I could take them off." She tried to pull them off her shoulders, but it was no good.

"Shall I have a go?" asked David kindly, although he did secretly think it would be a terrible waste.

"Yes," said Charlotte. But then she said "Ow!" and David had to stop trying.

"Bither, bother, bither!" said Charlotte crossly. Then she said, "I'm so hot!" But when she tried to take off her stripy jersey, she couldn't, because the wings were in the way.

"O dear, O dear," said Tot and her eyes filled with tears.

David stroked her left wing comfortingly. "When did you say Dilly would be back?" he asked.

"Not for three hours. And goodness knows how many minutes that is!" said poor Tot. "And I'm so hot!" she said again.

David kindly helped his sister get her two arms out of the jersey and then he undid the buttons at the side of the neck. But despite a lot of wiggling and pulling, he couldn't get it off her. She would just have to put up with it—and with the wings too, of course.

"Three hours isn't that long," he said encouragingly. "Mummy and Daddy aren't back until lunch, anyway. They're mending the pontoon and that always takes ages. You could wait here and I'll bring you some refreshments."

"I suppose so," said Charlotte.

"And you could practise flying," said David. "I bet you could go ever so high, now you're girl sized again." He looked longingly at his sister's wings; next time, he wanted to have a go, if Dilly would only magic him!

"I suppose I could," said Charlotte. She really didn't want Mummy and Daddy to see her with wings on, as she knew how startled they would be. And Ben would probably howl if he saw her. But would the fairy really come back in time? Supposing Dilly was late, or just forgot all about her? And what if she couldn't magic the wings away again?

"I bet you've had one hour already," said David. "So there's only two left to wait. Go on, see if you can fly up to that tree top." He pointed to a big oak tree growing high on the hill above the meadow.

Charlotte sighed. "All right then," she said. "But don't go away."

She found a nice clear place, without too many almond trees and practised lifting and fluttering her beautiful wings. Surprisingly, they didn't feel heavy, despite their great size. Then she felt a soft, warm breeze blowing upwards so she stood on tiptoe (just as she had done when she was tiny) fluttered her wings—and flew! It was easy! Up she went, higher and higher. The sunlight was all gold and glittery around her and it felt lovely. Charlotte decided that she was enjoying herself. Perhaps waiting for Dilly would be all right, after all. In no time, she had reached the top of the tall tree and landed on one of its great thick branches, covered in bright green leaves. She wobbled and steadied.

There was David, a tiny little figure down by the stream; beyond him she could see the even tinier shapes of her parents, bending over the pontoon. And could that be baby Ben sitting in his special seat? Up above, she could see one white, fluffy cloud making its way across the blue sky.

I wonder if I could fly up there, thought Tot. She lifted her wings and up she went! Very soon, she had reached it. The cloud was soft and pretty and it was wonderfully damp and cool. Charlotte felt much better. So she flew into and round it for a few times, until her hair and her jersey and even her wings were covered in little drops of fogginess.

Then she thought she had better get back. A startled buzzard passed by, mewing in alarm.

"It's all right, buzzard," shouted Charlotte, "I won't hurt you."

She swooped down and down and there was David waving encouragingly and then there was a bump. She had landed.

"That was lovely!" she said.

"You are lucky, Tot," said David.

"I suppose so," said Charlotte. "But I'm very thirsty now." She sat down in the shade of a hazel tree and folded her damp wings around her.

"I know," said David. "You wait here and I'll go and get some refreshments."

Off he went, running fast up the path to the house. Charlotte rested her head against the tree. Very soon, she was fast asleep.

Suddenly she woke up. Her left ear was buzzing and felt all tickly. She was just reaching up her hand to scratch it, when she realised that the buzzing wasn't buzzing at all, but the cross little voice of the tiny dandelion fairy.

"I went all that way," Dilly was saying, "as fast as I could—and you've gone and grown without me!"

"O Dilly," said Charlotte. "I am glad to see you! David found the bottle and so I did grow, I hope you don't mind. But my wings grew too!"

"Well they would, wouldn't they?" said Dilly. She didn't sound quite so cross now, as she was really pleased that the bottle had been found.

"Where is it?" she asked.

"I put it down there," said Charlotte, "as soon as I'd finished drinking." Dilly looked and yes—there was the little bottle, safe and sound. Quickly, she flew down from Charlotte's left ear, picked it up off the grass and put it safely away in her pocket.

Just then David arrived with his refreshments: a bottle of orange juice and some apple cake. Dilly wasn't at all frightened of him; she perched on his right arm and he fed her crumbs of cake with his left hand. She ate quite a lot, considering how small she was! But she didn't like the taste of the juice.

"Dandelion wine is much nicer," she said proudly.

"Can you magic my wings away?" asked poor Charlotte, urgently.

"I can," said Dilly. "You have to grow backwards this time. Lie down."

Charlotte lay down on her tummy. How big she looked and how tiny the little fairy looked as she whispered her instructions in Charlotte's left ear. David stepped back a bit to watch, which was just as well. He was exceedingly startled to see his little sister suddenly turn into a great brown bundle of a chrysalis! He counted carefully up to sixty chrysalises—and then watched in amazement as the chrysalis turned into a massive, wriggling caterpillar. Another sixty seconds of anxious counting—and there she was: a perfectly ordinary Charlotte again!

"Thank you, Dilly," said Charlotte. "I must go now and find Mummy and Daddy. And Ben."

"Can I have a go next time?" asked David.
But Dilly had already disappeared!

Chapter 9
The Sandpit

After her last adventure, Charlotte decided that it would be nice to have a **quiet** time playing near the house, where she could easily keep an eye on Mummy and Daddy. David was a bit disappointed as he couldn't wait to see Dilly again and ask her if *he* could grow small too. But there it was. Dilly was really Charlotte's friend, so he would just have to put up with it.

So David and Charlotte played in the sand pit and sometimes Ben helped too. That morning, they were working on a beautiful building project. In the middle of the sandpit was a very fine castle (*fit for a queen*, thought Charlotte!), with towers and turrets and steps and even hollowed out sand tunnels inside! In fact, it was so lovely that she started to sing, making up the new words as she went along.

Charlotty, Charlotty, where have you been?
I've been in the sandpit to build for a queen.
Charlotty, Charlotty, what did you then?
I built a fine castle and so did David-and Ben!

Then David fetched some water from the outside tap in his red bucket, so he could fill up the moat which he had built all around the castle; Charlotte decorated the towers with carefully chosen pebbles and flowers; and Ben started eating the steps.

Mummy came over to see what was happening and decided that perhaps Ben could do with a rest.

"Come on Ben," she said kindly, "time for your morning sleepus. And don't make such a fuss."

Off she went, passing David staggering under the weight of a full bucket of water for his moat.

"Bye Ben," said David cheerfully.

"Waa," replied Ben.

"Right then, out of the way, Charlotte," said David as he tilted the heavy bucket over the moat. He liked this bit. Whoosh went the water! Some of it got on one of Charlotte's best flowers, but most of it swirled nicely right around the castle, as it was supposed to. But what he hadn't expected was that the water would also find its way into the carefully hollowed out tunnels. And once it did that, the whole building started to shake and crumble! O dear!

Still, it was rather good watching it slowly collapse—although Tot didn't think so.

"David!" she cried indignantly. "What are you doing?"

Just then, they saw that the top turret was shaking and heaving in a most unexpected way, with cascades of sand flying out in all directions. Something seemed to be wriggling its way up through the castle. Or *worming* its way?

"David," cried Charlotte. "Do you think there's a worm inside? Or a snake?" And she hastily stepped back.

"Wow!" said David. And he leaned forward to get a good look.

But when the wriggling creature finally made its way out into the open, they could both see that it was not a worm nor even a snake, but a very cross and bedraggled fairy!

"Dilly!" cried Charlotte. "O dear!"

Poor Dilly was covered in wet sand: her lovely silvery curls were all muddy, her beautiful yellow petal dress was wet and filthy and so were her long green wings; one of her pretty pink sandals seemed to have got lost and the other one was all grimy and slimy.

For a moment, Dilly couldn't speak; then, she spat a mouthful of sand out and fairly howled in anger!

"I'm all wet!" she cried. "And I'm all sandy! And it's all your fault!"

"O Dilly," said Charlotte sorrowfully, "we didn't know you were there."

"I didn't think the water would reach the tunnels," explained David.

"Humph," said Dilly. "You said you were building a castle for a Queen! I heard you. So I came. And you said I was a queen—Queen Dilly, you said."

"I sang it, not said it," explained Charlotte. "It's different."

"I don't see why," said the fairy. And she burst into tears.

Fairies hardly ever cry, but when they do, they shed an awful lot of silvery tears. David watched in fascination as a silvery stream trickled down from the fairy's face over the collapsed tower and into his moat. Charlotte very gently reached forward and picked the tiny fairy up in her right hand. She blew soft warm air at her and tried to brush some of the wet sand away with her fingers. But Dilly just said,

"Leave me alone," and lifted her long green wings to fly away. Except that they wouldn't. Poor Dilly—her wings were so muddy and horrible that they just hung there lifelessly. Then she *really* began to howl.

Just like Ben, thought David, but he was careful not to say it out loud. He was surprised that such a small creature could make so loud a noise—but then the same could be said of Ben.

"O Dilly," said Charlotte.

And she stroked the little fairy so lovingly and gently, that in the end the howling died away. Then David went to get a fresh bucket of water and helped wash all the mud off the wings. But when they tried to clean the yellow petal dress, it went all limp. As for the sandals—well, it was no good having just one and in any case it was ruined.

"I'll get you some more," promised Charlotte.

"But what about my lovely dress?" said Dilly. And she started to cry again.

Chapter 10
Honey Bags

"I'll have to go shopping *again*," sobbed Dilly. "To get a new dress. Hic!" she hiccupped loudly. "And I haven't got any honey left to pay. Hic."

"We've got honey!" said Charlotte. "You can have some of ours."

"She means money," said David. "And we haven't got any."

"No I don't," cried Dilly. "Hic. Honey to pay the bee keepers."

"Bee keepers?" asked David.

"Bees that keep the shop, silly," said Dilly with a baleful glare. "Hic."

"O, I see," said Charlotte, even though she didn't. "Would you like us to get you some honey?" she asked kindly.

"Yes I would," said Dilly.

"You go, David," said Charlotte. "And I'll try to brush Dilly's hair." She had just spotted a little white feather which she thought would do for a brush.

"OK," said David helpfully and off he went.

Inside the house, Ben was still objecting to having his morning snoozle and Mummy was doing her best to cope.

"Can I take some honey please?" asked David politely.

"Yes, all right," said Mummy distractedly. "Only don't get it all sandy."

"Waaa," said Ben.

"I won't," said David. "Bye, Ben." And off he went, holding the jar carefully with both hands.

When he got back, he saw that Dilly was in a much better mood and that her hiccups had gone. Charlotte's feather had worked well and now the silvery curls were gleaming in the sun.

"Here's the honey," David announced. "But why do you need it?"

"To give to the bumble bees, of course, stupid," said Dilly. "You give them honey bags and then you can buy what you want." She peered at the jar, which was about half full. "There's enough honey there for loads of dresses," she admitted, "but I'll have to bag it up first. And you'll have to help. Come on." She tried to fly again, but it was no good: her wings were still too wet and heavy to lift properly.

"You'll have to carry me," she told Charlotte. "And you'll have to carry the honey," she ordered David. "It's the least you can do!"

Well, a quick listen in at the door of the house told them that Mummy would probably take hours settling Ben, so it looked as if the coast was clear. Unfortunately, though, Mummy heard them above Ben's bawling and called out. "David," she said. "Just run up to the pontoon, will you and ask Daddy how long he's going to be." (Daddy was still mending it!) "I want to know when to get lunch ready."

"O," said David. Then he said, "Bother," but quietly to himself so she wouldn't hear. "OK, then," he called out. In a whisper, he told Charlotte to go ahead and he'd follow as soon as possible.

So off went David to the pontoon and off went Charlotte, down the path to the flower meadow, carrying Dilly very carefully in her right hand and the honey pot in her left. When they got to the dandelion clump, Charlotte gently put the little fairy down on her flower.

"Right," said Dilly. "We need some spider webs. There's some huge ones over by the wild rose bush."

"O," said Charlotte. She wasn't quite sure about spiders and she knew their webs were horribly sticky; still, at least she was her proper girl size: just imagine if she'd had to get them when she was tiny!

"Go away," she said firmly to the spider; he scuttled off crossly, waving his eight legs at her. She scooped together a mass of sticky cobweb and plonked it down by the dandelion.

"Right," said Dilly again. "Now, you pass me clumps of honey and I'll make the honey bags."

Luckily, the honey was of the thick squidgy kind, so it wasn't too difficult for Charlotte to put little globules on her fingertip and pass them down. Dilly was very clever at weaving the cobweb round and making handles for the bags. After they had done six, Dilly said that was enough for the best dress in the bee shop.

"Now you'll have to grow small," she explained. "I'll need you to help carry the bags."

"O," said Charlotte again. She had been feeling nice and safe her own size, but she supposed it was only fair to do what Dilly wanted, after all that had happened. Anyway, it might be fun—only, no wings!

"I don't want wings," she said anxiously.

"You won't need them," said Dilly. "We'll walk together—I can't fly anyway and it isn't far."

"O good," said Tot. "But I thought you said it was three hours to the shops."

"No, stupid," replied Dilly. "That was to the wine shop, not the dress shop. It's quite different. Now, are you ready?"

Tot was and so Dilly produced the little bottle (luckily still in her pocket despite the sandcastle adventure), Charlotte took a gulp of slithery green wine—and there she was again: a tiny little girl! Dilly decided to leave the bottle behind, because of having to get undressed in the shop, so she hid it carefully under the dandelion flower.

"Right," said Dilly. "This way to the bank."

"But I thought we were going to the shop," said Charlotte.

"We are, silly!" said Dilly. "The shop is in the bank. I'll show you."

The two little creatures set off up a tiny fairy path that wound its way under the great grass stalks, round the corner by the spider web and onwards to the bank!

Chapter 11
Shopping

As the two friends made their way along the little fairy path, carrying the honey bags, Dilly explained about the bank. It was an old earth bank, she said, with brambles growing on it and it was where the bumblebees had their shop. You had to go down a little slope which led underground—and then there it was. It was by far the best dress shop around and had different dresses for all the different kinds of flower fairies.

How lovely, thought Tot. She wished she was wearing her fairy dress, instead of the shorts and t-shirt that had seemed more sensible for building a sandcastle.

It wasn't far to the shop, but the journey was exciting for a tiny girl. She liked looking up at the huge leaves and stalks above her head and down at the scurrying ants and beetles, being sure to keep out of their way. (*A bit like watching out for cars*, she thought.)

"Here we are," announced Dilly. She walked between two huge, prickly bramble stalks, found a little round hole in the bank and showed Charlotte how to slither down without dropping the honey bags. Inside it was dark and it smelled sweet; little beeswax candles flickered, showing rows of beautifully coloured dresses hanging from the earth walls.

"Aha! Bizzzzznessss…," came a soft buzzy voice from the darkness. It was the bumblebee keeper. He walked slowly forward on his six legs, his wings neatly furled. Charlotte was a bit frightened at first as he seemed so big and furry with huge shiny black eyes. But his voice was deep and kind and she soon relaxed and started to enjoy herself.

"Come in pleazzzze. Dandelion dresssezzzz over here," he buzzed, looking at Dilly, "sizzzzzes 3 to 5. And what sort of flower are you?" he asked Charlotte. "I can't make you out. It's very puzzzzzling." He peered at her t-shirt and shorts and shook his furry head disapprovingly.

"O, I don't need a dress," said Charlotte quickly. She would actually have loved a new fairy dress but she wasn't sure if there would be enough honey-money. "I'll just help Dilly look."

"You can browzzzzze, if you like," said the bumblebee kindly. "There are plenty to choozzzzze from."

And indeed there were. Charlotte could see beautiful silky bluebell dresses, lovely pink rose ones and a brilliant white daisy dress with a yellow petticoat. How she wished she could have one. She noticed that they all had extra holes for wings as well as arms, which would certainly make them easier to get on and off, if you were a fairy.

Meanwhile, Dilly, helped by a kindly assistant bee-keeper, had found a new dandelion dress that fitted beautifully ("The old one was getting a bit tight," she admitted) and had handed over the six honey bags in payment.

The two friends said goodbye and thank you to the bee keepers and set off back home along the little path. Dilly whirled and twirled, very pleased with her lovely new petal dress. Then she stretched out her long green wings and found, to her delight, that they were dry again and quite ready to fly.

"Hurray!" she cried. And in a joyful flutter and flurry she flew up, up into the blue air.

"Dilly!" cried Tot, "don't go—wait for me!"

But the dandelion fairy had disappeared.

Meanwhile, back on the finca, David had raced down to the pontoon and shouted out his message to Daddy. Daddy was looking very hot and muddy and the pontoon was looking quite muddy too, as well as wobbly.

"I've not nearly finished," said Daddy. "Tell Mummy 3 o'clock at the earliest."

"OK," said David and raced back to the house. It was surprisingly quiet. When he went in, he saw that Ben was fast asleep, lying on his tummy in the cot; and that Mummy was also fast asleep, lying on her back on the sofa. She looked so peaceful that he didn't like to wake her, so he wrote a message instead on a scrap of paper that he found in the waste paper basket. This is what it said:

Daddy says 3 for lunch. Gone to…

He didn't know how to spell Flower Meadow so he just wrote *f m;* he was sure Mummy would understand. Feeling very pleased with himself, he gently laid the message on top of Mummy's tummy, where she would be sure to see it when she woke up. At least, it would give him and Tot loads of time for an adventure! Then he tiptoed out of the house, hurtled down the path and arrived at the dandelion clump in next to no time.

But there was no one there.

"Charlotte!" he shouted. "Dilly?"

Not a sound. Bother.

He wondered if Charlotte had grown small again and he was just kneeling down to check that she wasn't hiding under the dandelion leaves, when he caught sight of the tiny, sparkling, two-headed glass bottle.

Wow! thought David. *I could grow small too!* He had watched his sister grow from small to big, so he knew what to do. It would be brilliant: sometimes he thought that adventures were wasted on his little sister. He wasn't sure if Dilly would be pleased, but as she wasn't there to ask he decided that she would have to lump it.

"OK," he said to himself. "Here I go!"

Very carefully, he picked up the tiny bottle. He undid the green glass stopper and took a gulp. Almost at once, he felt his tummy slide downwards—a bit like you do when you are in a fast lift in John Lewis. Then he saw two tiny feet, clad in black sandals, on the ground and he knew that he had done it! He looked up.

"Wow!" he said again. He was standing in a great green grassy jungle. A huge hairy fly flew past, startling him considerably. He could hear rustles and hums and buzzes and fluttery sounds all round him. It was brilliant!

Carefully, he put back the little green stopper and hid the bottle under the huge dandelion clump. He was ready for his adventure! Where should he go?

Then he noticed a little fairy path leading off round the corner by a massive spider web. He decided to follow it!

Chapter 12
The Frog

It was Charlotte's turn to be cross! Why did Dilly keep disappearing like that? It wasn't fair. Now Charlotte would have to find her own way back to the dandelion clump—and perhaps even have to grow big again all by herself. Bither, bother! She set off down the little fairy path, thinking that it would probably be better to sing than cry. So she did:

Where, O where has my little Dilly gone?
O where O where can she be?
With her hair cut short and her wings cut long—
O where, O whe-ere is she?

Deep down in the crumbly earth, a musical worm heard the song and wriggled his way up to the top so he could listen better. He squirmed his pink head at Charlotte as she passed by: "Lovely music," he whispered (worms can't speak loudly).

"Thank you," said Charlotte, determined not to be startled—and went on her way, still singing bravely as she followed the little fairy path…

Meanwhile, David was having a brilliant adventure! There were loads of grassy stalks that were excellent for climbing and that swayed excitingly in the breeze. There were masses of huge rocks (*Pebbles really, I expect*, he thought) on the ground to scramble up and then to slide down with a great whoosh on the other side.

Then, just as he turned a corner, he saw that his way was blocked! An enormous green frog was squatting right across the fairy path. It burped impressively.

"Wow!" said David. Then he said, "Please could you let me by?"

The frog stared at him with his great moist green eyes and blinked. But it did not move.

Bother, thought David. *Maybe it doesn't understand. I'll just have to climb over it, I suppose.*

He started to scramble up the frog's hind leg. This was not easy. The frog was slippery and it was difficult to get a grip. David had just managed to get one leg over the frog's back, clinging on to its neck with both hands, when there was a huge whumph and a great lurching and spinning all around. The frog had started to move! With its powerful hind legs it leaped high, high into the air—above the tops of the tallest grasses and up into the clear golden sunlight. David just managed to keep his hold on the slithery neck and dig his little heels into the slippery back. Then there was an enormous thudding crash that shook him from head to toe! The frog had landed! And it hadn't finished yet—it went on leaping and landing, leaping and landing, up the fairy path, with David clinging on desperately. He had slithered forward and sideways so his head was right up against the frog's neck and he could see one huge green frog's eye blinking in time to the leaps: up and down; open and shut! There was no way he could stop the frog, but at least he wasn't going to fall off. So he decided that he might as well enjoy the experience.

Then, as suddenly as it had begun, the leaping stopped. David took a deep breath and slithered down from the frog's neck. It was a relief to be back on firm ground again. And the first thing he saw was his tiny little sister Charlotte—there on the path just in front.

Charlotte had been very startled when she had heard a great crashing and seen, coming straight at her along the path, an enormous green frog with what appeared to be two heads! She didn't have time to be afraid or to get out of the way, so she just stopped, her mouth open in amazement. Then one of the heads disentangled itself and slithered down the frog neck onto the ground.

"David!" she cried in amazement. "What are you doing?"

They both turned to look at the frog. Its eyes were wide open and staring at Charlotte and its great green body was gently quivering. It blinked at her and the children were surprised to see two shiny tears trickle down its nose and land plop on the ground.

"What's the matter?" asked Charlotte gently, but the frog just gave a sorrowful croak, shook its great head sadly and, with a mighty bound, leapfrogged over the two children and away out of sight.

And then, there was a sudden fluttering in the air above and there was Dilly! She swooped down and landed on the ground beside the children. She looked suspiciously at David.

"How did you grow small without me?" she asked. "Have you taken my bottle?"

David told her what had happened, being sure to explain that he had carefully put the bottle back where he had found it. Then Charlotte joined in to tell Dilly about the strange sadness of the frog.

"What was the matter with him?" she asked.

"O, I expect he just wanted a kiss," said Dilly impatiently, "frogs usually do."

"O. I see," said Charlotte, although she didn't really.

Anyway, it was definitely time to be getting home. Ben would certainly be awake by now and even Mummy wouldn't sleep that long in the daytime. David and Charlotte walked back down the path to the dandelion clump, while Dilly flew round and round above their heads. Soon they had arrived.

"Right. Before you grow big again, I want your shoes," said Dilly to Charlotte as soon as she had landed. "You promised."

"O," said Charlotte. She had promised, it was true, but what would Mummy say if she came back without her new orange sandals? Mummy could hardly be expected to get her yet another pair! Still, a promise was a promise. Reluctantly she undid them and passed them over. Dilly was thrilled—and they did go well with her new dress and her freshly cleaned green wings.

Then it was time to find the two-headed bottle and drink the yellow wine to make them grow big again. Charlotte went first and then David. Soon the two children were making their way along the path to home. Charlotte had to go quite slowly, because of not having any sandals but David was very good about waiting for her!

Chapter 13
Cross!

It was a very hot afternoon and everyone was feeling cross. Daddy was cross because the pontoon *still* wasn't mended and he was getting exceedingly muddy trying to fix it. Ben was cross because he hadn't had his morning sleepus and he was tired, although he didn't like to admit it. Mummy was cross because Ben was cross. She had dumped him in the swing and told the children to look after him while she gave the house a good cleaning, which it certainly needed. Charlotte was cross because she had to wear her hot welly boots instead of sandals, as Mummy and Daddy had agreed that they wouldn't buy her *another* pair. She had gone to sit by herself at the bottom of the garden, where it was a bit cooler, to do some drawing. David was cross because no one would play football with him and it got a bit boring after a while playing on your own. So he decided to climb the old apple tree.

He managed the first bit quite easily; he had just got both legs and arms into a comfortable position, when he heard a very surprising sound coming from up above him.

"David!" came the sound. "Look at me!"

David looked up.

"Wow!" he said. "Dilly! Is that you?"

It was. Well, sort of. It wasn't a tiny fairy Dilly—it was a great big girl Dilly—pretty much the same size as Tot, only with wings, of course. There she was, sitting on one of the higher branches, swinging her legs and peering down at him.

"Aren't I clever!" exclaimed Dilly. "I wanted to see if I could grow as big as Tot, so I drank some yellow wine—and it was easy! I'm just like a proper girl aren't I?"

"Yes," agreed David. "Except for the wings," he added.

"And flying is brilliant!" said Dilly. "I can go much higher and faster now that I'm girl-sized!"

"Wow!" said David again.

Just then, he heard the door of the house bang and, peering through the lower branches of the apple tree, he saw Mummy coming across the grass.

"Shhhhh," he whispered to Dilly. "Keep still!"

David wasn't sure what Mummy would think about Dilly and he didn't want to startle her. Luckily, Mummy just went over to the vegetable patch, to survey the weeds. David quickly scrambled down the tree so that there would be no need for her to look upwards. Ben looked down to watch his brother land with a bump on the ground in front of the swing; then he looked up and saw a beautiful winged creature in the tree above his head. He laughed delightedly and stretched out his hands. Dilly scowled at him and stuck out her tongue, which made him laugh even louder and wriggle with delight.

"Shhh, Ben," whispered David—but Ben took no notice.

"Goo!" he gurgled happily and waved his arms.

Mummy came over.

"Well, at least he's happy," she said, "even if he's had no sleep since dawn! Where's Tot?"

"At the bottom of the garden," explained David. If only Mummy would go down there, he would have time to tell Dilly to go away and wait for them in Flower Meadow.

"She probably wants to show you her drawings," he went on hopefully.

"Well, I'll just go and see," said Mummy, "and then I really must get going on the vegetable patch. Just look at all those weeds."

As soon as Mummy had gone away, David looked up. Dilly had moved and she was now leaning down from the lower branches of the tree and swinging Ben's ropes with her two big hands.

"Dilly, go away," hissed David urgently.

"No!" said Dilly. "I won't."

"Doo," said Ben, happily.

"Please, Dilly," whispered David. "Mummy's never met a fairy before and she might be startled."

"No!" repeated Dilly. "I want to see inside your house. I've never been inside one before!"

And with that, she gave Ben's ropes one last swing, jumped down from the tree, ran over to the house, opened the blue door, went in—and banged it shut behind her!

"Waaa!" said Ben.

"Bother!" said David.

Mummy and Tot came back from surveying the drawing and walked over to the apple tree.

"Do stop crying, Ben," said Mummy. "I suppose you really do need a sleepus. Come on."

"I'll take him," said David quickly. "Then you can get on with the weeding. Charlotte can help. We'll play with him and then if he looks sleepy, we'll call you."

"All right then," said Mummy, looking surprised but pleased. "Thanks, David."

"Come on Ben," said David. Mummy lifted him down from the swing and he crawled excitedly over to the house: he had seen the lovely yellow and green creature go inside—and he wanted to have a closer look!

"Come on, Charlotte," said David—and to his relief she didn't make a fuss but followed happily.

"I want to put my lovely drawing on Daddy's pillow," she explained, "so he can see it when he gets back from the pontoon."

By this time, Mummy was down on her knees beside the vegetable patch. All three children went inside the house. David shut the blue door with a sigh of relief.

Chapter 14
Playing with Dilly

Quickly, David explained what had happened.

"Golly!" said Tot. "So where is she now?"

The three children peered through the gloom of the house—it always seemed particularly dark when you first came out of the bright sunlight. David reached up to turn the light switch on.

"There she is!" cried David. "Wow!" He pointed upwards. Dilly was perched on top of the banisters, dangling her great legs over the edge of the stairs, her long green wings fluttering gently.

"It's a brilliant house!" cried Dilly as, with a flutter of wings, she swooped down to land beside Tot. "Look, I'm as big as you now!"

"Did you drink the yellow wine?" asked Tot.

"I did!" said Dilly proudly. "And now I'm a girl!"

"Except for the wings," said David. "You really ought to hide them. If Mummy comes in, they'll be the first things she'll notice. Can't you take them off?"

"Of course not, silly," said the fairy. "They're part of me; they grow big when I do!"

Ben chortled delightedly: he thought Dilly was brilliant! But David and Charlotte were worried.

"You really don't look terribly like a girl," explained Tot. "Girls don't have wings. And they don't have lovely petal dresses either."

"O well," said Dilly. She wasn't at all bothered about Mummy and she really did want to see what it felt like to be a proper girl in a proper inside house.

"Can I wear one of your dresses?" she asked Tot.

"I suppose you can," said Tot. But when Dilly tried to put the blue denim dress on, it was far too tight to fit over the petal dress let alone the wings and it wasn't nearly long enough to hide them.

"It's hopeless," said David. "Anyone could see she isn't a girl."

"I know!" cried Tot. "I've got a brilliant idea. She can wear my nightie!"

Charlotte had a pretty flowery nightie, which was nice and loose for sleeping in and which reached right down to the ground.

"Then, if Mummy does see her," Tot went on, "she'll just think it's a friend come to stay the night."

"I suppose so," said David doubtfully. But he couldn't think of a better idea so they agreed to try it. Even the loose-fitting nightie wouldn't fit over the petal dress, so Dilly had to take it off. She laid it carefully on David's bed and cleverly remembered to take the two-headed bottle out of the petal pocket and put it into the nightie pocket, in case she needed it in a hurry. She furled her two green wings neatly behind her back—and the nightie covered them up beautifully. You probably wouldn't guess that she was really a fairy and not a little girl! Except that her eyes were strangely green and glowing and her hair was remarkably silvery for one so young; still, apart from that, she might be a friend come to stay the night. (Although, of course, it wasn't night yet.)

"You should take my sandals off, though," said Charlotte. "You don't wear sandals in bed."

"No!" said Dilly. "They're not your sandals, they're mine. And anyway, I'm definitely not going to bed. This is much too exciting."

She tried to lift her wings to fly up to the ceiling and inspect the light (she had never seen one before). But of course, she couldn't because of the nightie getting in the way. So she climbed up the stairs instead and peered down at it from the children's bedroom. Ben tried to climb after her, which he wasn't allowed to, so David told her to come down.

"We'll show you our toys," he said. "Come on!"

So the three children and the fairy-girl had a brilliant time getting all the toys out all over the floor. Dilly liked Ben's rabbit best. She also liked the animal jigsaws; at least she liked pulling the bits apart—she didn't even try to fit them together again.

She was good at bricks, though, balancing them cleverly to make a massive tower and not making a fuss when Ben knocked them all down. She obviously didn't understand what books were for and had no idea how to read, but she liked looking at all the pictures, once she had got the hang of turning the pages over. When David played her *Michael Finnigan* on the piano, she was amazed at the sound, although she didn't understand what the words meant!

"Why has he got whiskers?" she demanded. "I thought that was rabbits."

David had just started to explain, when they all heard, quite clearly, a loud knocking on the kitchen window!

Chapter 15
Hiding

"It's Mummy," hissed Charlotte. "Quick—hide in my bed! Upstairs!"

David ran over to the window. He stood on a chair so he could see Mummy better and she could see *him* but not the stairs!

"What do you want?" he asked.

"Is Ben all right?" asked Mummy. "I don't suppose he's feeling sleepy, is he?"

"He's fine," said David. "We'll call you if he gets sleepy."

"Well," said Mummy. "I've done quite a lot of weeding, but there are still loads left. Are you OK for a bit longer?"

"We're fine," said David.

"We're fine," said Charlotte, who had bundled Dilly under her duvet and scampered down the stairs again.

"Doo!" chortled Ben, happily.

"Well, that's good," said Mummy. "I think I'll just come in and get a drink of water before I get back to the weeds."

"It's all right," said David. "I can pass you one out of the window." And he knelt down on the chair to reach for a full glass which happened to be standing nearby on the table.

"I expect you're muddy," said Charlotte. "And you don't want to get the house dirty after all that cleaning!"

"I certainly don't," agreed Mummy. "Thank you, David," she said. She drank the water in two great gulps and set off back to the vegetable patch.

"Wow!" said David. "That was close!"

"You can come out now, Dilly," said Charlotte.

"I do like your bed," announced Dilly, who had emerged from the soft white duvet and slid down the banister. "Can I really stay the night with you?"

But before the children had time to answer, they all heard another noise. Squelch, squelch, squelch it went, coming from the direction of the pontoon and getting nearer and nearer!

"It's Daddy!" cried David who, still on the chair, was peering out of the open window. "He's all muddy! He must have fallen in the mud—and he's coming this way!"

There was no time to hide! The two children and the big fairy stood rooted to the spot; Ben stood up excitedly for a whole thirty seconds, which was a record, only no one noticed.

"Da!" he said.

Everyone (except Ben) listened with bated breath to the footsteps. Squelch, squelch, squelch they went, down the little hill, up to the patio bit, past the blue door and round the back of the house. Then they heard the squeak of the bathroom door and the gurgling of pipes.

"He's having a bath," said David! "Thank goodness."

But the danger was not over yet! There was a tap-tap at the window—Mummy, looking hot and weedy!

"I'm going to have a bath with Daddy," she said. "We won't be long. OK?"

"OK!" said David, still on his chair.

"Ba!" said Ben from under the table.

The two girls didn't say a word or move a muscle. And the amazing thing was that Mummy didn't even notice that there were two little girls in her kitchen, instead of the one which she knew about. Extraordinary! But then, she never had been much good at counting, or sometimes even remembering which child was which. They all (except Ben) listened anxiously for the squeak of the door which meant that she too had safely gone into the bathroom.

Then David sprang into action.

"This is our chance!" he cried. "Go on Dilly, quick! Off you go."

"I don't see why…" Dilly began, but when Charlotte said "Please, Dilly, you really can't stay," she saw that it was no good.

As quickly as she could, she wriggled out of the nightie, flinging it wildly away when she had finally freed her wings. (It landed on the lightshade!) Meanwhile, Charlotte had fetched the petal dress from David's bed and helped Dilly on with it.

"We'll come and see you tomorrow," she said. "We promise!"

"Humph," said Dilly. Then David carefully opened the door (this one, luckily, didn't squeak at all) and she was off, flying swiftly over the trees to Flower Meadow.

Chapter 16
Cross Again!

"Phew!" said David. "Come on, Tot; we'd better start clearing up."

And indeed the room was a complete mess! All the toys were scattered over the floor; and Ben had clearly been investigating the Weetabix packet under the table when they had been too busy to notice. But the children had scarcely begun the tidying when the door opened and in came a lovely clean, pink Mummy.

"Daddy's still getting his mud off," she began, "so he…O, no! Look at this mess! And I've only just tidied up! Whatever have you been doing?"

"Um," David began, but Mummy was too cross to wait for an answer.

"Right!" she said. "Tidy up now, then bath for both of you and you can get changed into your night clothes and then early bed. And that means you too, Ben. Look at all that Weetabix! And no supper, either. Charlotte, what is your nightie doing on the lampshade?"

"Um," Charlotte began, but Mummy was in no mood for listening.

"Just get on with it!" she said.

So they did.

The bath was a bit muddy round the edges, but never mind. David and Charlotte had a quiet wash without too much in the way of splish-splash. Then, as ordered, they got straight into their night clothes.

And it was then that Charlotte suddenly realised. She felt something unexpectedly hard in her nightie pocket and, reaching her hand in, she pulled out the little two-headed glass bottle!

"O, no!" she said. "The bottle! Dilly must have put it here when she got changed."

"But that means she must still be big," said David. "She can't grow small again without it."

"O dear!" said Charlotte. "She'll have to be small to sleep in the dandelion. She'll need it! What shall we do? Mummy will never let us go to Flower Meadow now."

"No," agreed David. "Not now we're ready for bed."

He thought hard. And then he had a brilliant idea!

"I know," he said excitedly. "Your sandals!"

"What?" asked Tot.

"Your sandals!" cried David. "Dilly was wearing them wasn't she? So they'll still be big too. We'll tell Mummy we've just thought where they might be (which is true!) and she's bound to go and let us look."

"I suppose so," said Charlotte. She remembered all the fuss there had been after she had reported the loss of the second pair.

"But will Dilly let us have them back again?"

"She'll just have to," said David. "And anyway she'll be so pleased about getting the bottle back! Come on." So that is what happened.

Mummy and a beautiful pink and clean Daddy agreed that the children should go and find the sandals straight away, as they really couldn't afford another pair. So Charlotte and David hurtled down to Flower Meadow in their night clothes (Tot wore her welly boots so she could go quickly). At first, they couldn't see Dilly anywhere, despite her great size, but then David remembered where she had been earlier and he looked up at the hazel tree. Yes, there she was, curled up on the top branch with her great green wings and long legs dangling down the trunk.

She was so pleased to get her bottle back (trees make very uncomfortable sleeping places) that she agreed almost at once about the sandals. They said goodnight and David and Charlotte walked happily back along the little path. Charlotte was wearing her lovely orange sandals and singing happily:

Wee Dilly Dinkie
Made such a mess,
Upstairs and downstairs
In her night dress.

Tapping at the window ("Only that was Mummy," she said)
Crying through the door ("There isn't a lock on our door," she explained)
Are all the children in their beds

Or are there any more…? ("Dilly's really a child too," she said, "and she's not in bed."

"Nor are we," said David.

But they were soon!

Chapter 17
Egg

David and Charlotte had promised they would see Dilly the very next day, so they set off straight after breakfast, down the little path to Flower Meadow. Charlotte was very pleased to be wearing her lovely orange sandals again, instead of those horrible hot welly boots. Dilly was still a bit cross about giving them back, but she was in a reasonably good mood, considering and ready for an adventure. The two children sat down and Dilly settled comfortably on David's right knee.

Charlotte wasn't so ready for an adventure; she thought a nice day just being her own size would be restful. But David was extremely ready—and he had been thinking!

"Dilly," he said, "I want to fly! It's my turn. But I don't want butterfly wings. Can I have bird ones please?" David was very interested in birds and had learned a lot from Daddy about their different ways. "Can I be a blackbird?" he added hopefully. He loved blackbirds because of their beautiful singing and friendly nature; and they also flew very well—not too fast like swifts, but quite fast enough for a beginner.

Dilly considered. "You can," she said, a bit doubtfully. "Of course, you'll have to be an egg first and then a nestling and then a fledgling. And it takes much longer than growing butterfly wings, even in fairy time."

"O," said David. "How long?" He knew that in proper time, each stage might last as much as twelve days, but he had hoped fairy time would be much faster.

"Thirty minutes for each bit," explained Dilly. "That's ages to wait."

"O," said David again. It was quite long—but there wasn't really any hurry, as it was ages before they would be expected back for lunch. He tried to work out how many minutes three lots of thirty would be. Hmmm. Too many to count on his fingers, but probably not too many to be OK for lunch.

"Yes please!" he said politely.

"Not me, thank you," said Charlotte politely. "I'll just wait here and watch."

"Well," said Dilly, "there's a blackbird nest in the hazel tree over there. Listen!"

They listened. Yes, they could hear the lovely singing of the father bird above all the humming and buzzing of the meadow.

"Hurray!" said David excitedly. How lovely it would be to have wings and swoop and zoom around and then perch on a branch and sing!

"Right," said Dilly. "The first thing is to get you into the nest. You have to be in the right place for being an egg. Because you'll need sitting on."

"O," said David. He hadn't thought about being sat on. Still, he was sure it would be worth it. He peered up at the tree. "I could easily climb up," he said. "Only then I'd be far too big to fit in the nest!"

"That's all right," said Dilly. "You climb up; I'll fly up and once you're on the branch you can grow small and get into the nest."

"I'll wait at the bottom," said Charlotte. "Just in case."

So that is what happened. Boy-sized David climbed up the tree and made his way carefully along the branch where the nest was. He did startle the mother bird, who went taktak taktak at him and flew off in a huff, but that was probably just as well, as she would be a much better egg-sitter if she didn't realise she was actually hatching a boy!

Dilly flew up to the nest and saw that there were already three lovely speckled eggs in the nest. She explained that that was good, as it meant that the mother bird would be bound to come back soon. It would be a bit crowded but she was sure David could manage.

"Are you ready?" she asked.

"Yes," said David bravely.

Dilly gave him the little two-headed bottle and he took a quick drink from the green side. In no time at all, he was a tiny David, still his own boy shape, but much more the size you would expect of an egg.

"In you get then," ordered Dilly. "O, you'd better take your sandals off," she added. "You won't need them for flying. I'll look after them for you," she promised.

Getting in was actually more difficult than climbing the tree had been! The nest was prickly and scratchy—and seemed very large, with high curving walls guarding its centre. Tiny David scrambled his way up—and then rolled over the top and down into the middle, landing with a bump on a nice feathery patch next to the eggs.

"I'm in!" he cried to Dilly, who was standing on the nest edge, fluttering her long green wings.

"Lie down, curl up into a ball and shut your eyes," she said. And so he did.

All this while, Charlotte had been standing anxiously at the bottom of the tree, peering up. She couldn't see inside the nest, but she did see David grow small, take off his sandals, climb up and then roll over the top and disappear inside.

Then down flew Dilly and landed on her left hand.

"Is everything all right?" asked Charlotte.

"O yes," said Dilly carelessly. "Now, I'm off!"

"What? Why?" said Charlotte. "Where?"

"I don't know yet," said Dilly. "But I can't possibly wait three lots of thirty minutes! It's far too boring."

"O, Dilly," said Charlotte. "But what if something happened to David? He might need you!"

"Well, of course something's going to happen," said Dilly impatiently, "he's going to grow bird wings. Look, I'll let you have the bottle, if you like. Just in case."

"OK," said Charlotte. She supposed that was better than nothing. Carefully she took the bottle from her tiny friend and placed it gently in her pocket.

"I'll see you later," cried Dilly—and off she flew!

Charlotte sat down under the hazel tree. She decided to sing—that was always the best thing to do if you were feeling anxious. This is what she sang:

Sing a song of blackbirds,
A pocket full of bottle.
David is a blackbird,
But I am just a Tottle.
While the egg is hatching,
I shall wai-ait here,
And listen for the blackbird singing,
Wi-ith my-y ear!

Chapter 18
Nestling

Being an egg was actually quite peaceful. It was dark and soft and warm and there was plenty of gooey stuff to eat. David had always liked eating soft boiled eggs and even though there wasn't any toast, the eggy bit tasted pretty much the same. It *was* a bit boring, because thirty minutes is a long time when you have nothing to do, but David was sure it would be worth the wait. In any case, a good rest would set him up for the flying adventure that lay ahead. He couldn't hear anything—not even Charlotte's lovely song or the surprised squawk of the mother bird when she flew back to discover an extra egg in her nest. That was puzzling for her—but birds aren't particularly good at counting and she supposed she must have made a mistake when she had totted the eggs up earlier. David *did* feel a heavy whump when she sat down on top of him but he didn't feel at all squashed or uncomfortable.

After a long time of waiting, things started to happen quite fast. Crack went the eggshell above his head! David's nose started to itch and, without thinking, he started to scratch it furiously on the shell. Crack! Crack! The whole shell broke open—and suddenly a bright light streamed into the darkness, dazzling him. He shouted in surprise—at least he let out a rather feeble cheep cheep—and scrambled out of the last bit of shell. He looked around. The other three eggs were still slumbering peacefully, but the mother bird was perched on the edge of the nest, looking down at him with her bright beady eyes and shrieking with delight and pride! She wasn't actually black at all; she was dark brown with yellowish spots but, thanks to Daddy's teaching, David knew that was only to be expected from female blackbirds. Once he grew up, he'd have lovely shiny black feathery wings! At the moment he was still wearing his brown t-shirt and shorts, which fitted very well and wouldn't startle the mother bird too much and his little wings were a raggedy, downy brown.

Another thirty minutes to wait, he thought. *O well, at least I can move a bit, this time.* He couldn't see over the high wall of the nest, but above him he could see the great green leaves and swaying branches of the hazel tree and above that the beautiful blue sky.

It will be fine, he thought to himself.

Only, unfortunately, it wasn't!

The first problem was food! David was feeling ravenously hungry, now that he had hatched. The mother bird clearly understood this. She went zooming off, presumably to go hunting; when she got back she was holding a horrible wriggly fly in her shiny yellow beak. She obviously wanted David to eat it—but, hungry as he was, he just couldn't!

He opened his mouth to protest and she deftly slipped it in! David tried to spit it out but she had poked it in too far. He could feel it wriggling its way down his throat and into his tummy. Yuk! He really hoped there wouldn't be another meal during the next twenty-five or so minutes.

The next problem was the other eggs! David had just got over his meal, when he was startled by a very loud crack! crack! crack! His brothers (or sisters?) were hatching! The new nestlings were not beautiful—they had thin, cross-looking faces and baldish brown bodies, all gooey with bits of eggshell. They had huge sharp beaks, which they opened wide to make the most angry-sounding cheeping and squawking David had ever heard. They just gobbled down the flies that the mother bird was bringing. Well, that was all right, as it meant that David didn't have to—but they were not at all friendly! They scratched little David with their sharp little claws and pushed him with their great sharp beaks.

I'm much nicer to my brother and sister, thought David indignantly. His own little hands and feet, not to mention his own little nose, were not nearly as sharp and it was difficult for him to fight back. There really wasn't much room in the nest; obviously, it had been built for three nestlings and that was how the nestlings wanted it. They behaved reasonably well while their mother was keeping an eye on them but as soon as she left to go hunting, they just went for him. To get out of their way, David scrambled up the steep side of the nest and perched on its edge. He looked down. The ground seemed miles away and so did the bright curly head of his proper sister! David knew his poor little stumpy wings weren't nearly ready to fly with. He clung to the edge with his tiny hands and feet.

The biggest and ugliest nestling had started to jump up and down in the nest and poke at him with its sharp beak. David wasn't sure how long he could hold on. *There must be at least fifteen minutes left*, he thought desperately. What could he do?

"Charlotte!" he shouted down. Except that it wasn't really a shout, more of a pathetic cheep! The head didn't look up—and now David could hear her singing:

Sing a song of blackbirds
A pocket full of bottle...

If only, she would stop singing! She would never hear his cheep above the sound of her own voice! How could he get her to look up? Then David saw a big hazelnut growing on the branch just above him. If he stood up on his tiptoes, he could probably reach it. He felt a bit dizzy and wobbly, but he managed it. Pulling with all his might, he picked the nut and hurled it down at Tot. Luckily, David had a very good aim (all that cricketing practice with Daddy) and it hit Charlotte right in the middle of her great curly head!

David is a blackbird,
But I am just a... ow!

She looked up! Hurray!

"Charlotte," cheeped David urgently. "Can you hear me?"

Now that she had stopped singing, she could—just!

"You'll have to climb up the tree and rescue me!" he cheeped.

"I can't!" wailed Charlotte. "It's too high up." But then she had a brilliant idea. The bottle! She would just have to grow really big—bigger even than girl size—as big as the yellow wine would let her! Brave Charlotte took a deep breath, carefully took off the little stopper—and drank the whole of the yellow side up in one great gulp!

Chapter 19
Fledgling

The result was dramatic! Charlotte felt her whole body rising upwards and upwards. Her orange sandals were getting further and further away and her fingers, still clutching the glass bottle, were growing huge. Suddenly, she stopped. Her nose was now level with the top of the hazel tree and she could see above it to her house and the garden just beyond. In fact, she actually had to bend *down* to make out the little nest and her tiny brother clinging desperately to its prickly edge!

"David!" she cried, "here I am!" and her voice sounded like a great cathedral bell, while the rush of air from her mouth almost swept poor David off his perch.

"I know!" gasped David, struggling to keep his balance. The other nestlings had stopped jumping and scratching and were standing quite still, staring upwards, open-mouthed in amazement; and the poor mother bird, flying back from yet another hunting expedition, was so astonished that she opened her yellow beak in surprise, letting slip the slithery pink worm that she was carrying.

"Ow! Careful!" cheeped David as Charlotte grasped him firmly by his waist. She lifted him right up above the tree and then down in a great swooping curve. It was like being on a massive slide. At least he was safe now, even if it was hard to breathe!

Charlotte couldn't fit under the tree, so she took a few enormous strides out into the open meadow before she sat down with a mighty whump. She let go her grip and David slithered down her huge pink finger and onto the grassy ground. What a relief!

The first thing Charlotte did, now that the rescue was over, was to lift the glass bottle up to her mouth. She didn't at all like being so huge and was anxious to return to own size as soon as possible. It was difficult getting the tiny glass stopper off, with her great fingers, but she managed it in the end and drank the whole of the green side up. It didn't seem like much at all—barely a drop in her great pink mouth—but it worked. Thank goodness! She felt herself slithering rapidly downwards, her sandals came back into view—and in no time at all she was herself again!

"Wow!" cheeped David. "Thank you, Tot."

"It's OK," said Charlotte, picking him up again so he could perch on her knee. "But the bottle's empty—what will Dilly say?"

"Where is she, anyway?" asked tiny David.

"I don't know," complained Charlotte. "She just flew off."

"O well, she'll be back," said David. "And I bet my thirty minutes of nestling time are nearly up."

He was right. Charlotte watched with interest, as her brother's stumpy, bald wings started to grow soft little brown feathers and become longer and stronger! David stretched his new fledgling wings.

"I should be able to fly a bit," he said. "Of course, I ought to be pushed out of the nest by my mother, but I'm not going back there!" He shuddered. "Why don't you lift me up on top of your head? That would make a good launching pad!"

"All right," agreed Charlotte. "Only, don't kick me."

And she lifted him up and plonked him on top of her head.

David cautiously hopped over to the edge. The curls felt soft and slippery under his bare feet, but he could feel her hard head underneath. He took a deep breath, lifted up his soft feathery wings and leaped into the air. It wasn't as easy as he had expected. He fluttered wildly, veering sharply to the left and toppling head-over-heels, before he managed to straighten up, just before his bare feet hit the ground with a soft whump.

Charlotte couldn't help laughing—he looked so small and clumsy. But David was determined to learn and she kindly lifted him up again and again, onto her soft launching pad; and each time David managed a bit better and flew a bit further before coming down. After a while, he decided he needed a rest. He was also extremely hungry!

"Have you got anything to eat, Tot?" he asked, as he perched on her bare knee.

She rummaged in her pocket, taking great care not to break the bottle—even if it was empty—and found an elderly ginger biscuit. David and Charlotte took it in turns to eat and she kindly crumbled his share up so he could manage.

Then David decided he was thirsty. "I'll just dash over to the stream," he said. It wasn't far and he liked the idea of standing in the cool water in his bare feet while he had a little sip.

He set off, hopping across the sun-baked earth. But that was when the trouble started…

Charlotte was the first to notice the great black shadow of a buzzard moving fast over the distant fields. David was far too small to see above the grass stalks, so the first he knew of any danger was when the whole sky above him seemed to suddenly grow black and thundery and he heard the great wild beating of enormous wings.

"Look out, David!" cried Charlotte, standing up and pointing. But it was too late. With a triumphant mew, the buzzard picked tiny David up in his massive curved claws; he held him quite carefully by the waist, so although David felt squeezed he wasn't hurt. You see, just as small birds like wriggling insects and worms to eat, so do the bigger birds like their food live and warm! And the buzzard had decided that the little fledgling would make an excellent lunch for his two hungry nestlings!

Up, up, up the buzzard flew, flapping slowly with heavy wing beats. Charlotte could see her little brother being carried away towards a great oak tree that stood on a far-off hill. There was nothing she could do. The tree was too far away, the buzzard was flying too quickly—and in any case the two-headed glass bottle was now completely empty.

"Dilly!" she shouted with all her might. "Dilly, where are you? Help!"

And then her heart leaped as she heard the familiar flutter and whoosh—and there was the little fairy coming to land on her shoulder.

"Quick!" shouted Charlotte. "The buzzard's got David. Look—over there!"

Dilly looked. She knew all about buzzards and didn't seem alarmed; in fact the light of battle was shining in her green eyes.

"Right then!" she cried and flew after it, fluttering her long green wings furiously.

Chapter 20
Bird

David was too surprised to feel really afraid. One moment he had been hopping happily towards the stream; the next moment, he was high, high in the blue air with the sunlight warm on his little brown head. It was such a glorious feeling that he quite forgot his danger. Until, that is, they neared the massive buzzard nest built high in the green oak tree. Then he could hear the frantic squawking and mewing of the two buzzard nestlings and he could see below him their wide-open beaks—and he knew what *that* meant!

"I'm not your dinner," he shouted, "I'm a boy. Let me go."

But it is doubtful if the buzzard even heard, let alone understood, his words. Another great flap of the heavy wings and they had arrived.

But so had Dilly! Like an angry yellow and green wasp, she zoomed round and round the buzzard's head, as it stood perched on one claw on a great oak branch; then she zoomed round and round the nest, just out of reach of the hungry nestlings, who snapped and shrieked at her wildly; then she flew straight at the big buzzard's claw—not the one grasping the branch, but the one holding David. She had picked a sharp twig from the tree which she used as a sort of spear to attack the claw. (She was quite careful not to hit David.)

"Mew-ow!" cried the buzzard in pain and let go of his hold.

"Fly, David, fly!" cried Dilly, as she zoomed out of reach of the buzzard's snapping beak.

And he flew!

His last thirty minutes must have passed already, because once he was set free in the beautiful warm blue air, he felt a great surge of strength—and, glancing to the right and left, he could see his two beautiful black wings shining in the golden sunlight!

"Wow!" he cried joyfully. "I'm a bird! I can really fly!"

It was brilliant. He soared and he swooped and he swooped and he soared. It was every bit as good as he had ever imagined. Soon Dilly joined him, laughing with glee at her own cleverness in outwitting the buzzard; together they raced over the fields and meadows, over the oak wood and finally right over the children's house and garden! David could see his parents and Ben weeding the vegetable patch and he called down to them but only Ben bothered to look up.

"Doo! Doo!" he cried in delight, waving both arms!

At last, David began to feel tired, so together the two friends made their way slowly back to Flower Meadow, where Charlotte was anxiously waiting.

"Are you all right, David?" she asked, when they were all sitting comfortably. Charlotte was leaning her back against the hazel tree and David and Dilly were perched on her knees.

"Yes! It was brilliant!" said David, forgetting all about the scary bits and thinking only of the glorious flight through the blue air.

"I rescued him," said Dilly smugly.

"Yes, she did," explained David. "She was very brave." And they told Charlotte all about it.

She listened carefully, but was secretly quite glad not to have been there!

"And I rescued David before," she said, once they had finished.

"Yes, you did," agreed David. "You were brave too!" And they told Dilly all about it.

"Where were you, Dilly?" asked Charlotte, "before you came back for the rescue?"

"Talking to Ben," said Dilly mysteriously. She didn't explain—and anyway, that's another story!

David decided to take one last joyful flight. He wanted to visit his own nest again and say hello to his bird family. The three nestlings were still squealing for food with their great open beaks, but the mother bird was nowhere to be seen.

Probably gone hunting again, thought David. How hard mothers had to work! Then he had a good idea. He swooped down and picked up the crumbs of ginger biscuit from the ground under the tree, swooped up again and kindly fed them to the hungry nestlings. With his excellent aim, he lobbed the crumbs straight into their open mouths and saw them disappear down their great red gullets. Then he perched on the branch, opened his little mouth and sang! There were no words, just beautiful music pouring forth out of his heart and soul.

Charlotte, sitting on the grass below, thought she had never heard anything so lovely!

Then it was definitely time to become a proper boy and grow big again. They all decided it would be much more peaceful to do this in the shade of the tree.

"And you don't need sitting on now," explained Dilly, "although it will still take the same time."

So David became a little fledgling again for thirty minutes. This time he got his river drink, while the others kept a sharp lookout for him. When he became a nestling, Charlotte took him on her lap and gently stroked his fluffy, stumpy wings, while Dilly had a quiet snoozle. David himself went to sleep while he was an egg, but Charlotte stayed faithfully awake, keeping him warm and safe in her soft pink hands. And then there he was—his own boy shape again, only still tiny, of course.

"O, no!" cried Charlotte. "The bottle's empty! Dilly, wake up!"

But it was all right. Dilly had bought another bottle (when she thought the other one had been lost, if you remember) which hadn't even been started yet. She fetched it from her dandelion flower, unstoppered the yellow side—and soon David was back to normal.

"Thank you, Dilly," cried the two children and set off, running, for home. And it was only when David trod on a bramble by the bonfire patch and said *ow* that they remembered that Dilly had taken his little black sandals.

But by then Daddy had seen them and it was too late!

Chapter 21
Talking to Ben

As soon as she had said goodbye to Charlotte, Dilly flew up and away. She zoomed straight across the stream, over the little path, heading for the old apple tree by the house. She landed on the topmost branch and folded her green wings neatly. What could she see?

There was the children's mother, having a quiet snooze on a wobbly grey plastic chair, just underneath her! And over there was the children's father, making a strange buzzing sound as he wrestled with some enormous brambles by the vegetable patch. But where was Ben? Dilly had been particularly taken with Ben, when she had spent her day playing with the children in the house. She thought he made interesting noises and she especially liked his big gurgling laugh. She hadn't really heard him bawl yet—because the truth was that Ben had been particularly taken with Dilly: when she was there, he just didn't feel like crying at all! She also liked the way he stood up, wobbled and sat down again—and the way he moved on all four paws. Anyway, she was very keen to see him again and get to know him better.

But where was he? The little swing below her, where she had first met him, was empty. There was no one in the sand-pit or on the patio. Just then she heard an angry *waaaa* coming from the direction of the house. That must be Ben! Another really interesting noise! She watched Mummy stir uneasily in her sleep, but she didn't wake up. Presumably Daddy was too busy buzzing to hear. This was her chance! Dilly lifted her long green wings and flew over to the house. The little blue door and kitchen windows were shut, but she found a nice open window by the children's bedroom, that was easily big enough to allow her to slip through.

She flew round the room, with just a quick stop to inspect the electric light and then she swooped down and landed on the top of Ben's cot. The interesting *waaaa* noise was much louder now.

Ben looked cross. He was standing up in his cot and shaking the side bars angrily.

"Waaaa," he continued. Then he saw her and stopped in mid howl!

"Waa…Doo! Doo!" he shouted in delight and gave his lovely gurgling laugh! He reached out his two little hands.

"Hallo, Ben," said Dilly and she fluttered down and landed elegantly on his thumb.

That was a mistake. Ben grabbed her waist between his thumb and forefinger—and lifted her up to his mouth.

"Doo!" he chortled. Dilly got an alarming glimpse of six huge shiny teeth and a great big tongue. Just in time she gave him a kick on his nose. It was a good kick as, luckily, she was wearing David's nice black sandals, so although she was too little to hurt Ben, she did startle him! He let go of his hold and she flew up, landing neatly on the far end of the cot. Ben wobbled and sat down unexpectedly.

Dilly was a bit startled too: she didn't know that babies always like to put new and interesting things in their mouths and that she would probably only have got a bit wet, not eaten up entirely! She thought it would be a good idea to make Ben grow small, but then she remembered that she had given her bottle to Charlotte to use just in case. Never mind: Ben was quite safe as long as she stayed out of reach of those huge hands—and she was a good deal faster at getting around than he was! Anyway, he clearly meant no harm and was still laughing happily.

Then Dilly remembered all the lovely toys! Yes, there was Ben's whiskery rabbit, looking much bigger now, on the tiled floor beside the cot. She darted down beside the rabbit and tried to fly up again, holding its floppy left foot in her two little arms while her green wings beat frantically. After a lot of effort, she managed to hoist it over the edge on the bars, where it flopped down into the cot. Ben was delighted!

"Goo!" he cried. He picked up Rabbit, stood up again and hurled it joyfully across the room, where it landed on top of a tall cupboard.

Humph! thought Dilly. She was too tired to lift it up again so she decided to explore instead. There was a very interesting smell coming from the far end of the room—something wonderfully sweet and gungy. She decided to look. Over she flew and landed beside a huge tray of great golden brown, squidgy things. Dilly didn't know they were flapjacks, as she had never seen, let alone tasted, a flapjack before in her life; but Ben knew all about them.

"Doo! Goo! Ummmm!" he cried excitedly and opened his great pink mouth. It was easy to see what he wanted. Dilly obligingly broke off a corner, held it tight in her little right hand and flew back to the cot.

"Here you are, Ben!" she said and popped it onto his great pink tongue. Ben was thrilled.

"Goo! Ummmmm!" he cried, as soon as his mouth was empty enough to make a noise.

"I'll get you some more," said Dilly. "Only I want a taste too!"

Luckily there were loads of the things. Dilly thought she had never tasted anything so delicious and Ben thought they were his favourite food except perhaps for Weetabix. After several more journeys between the cot and the table, Dilly was full to the brim and Ben was sticky and happy. He was also a bit itchy as crumbs had got all over his cot sheet and onto Rabbit, but it was definitely worth it.

Then, of course, they both felt thirsty. Dilly whizzed around the room looking for some water, but she didn't understand about taps. Luckily, Ben's yellow and blue drinking cup was on the table—and Ben knew exactly what was in it! He waved his arms excitedly.

"Woo!" he cried. "Wooooo!"

Dilly stood up on tiptoe and peered through the yellow plastic spout. Yes, there was water inside. Only how to get at it? She pushed the cup with all her might until at last it toppled over and rolled off the table and onto the floor. A trickle of water oozed out of the upturned spout—quite enough for a thirsty fairy to lap up, but frustrating for Ben to watch. After all, it was his cup!

"Woooo!" he cried again. And then, more ominously, "Waaaaaa!"

Outside, Mummy stirred in her sleep. *O dear, was that Ben?* she wondered. She had better get up and see.

Dilly was trying to fly the cup over to Ben, but it was proving very slippery: she couldn't really get a good hold of the blue handle. It was also much heavier than Rabbit. She did manage to roll and push the cup over the floor to the cot, but she just couldn't lift it up. Bother! If only she hadn't given Charlotte the bottle! Just then she heard a loud squeaking noise behind her and a great burst of dazzling light flooded the dark room. Heavy footsteps sounded across the tiled floor and Dilly could make out two enormous brown sandals.

Even bigger than David's, she thought excitedly.

It was Mummy. Luckily, she didn't look down! She had caught sight of the state of Ben's cot and of his face and hands. There were crumbs everywhere! And Mummy knew at once what they were.

"Ben!" she said crossly. "How on earth did you get hold of a flapjack?" She lifted him up, carried him over to the tap and washed down his sticky face and paws. Dilly watched curiously: so that was where water came from!

"I suppose David and Charlotte must have been in," said Mummy, "while I was having a snoozle. Did they feed you, Ben? Naughty children! I was keeping those flapjacks for tea. And you were supposed to be asleep."

"Doo! Doo!" cried Ben—and he waved his arms about. But he hadn't really learned how to point yet, so Mummy still didn't look down. There were still enough flapjacks left for tea but she didn't see why David and Charlotte should be allowed any.

"They need to learn to wait," she said disapprovingly. "And you too, Ben." She dumped him down on the tiled floor, while she covered up the remains of the flapjacks with a fresh t-towel.

Free at last, Ben made a bee-line for Dilly!

"Doo!" he chortled. "Woo!"

Dilly pushed the cup over to him, gave him a quick kiss on his nose (fairy kisses are very light and shivery) and flew off out of the open door and away. It was time to be getting back; she ought to see how David was getting on with being a blackbird.

"Waaaaa," protested Ben—but it was too late. The fairy had flown.

Chapter 22
The Dandelion House

David was busy brambling. He was wearing Mummy's heavy gloves which reached up to his elbow and stopped most of the prickles from getting at him. Daddy did some strimming and then David heaved the bits into the wheelbarrow and took them down to the bonfire patch. There was already an enormous pile of brambles and David was looking forward to the time when the bonfire would be lit. But it wasn't ready yet; so back he went with the empty barrow for another load. It was extremely hot and muggy and, despite the gloves, every now and then a particularly awkward bramble would scratch him.

He was very glad when Daddy finally turned off the strimmer, took out his ear plugs and wiped his brow.

"Well done, David," he said. "You have been really helpful!"

"Is that it?" asked David hopefully.

"No," said Daddy. "There's loads more to do—but it must be getting on for lunch by now. Let's go and see."

Together they walked over to the little house. Ben had only just woken up Mummy so lunch hadn't been made yet—but it wouldn't take long.

"About half an hour," Mummy said. "David, can you go and find Charlotte and tell her?"

"All right," said David helpfully. He had a drink of water and a quick biscuit, just to keep him going; then he set off down the little path to Flower Meadow. He was wearing his new blue sandals, which his parents had reluctantly bought him, so it didn't matter when he stepped on some of the brambles that had escaped the bonfire pile. Only half an hour to lunch—it wasn't too long, although, despite the biscuit, he was feeling exceedingly hungry! He hoped Charlotte would be ready and waiting.

Charlotte had gone down to Flower Meadow straight after breakfast. She wasn't that keen on brambles and she was looking forward to the chance of spending a peaceful morning with Dilly. But when she got to the little dandelion clump, Dilly was nowhere to be seen. Charlotte had to sing her Dilly Dilly calling song through several times. At last, the tiniest yellow petal in the very middle started to swirl and grow upwards—and there was Dilly, sitting on top of the flower, dangling her legs and wings.

Dilly was still sleepy. She didn't particularly like getting up in the mornings. She threw the little glass bottle down on the ground.

"Can you grow small?" she asked with a yawn. "It's far too tiring talking to you when you're so huge!"

"All right," agreed Charlotte, bending down to pick up the little bottle. She took a sip from the green side and in no time at all she was the same size as her fairy friend. Dilly leaned over the edge of the flower and gave her a hand and Charlotte scrambled her way up the stem. She had remembered to bring the empty bottle with her, so she gave it back to Dilly who put it safely in her pocket. The two friends sat side by side on the flower in the hot golden sunlight.

At first, they just sat there, peacefully watching the buzzy bees and the fluttery butterflies go about their business and listening to the whoosh and splutter of the stream over the rocks. Dilly wasn't thinking about anything much, but Charlotte had been wondering.

"Dilly," she said, "what happens to you at night time? Where exactly do you go?"

"Well," said Dilly, "first I grow tiny; then I slither down through the hole in the middle of my flower—and into my bedroom."

"But where?" asked Charlotte.

"Haven't you noticed? Underneath the flower there's a round green pod. That's where I sleep. And when it gets dark, my flower house curls up around me and keeps me nice and warm."

"Goodness!" said Charlotte. She liked the idea of having a house that opened and shut according to the time of day. In her house, you could open and shut the windows and door but that was about it.

"Would you like to see?" asked Dilly.

"O, yes please," said Charlotte. She would love to see inside a fairy house!

"Well, we'll both have to grow really tiny," said Dilly, "but there's plenty of wine. I'll go first. Watch!"

Charlotte watched as Dilly stood up tall and took a sip from the green side of the bottle; then she lifted her wings and arms straight up above her head. Almost at once she started to shrink downwards and inwards until she was the same size as the middle petal of the dandelion flower; then she gave a wriggle and disappeared down the hole!

"Don't forget to bring the bottle!" came a whispery cry, as her little silvery head vanished from view.

Charlotte stood up tall, took two sips of green wine—and had just enough time to close the stopper and lift her arms up high, before she felt a slithery whoosh; the bright blue sky turned to a dim green glow—and she landed with the gentlest of whumps on a bed of soft silvery down. She sat up. All around her and above her head, curving green walls cut out the bright light. Just a pinpoint of sunlight came through the little hole, but inside the bedroom it was beautifully cool. It felt a bit like being under water. She could see why Dilly liked sleeping!

"It's lovely," she said. "But haven't you got any toys or anything?" Charlotte wasn't expecting books or jigsaws because she remembered that Dilly didn't know what they were, but she had been hoping for a few fairy toys.

"Don't need them," said Dilly. "This is just for night times—or if it gets really wet. I do all my playing outside: sailing and racing other fairies and hunting and hitching lifts on swallows and suchlike."

"I see," said Charlotte. She wondered if Dilly would ever ask her and David to play with other fairies! That would be exciting—but meanwhile it was lovely just being inside a real fairy bedroom.

"Now," said Dilly, "I'm going to have breakfast. Do you want some?"

"Yes please," said Charlotte. She wasn't really hungry, as she had already had one breakfast, but she was curious. She couldn't see any of the breakfast things you would expect: packets and bowls and a cooker and kettle. She watched as Dilly made a little space in the centre of the fluffy silvery bed; then she saw a little grass stalk, just peeking out of a hole in the middle of the floor. *Dilly lifted it to her mouth and sucked—just like sucking through a straw*, thought Tot.

"Yum!" said Dilly. "Your go!"

"But what is it?" asked Charlotte. It would be useful to know exactly what you were sucking, before you did.

"Dandelion nectar juice," said Dilly. "It comes up from the dandelion roots and through the stem and into the leaves and flowers; but I take a bit of it through my grass stalk. Did you know dandelion roots grow really deep? That's how they get all the good stuff out of the earth. And that's why dandelion wine is the best! All the other fairies have to use dandelion wine to grow with, because it's really strong!"

"I see," said Charlotte. She put the little grass stalk in her tiny mouth and sucked: yes, it was lovely—sweet and tingly. It would do for being thirsty as well as hungry. After taking it in turns a few more times, they had both had enough. Dilly poked the grass straw back and covered up the hole.

And there isn't even any washing up! thought Charlotte.

Just then, the little room started to sway gently.

"What's happening?" asked Charlotte.

"It's only the wind," explained Dilly. "It's nice when it rocks my house."

Once Charlotte had got used to the swaying, she thought it felt nice too, like sailing in a boat on the sea—or like being in a cradle. The words of the nursery rhyme came into her head and she started to sing:

Rock-a-bye Fairy
On the flower top,
When the wind blows
The flower will rock,
When the…

Charlotte thought it would be better to stop there; she didn't like to think of the flower house breaking and Dilly falling down.

And then, in the sudden silence, there was a noise of heavy running footsteps, coming from outside and then an extremely loud voice.

"No!" shouted the voice. "Stop! Stop! Go away!"

It sounded like David's voice. But why was he shouting? What on earth was going on?

And then, quite suddenly, the whole house began to shake!

Chapter 23
Goat

"Bother!" said David to himself, when he had reached Flower Meadow. "I wonder *where they've gone*." He didn't even consider that they might be *inside* the dandelion house; he supposed they must have gone off to play somewhere. He surveyed the scene carefully, but there was no sign of a tiny sister and her fairy friend. But what he *did* see startled him considerably!

A large, bearded goat was busy munching its way through Flower Meadow. David knew quite a lot about goats, as there were lots of them on the farm nearby. But this goat wasn't part of a flock with bells; it was all by itself and didn't have a bell. It did have two large curving horns and it looked fierce. It lifted up its old face, staring at David with its yellow eyes. David noticed the black slits in the middle of each eye and the wispy grey beard, as well as the two sharp horns. The goat finished its mouthful, gave a weary bleat (David could see its old yellow teeth) and ambled down the meadow. It stopped again, lowered its head and got on with its munching. Suddenly David realised. The goat was standing right next to Dilly's house—and it was munching dandelions!

"No!" he shouted at the top of his voice. "Stop! Stop! Go away!"

But it didn't. It took absolutely no notice of David; what it did take, was a large mouthful of dandelion leaf! The whole clump shook violently. David knew at once that he would have to be quick. Of course, he didn't know that Dilly and Tot were inside and about to be eaten up—he just wanted to save Dilly's house.

He grabbed a large stick that was lying under a nearby hazel tree and went hurtling down the slope. He gave the goat a huge whump on its bottom. The goat turned, looked at him angrily with its old yellow eyes, lowered its head—and charged! David just had time to leap out of the way of the two fierce horns—and he also managed another whump with the stick. The goat wheezed angrily, gave a sort of goatish cough and scrambled its way up the little hill and out of sight.

Thank goodness for that! David wondered if the goat had escaped through the farm fence and somehow managed to get rid of its bell; or whether it was a wild goat from the moor and had always lived by itself. Well, at least it was gone now. He did hope Dilly's house was all right. He was just bending over, examining it anxiously for damage, when to his surprise the tiniest petal in the middle of the flower started to swirl and grow—and out popped a tiny Dilly and then a tiny, tiny Tot!

In no time at all, they took a sip of green and grew to normal fairy size (nearly as big as David's hand). Dilly stood up in the middle of the flower; Charlotte sat down (she wasn't quite so good at balancing).

"David!" shouted Dilly angrily. "What have you done to my house?"

"It wasn't me," explained David, "it was a horrible goat. I rescued your house!"

"I can't see any goat," Dilly went on crossly. "And just look at my leaves—they're all broken. How could you?"

David sat down. "That was the goat," he explained. "I wouldn't break them! Look, they're not broken, they're chewed. You can see the teeth marks."

Dilly flew down to get a better look.

"There!" said David. "And look, you can see his hoof marks on the ground. It was a goat!"

He felt a bit angry with Dilly: after all, he had bravely saved her house, not tried to eat it up!

Dilly examined the marks. Yes, you could clearly see the great cloven foot marks in the earth—quite unlike anything a new blue sandal would make. You could also see how they went up and over the hill.

"O," said Dilly. "Yes, I do see. Sorry, David."

"That's all right," said David kindly. He supposed anyone would be upset if their house got chewed. "I whacked him with this stick and he went charging away."

"Well done, David," said Charlotte. "You rescued us too. We were inside!" She wondered what it might feel like to be eaten by a hungry goat; she was very glad David had got there in time!

David lifted her down from the flower and they all set about inspecting the damage. Some of the leaves were badly chewed, but the flower and its round green pod seemed to be all right.

"It's funny," said Charlotte, "but even the good leaves look a bit chewed, as if someone had bitten them!"

"That's why they're called dandelions," explained Dilly. "It's French for lions' teeth. Dents de lion!" she explained when the two children looked blank. "The lions think that our leaves look like lion teeth and our flowers look like lion manes!"

"O!" said Charlotte. She hadn't really understood; what lions? She decided that she would have to ask Mummy about the French bit.

"Anyway," said David, "the house should be OK. And it's lunch time. Come on, Tot, you'll have to grow big quick."

Then he felt a drop of warm rain on his bare arm. He looked up: most of the blue had gone and dark grey clouds were hurtling across the sky.

"Bother," said Dilly crossly. "I hate wetness. I'm going back to bed."

She took the little bottle from Charlotte and flew back onto the flower. Just before she grew tiny, she said, "Thank you, David; sorry I was cross," which made everyone feel much better.

And then it started to rain in earnest.

Chapter 24
Wet

Lunch was tuna and corn rolls with tomato salad and blackberries for pudding. (You might as well pick some of them while you were brambling.). It was good and David ate loads, but Charlotte wasn't feeling hungry after her double breakfast. Ben was *extremely* hungry after an unusually long sleep and so were Mummy and Daddy.

While they were eating, it got darker and darker outside and by the time they had finished the last blackberry, the rain was simply pouring down.

"No more strimming today," said Daddy. Luckily, he had noticed the black clouds while Mummy was getting lunch and he had put the strimmer safely away in the barn.

"Just listen to it!" said Mummy.

Mixed through the wind and rain they could make out a few thundery roars.

Like a lion, thought Charlotte and wondered how Dilly was getting on in her bedroom. She remembered her rock-a-bye song and hoped the last two lines wouldn't be needed after all.

Rainy afternoons were actually quite nice and certainly made a change from the usual hard work on the garden. Charlotte settled down at the table with her crayons and drawing paper. She drew lots of different flower fairies; not that she had seen any, apart from Dilly, but she liked to imagine what they would be like and she had seen some of the dresses. David snuggled up on the sofa with one of Daddy's bird books. He looked at the pictures of blackbirds and buzzards and even managed to read some of the words underneath.

Ben was feeling particularly energetic after his long sleep. He practised standing up without holding on and increased his record to almost sixty seconds! Not bad. Then he practised climbing up onto the big sofa and down again backwards. After that, he decided to tackle the steps up to the bedroom, but

Mummy hoiked him down before he had a chance to climb more than three. Then he found a marble which he chased around the room on all four paws, until it rolled under the piano.

"Come on then, Ben," said Daddy. He sat Ben on his lap and played all through the nursery rhyme book and Mummy helped with the singing. When they got to *I hear thunder,* the whole family joined in the musical round.

So the afternoon passed peacefully; and then it was bath time. This was quite exciting as it was still pouring down outside, with the odd clap of thunder and flash of lightning. Mummy decided the sensible thing would be for the children to take all their clothes off and let the rain wash them instead! It was fun feeling the warm rain tingling on their backs and tummies and the children ran (or crawled) twice around the grassy bit to get nice and clean. Except that Ben got remarkably muddy and had to be washed in the bath after all.

And then it was time for supper and stories and bed.

And it was still pouring outside!

Charlotte and David had wanted to go splashing down the little path to Flower Meadow to see if Dilly was all right, but they just didn't get a chance to slip quietly off. Anyway, Dilly was very tough and probably used to it. David wondered how the goat was getting on; he was definitely tough and might even enjoy a good wetting!

As she lay snugly under her soft white duvet, Charlotte thought about the dandelion house. By now, the petals would have curled up tight, keeping Dilly nice and warm. The leaves wouldn't mind the rain—they might even be glad of a good drink. And inside the green pod, it would surely be soft and warm and snug. *Dilly would get a good rock-a-bye*, she thought, as she listened to the wind outside…as long as the bough didn't break and the little fairy fall down!

Chapter 25
Night

Charlotte woke up suddenly. She listened. Inside the house, everything was quiet, except for the heavy breathing of the rest of the family. But outside, there was the crying of the wind and the pounding of the rain. And there was another noise too, coming from her bedroom window: *tap, tap, tap*. Perhaps it was just the branches of the apple tree which grew right beside the house. *Tap, tap, tap*...did that sound like an apple branch? Then she remembered the words of her song:

Wee Dilly Dinkie
Made such a mess,
Upstairs and downstairs
In her night dress.
Tapping at the window
Crying through the door
Are all the children in their beds
Or are there any more...?

Perhaps there was a terrible mess in Dilly's dandelion house; perhaps Dilly was flying around outside Charlotte's house, trying to get in; perhaps she was tapping and crying and wondering if the children were all in their beds asleep— or whether perhaps someone might be awake to hear her.

Tap, tap, tap...

Charlotte could bear it no more. She wriggled out of her soft warm duvet and carefully crept over to the little bedroom window. It was, of course, quite dark, so she didn't see David's foot until too late. Somehow, David's left leg had slithered off the mattress and onto the floor.

"Ow," said Charlotte as quietly as she could, as she stumbled and hit her knee on the cupboard. But David didn't say anything: he just sighed and turned over and snuggled even deeper under the duvet.

She reached up to the little window. Usually it was left open but Daddy had shut all the windows that afternoon so that the rain wouldn't get in. Could she manage the handle? Yes, she could! With a heave and a twist, the handle turned and the little window opened. A great gust of warm wet wind blasted through—and fluttering in the middle of the blast was a small, bedraggled fairy!

"Dilly!" whispered Charlotte excitedly. "I thought it might be you!"

"Humph!" said Dilly crossly—and not that quietly! "I've been tapping for ages. And I'm all wet."

"Shhhh," said Charlotte comfortingly. "I'll dry you—but please be quiet, because the others are all asleep."

Very gently, she lifted the shivering little fairy by her waist and carried her over to her bed, being careful to mind David's foot on the way. Then she dried Dilly's long wet wings with a handy t-shirt that was lying around on the floor and blew warm breath over her lovely petal dress. She couldn't find a feather to brush Dilly's hair, so she used a toothbrush instead and it worked very well. She couldn't see much of Dilly in the darkness but she could feel the shivering gradually getting less and less, until it finally stopped.

"Are you all right now?" she asked in a whisper. "What happened?"

"The stream flooded," said Dilly. "I told you dandelion roots are strong and deep—and so they are—but the water rose and swept all over my house! Whoosh! There I was, one minute fast asleep—and the next minute—freezing cold water rushing through my bedroom."

"How horrible!" said Charlotte. "What did you do?"

"Well, it was quite exciting," said Dilly. "I managed to save the dandelion wine bottles—they're in my pocket—but then I got swept away by the water. I knew I had to grow bigger, because I was so tiny I didn't have any strength. In the end, I got washed up onto an oak leaf, so I could get at the bottle. Then I flew over here. Luckily, the wind was blowing in the right direction. My wings were so wet they weren't much good."

"Goodness!" whispered Charlotte. "Do you feel dry now?"

"I do!" said Dilly. "Thank you, Charlotte," she said and Charlotte felt pleased and proud.

"Can I sleep here?" asked Dilly. "Then tomorrow, I'll find another house."

"Of course you can," said Charlotte.

She decided that Dilly should sleep on her pillow; she could easily manage without it and she didn't want to roll over in bed and squash the little fairy by mistake! So she put her pillow on the floor next to the mattress and covered Dilly up with the dry part of the t-shirt. In no time at all, the two tired friends fell fast asleep.

Later in the night Daddy woke up; he had heard the upstairs window banging in the wind. *That's funny*, he thought. *I could have sworn I shut that window.*

He heaved himself out of bed, took a torch off the piano, climbed the stairs and reached up to shut it. He bent down to tuck David's leg under the duvet. It was a bit damp, but David clearly didn't mind as he was still fast asleep. Then Daddy walked quietly over to check on Charlotte. Yes, she was fast asleep too. He did notice that her pillow was beside the bed, not on it.

"Silly Tot," he said fondly to himself.

But as she didn't seem to want it, he let it be!

Chapter 26
Breakfast

Next morning, Dilly was the first to wake up. Where was she? When she opened her eyes, she saw sunlight on a huge white wall and a great wooden roof far up above her head. Where were her soft, curving green walls? Then she remembered. Her lovely dandelion house had been swept away in the flood! Now here she was, lying on Charlotte's pillow with a heavy red t-shirt covering her up. She listened: only the sound of breathing and the wind in the trees outside.

Normally, Dilly would lie in bed lazily, until the sunlight came right through the little hole above her sleepy head and dazzled her into getting up but, of course, today was different. She heaved the red t-shirt off the pillow, sat up and looked around. Yes, there was Charlotte, next to her, fast asleep, with just the top of her head poking out of the great white duvet. And over there she could make out David's brown hair and dangling left foot.

Right, thought Dilly. *Time to go home!* Except that she didn't have a home any longer! Nor could she get out. The window by the children's beds was shut tight (Dilly could have sworn Tot had left it open last night) and so were the downstairs windows and door.

Bother!

She flew upstairs again and burrowed under the duvet, settling on Charlotte's left ear.

"Charlotte!" she whispered urgently. "Wake up! I can't get out."

Charlotte rolled over onto her other side, but she didn't open her eyes. Dilly tried again. When there was still no response, she pulled Charlotte's hair. That worked well.

"Dilly!" said Charlotte, wide awake all of a sudden. "What's the matter?"

"I want to get out," explained Dilly, "and the window's shut."

"OK," whispered Charlotte. "Hang on."

Charlotte heaved back the duvet and climbed out of bed. She made her way over to open the window, but she forgot about David's foot! She tripped, stumbled and fell—right on top of him!

"Ow!" said David.

"Shhhh!" whispered Charlotte urgently. "Don't wake the others."

"What's the matter?" yawned David sleepily. He had slept right through the storm and Dilly's unexpected arrival in the night. Charlotte explained what had happened. Then, as quietly as they could, the two children pushed open the little window.

"OK, Dilly, out you go," said Charlotte. "We'll come down to see you after breakfast."

"All right," agreed Dilly. "See you after breakfast."

But then she thought, "What breakfast? I haven't got any breakfast because my lovely green house and my grass food straw have been washed away in the river."

"I'm so hungry!" she complained loudly. Luckily, her fairy voice was smallish, otherwise she really might have woken up the others. "And I haven't got any breakfast."

"We'll get you some," whispered Charlotte kindly. "Only we can't wake the others up. They might see you."

"I don't expect Mummy and Daddy will wake up," said David who was also feeling hungry, "not unless Ben does, anyway. He's the key."

"But he might wake up any time," said Charlotte, "And if he does, he'll probably bawl. You know what he's like."

"I've got a good idea!" said Dilly. "I'll make him grow small. Then you can easily carry him upstairs and hide him. And if he does cry, they probably won't even hear it, he'd be so tiny."

"Hmmm," said David doubtfully. "It wouldn't work. You'd have to wake him up to get him to drink the wine. And he always bawls as soon as he's awake—or nearly always."

"And I don't think he'd drink the wine," agreed Charlotte. "Not without a fuss. It's quite difficult getting him to drink something he doesn't want."

"We could pretend it's green ice-cream," suggested David. But he didn't really think it would work.

"Look," he told Dilly. "Ben really likes you. He probably won't cry if he sees you. You go on Ben-Watch. Stop him crying if he wakes. Me and Charlotte will get you some breakfast. Do you like Weetabix?"

Dilly didn't know, but she was willing to try, especially if it tasted anything like flapjacks! She flew down and perched on the cot rail above Ben's head. Charlotte and David crept down the stairs into the kitchen and, ever so quietly, started to sort out bowls and cereal and milk and sugar. They were almost ready to sneak them upstairs, when their little brother sneezed, opened his eyes and…laughed!

"Doo!" he cried in delight, standing up and reaching out his two big arms. "Doo! Doo!"

"Shhhh," said Dilly, leaping out of the way just in time.

"Ben?" came Mummy's sleepy voice from upstairs. "Why are you laughing?"

"Doo!" explained Ben, but luckily Mummy didn't understand. She rubbed her eyes and sat up.

"David! Charlotte!" she called. "What are you doing downstairs?"

"Um," explained David, nervously. But Charlotte was made of sterner stuff.

"Would you like some breakfast, Mummy?" she called up sweetly. "And Daddy too, of course. We thought that you'd like breakfast in bed today. You must be tired after all that brambling. We can all have breakfast in bed. You too, Ben," she said sternly to her little brother. "You can come in our room and have it with us."

"Well," said Mummy, "that would be just lovely! Darling children," she added fondly.

So that is what happened. Mummy lay down again and shut her eyes with a contented sigh. Daddy had, as yet, barely opened his. Ben gurgled happily at Dilly, until the children arrived with bowls of Weetabix for their sleepy and grateful parents. Then, while they were all busy trying not to spill the bowls, Dilly quickly zoomed into Charlotte's room and hid under the duvet, just in case. David and Charlotte carefully carried their own breakfast upstairs, including the remains of an apple cake and a ginger biscuit to keep Ben quiet. The three children and Dilly enjoyed a fine and crumbly feast under Charlotte's white duvet.

"Thanks," cried Dilly, as soon as she had finished her crumbs. "I'll see you later."

She gave Ben a quick fairy kiss on his nose and flew out of the open door and down to Flower Meadow.

Chapter 27
The Last Day

Flower Meadow looked very different. The sky was blue again now, after last night's storms, but it was still quite cold and windy and the stream was racing noisily across the rocks, white spray dancing on the waves. Dilly's house had completely disappeared. There were lots of mud and pebbles where once the dandelion clump had grown. But the biggest change was in all the other dandelions. No longer was the meadow bright with yellow flowers; instead, round, feathery dandelion clocks waved in the wind, their flying parachute seeds making silvery clouds in the air.

O dear! thought Dilly. She had been planning to find a new house. But overnight, the season seemed to have shifted from bright summer to cold autumn. There was no point in settling down in a new home now. The summer was over and it was time to go.

Just then, she heard the noise of running feet—and there were David and Charlotte racing down the path. She flew over to meet them. The children sat down on a rock and Dilly perched on David's left knee.

"I'll have to go," said Dilly. "My season's over."

"Go?" cried Charlotte in dismay. "Go where?"

"What season?" asked David, anxiously.

"Summer, of course," said Dilly. "It's time to change into a seed and fly away. Look!" And she pointed at all the silvery dandelion clocks.

"O," said David. He and Charlotte knew about dandelion clocks. They had often picked them and seen how many goes it took to blow all the seeds away.

"But how do you change into a seed," asked Charlotte. "And why do you?"

Dilly explained. She had a special one-headed bottle of white dandelion wine. When the right time came, she would drink it up and change into a tiny seed in the middle of a silvery puff ball. She didn't know that the children called them clocks, but she agreed about them blowing away in the wind.

"You have to be blown as far as you can," she explained. "So a windy day is best! Then, wherever you land, that's where you burrow deep into the ground. Then you have a long, long winter sleep. And when you wake up, it's spring and time to start growing again."

"So, won't you grow here?" asked Charlotte sadly. "Then we could see you next spring."

"O, no," said Dilly firmly. "You have to go as far as the wind takes you. And sometimes it's miles away!"

"Do you have to do it now?" asked David.

"Well, soon," said Dilly. "This is definitely the last day."

"I know!" said David. "Let's have one last adventure together. Can we?"

"All right," Dilly agreed. "It doesn't look as if the wind's going to drop. I'll go this afternoon."

The two children and the tiny fairy sat quietly in the meadow, watching the dandelion puff balls drift away in silvery clouds. Soon it would be Dilly's turn. What could they do on their last morning together?

"What would you like to do, Dilly?" asked Charlotte. She felt so sad that her fairy friend would have to go away. She wanted Dilly to be happy on her last day in Flower Meadow.

"I know!" cried Dilly, brightening up suddenly. "We'll go fairy sailing. It's a brilliant day for sailing."

"It is!" agreed David. There was a lovely wind and a bright sun and the sound of the stream racing over the stones was exciting.

"How?" he asked eagerly.

"Don't forget we haven't got wings," said Charlotte. "So we can't fly away if the leaf sinks!" She was remembering her first dangerous adventure with the fairy.

"It's all right!" said Dilly. "We'll go on a branch. They don't sink so much. And there are loads of them lying around after the storm."

And so there were. Fallen hazel branches, still with their leaves on, littered the ground under the trees.

"You'll have to grow small later," said Dilly, "to save time."

She got David to pick up a nice strong branch, with two big spiky twigs growing out of it.

"Is that going to be our boat?" asked Charlotte doubtfully. "What about life jackets? Daddy says we have to have them on boats."

Dilly didn't know about life jackets, but once Charlotte had explained, she saw their point. After all, if you didn't have wings you might very well end up in the water, in which case life jackets would be useful.

"I'll make you some," she promised. "Acorns will do, I expect. And cobwebs."

The children watched as Dilly flew over to a big oak tree, on a ridge above the valley and collected two fat acorns. She managed to fly down again, holding them in her arms, although they were quite big for her to carry. Then she zoomed over to the spider to pinch some strands of cobweb.

"You carry the branch, David," she said. "Charlotte, you carry the cobweb. And the acorns. We'll go upriver and then, when we've found a good place to launch, you can grow small."

So they set off upstream and round the corner, Dilly flying ahead. The stream raced happily past them and at one point David and Charlotte had to paddle, as the path was still under water. Luckily, they both had their sandals back now and could manage the sharp stones. They found a place where the water lapped gently in a little sandy bay.

"This is perfect," announced Dilly, fluttering down. "Put the branch boat in the water, only with one end still on the sand. It's time for you to grow small."

Chapter 28
Sailing

Dilly took the two-headed glass bottle out of her pocket. David and Charlotte each had a sip from the green side and soon they were fairy size. Then Dilly made the life jackets. She wrapped the sticky cobweb round the acorns and then round the waists of the two children, tying them neatly in a bow at the back.

"Acorns float quite well," she explained. "So, if you do fall in, you won't sink." She looked at their feet. "But I think you ought to take your sandals off," she went on, "you get a much better grip with bare feet."

So they did.

"You get on board first," she said helpfully. "And I'll push off and then fly on at the last minute."

"OK," agreed David and Charlotte. They were quite used to boats and knew how to sit nice and still. Except that they wouldn't be sitting!

"It's much more fun standing up," said Dilly. "You can hold on to your leafy twig for balance. You'll be fine. Ready!"

It was more of a command than a question. Carefully, David stepped up onto the wobbly boat. He steadied his bare feet on each side of his twig, which he held firmly in both hands. Just behind him, Charlotte did the same. Then Dilly gave a great heave, flew up and over and landed in the bows (the front bit of the boat). She stood tall, spreading out her two green wings as sails. The current caught the little boat, the wind blew in her sails—and they were off!

Once they got used to it, it was brilliant. Dilly was very good at steering, leaning from one side to the other as the boat hurtled past great rocks. Soon, David and Charlotte got the idea and they too leaned over, following Dilly's lead and the boat responded beautifully. The wind seemed gale force, now they were tiny and the foamy stream seemed like an ocean of mountainous waves!

"It's brilliant!" shouted David, but his little voice was drowned by the roaring wind.

"I'm holding on tight!" cried Charlotte, although no one could possibly hear her. She held her twig with both hands and found that she could keep her balance really well. All the same, she was glad of the comforting acorn nestling snugly next to her waist. Just in case!

All too soon, they reached the meadow. Dilly steered the boat away from the main current and into a smoother bit, right by the bank.

"Out you get!" she cried. "Quick! I can't hold the boat for long."

The children jumped out. They had almost reached the bank and didn't have far to swim. The life jackets worked brilliantly, keeping them afloat above the waves. Then they were able to grab hold of a great tuft of grass and scramble their way up onto dry land. The branch boat hurtled off downstream and Dilly flew up and then down and landed beside them.

"Thank you, Dilly," said Charlotte.

"It was brilliant!" said David.

"I expect you'll dry soon," said Dilly. "It was good wasn't it!"

As they sat on the grass, recovering, Charlotte quietly sang:

Sail, sail, sail your boat
Quickly down the stream;
Splishily, splashily, hippily, happily,
It wasn't just a dream!

David joined in, once he'd got the hang of the words to make it a round. They tried to teach Dilly how to do it—but she wasn't very musical! Most fairies just aren't. They enjoy listening to singing, but they can't do it themselves.

Chapter 29
Goodbye

And now it really was time for Dilly to go.

"The best thing," she said, "is for you two to grow big *now*. Then you can watch me change. Otherwise, I'll blow away with the bottle and you'll have to stay small for ever."

"O no," said Charlotte, "we can't do that!"

"They'll be expecting us back for lunch," said David.

"All right. Listen carefully!" said Dilly. And she explained exactly what they had to do.

First, they had to get back to their usual size. This was easy. There was plenty of yellow dandelion wine left. David went first. Before Charlotte took her sip of wine, she gave her friend a big wet hug.

"Thank you for everything, Dilly," she said. "I do hope we will see you in your next summer season."

"I hope so too," said Dilly. "If I hear you sing, I'll find you. It's just I never know exactly where I'll end up."

Then Charlotte drank her wine. She just had time to give the little bottle back to the fairy before she felt the familiar slithery feeling—and there she was, her own girl size again.

The next thing was for Dilly to change into a silvery seed. The two children sat down together on the grass and watched. Dilly took a little one-headed glass bottle out of her other pocket. It was full of bubbly white wine. She lifted back her little silvery head and drank it all up.

Almost at once, she started to change. The yellow petal dress faded and dropped; the long green wings shrivelled away. She grew smaller and smaller and more and more feathery. They could just make out her little silvery head peeping out above a strange new silvery dress. She still had David's old black sandals on, but now they were a soft brown colour. All around her, other little seeds grew, clinging to the faded green pod of the dandelion clock. They all trembled in the wind.

The next thing they had to do was to carry the clock up the slope to a nice windy bit. David went first and Charlotte followed, carefully holding the stem. Very slowly they climbed up and up, until they reached the bare hillside. This would make an excellent launching place. They could see for miles around and a good strong wind was blowing.

"Now we have to take it in turns," said Charlotte. "You go first."

She held out her hand, clutching the little brown stem. David took a deep breath and blew.

"One!"

It was a good strong breath and over half of the little seeds whooshed away. But right in the middle, Dilly was still there, clinging to the faded green pod.

"Your go," David whispered.

"OK," said Charlotte. "Goodbye, dear Dilly."

She took a deep breath and blew as hard as she could. The rest of the seeds, including the middle one, whooshed away and away.

"Two!"

Charlotte was left holding the bare stem. They watched the silvery cloud whoosh up with the wind and over the hills and far away. They couldn't see where it landed. Perhaps in the next valley, but it was difficult to tell.

"Maybe she's still flying in the wind," said Charlotte.

"She might be," agreed David. "When she lands, she'll burrow deep into the earth."

"It's a long time till spring," said Charlotte. "We don't even know what we'll be doing then."

"We don't," agreed David. "Anyway, we'll still be here and we can go on an adventure and look for her."

"OK," said Charlotte. "And I can sing my Dilly Dilly song."

"I wonder what the time is now," said David. "Do you think it's lunch time?"

"It must be!" said Charlotte excitedly. "Do you remember what the dandelion clock said? Two o'clock! We'll be late."

"Come on then," said David. "We'd better run."

And it was only when they got to the brambly bit by the bonfire that they remembered that they had taken off their sandals upstream.

"We can't go and get them now," said Charlotte. "We'll be even later."

Mummy was not best pleased to see two wet children, in bare feet, appear for a late lunch! But she was still feeling grateful for the unexpected breakfast in bed, so she wasn't too cross.

After lunch, David and Charlotte went to find their sandals. But it wasn't till they got there that they remembered. Two tiny blue sandals and two tiny orange sandals lay neatly on the river bank. But the fairy had flown and there was no way of making them bigger, ever again!

Hannah Goes to School

Chapter 1
The Rabbit

Hannah had had an excellent morning at school. She had painted a beautiful chicky bird, carefully dipping her brush into the yellow and blue paint pots and being sure to wipe it clean between each dip, so that the bird didn't come out a sludgy green by mistake. She had taken her picture home for Daddy and Mummy to admire and when they had finished, which didn't take long considering, Mummy had helped her hang it up in her bedroom. Then Mummy had given her a cheese baguette, a handful of raisins and a banana for her lunch. She ate it on the swing outside, rocking gently and talking happily to herself in between munches. Hannah had a high, clear voice—and what with all the talking and the munching, she was making quite a lot of noise: too much noise to hear anything else.

"O no, O no, O dear," came an unexpected voice from the geranium patch just in front of her. But Hannah didn't hear it. She had finished her baguette by now, but there was still a lot of talking to do, (not to mention a lot of banana to eat and two remaining raisins). Sometimes, Hannah went on for ages and not everyone knew exactly what she was talking about, for she used an interesting mixture of English and her own Hannah-words.

"O no, O dear, O what shall I do?" the strange voice continued. It was a squeaky sort of voice, not nearly loud enough to be heard above Hannah's talking.

"Banana, sultana, tuna and Bear," said Hannah loudly. "Buttery butter gets into my hair. A bither, a bother, a bother a bith…**oh!**"

Hannah gave a startled gulp, as the last bit of banana slithered down her throat. For she had noticed a strange stirring among the tall green leaves of the geranium flower bed.

"Help!" squeaked the voice, quite loudly. This time Hannah heard it; it was coming from the middle of the geranium patch. What could it be? She jumped off the swing, scampered a few paces to her right and leaned down to see. **Something** was squirming and wriggling underneath the tall geranium leaves. Something grey and furry with quivering whiskers, a little black nose and two shiny black eyes, which were looking straight up at her…

"It's a rabbit!" exclaimed Hannah. Whatever was it doing there?

"Hello, Rabbit," said Hannah. "Whatever are you doing here?"

"I'm stuck," explained the rabbit. "And I'm late for school. O dear, O dear."

Hannah knelt down to get a better look. She brushed aside the geranium stalks. Some of them got a bit bent, but never mind. She was sure Mummy would understand. She saw that the rabbit's four little legs were all tangled up in a piece of string. However had that got there? Maybe it was the string from her brother David's bow? Or perhaps it had come from one of Ben's home-made aeroplanes; these often landed where they weren't supposed to, coming apart quite easily and not always being picked up properly. Anyway, it was quite clear that the poor rabbit couldn't move.

"Does it hurt?" asked Hannah.

"Only a bit," said the rabbit. "But I'm late. Can you unstick me?"

"I'll try," said Hannah helpfully. "Up you come."

She leaned forward and lifted the rabbit up in her arms. It wasn't too heavy and felt lovely and soft. She could feel its little heart beating fast underneath the grey fur.

Carefully, she carried it over to the swing, settled it on her lap and started to untwist the string. This wasn't easy as it was tight and tangled.

"Ow!" said the rabbit.

"Keep still," said Hannah. "If you don't wriggle, it won't hurt." *A bit like hair-brushing*, she thought (at least that's what Mummy always claimed, although Hannah had her doubts). The rabbit's whiskers quivered and its black eyes blinked and its nose twitched and its little heart pounded, but otherwise it lay quite still. At last, Hannah managed to untangle the string. With a squeak and a bound, the rabbit leaped off her lap.

"Thank you," it gasped—and then hoppity-hopped as fast as he could on its four legs, over the tiles, up the steps and round the corner.

"Stop, wait for me," cried Hannah. And with a leap and a bound she ran after, as fast as her two legs would carry her.

Chapter 2
The Schoolroom

The rabbit hopped past the bonfire patch and along the little path which led towards Frog Pool. Hannah raced after it; probably it was going a bit more slowly than usual because of its recent entanglement, for she had almost caught up when it suddenly left the path and hurtled down the steep bank. Hannah watched as it leaped across the little stream at the bottom and then disappeared into a huge mass of brambles.

"Bother," she said to herself. But she was a determined little girl and not easily put off. She scrambled down the bank, sliding on her bottom when it got particularly steep and then jumping right over the little stream, without even getting her shoes wet. Then she stopped just in front of a great mass of brambles. Hannah knew all about brambles and how scratchy and sharp they could be. Just then, a little chicky bird (really very like the one she had painted at school that morning) fluttered down from the blue sky, hovered for a moment in front of a particularly fierce bramble stem—and then tugged at it with its little beak. At once, a great curtain of brambles swung open—and the little bird flew inside. Hannah just had time to glimpse a great dark tunnel before the bramble curtain swung back into place. Good heavens! There was a tunnel leading right into the heart of the massive bramble thicket! Cautiously, she pulled at the branch, taking great care not to hold the prickly bit; and to her great delight, it swung smoothly aside and there behind it was the tunnel!

"Here I go!" said Hannah bravely and she stepped inside, letting the bramble curtain swing shut behind her. The tunnel was taller and wider than she was; and it wasn't completely dark after all, as a few dim rays of sunlight sneaked in through gaps in the brambles high above her. On the floor was a little stone path, its white pebbles gleaming in the faint light. In the distance, Hannah could hear a noise—a confused kind of noise with lots of gurgles and squeaks and mutterings. Excitedly, she followed the path—along a bit and then round a corner—and there, just in front of her, she saw the most unexpected sight!

A dazzle of sunlight poured through a round hole high up in the bramble roof; and Hannah could see a big round room with curving green walls and a floor made up of soft dry earth; and sitting on the floor was a circle of…animals! She gasped in surprise. There was her rabbit, still out of breath as it joined the circle; and there was a little pink piglet and a small grey goat with a beard and a bell around its neck; and over there was a whole line of small frogs, burping; and opposite them two little brown mice; perched on a bramble stem was the little chicky bird; and there was a sweet little round turtle, its shell glistening in the sunlight and a lively young stork with a feathery tuft on his head and a shy little deer with great brown eyes. Hannah recognised the donkey from the next-door field, where she often saw him. He smiled at her, rather shyly. And standing upright on three legs and waving its fourth leg in the air stood—a very fluffy white sheep.

"Goodness!" exclaimed Hannah. Whatever was going on? And at the word goodness, all the creatures turned round and stared at her and for a moment there was complete silence. Then everyone got up and started braying and bleating and croaking and whistling and squeaking and turtling: what a din!

"Be quiet!" cried the sheep, who seemed to be the teacher. "Sit down, all of you!"

The creatures stopped talking and slithered back down onto the floor; but still their bright eyes stared at Hannah. Hannah sat down too, in the space next to her rabbit who grinned toothily up at her but didn't say anything.

"It seems we have a new pupil," said the Sheep with a kindly smile. "A human. Are you a boy human or a girl?"

"I'm a girl," explained Hannah firmly.

"Why so you are, my dear," said the sheep, peering down at her. "A great big girl. And what's your name, girl?"

"Hannah," said Hannah. "Only sometimes I'm called Small. Or Bear."

At the word 'bear', a whispery shiver ran round the class and several of the smaller animals started whimpering.

"O, I'm not a real bear," explained Hannah hastily, "it's just what they call me. Only sometimes, not always," she explained. "You don't have to, if you don't want to."

"We don't," said the Sheep. "We really can't have any bears in our school. And we can't really call you Small either, my dear, because you aren't."

And indeed she wasn't. Looking around, Hannah saw that only the deer and the donkey were bigger than she was. Most of the creatures were much smaller—and, although the Sheep and the piglet were a lot rounder, they weren't as tall.

"We shall call you…er, what did you say your name was, my dear? I've forgotten."

"HANNAH," said Hannah. "It begins and ends with an H and it's got two *a*s and two *n*s. And I can write it! It goes the same backwards as forwards."

"O dear!" said the Sheep, rather sheepishly. She didn't really understand spelling. (Actually, she couldn't write and didn't really understand what writing was for! She couldn't read either—it wasn't that sort of school, as you will see.)

But she had managed to remember the name.

"Hannah!" she said. "Now then, everyone, say after me: HANNAH!"

And all together, they did: the frogs croaked it and the little mice squeaked it and so did the rabbit and the donkey brayed it and the turtle turtled it and the piglet oinked it and the deer mewed it and the stork squawked it and the chicky bird sang it most beautifully! What a noise they made. But it was definitely her name all right.

"You can call me Teacher," said the Sheep, "And we will all tell you our names. But only one each morning, otherwise you'll never remember. Whose name would you like to learn today?"

"Me, me, me," cried the frogs; and everyone looked up at her hopefully, pleading with their shining eyes.

But Hannah wasn't sure about frogs. "The rabbit!" she said. "Because I met him already."

At this, all the animals burst out laughing. "But I'm not a him, I'm a **her**," squeaked the rabbit. "And my name is Hurtle."

"Hurtle," said Hannah wonderingly. She thought it was a good name for a *her* rabbit; and of course the rabbit had really **hurtled** down the steep bank. **And it began with an H, just like her own name!**

"There we are," said the Sheep, approvingly. "And now, my dears, it is time for today's lesson. Follow me. Two by two, if you please—and no talking."

Chapter 3
The Singing Lesson

Noisily, the creatures scrambled to their feet and formed a line, the littlest ones (the two brown mice) at the front and the tallest ones (the donkey and the deer) at the back. But Hannah walked beside Hurtle, even though she was much bigger than her new friend; she tried to lean down to hold Hurtle's hand, but after a bit this made her back ache, so she just picked the little rabbit up and held her tight, enjoying the feel of soft fur on her bare arms. Hurtle grinned toothily at her, but she didn't say anything: "No talking," the teacher had said and Hurtle (unlike some of the others) wasn't one to disobey. Nor was Hannah. She quietly followed the creatures in front, looking curiously around her as the procession passed through a different tunnel, a much bigger one, which wound its way through the bramble thicket and out into the sunlight.

Why, it's Flower Meadow! thought Hannah to herself as she recognised the little stream and the hazel trees and the long grass waving in the breeze. But she didn't say it out loud. The Sheep led her pupils to a grassy spot under the shade of a tree. Hannah put Hurtle down and everyone settled expectantly on the grass.

"Today we are going to learn singing," said the Sheep.

"O, I know how to sing!" exclaimed Hannah excitedly. "Listen." And she sprang to her feet and sang Baa Baa Black Sheep (which was the first song that came into her head) in her lovely high clear voice. Some of the pupils giggled when she got to the "One for the little boy" bit, but the Sheep was puzzled.

"I don't understand," she said. "I thought you said you were a girl."

"O," said Hannah, "Yes, I did—I am." She sat down again. Hurtle snuggled up against her comfortably.

"Don't worry," whispered the little rabbit. "She's not very good at understanding. And I thought you sang beautifully!"

"Thank you," said Hannah, feeling much better.

"The Teacher can't sing at all," Hurtle went on, "she just bleats."

Hannah thought it was quite strange having a teacher who couldn't read or write or even sing, but she didn't say anything.

And just then, the most beautiful music came floating through the air. The Sheep pointed with her front leg and everyone looked up to see a gleaming blackbird perched on the branch of the tree just above them, singing his heart out. When he stopped, there was a great silence and then everyone clapped enthusiastically. (Have you ever heard a piglet clapping? It makes a lot of noise!)

"What beautiful singing!" beamed the Sheep. "Now, my dears, I want you all to practise. Stand up, take a deep breath and try to copy the blackbird."

Well, that was easier said than done. Actually, Hannah managed quite well, because she was used to singing, but some of the animals found it really hard. The frogs, for instance, made a pretty ghastly noise, while the poor donkey could only manage a horrible bray. Hurtle was **quite** good, only her voice was a bit wobbly, not lovely and smooth like the blackbird's (or indeed Hannah's).

After a bit, the teacher told them all to sit down again.

"Now my dears," she said. "Who knows why singing is important? Paws up, please!"

Hurtle stuck a front paw up into the air. "Because it's lovely," she volunteered.

"Well, yes, it is," agreed the Sheep. "Anyone else?"

"Because it helps you make friends?" suggested the smallest mouse. He had only been able to manage a tiny squeak; he was very shy and he really wanted to have more friends. If only he could learn to sing like the blackbird! He decided he would practise every morning before school.

"That's a nice thought," said the teacher encouragingly. "Anyone else?"

"Because when you sing, it tells the other creatures that it's your home?" suggested Hannah, waving her hand in the air. She loved singing in her home and so did her big sister Charlotte.

"Yes it does!" agreed the Sheep and Hannah felt pleased and proud. "Good answer. Now, all of you, look up into the tree and tell me what you can see."

Everyone looked up.

"I know!" cried Hannah excitedly. "There's his nest! It **is** his home!" For high up in the branches she could see a lovely round nest.

"Yes!" said the Sheep. "Well done, Hannah. When the blackbird sings, the other birds know that the tree belongs to him and his family. Now I expect it's time to go to your homes. Who knows what time it is?"

Hannah didn't know but the piglet did! He sprang up. He had been hopeless at singing, but he was the best in the class at counting—he could count all the way up to five. Every evening before bed he would practise *this little pig*gy using his four trotters and his tail to make five. He ran over to the goat and rang its bell with his snout, counting carefully—bong, bong, bong. Three o' clock.

"Off you go, my dears," bleated the Sheep, who couldn't count herself, but always relied on the piglet to tell the time and the goat to ring the bell.

And with that all the little creatures leaped or scurried or ambled or hopped or flew away, until only Hannah and Hurtle were left.

"Can I come home with you?" asked Hurtle. "And then you can sing me some more."

"Of course you can," cried Hannah delightedly. "Follow me!"

Chapter 4
Bedtime

So Hannah ran ahead and the rabbit hopped behind—back along the little path to her house. She did share the house with her parents and her older brothers and sister, of course, who would probably be back from their school by now, but she was sure they wouldn't mind a visit from a friendly rabbit. And they didn't!

"Wow!" said Ben as Hannah and the rabbit came happily into the sitting room. Ben was sitting on the floor working on a new paper plane. This one didn't have string, just cleverly folded paper. "A tame rabbit!"

"She's called Hurtle," explained Hannah, "she got stuck this morning and I rescued her from the geraniums. Her legs got tied up in string."

"Was it hurt?" asked Charlotte anxiously, peering over the bannisters from the stairs.

"Not much," explained Hannah. "Because I untangled them."

"Is that why her name's **Hurt**—le?" asked David, who liked making jokes. He was sitting at the table mending his bow; the old string had mysteriously disappeared only that morning.

"No it's not!" exclaimed Hurtle indignantly. "It's because I'm the fastest runner in the whole family."

"Wow!" said Charlotte, climbing rapidly down the stairs. "It can talk!"

"It's a she not an it," said Hannah.

"Is that why **she's** called **her**-tle?" laughed David.

"Don't be silly, David," said Hannah crossly. "It's because she **hurtles.** I bet she can run faster than you! And she can sing and she goes to school. And I went to school too! I mean, to the animal school, not the ordinary one. (Well, I went there too, of course, but it wasn't as exciting.) The teacher's a sheep! Not the ordinary teacher, the animal one!"

And she told her sister and brothers all about the afternoon's adventure. As she explained, the little rabbit nodded her head and wiggled her little round tail.

"Can you really sing?" asked Ben.

"Like a blackbird?" asked Charlotte.

"Well, I'm not very good," admitted the rabbit. "But I can a bit. But Hannah's much better—she knows a song about a black sheep!"

"We all know that—even Ben," said David. "And I can play it. Listen." He got up from the floor, sat down on the stool and played the music on the piano and all four children sang the words. Hurtle thought it was amazing!

"Have you ever seen a black sheep?" she asked, wonderingly, when they had finished.

"I think so," said Hannah doubtfully—but the other three children thought they definitely had.

"But we've never seen a talking rabbit before," said Charlotte. "Can all your family talk?"

"Of course they can," said Hurtle. "Only the little ones don't go to school yet, because they're too little. What are their names?" asked David.

"Hop and Scotch," explained Hurtle.

"Can we go and see?" asked Charlotte longingly. But Hurtle said she wanted to see where Hannah lived and there hadn't been time to look around properly yet.

So Hannah carried her up the steps to her bedroom and showed the rabbit her bed and her best toys and books. Hurtle didn't know about reading but she liked the pictures and she particularly liked the soft warm duvet on Hannah's bed. She snuggled down—shut her bright black eyes—and, in no time at all, fell fast asleep!

But Hannah was hungry. She didn't feel at all like sleeping yet; so when Mummy called them down to the kitchen for supper, she tucked up her friend and ran after the others. Supper was baked potatoes and beans (not bad) and treacle pie for pudding (yum). And then there was cleaning-teeth-and-washing-face in the bathroom. And then the time came for a bedtime story. Usually, Mummy would come up and sit on the bed while Hannah snuggled up inside it, under the duvet. But supposing Mummy sat on Hurtle by mistake? That would never do. Hannah raced ahead and scrambled into her room. She was just in time.

Hurtle was still fast asleep, so Hannah jumped into bed and—quickly but gently, so as not to wake her up—she pushed the little rabbit right down to the bottom of the bed with her feet. That made a nice big space for Mummy next to the top of the bed and she listened quietly to her favourite Red Shoes story, about the girl who couldn't stop dancing. Half way through, Hannah felt the rabbit stirring at her feet. The fur was tickling her toes and it was hard not to laugh. Luckily, Mummy was too busy reading to notice the unusual movement at the far end of the bed. Hannah put her bare feet firmly on top of the rabbit's warm back and pressed down gently, until at last Hurtle settled down quietly.

"That's funny!" said Mummy, when she had finished. She had just noticed the round hump at the bottom of the bed. "I don't remember making you a hot bottle. I must be getting more absent-minded than I thought."

And she kissed her youngest daughter goodnight and went back to the kitchen to get on with the washing up.

Chapter 5
Run, Rabbit, Run!

As soon as Mummy had gone, closing the bedroom door firmly behind her, Hannah peered under the duvet.

"You can come up now," she called.

Up came the little rabbit, settling down happily on Hannah's pillow.

"I loved the story!" Hurtle sighed. "I know, let's ask Miss if we can have dancing lessons tomorrow."

"O yes," agreed Hannah. That would be fun.

"Can the tiny brown mice dance?" she asked curiously. "Could they show us?"

"I don't **think** so," replied Hurtle. "They just wriggle and squeak. But you never know."

Perhaps the Sheep is a good dancer, wondered Hannah, though she doubted it. As far as she could see, her animal teacher wasn't good at anything much. And just imagine a wobbly woolly sheep doing ballet! She'd never be able to get up on her pointed toes. She probably didn't even have any toes, just clumsy hooves.

Just then, in came Ben. He was next to go to bed, after Hannah. Mummy didn't have to read him a bed-time story, as Ben was a very good reader himself. Tonight, however, he was much more interested in Hurtle than in reading. And neither he nor Hannah were feeling at all sleepy. Ben wanted to show Hurtle his paper aeroplanes—and he did a few excellent demonstration flights from the bedroom. Hurtle watched in delight as the aeroplanes soared and swooped downwards, landing on the patio floor below.

"I wish I could fly," said the rabbit longingly. "Like birds and aeroplanes."

"So do I," agreed Hannah. But she knew that humans could only fly **in** aeroplanes, which wasn't the same thing at all. And rabbits couldn't even do that.

"Anyway," said Hurtle, "I'd better be getting back to the burrow. They'll be wondering where I am."

"OK," agreed Hannah. She felt a bit sad at first, but then she thought that she would see her new friend at school, tomorrow afternoon. She got out of bed, climbed down the stairs and opened the door. Hurtle followed, hopping cautiously from step to step and managing not to fall down.

But, although Hannah and Ben knew perfectly well that it would be dark by now, the rabbit was startled. She had no idea how much time had gone by, as she had been fast asleep for most of it. And she didn't know about electric lights, so she thought it was just ordinary sunlight in the bedroom.

"O dear, O, no!" she exclaimed. "It's night time."

"Well of course, it is," explained Hannah. "I don't go to bed in daylight!"

"But I'm not supposed to go out in the dark," said the rabbit.

"I thought rabbits could see in the dark," said Ben.

"Well, they can, it's true. But my daddy said I'm too young and it might be dangerous on my own. O dear, O dear." And the little rabbit started to cry.

"It's all right, Hurtle," said Hannah kindly. "I'll come with you. If it isn't too far." "Can you see in the dark too?" asked Hurtle hopefully.

"Well, not really," explained Hannah. "But there might be a moon tonight."

"There isn't," said Ben, who had come downstairs after them. "But I've got my head torch. I'll come too."

"Thank you, Ben," said Hannah gratefully. She didn't mind the getting there with Hurtle, but what about the coming back? Especially as there was no moon. Then she had a good idea. She ran into David's room and took the head torch which was lying on his pillow. Then she would be able to see too. And David wouldn't go to bed for ages yet—he and Charlotte had masses of homework, which they always did downstairs.

Quickly, Ben and Hannah put on their welly boots (better than sandals for darkness, as you never knew about prickles) and Hannah put on a warm jersey over her pyjamas. Ben, of course, was already dressed.

"So where exactly **do** you live?" asked Ben.

"Well, you know where the school is?" said Hurtle.

"No, I don't," said Ben.

"I do," said Hannah. "I know exactly where." She remembered sliding down the steep bank and jumping over the little stream at the bottom. "Is it near there?"

"It's on the other side of the path," explained Hurtle. "It's **up** the steep bank, not **down** it. Under an oak tree."

"That's easy," said Hannah. "Come on, let's go."

Together, the two children and the little rabbit crept past the house; they could see the lamp lighting up the sitting room and hear the gentle clink of washing-up. Hannah went first, as she knew the way to the school. David's head torch felt a bit loose on her head, so she carried it instead, pointing it down at the path, so she wouldn't stumble over any stones by mistake. Then came Hurtle, her green eyes looking all around, as she tried to remember the landmarks. Finally, came Ben, his head torch pointing straight forward at his little sister's back.

Although they were going slowly and carefully, it wasn't that long before Hannah recognised the place where Hurtle had scrambled down to the blackberry thicket; she could hear the sound of the stream tinkling below. But Hurtle had said her warren was up the steep bank, not down it.

"I think we go upwards here," she whispered. Somehow, she felt like whispering in the dark night; she knew that the family was miles away by now and couldn't possibly hear them, but there might be other creatures awake and listening.

"Hurtle, you go first now and show us the way."

"All right," whispered the little rabbit.

Up they went—Hurtle, Hannah and Ben. It was quite hard going for the children, as it was very steep and overgrown with bushes and plants. But now that Hurtle knew the way, she bounded ahead. Having four paws meant she was much faster than the children.

"Come on!" she cried, turning round to face them, "we're nearly there!" Her two green eyes shone brightly in the darkness.

But Hannah and Ben weren't the only creatures to see them! Just then, Hannah heard an eerie hooting cry and the swish of beating wings in the dark sky.

"It's an owl!" she exclaimed. The owl swooped low and swept right past her, so close that it ruffled her hair with its great feathery wings. What was it doing? Then she realised.

"Hurtle! Run! Quick!" she cried. Because, as Hannah knew, owls hunt at night—and what they like best are small, furry animals.

"Run, Hurtle, run!" echoed Ben, who saw the danger too.

The children watched, holding their breath, as Hurtle turned tail and **ran!** Now they could see why she was called Hurtle. The owl was mighty quick, but the little rabbit made a wild dash for the safety of the burrow. In no time at all, she had disappeared down the hole. Thank goodness!

"That was exciting," said Ben. They watched the owl flap its great wings and circle up again into the night sky. It would have to find something else for its supper tonight. The children stared anxiously up the slope, but Hurtle must have decided that it was too dangerous to come out and say goodbye. So they set off, back along the little path to their house—and into their nice snug beds.

Hannah didn't get to sleep straight away; she lay awake remembering her exciting day and all the things that had happened.

"And tomorrow afternoon, I'll go to Animal School again," she decided. That will be fun!

Chapter 6
Can You Dance?

Hannah couldn't wait for her second afternoon at Animal School. But first, of course, she had her ordinary one to go to. That day, the teacher (the human one) taught the class a new dance. She wanted the children to be ready for the Easter parade, in a few weeks' time. It was a lovely dance with lots of clapping and spinning and twirling to the music of guitars and drums. By the end of the lesson, the children were quite tired—and very thirsty. So they had their snack (apple juice and a flapjack for Hannah) and settled down for some peaceful colouring. Hannah was given a picture of a lovely Scottish dancer in a twirly tartan kilt—and she coloured it in beautifully. And then it was time to go home—and there was Mummy waiting for her at the bottom of the school steps.

"I've got masses of digging to do this afternoon," explained Mummy as they walked home together. "I've got to get the vegetable patch ready for planting strawberries. Do you want to help?"

Hannah considered. She loved eating strawberries, but digging was hard work. And anyway, she really wanted to go to Animal School again to see if Hurtle was all right after last night's adventure with the owl.

"Well, you see," she explained. "I really want to go to school this afternoon."

"To school?" echoed Mummy in surprise. "But you don't go to school in the afternoons."

"Yes I do," said Hannah. "It's called Animal School and it's under the brambles and my best friend is a rabbit and the teacher is a sheep, only she's not very good at spelling. And there are lots of other animals too."

"Are there indeed? Well, I'll just have to dig on my own, I suppose," said Mummy.

"Daddy's busy today, so he won't be any help either."

"You don't mind, do you Mummy?" asked Hannah. "It's just that we might do dancing. I'm going to ask if we can."

"Well, as long as you can amuse yourself," said Mummy.

"I don't need to amuse **myself**," said Hannah, "because all the others will be there."

But Mummy didn't really understand.

"Anyway, lunch time first," she said. "And then I really must get going."

So they had lunch together—scrambled egg on toast with fresh tomatoes followed by lemon yogurt. They sat outside on the patio as it was another bright day. Hannah stared hopefully at the geranium bed, but there was no sign of a little furry rabbit beneath the tall green stems. As soon as she had finished her lunch, Hannah stood up.

"I'm going to school now," she explained. "And I might be some time. Goodbye." Happily, she skipped down the little path and slithered down the steep bank and jumped over the trickling stream and opened the bramble curtain and walked along the long tunnel—and there she was, in the Animal Schoolroom.

The Sheep was already there, waving her front paw as she greeted her pupils.

"Hello, Hannah," she bleated cheerfully, very proud that she had remembered the girl's name. "You can sit next to Hurtle, if you like."

Hannah **did** like! Definitely.

"Were you OK last night?" Hannah asked her furry friend. "The owl didn't scratch you did it?"

"It didn't, but it nearly did," said Hurtle. "Thank you for warning me. Otherwise…" She shuddered. "I might have been snatched! And eaten!"

"Did your parents mind you being late?" asked Hannah.

"Well, they were a bit cross at first, but I said I had been visiting a new friend and gone to sleep by mistake. And I said you had seen me home and saved me from the owl. So then they said you could come back to tea after school."

"Hurrah!" said Hannah. She would love to see inside the rabbits' burrow and meet Hurtle's family. She wondered what rabbits had for tea…hmmmm.

By now, all the other creatures had arrived and it was time for Hannah to choose one so she could learn its name.

"Um…The mice," she said. That meant **two** new names, but she was sure she could remember them. Well, the little brown mice were very timid. They wriggled and giggled nervously when asked to say their names.

"Speak up, loud and clear, my dears," said the Sheep encouragingly. "Tell Hannah your names."

"Bubble and Squeak," they giggled in unison.

"Bubble and Squeak," repeated Hannah. She wasn't sure which was which, though. Or even if they were boy names or girl names. But it didn't matter—they seemed to do everything together anyway.

"Can you dance?" she asked eagerly. "Can you stand on tiptoes like this?" And she stood up on her tiptoes and waved her arms elegantly in the air and did a beautiful twirl.

The mice giggled.

"We can, we can!" they squeaked. "Look!"

To everyone's surprise, the tiny mice stood up on their hind legs and, holding each other's front paws, turned circles—right there in the middle of the room! Round and round they went, waving their tails and blinking their bright eyes and laughing happily. They were excellent dancers!

And then of course, everyone wanted a go. The piglet and the goat and the donkey were very clumsy and kept falling over, nearly squashing the frogs, who leaped away just in time and then continued leapfrogging up and over all the dancers. The deer was a bit better, but she wobbled after only a few seconds, coming to land on all four hooves, which was just as well as they were sharp and shouldn't really be waved around in the air; the chicky bird couldn't exactly dance but he flew round and round in circles, cheeping excitedly; as for the stork, he stood on one leg and hopped. It wasn't really dancing at all and it certainly wasn't beautiful—and he kept tripping over the other creatures with his enormous feet. The turtle went round and round in circles and kept getting in everyone's way. Little Hurtle was good at jumping up high but no good at turning circles, so in the end Hannah lifted her up and danced round and round with her in her arms. As for the Sheep—well, she didn't even try to dance—she just stood there on all four stumpy legs bleating "Do be careful! Look where you're going! Stop it, all of you!"

But no one could hear her above the rumpus. What a commotion they all made: bumping and giggling and squeaking: "Look out! Don't tread on me! Mind your backs! Ough! That hurt!"

The goat's bell was swinging and ringing wildly, which added to the confusion. O dear!

Then, echoing through the back tunnel, they heard a mighty bellow: **"Silence! All of you. Now!"**

There was a sudden silence as the creatures froze in mid-twirl (*a bit like musical statues*, Hannah thought). Who could it be?

"It's the Head!" whispered Hurtle. "O dear, O dear."

"Outside, all of you! Now!" came the mighty bellow.

And outside they all crept, not daring to say a word.

Chapter 7
The Head

Hannah wasn't at all sure what a Head was. She thought it seemed very odd: how could you have a head on its own, without a body as well? The Head must have ears and a mouth, because it had clearly heard the kerfuffle and it could bellow very loudly—and she supposed it would have eyes as well. But what sort of a creature was it? She wanted to ask Hurtle, but she knew she wasn't supposed to talk. No one was making a sound and the animals looked quite scared. Even the Sheep looked nervous as she hooshed her pupils through the green tunnel and out into the bright light of Flower Meadow.

And there, standing huge against the dazzling sun, stood…a great black bull! Hannah had only seen bulls in pictures before and she had never met one face to face. But at least it had a body, with four great strong legs and a long black tail, as well as a great black head with two horns growing out of it. She was glad it looked like a proper animal should, even though it was very big—much bigger than she was and much bigger than all the other animals, even the donkey. No wonder it had made such a loud noise.

"I am sorry, Sir," bleated the Sheep nervously. "We were having a dancing lesson and the animals were naughty and they wouldn't listen when I told them to stop."

"Dancing, hey?" bellowed the Bull. "Dancing is a very fine thing, but it has to be done properly. Which of you think you can dance, hey?"

Well, the two little mice were much too shy to say anything, even though they were very good dancers. But Hannah was made of sterner stuff.

"Please, Sir," she said, raising her hand, "I'm a good dancer."

The Bull looked at her with his piercing black eyes.

"A human!" he said. "So you think you can dance, hey? Then you must show us."

"I will," said Hannah.

She stepped forward and twirled and swirled and whirled, standing up on tiptoes and waving her hands in the air most beautifully. She would have liked some music to dance to, but there was just a great quietness as all the animals stood still and watched her. But when she finished, with a lovely low curtsey, do you know what? Everyone cheered and stamped their hooves and paws on the ground, which was their way of clapping without hands. Even the Bull stamped his four great hooves, making the earth tremble.

"That was very good," said the Bull and Hannah felt pleased and proud. Perhaps the Bull wasn't so scary after all. But why was he called the Head?

"Please, Sir," said Hannah, "why do they call you the Head? I don't understand. Because you aren't **just** a head, are you?" At this, the Bull gave a great bellow—but it was a bellow of laughter not of anger.

"I am Head of the school," he said in his deep voice. "I am the Head Teacher. This is my school. And everyone who comes must do as I say. Will you do as I say? Hey?"

"Yes, Sir Head," said Hannah. "I will."

"Now," said the Bull. "We have just seen some beautiful dancing! It is time for you all to try. But if you have four legs, then you must use them all. And if you have wings, then you must use them. And do not bump into each other! I will provide the music."

And at that, the Bull opened his huge mouth and started to sing! He had a very deep bottom bass voice and as he sang, he stamped his four hooves on the ground, making a deep thudding sound, like a drum. Hannah knew the tune, as it was just like the one she had danced to that morning in her human school. The words were different, though; they went like this:

Animals, animals, animals dance;
Up on your four legs and circle and prance;
Up on your two wings and stretch right up high,
Dance to the music and reach for the sky.

Now that the creatures realised that they could use **all** their legs (not to mention wings) and now that there was enough space in the lovely meadow, the animals found they could dance pretty well, considering. The goat turned his head from side to side so that his bell rang in time to the hoof-beat, as he galloped round and round. The chicky bird and the stork lifted their wings and spiralled higher and higher in the blue air. Even the Sheep had a go—and managed to walk round in a circle, her tummy wobbling and her tail swinging and not bumping into anyone. The Donkey did his best, although he was quite clumsy and kept stumbling over the little turtle who wasn't really dancing at all, just going round and round in circles, chasing his tail. As for the little mice—well there they were, right in the middle, up on their back paws and dancing like anything. And as for Hannah, well she just loved it: how she whirled and twirled to the music:

All of us creatures can dance and can sing,
Whether we move with a leg or a wing;
Join in the music, all singing together—
For dancing and singing can go on forever.

And they all sang and danced, on and on. High up above them, in his almond tree, the musical blackbird sang his heart out and even higher up on the rocky crag above Flower Meadow, two yellow eyes watched intently. The eyes belonged to a wild cat who had never seen anything like this before! And high, high up in the sky, a flock of birds joined in the dance, spiralling and swooping and turning together, the way only birds can. It was brilliant.

But it couldn't really go on forever. One by one, the tired animals dropped out of the circle and sat down on the grass to watch; Hannah picked up little Hurtle and danced with her in her arms, until she too sat down, exhausted. Only Bubble and Squeak, the two little mice, remained, circling and circling together, until at last they had had enough.

The music stopped and there was another great quietness.

"That was a very good lesson," said the Bull. "Goat, ring your bell—it is time to go home."

And with that, the Bull bounded off and away into the distant hills. All the creatures said goodbye and went off to their homes. The Sheep saw them off safely and then waddled back to her grassy field.

"Can I really come home with you?" Hannah asked Hurtle. She did want to see the burrow and the other members of the rabbit family.

"Of course, you are **expected**!" grinned Hurtle. "Follow me."

Chapter 8
Vegetables

They reached Hurtle's burrow in no time: Hannah knew that the entrance was a round hole in the steep bank, but what was it like inside? Hurtle said it got much bigger underground and she thought that Hannah could probably squeeze through the first bit of tunnel. So Hurtle went ahead to warn the family and Hannah lay down on her tummy and wriggled her way in, like a very large worm. The tunnel was quite dark, but enough light came through the hole to show her the way. It felt slithery but quite warm. And then the tunnel widened out into a big round room—not big enough for Hannah to stand up in, but just big enough for her to sit down cross-legged, if she minded her head on the roof.

And there, staring at her with their bright green eyes, was the rabbit family!

"She looks quite nice!" said a small rabbit, presumably one of Hurtle's siblings.

"Of course, she's nice," said Hurtle indignantly, "she saved me from the owl. And she can dance beautifully."

"O show us, please show us," squeaked the second little rabbit.

"I can't," explained Hannah, "I can't even stand up, let alone dance."

"O," exclaimed the rabbit, disappointed.

"Well, it is very nice to meet you," said Mother Rabbit; and she held out a furry paw for Hannah to shake.

"Thank you for looking after Hurtle," said Father Rabbit. "Let me introduce you. This is our youngest daughter, Scotch; and this is our only son, Hop."

Hannah shook paws with all the rabbits.

"Would you like some supper?" enquired the mother Rabbit.

Well, Hannah wasn't very hungry, as she usually had her supper much later; but she was curious about rabbit meals, even though she wasn't quite sure that she would like them.

"Yes please," she said politely.

The mother Rabbit went out to the kitchen and came back a minute later, pushing a huge pile of vegetables into the centre of the room with her two front paws.

"Help yourself, Hannah," she beamed. "Scotch and Hop, wait for your turn. Guests go first!"

Hannah surveyed the pile. She could make out raw green cabbage leaves and raw orange carrots and purple radishes and long white leeks and fat onions, still in their brown skins and fierce looking nettles. O dear! Rabbit food did look a bit difficult, but she didn't want to be rude.

"I'll have a carrot, please," she said. Surely she could manage a carrot? She picked the smallest one she could see and remembered to say thank you politely.

Then all the rabbits made a dash at the pile and started to grab and gobble like anything! In no time at all, the pile had disappeared. Hannah took a bite of her carrot, which didn't taste **too** bad. Then she quickly broke the remains into two bits and passed them secretly to Scotch and Hop, who disposed of them in a great gulp. Hannah didn't think the other rabbits had noticed. Luckily, there didn't seem to be any pudding.

"It was lovely," she said bravely. "Thank you for my supper."

"We saved up the best vegetables for you," Skotch boasted. "We all went vegetabling while Hurtle was at school. It was fun!"

"Where did you find them?" asked Hannah.

"Hurtle told us where to look," explained the father Rabbit. "She discovered it yesterday: a beautiful vegetable patch, all neatly dug, with soft brown earth and masses of vegetables all in neat rows. Perfect!"

O no, thought Hannah, *it must be our vegetable patch.* She knew that Mummy wouldn't want rabbits to eat it all up. Not after all that hard work. But she didn't say anything. Guests were supposed to be polite.

"We had to be careful," said the mother Rabbit. "There was a very big human digging away in another bit of ground nearby, but we sneaked behind it when it wasn't looking."

"It was easy," cried Hop. "It didn't hear a thing. We're very good at sneaking."

Poor Mummy, thought Hannah. But she didn't say anything. "Did you take **all** the vegetables?" she asked anxiously.

"O, yes," boasted Scotch. "Every single one. Because we knew you were coming to supper and we wanted to have a feast!"

"We would have taken them anyway," said Hop. "They looked delicious."

O dear, thought Hannah again. She didn't mind too much about the vegetables, but supposing it had been the strawberries? Hannah loved strawberries! Perhaps she had better tell Mummy about the rabbits sneaking up? But Mummy might be cross. She didn't know what to do.

"I think I should go now," she said. "Thank you for having me." And she wriggled down on her tummy and wormed her way out through the tunnel. Hurtle came too, to wave her goodbye. It wasn't dark yet and there was no danger of owls.

"See you at school tomorrow!" cried Hurtle.

"OK," said Hannah. "Thank you."

She ran quickly along the little path and stopped to survey the vegetable patch. There wasn't a vegetable to be seen—just soft brown earth and…rabbit footprints! On a nearby patch of ground, were neat green rows of strawberry plants. Mummy must have been busy. It was too early in the year for actual berries, or even flowers, but anyone could see that there would be a delicious crop one day.

Anyway, there were the others, back home from sport and starving! Daddy wasn't back yet and Mummy was busy cooking. She gave them each a biscuit to keep them going and told them that they would have to wait for supper.

"I'm making a casserole," she said. "And I need some vegetables. Ben, could you go and pick some? Here's a basket. I want carrots and leeks and onions, please. David and Charlotte, you can get started on your homework."

"I suppose so," said Charlotte.

"Can I use the computer?" asked David.

"OK," said Ben.

"I'll come too," said Hannah and she put on her sandals.

So she and Ben set off for the vegetable patch.

As soon as they were out of earshot, Hannah explained everything.

"Wow!" said Ben, very impressed. "Did you really have supper with the rabbits?"

"Yes I did," said Hannah. "But it was horrible—all raw vegetables and nettles. And where do you think they got the vegetables?"

"I don't know," said Ben. "I'm not a rabbit. I suppose they just dug them up."

"Yes, but where from?" asked Hannah. By now, they had reached the vegetable patch. "Look!" And she pointed.

"Look where?" asked Ben. "I can't see anything."

"But that's the point," said Hannah, almost in tears. "You can't see anything because there isn't anything to see! The rabbits have taken it all!"

"Golly!" said Ben. He knelt down and peered at the soft brown earth. "Footprints!"

"I know," said Hannah. "It was the rabbits. What are we going to tell Mummy?"

"I don't know," said Ben. "She might be cross. She likes vegetables. So does Daddy. Especially in casseroles." He thought some more. *I suppose it might have been a fox*, he wondered, *or a stray goat*.

"No, it was the rabbits," said Hannah. "They said so. They sneaked up behind her when she was planting the strawberries and she didn't notice a thing."

"Don't worry," said Ben. "I expect there's a tin of corn she can use instead. Actually, I prefer tinned corn."

Just then Daddy came marching around the corner.

"Mummy says can you get a move on? She wants to put the vegetables in the casserole; otherwise, they won't get cooked properly."

"But Daddy," cried Hannah, "there aren't any!"

"Good grief, so there aren't!" exclaimed Daddy. He leaned forward. "Footprints!" he cried. "Rabbit footprints, unless I'm much mistaken. The little devils!"

"They might be foxes," said Ben hopefully, "or goats."

"Definitely not goats," said Daddy. "Hmmm. We'll have to lay some netting tomorrow. That'll stop them."

"O dear!" said Hannah. She was remembering when Hurtle had got her paws caught up in Ben's string. Surely netting would be even worse? Supposing little Skotch and Hop got all tangled up? She would have to warn the rabbit family. Or, she would have to explain everything to Daddy and Mummy. What should she do? What would be best? She couldn't decide.

Well, casserole with tinned corn is actually very good and Mummy didn't make *too* much fuss, considering. But Hannah wasn't hungry. She listened anxiously as Daddy explained his netting plans to Mummy. He would go into the town first thing next morning to buy some nice green netting and then they could spend the rest of the morning setting it up, while the children were at school. That should stop the rabbits.

"Or foxes," said Ben.

"Whatever," said Daddy. "The point is, those are our vegetables and Mummy has worked really hard growing them."

"Would it hurt the rabbits?" asked Hannah. "If they got tangled up?"

"No, I'm sure it wouldn't," said Mummy. "Don't worry about rabbits—they can look after themselves. Daddy's right—we have to stop them. Supposing they got at the strawberries? You wouldn't like that, would you?"

She was right: Hannah wouldn't.

Lying in her snug little bed that night, Hannah still couldn't decide what to do.

But then she had a brilliant idea…

Chapter 9
Digging

Hannah climbed out of bed and clambered down the stairs. There were David and Charlotte sitting at the big table, doing their homework. Daddy was in the kitchen washing up; Mummy and Ben were doing spellings on the big green sofa.

"Hannah!" exclaimed Mummy. "You're supposed to be asleep."

"I know," said Hannah. "But I couldn't. You see, it's about the rabbits." And she told Mummy everything—all about finding Hurtle under the geraniums and going to Animal School and the Sheep and the owl and the Head and the singing and dancing lessons and having supper with the rabbits…It was quite a long telling and as she went on David and Charlotte and Daddy came over to listen (of course, Ben knew most of it already, but he listened too, with only a few interruptions). So now everyone knew everything and Hannah felt much better.

"But we still have to do the netting," said Daddy. "We can't have rabbits eating all our vegetables."

"Or strawberries," added Charlotte and everyone agreed.

"I know," said Hannah, "but I've got a brilliant idea. I'll explain everything to the rabbits and then we can help them make their very own vegetable patch. And they can grow whatever they want in it—even nettles."

"They don't need to grow nettles," said Daddy, "they can help themselves to all the nettles they like."

"It's a very good idea," said Mummy. "We can help them make their own patch and they can help us with all the nettles. That would save a lot of work weeding."

"Rabbit poo is good for composting," said David. Everyone laughed, but Mummy said that David was quite right—the rabbits could help with the compost heap too!

"And then I can meet the baby rabbits," said Charlotte. "Brilliant!"

"I'll go into town tomorrow and get some seeds," said Daddy. "We won't need the netting after all."

"And some more strawberry plants," added Ben.

And so it was agreed.

Next morning, Hannah woke up feeling very excited. She couldn't wait to see Hurtle and tell her of the plan. But first, of course, she had to go to Human School in the village. And, actually, she had a very nice morning. The Teacher told the class a lovely story about Jack and the Beanstalk and then everyone had to draw the great beanstalk reaching up into the sky, with Jack climbing up it and his mother waiting anxiously below. Hannah decided to show it to Hurtle, to explain what fun it would be growing your own vegetables. Perhaps Daddy would buy a magic bean when he went shopping!

After lunch (the remains of yesterday's corn casserole), Hannah ran off to Animal School, happily clutching her drawing. The Sheep was very interested to see it and thought that Hannah could tell the whole class the story, as today was storytelling day. So they all sat round in a circle, while Hannah told them about Jack and the poor cow and the magic bean and the great giant in the sky. Then she taught them how to say the giant's fierce poem:

Fee, Fi, Fo, Fum
I smell the blood of an Englishman;
Be he alive, or be he dead
I'll grind his bones to make my bread!

It sounded especially fierce with all the animals chanting the words at the tops of their voices. Bubble and Squeak were quite frightened and huddled close together. Then it was time for Hannah to choose her next animal, to learn its name. But before she could decide, the Donkey looked round shyly and said:

"She knows my name, already. But I can't remember hers."

"I do," agreed Hannah shyly. She had never talked to him before, though. He didn't seem nearly as fierce as she had thought.

"You're called Donk," she said. "And you live in the field next door! And I'm Hannah."

"Ah!" exclaimed the Donkey, with a big smile, which showed up all his yellow teeth.

Hannah was so pleased that he seemed so friendly, after all. Next time she went to visit next door, she definitely wouldn't be frightened.

And then it was time to go outside. The sheep explained that they all had to pick three different leaves from the trees in Flower Meadow and say their names. Hannah went with Donk and helped him say the names over and over until he could remember them.

"A hazel leaf, an oak leaf and a beech leaf," she said. She couldn't reach up to pick the beech leaf but Donk could; he picked it with his great yellow teeth and felt pleased and proud. He liked Hannah very much, even if he found her name difficult.

"Hannah," she explained. "It's spelt the same forwards as backwards." But the donkey didn't know about spelling.

The Sheep said they could take their leaves home with them, so, after the pig had counted three and the goat had rung his bell, Hannah and Hurtle scampered off together, clutching their tree leaves and Hannah's lovely picture of the beanstalk. And as they went, she explained the plan about the vegetable patch. Hurtle was very excited. They didn't need to go inside the burrow this time, as the whole rabbit family were outside, enjoying the afternoon sunshine. Hannah explained the plan and kindly said that the little rabbits could have her picture as a present to inspire them. So Scotch and Hop scampered inside the burrow with the picture and the leaves which, they said, would look just lovely in their tunnel bedroom. As soon as the rabbits had understood the plan, they bounded excitedly down the steep slope and along the little path. And there was Mummy waiting for them with a big smile on her face and a big spade in her hand.

Hannah introduced her to all the rabbit family and Mummy leaned her spade against a handy apple tree so that she could shake all the paws. Like her youngest daughter, Mummy was very good at remembering the names.

"The others aren't back yet," she said. "But we can get started with the digging." And with a mighty grunt, she struck the heavy spade into the soft earth. This was going to be hard work.

But it wasn't! The rabbits were brilliant at digging. After all, they were used to digging burrows. With their four paws and strong legs, they set to work with a will, sending up great clouds of dust as they dug deep into the soft earth. Mummy stood back, leaning on her spade and smiling happily. What a good idea this was—and what a very clever daughter she had! In no time at all, a lovely square patch had been dug, near her own patch but not too near, so it would be very clear which was which! When it came to refreshments, the rabbits were very happy with nettles—there were plenty growing around, just as Daddy had said—while she and Hannah had a slice each of an excellent lemon cake which she had made that morning.

And then, with a cheerful shout, down the path came Daddy and the older children, back from school. Daddy had brought lots of packets of seeds, with bright coloured pictures on the front and six green strawberry plants. And he **had** bought some bean packets—hurrah! Some of the packets were for Mummy (to make up for the lost vegetables) and some were for the rabbits. Well, the rabbits were no good at all at sowing the seeds. Paws just aren't the same as fingers and thumbs, for tricky manoeuvres. So they watched curiously as the children made nice long runnels for the seeds to be planted. Ben was in charge of watering them and he tried to explain how the hose worked to the father Rabbit. Unfortunately, he squirted him by mistake, just as the poor rabbit was leaning forward to get a better look at the tap. Never mind. The father Rabbit was too polite to make a fuss and he had been feeling thirsty anyway. And then, of course, all the rabbits wanted a drink and some of them got very wet in the process. Not to mention the children. Still, in the end, the seeds got nicely watered and so did the strawberry plants which Daddy had planted at the edge of the rabbit patch.

They all stood back to survey their handiwork: excellent! A beautifully smooth and well-watered patch. Mummy explained that they would have to wait a few weeks before the seeds grew into proper vegetables, but meanwhile, they could help themselves to nettles; Daddy explained that while he was in town, he had bought a big packet of raw carrots and another one of onions. The rabbits were welcome to have some and so were the children. But Charlotte said she preferred ginger biscuits and so she dashed off to get a packet from the kitchen. Everyone sat down, tired but pleased with all their hard work and ate raw carrots, onions or ginger biscuits, according to their natures, in the last rays of the setting sun.

And that night, as she snuggled under her soft white duvet, Hannah thought that after all the bother of yesterday, today had been just brilliant!

Chapter 10
The Listening Lesson

High up on a rocky crag above Flower Meadow lived a yellow-eyed cat. Unlike most cats, she didn't belong to a human family and she didn't have a family of her own. She was a wild cat who lived by herself. Her home was in a little rocky cave; it was snug and dry here, even in the wettest weather. But when the weather was lovely and sunny, the cat enjoyed stretching out on the warm rock in front of her cave. Sometimes she would curl up and go to sleep; other times, she would watch what was happening in the flower meadow below. She liked watching the Animal School creatures. She could see them clearly, but they couldn't see her. Her fur was the same soft grey colour as the rock, so she was hard to spot, while her yellow eyes might look like sunlight, if you happened to look upwards, which the creatures hardly ever did. Sometimes the cat felt lonely and wanted to be a part of the school. But, most times, she liked to stay by herself.

The next day, the Sheep took all of the animals—and Hannah too, of course—outside for their lesson. She told them that this was to be a listening lesson and that outside would be better, as there would be more noises to listen to.

"Why is listening important?" she asked the class.

"So you can hear your enemies coming," answered the Deer, "even if you can't see them."

"Good answer, my dear," said the Sheep. "Anyone else?"

"So you can listen to the lovely music," suggested Hannah, remembering the first lesson outside and the blackbird's beautiful song.

"Yes, my dear, that's right," baaed the Sheep. "Anyone else?"

"It's because when you are listening you have to keep very still or else you don't hear anything and keeping still is good because that means your enemies don't see you because you're camouflaged. Well, you might be," continued the

Stork, who was really rather clever, despite his gawky appearance, "if you were standing in the right place to match your colour. Or sitting. Or lying."

The Sheep looked puzzled.

"I think that is a good answer, but I didn't quite follow it," she admitted. "Anyone else?"

"So everyone will listen to my jokes!" giggled the goat. And at that everyone laughed uproariously.

"That," said the teacher "is a very silly answer. Now behave yourselves, all of you."

She told them to lie down and shut their eyes and listen to all the noises around them.

At first, the animals were still a bit giggly and silly.

"I can hear the piglet snoring!" said the goat, cheekily. Then he rang his bell on purpose, which quite spoiled the peacefulness of the afternoon.

"I can hear my tummy rumbling!" squawked the stork.

Then the goat did a burpus-on-purpose, which sent all the animals shrieking with laughter. And then all the frogs started to copy him, burping away like anything: *Brekakorax, korax, korax.*

"Shshsh," said the Sheep. "Silence!"

And at long last, everyone settled down and there was a great quietness.

Hannah lay on her back in the shade of a hazel tree. She liked this lesson. She felt warm and drowsy. Little Hurtle lay beside her and Hannah could feel the rabbit's soft fur tickling her bare legs. She listened intently. She could hear the drowsy buzz of flies and bees, winging their way through the grasses; the faint and faraway clanging of bells—a flock of sheep, probably; the putter putter of a little boat engine, which must be coming from the river—perhaps it was Daddy, on his way downriver. But there was no beautiful singing from the blackbird in the tree above. Why wasn't he up there sitting on the eggs in his nest? But then, as Hannah listened and listened, she heard the most wonderful thing: the faintest cheep cheep cheep—it must be the baby birds—they must have hatched! And the father blackbird must be busy hunting for food for his new nestlings. How Hannah wished she could see them.

Just then, she felt a tickling on her nose; she mustn't sneeze, or the Sheep would be cross. Slowly she opened her eyes and saw that a pretty dandelion seed had floated down and landed on her nose. Gently, she brushed it away. She was just going to close her eyes again when she caught a glimpse of sparkling yellow, high up on the rocky crag. What could it be? It might be just the dazzle of sunlight in her eyes, but it seemed different, somehow. Very gently, so as not to disturb the others, she raised her head to see better. There, staring straight at her, was a furry-grey, yellow-eyed cat! How extraordinary! But Hannah couldn't say anything—she had to keep quiet—so she shut her eyes again and listened some more.

And then she heard a soft whispery sssss, from among the long grasses. It was getting louder and nearer: SSSSSSSSS. A snake? Hannah sat up with a start. She knew that snakes could bite. Yes, there it was, a long, green grass snake, winding its way towards Bubble and Squeak, who were curled up together, eyes shut tight. Hannah also knew that snakes liked eating mice.

"A snake! Look out!" cried Hannah. Everyone sprang to their feet in alarm. Hannah reached down and quick as a flash picked up the two little mice, just before the snake could get at them with its flickering tongue.

"Hsssss," went the snake crossly, as it slunk away into the long grass.

"Well done, Hannah!" said the Teacher. "That was a very good example of listening out for enemies!"

"Thank you, thank you," whispered the two little mice. Hannah could feel their tiny hearts thudding and their whole bodies shivering with fear.

"You're all right now," she said, as she placed them gently back on the ground.

High up above, the cat stretched and got to her feet. She too liked eating mice—and baby birds. From her perch, she had a good view of the new nestlings. Hannah saw her yellow eyes glinting as she surveyed the scene.

But then it was time for her to choose her next name and, for the moment at least, she forgot all about the cat.

"Um…the turtle," she decided. "What's your name, turtle?" she asked.

"My name is Tut and I live in Turtle River," turtled the creature in a squeaky voice. "And I'm very good at swimming. Can you swim?"

"I can a bit," said Hannah. She couldn't really swim properly yet, unlike her older brothers and sister, but she enjoyed a good splash about with her arm bands on.

The piglet and the goat were giggling together.

"Say it's three now," bleated the goat. "Go on. Miss can't count—she won't realise."

"OK," chortled the piglet.

"Time to go home!" he announced and rang the goat's bell.

At the sound of the bell, all the animals said a cheerful goodbye and rushed off home.

"Would you like to come to the burrow for tea?" asked Hurtle. "Your daddy gave us loads of raw onions and carrots yesterday, so there'll be plenty to eat."

"Um," said Hannah. She wasn't quite sure about raw vegetables. "Well, actually, I've got something important to do first. See you tomorrow!"

"OK," said Hurtle and she turned tail and hurtled eagerly homewards. She was looking forward to her tea.

Hannah really *had* got something important to do: she was going to climb the rocky crag and find the cat!

Chapter 11
The Yellow-Eyed Cat

Hannah was good at climbing rocks. She scrambled upwards using both hands as well as both feet as she went higher and higher. Finally, she heaved herself onto the narrow rocky ledge, quite out of breath.

"Here I am," she gasped. "I'm Hannah. I saw you watching us. Who are you?"

But to her dismay, the cat arched its back and extended its sharp claws and opened its mouth, displaying its great white teeth and hissed.

And then it slunk away, back into the darkness of the cave.

Hannah was surprised and upset. No one had ever talked to her like that before; everyone was always glad to see her—well, almost always! Was the cat an enemy, like the snake, or a friend, like all the other pussycats she knew? She wasn't sure. But she was curious and determined to try again. She crawled over the rocky ledge and peered into the gloom of the cave.

"Please don't be cross," she said. "I was being friendly. I thought perhaps you might want to come to Animal School too. Do you? It's fun!"

No answer. Hannah could see two gleaming yellow eyes staring back at her from the darkness.

"Please come out again, pussycat," she pleaded. "I do love cats and I won't hurt you."

Secretly, she wondered if the cat might hurt her instead. After all, it did have very sharp claws and teeth. She knew cats could scratch, even tame cats—and this was clearly a wild one. But she felt sorry for the cat, living all by itself. She tried again.

"I could stroke you, if you liked. Don't you like being stroked? Has anyone ever stroked you?"

No answer. But surely the yellow eyes were a bit nearer now?

She wondered what cats liked to eat. She felt in her pocket. There were a few flapjack crumbs there, left over from her snack that morning. Surely everyone, even wild cats, liked flapjacks?

"Look," she said. "I've found some flapjack crumbs. They're delicious!" And carefully, she spread them out on the sunlit rock.

No answer, but now those gleaming yellow eyes were really close now and she could make out a little black nose and two velvety grey ears and the glint of white teeth.

"Please come," said Hannah.

And then—out it came!

It didn't eat the crumbs and it still didn't say anything, but it did stand quite still next to Hannah, staring at her. So the little girl picked the crumbs up and held her hand out, nice and flat.

"Go on, they're lovely," she said. "Haven't you had any flapjacks before?"

No answer. But then the yellow-eyed cat put out its rough pink tongue and licked Hannah's outstretched hand. The tongue felt rough and tickly but Hannah kept her hand quite still until all the crumbs had gone.

"There. That was lovely, wasn't it?" she asked. "Shall I stroke you now?"

The cat didn't say anything, just stared at Hannah with its yellow eyes. But then it sat down, right next to her. So, very gently, Hannah stroked the soft grey fur—starting with the head and then down the curving back and through to the tip of the long tail…

And after a few minutes of this, the cat started to purr! It was a very small purr, but Hannah knew it was the sound cats make when they are happy. She felt very excited!

Then she wondered if the cat could actually talk. She knew ordinary pussycats couldn't, but this was surely a special one, like all the animals at school—they could all talk, even the silly ones like the goat or the tiny ones like Bubble and Squeak.

"I'm Hannah," she tried again, still stroking the soft grey fur. "And I live in the house down there and I go to Animal School in the afternoons. Who are you? What's your name?"

And then, to her delight, the cat spoke:

"No name. Live alone. Walk by myself. Don't want school."

"I could find you a name," said Hannah eagerly. "Are you a boy cat or a girl cat?"

"Girl, of course," hissed the cat angrily and she stood up suddenly and arched her back, shaking Hannah's stroking hand off. Just for a moment, Hannah thought the cat was going to slink back in the cave again.

"Don't be cross," she pleaded. "I want to be friends. You don't have to come to school, if you don't want to. But I could come and see you sometimes, when it's finished. At three o'clock. And I shall call you…" She thought hard. "I know, Alona—it's a pretty name and you do live alone. But aren't you ever lonely?"

Well, in fact, the cat **was** often lonely, especially when she watched the animals having such fun in Flower Meadow, dancing and singing and giggling. But she was a proud cat, proud of managing by herself and not needing anyone to help her.

"Not lonely," she hissed. "**Like** living alone." And then, after a long pause, "See me again."

"O good!" exclaimed Hannah. "And I can bring you some more flapjacks. What else do you eat?"

"Rats and mice and baby birds," said the cat. "Hunt at night, best time to catch. Birds who have fallen out of their nests and can't get back; mice who are lost in the darkness; rats who try to sneak up and get inside my cave."

That was by far the longest thing the cat had said and Hannah felt pleased and proud. But she also felt alarmed. If the cat was going to eat baby birds and little mice, then she must be an enemy after all. But she didn't say this out loud. She would like to become a friend and then she could explain that birds and mice were her friends too. She wasn't sure about rats, never having met one.

She decided to change the subject.

"Don't you have any friends, Alona? Or family?"

"No family. No friends. Nothing."

"Well, you can have me as a friend," said Hannah. "Would you like that? Shall I come again?"

Alona stared at her with her gleaming yellow eyes. Then: "If you must," she said.

And then, with a whisk of its tail, she turned and crept back into her cave.

So Hannah scrambled back down the rocky slope and ran, helter-skelter, all the way back to her nice, warm, friendly home. How glad she was that she had a family to live with!

Chapter 12
Friend or Foe?

That night Hannah lay awake in bed until David, Charlotte and Ben finished their homework and came upstairs to say goodnight. She wanted to ask them about the cat. The children snuggled down to consider the problem.

"You see," said Hannah, after she had explained all about the unsettling meeting on the rocky ledge, "I don't know if she's a friend or an enemy."

"Friend or Foe?" muttered Charlotte dreamily.

"What's a foe?" asked Hannah.

"You know," said Ben, "Fee, Fi, **Foe**, Fum…it's an enemy. You have to grind its bones!"

"No!" protested Hannah. She certainly wasn't going to grind the pussycat's bones. Whatever it meant, it sounded horrible. She remembered the gentle tickle of the cat's tongue on her hand and the softness of its fur as she stroked it. "What do you think, David?"

"Well, cats are sort of tigers," explained David, "and they can be ferocious killers. But they can also be pets—it all depends."

"Depends on what?" asked Charlotte.

"On how they've been brought up, I suppose," said David.

"I think my cat is in the middle," explained Hannah. "She is a sort of killer because she hunts at night and eats baby birds and mice and rats—but she really liked having her back stroked and she purred a bit and she tickled my hand with her tongue. I don't think she's really a foe, but she isn't quite a friend either." She thought some more. "She said I could come back if I must," she added. "Perhaps she wants to be a friend but just isn't one yet."

"It can take time to become a friend," agreed David.

"Or an enemy," added Charlotte. "You don't always know straight away. I wonder who her family were—she must have a family somewhere."

"She said she hadn't," said Hannah.

"The important thing is the hunting," said David. "You should warn the blackbird and the mice—just in case."

"Yes, I suppose so," agreed Hannah. It would be awful if Bubble and Squeak got eaten—or the baby birds. Or even the little rabbits. She remembered the Owl and shuddered. She thought that Alona was probably quite capable of grinding bones with her sharp teeth.

"Let's go and warn them now," said Ben. "It would be an adventure."

"Not in the dark," said Charlotte, sensibly. "Hannah's supposed to be asleep and so are you, Ben. Hannah can warn the mice at school tomorrow and I'm sure the baby birds are too young to fly yet, if they've only just hatched, so they won't fall down. They'll be safe."

And so it was agreed. Hannah would warn the little creatures tomorrow.

And after school, she thought, *I'll go and talk to the cat again.*

Chapter 13
The Warnings

Hannah woke up suddenly. She had been dreaming about the yellow-eyed cat, Alona. In the dream, Hannah had been gently stroking her, when suddenly the cat had stood up and bared its teeth at her—and when the cat stood up she grew enormous, much taller than Hannah and the gentle purring turned into a terrible tigerish roar.

Hannah went over to Ben's bed and snuggled down next to him.

"Ben," she whispered, "wake up."

"Humph," said Ben crossly. He turned over to get back to sleep, but found a pajamaed small sister in the way. "What do you want?"

"Listen," said Hannah. "I can hear birds singing. It must be getting light. Let's go and find the blackbirds and warn them about the cat. The babies might start trying to fly and they might fall out."

"OK," agreed Ben, who was now fully awake. "We'd better get dressed, it's cold."

Ben and Hannah put on warm clothes and shoes. Charlotte never woke up unless you bounced on her and David's room was along the corridor, so he wouldn't hear them. As for the parents, well, there was no sound coming from their room as the children crept past in the cold grey light of dawn.

When they got to Flower Meadow, Hannah looked up at the rocky ledge, but there was no sign of the yellow-eyed cat. **Probably** she was fast asleep inside her cave—although she **might** still be out after a long night's hunting. They couldn't see the father blackbird anywhere. Or the mother, come to that.

"Listen!" whispered Hannah. The children held their breath in the early morning mist and listened with all their might. Yes, faintly but clearly came the cheep cheep of baby birds, from the nest above them.

"Thank goodness," said Hannah. "They're OK."

"How many are there?" asked Ben. But Hannah didn't know. "It's difficult to count," she explained, "because they all cheep together."

Just then, there was a flutter and a swoosh and down flew both blackbird parents. They landed on the hazel tree branch where the nest was, shaking the fresh green leaves. The mother blackbird held a worm in her beak, while the father held a wriggling fly. And then how those hungry baby birds cheeped! Anyone could hear them, even without having had listening lessons.

After the noise had died down, Hannah remembered her singing lesson and tried to copy the father blackbird's singing:

Sing a song of blackbirds
On a foggy morning;
Listen to me, blackbirds,
Listen to my warning.
Flutter down and talk to us
We're here on the ground;

We don't want to make a fuss ("Well, I suppose we do, really," she whispered.)

Just to tell you what I found. ("'cos it was only me that found it," she explained.)

Ben was impressed; sometimes, he thought his little sister was quite clever, after all.

The blackbirds must have been impressed too, for in no time at all, there they were, standing on the ground beside the children.

Hannah started to explain, but the blackbirds just shook their heads.

"They want you to sing it, I expect," said Ben. "They probably can't understand if you just speak it. Just like we can't understand what they're singing about."

"Good idea," agreed Hannah. She thought a bit and then started to sing in her best voice, using the same tune:

I have found a pussy cat
In a rocky cave;
She says she's a hunter,
So you must be brave.

Look after the baby birds
You have to keep an eye;
Listen to my warning words
Because the cat might try.

"Try what?" asked Ben.

"To catch them of course, silly," said Hannah. "But I couldn't think of a rhyme for catch."

"Snatch," suggested Ben in a moment of inspiration. "And patch."

But the birds seemed to have understood Hannah's song perfectly, even if Ben hadn't.

The mother bird looked at the children with her bright black eyes and nodded her head three times. The father bird flew straight up to the nest, presumably to keep an eye on the babies. From now on, they would only hunt one at a time.

Pleased with themselves, the two children left the family in peace.

"What about the mice?" asked Ben.

"I don't know where they live," explained Hannah.

"But you know their names, don't you?" said Ben. "Isn't there anyone you could ask?"

"I could ask Donk, I suppose," said Hannah.

"Good idea. Come on then."

And as the two children jumped over the stream to find the donkey's field, Ben started to sing the blackbird song, with his new improved words:

We know a furry pussy cat
Who comes out at night;

("**You** don't know her," protested Hannah. "Shhh," said Ben, "I'm busy.")

Hannah says she might be a friend,
But she's a foe all right.

("Not necessarily," argued Hannah. "Shhh," said Ben. "I'm thinking.")

She's fie-ierce hunter,
She can snatch and catch—
And you don't really wa-ant he-er
O-on you-our patch!

"Brilliant!" said Ben, feeling very pleased with himself.

"Hmmmm," said his little sister.

But there was no time to argue about whose song was best. They had reached Donk's field and there he was, busily chomping away at some of the few weeds that had escaped the farmer's attention.

"Do you know where Bubble and Squeak live?" asked Hannah importantly. "We want to warn them."

Donk stopped chomping and thought hard. Yes, he did know where they lived—but it was difficult to explain in words.

"Follow me," he said, after once last mighty chomp, "it isn't far."

He led the way across the beautifully tended field into an area of tall golden wheat.

"I won't go any further," he said, "because I might startle the mice with my great hooves. But you can see their house from here."

And he swivelled one of his great ears forward and pointed. There, swaying gently in the breeze, attached to a tall stalk of wheat, was the most beautiful, round golden nest, cleverly woven out of stalks, with a tiny hole at the top for a door.

As quietly as they could manage, amidst the rustling of the wheat, Hannah and Ben tiptoed forward.

"Let me do it," said Hannah, "they know me and they don't know you." She knelt down and whispered through the hole. "Bubble? Squeak? Are you there? It's me, Hannah."

There was a rustling, whiskery sound—and then out of the hole popped the two tiny mice. They stood side by side on top of their beautiful nest, gazing up at Hannah with their four bright eyes. Hannah picked them up. She could feel their little hearts beating, but they trusted her and weren't really afraid.

"I've come to give you a warning," she explained. "I found a pussycat on the rocky ledge just above the school. She's OK in the daylight, but she likes hunting at night. So don't ever go near there in the dark! Stay safe and sound in your nest."

"We will, we will," squeaked the little mice together. Hannah still hadn't worked out which was which.

"She might become a friend," explained Hannah. "But she isn't really one yet; it might take some time. So be careful."

"We will, we will," squeaked the mice.

Ben took a step forward. He would love to hold the tiny creatures. But as soon as he moved, Bubble and Squeak disappeared down the hole into their house.

"Bother," said Ben.

"Oh Ben!" said Hannah crisply. "Never mind—they got the warning and they definitely understood."

By now, the sun was rising quite high in the sky and all the fogginess was vanishing fast. Definitely time for breakfast!

Together the children waved goodbye to Donk, jumped back across the stream and arrived at their house, just as Mummy was laying the table. David and Charlotte were still asleep, so Hannah and Ben got in first for hot chocolate and honey toast. Delicious!

Chapter 14
Hide and Seek

After breakfast, Mummy walked the children to Human School, while Daddy got on with some strimming. Hannah learned how to write B for Ben, C for Charlotte and D for David; she knew about A already, as it was in her name (twice). At break, the children played hide and seek. Hannah was particularly good at seeking; now that she had learned how to listen properly, she could catch the slightest sound from the hiders—a cough or a sniff, the slightest crack of a twig, or the gentlest of breathing. Then there was drawing (Hannah drew a grey cat with yellow eyes) and then it was time to go home. Mummy picked her up; she had had a useful morning in the village doing shopping and washing. For lunch, there was bread and cheese and tomatoes, with oranges for afterwards.

"Please can I have a flapjack to take to Animal School?" asked Hannah, as soon as she had finished her last piece of orange. "I want to give it to the cat."

"What cat?" asked Mummy and Hannah remembered that she hadn't explained about Alona yet.

"I'll tell you later, Mummy—I don't want to be late," cried Hannah as she snatched a flapjack from the tin and stuffed it into her pocket. She reached the little path just as Hurtle came hurtling along. Together, the two friends slithered down the steep bank. Then Hannah remembered that she hadn't told Hurtle about the yellow-eyed cat either.

"I met a wild cat yesterday," Hannah explained, "as they made their way across the little stream. You must be careful because she hunts at night. I don't think she eats rabbits though, not like the Owl."

"Cats couldn't catch rabbits," said Hurtle. "They wouldn't dare. We can kick really hard."

"O good," said Hannah. "And I warned the blackbirds and the mice, so they're all right. I want her to become a friend, but it might take some time."

"I bet she won't," said Hurtle. "Anyway, I'm your friend aren't I?"

"Yes, of course you are," explained Hannah. And she picked the little rabbit up to give her a quick cuddle, before opening the bramble curtain and entering the long green tunnel that led to the schoolroom.

"Well, my dears," said the Sheep, once they were all finally settled. "Today we can play a game outside. Who wants to choose?"

"Me, me, me," shouted all the animals. The stork wanted to play football—except that there wasn't a ball; and the piglet wanted to play Piggy in the Middle, but you need a ball for that too. The goat wanted to play Rough and Tumble, but the Sheep said it wasn't a proper game and the little ones might get squashed. So Hannah suggested Hide and Seek. None of the animals had heard of it, but Hannah explained the rules and everyone thought it was a good idea.

The Piglet was the first seeker, but as he could only count up to five it was hopeless: no one had a chance to hide anywhere (except the frogs who leaped headlong into their pool and were not seen again for the rest of the afternoon). So everyone said that Hannah should be the next seeker as she could count for ever. So it was agreed. Hannah shut her eyes and started to count. She knew that she was supposed to keep going up to fifty, but she wasn't quite sure about what happened after thirty-seven, so she decided to use her fingers and count ten several times. That would probably be about right, she decided. When she had finished, she shouted, "Coming! Ready-or-Not!" and opened her eyes again.

She looked around her. High up on the rocky crag she caught a glimpse of gleaming yellow eyes, but she couldn't go and see the cat now—there was business to be done. She found Donk first; he had ambled slowly off in the direction of his field, but hadn't got very far. Donkeys **can** run, of course, but I don't think he understood the game properly. Anyway, it was easy for Hannah to follow his hoofprints a short way up the bank on the other side of the stream and round the corner—and there he was, not hidden at all.

"I found you!" cried Hannah triumphantly. "Now you have to come back and wait for the rest."

The Donkey was puzzled, but as Hannah seemed to know what she was doing, he humbly followed her back to Flower Meadow and waited. Hannah found the Sheep very quickly too; she was too big and wobbly to get far, even with a count up to fifty and she had hidden behind the trunk of a nearby oak tree. Unfortunately, she forgot that she was considerably wider than the tree trunk and that most of her back part could be seen sticking out. As for the goat, well he was easy, as he just couldn't keep his bell from ringing; he was balanced on a rock, a little way upstream, but it was a particularly wobbly rock and he had to keep shifting his weight to maintain his balance. Hannah bet she knew where Hurtle would have got to—and she was right. When she knelt down and peered through the hole in the burrow, there was her furry friend staring back at her.

"Out you come, Hurtle," said Hannah cheerfully. "I found you!"

Hannah found the two mice by accident; she was slithering down the steep bank from the burrow on her bottom when she felt something soft and squidgy: she had slithered right over Bubble and Squeak! Never mind, they weren't squashed, only a bit breathless, so Hannah picked them up and ran happily back to Flower Meadow so they could join the others. When Hannah got there, she discovered that the naughty goat had decided to break the rules; now he had been discovered, he just couldn't be bothered to wait for the others to be found. He had rung his bell three times and the animals had thought that school was over and the game finished so they had come rushing out of hiding: the chicky bird, the deer, the turtle and the pig—all very cross that they had been tricked. But the stork was too clever to be fooled; he was still hiding—where could he be?

Well, actually, the stork had flown right over to the house and had perched on top of the roof. Looking down, he saw the most wonderful thing—a beautiful white and black football! Forgetting all about the Hide and Seek game, he flew down to investigate. He started to kick it with his enormous feet (all young storks have huge feet) and it just zoomed through the air, narrowly missing the kitchen window and bouncing off the wall to go rolling down the path. Brilliant!

Five minutes later, while Hannah was still carefully checking out the trees in case the stork was hiding up one of them, there was a great splash as a black and white ball came zooming through the air to land in the stream, shortly followed by the triumphant stork, running flat-footedly down the path to Flower Meadow.

"Brilliant kick!" he cried. "One nil to me."

"That's our ball," objected Hannah, but she didn't really mind.

Nor did the stork! "Who wants a game?" he cried joyfully.

Well everyone did—or nearly everyone. The Sheep, the turtle and the little mice just watched but all the others (except the frogs, of course, who were still nowhere to be seen) joined in. The goal was the stream and the stork was the goalkeeper and everyone else had to try to kick the ball past him into the water. Even Hannah lost count of the number of goals, but a good many were scored before the piglet announced that it really was three o'clock and time to ring the bell.

"But I haven't chosen my animal yet!" protested Hannah. "What's your name?" she asked the beruffled stork.

"My name is Kaka," he said. "Because I'm a very good kicker and brilliant at football."

And so he was.

Then the bell was rung and the animals ran happily homewards. Luckily, you can't fly carrying a ball, so the stork regretfully had to leave it behind; Hannah would take it back when she was ready. She knew her brothers would be cross if it disappeared.

But she wasn't ready yet. There was the flapjack, still warm and sticky in her pocket—and there were the gleaming yellow eyes of the wild cat still staring right at her from high up on the rocky crag.

Chapter 15
Friend?

Up the great crag climbed Hannah. The yellow-eyed cat watched her as she came closer and closer to her rocky ledge. But this time, she didn't hide inside her cave. She just stood there, tail swishing, eyes staring, fur bristling. Would she be a friend or a foe? Hannah wasn't sure.

"I've brought you a whole flapjack," she said breathlessly. "Here you are." She sat down on the ledge, crumbled the flapjack up, held out her hand and waited. Slowly, slowly, the cat crept forward. Then she opened her mouth and started to lap up the crumbs. Hannah loved the feel of the cat's rough tongue licking her hand. At last, there were no crumbs left. The cat turned round and was just about to retreat inside the cave, when Hannah cried:

"No, don't go! Would you like me to stroke you again?"

Slowly, the cat turned back again and stared at Hannah.

"I wonder *what she's thinking*," said Hannah to herself, but she didn't say the words out loud.

"Do you want me to go?" asked Hannah. She would love to be friends with the cat, but perhaps it wouldn't be possible after all. You can't be friends with someone who doesn't really want you there.

The cat didn't say anything, but she turned round in a circle and then sat down on the ledge. Hurrah! Gently, Hannah reached over and started to stroke the soft fur. And after a bit, Alona started to purr—quietly at first, but then louder and louder!

Then, greatly daring, Hannah said: "I can reach better, if you sit on my lap. Would you like to?"

Slowly, silently, the cat got up, shook her head—and then settled down in a lovely curly heap on the little girl's lap! How warm and soft and heavy she felt; and how smooth Hannah's fingers felt as she stroked the glossy fur.

"I can sing, if you like," said Hannah. "Listen!"

And, still stroking, Hannah sang in her lovely high voice the nursery rhyme which she had known ever since she was a baby. She changed the words a little, because she thought that the real words didn't quite fit. The tune was the same, though:

I—I love grey Alona,
Her fur is so warm;
I never would hurt her,
Though she might do harm.
I'll sit on her ledge,
And I might be her friend,
And she might love me ba–ack,
And that is the–e end.

She stopped stroking and waited, wondering what would happen next. The cat got up from Hannah's lap and walked a few paces away. But she didn't go back into the cave.

And then, at last, Alona spoke:

"Why friend? Don't want friends."

"I know," said Hannah. "But that's why, I suppose. You see, I have lots of friends and it must be sad and lonely not to have **any**. And I have a big family but you don't, which makes it sadder, I expect."

"**Like** living alone," said the cat. "Walk by myself. Told you."

"I know," said Hannah again. And then, greatly daring she said, "But you could still live alone and walk alone. I could just meet you here. After school. And we could just have a little talk and then I could go away again. And I won't tell the other animals, I promise. You did like the flapjack, didn't you? And the stroking?"

"I liked the singing," said Alona. "Sing me some more."

She didn't say please, but Hannah didn't mind. Alona liked her singing! Surely that was friendly?

So she sang; and as she did, Alona crept near and sat down and leant her soft grey head on Hannah's lap and closed her yellow eyes, the better to listen.

This is what Hannah sang: the tune was an old one, but the words just seemed to come out by themselves:

Wildycat, Wildycat, where have you been?

I've been out hunting, but no one has seen;

Wildycat, Wildycat, will you be my friend?

Nobody knows what will be at the end.

Wildycat, walking alone through the night,
Softly she goes, with her eyes burning bright;
Mouses and chicky birds tremble with fear
Alona the wild cat is creeping up near!
Wildycat, Wildycat, where do you go?
Are you an enemy, are you a foe?
Wildycat, Wildycat, will you be my friend?

Nobody knows what will be at the end.

Hannah finished singing and there was a great quietness. Then the cat, got up, stretched, stared at Hannah with her great yellow eyes and turning tail, disappeared into the darkness of her cave.

Hannah scrambled down the slope, stopped at the bottom to pick up the football and then ran helter-skelter back to the house, where her lovely family was waiting for her.

Chapter 16
Turtle River

Next day was Saturday—so no Human School. Hannah supposed there wouldn't be any Animal School either, although the Sheep hadn't said anything. But then she **was** rather forgetful. Anyway, the family had plans for the day. They were going to take the boat upstream to Turtle River, packing a lovely picnic and their swimming things. By now, it was almost Spring time and really quite sunny. Ben said it was easily warm enough to swim and David and Charlotte agreed. Mummy said that she and Daddy would watch, but that Hannah could certainly take her swimming things and arm bands, if she wanted to.

"I might as well," said Hannah. "I can always just watch too, if it really is cold."

Everyone loves an expedition to Turtle River. It is such a beautiful place, with the rushing stream and the deep pools and plenty of warm rocks to sit upon and little gravelly beaches and grassy green banks. As the boat nosed its way slowly through the water, Hannah noticed lots of tiny turtles diving hastily into the water from the rocks. She remembered that Tut the Turtle lived here—but it was difficult to tell whether or not he was one of the divers, as they all looked so alike.

Ben was the first to jump into the water; he always got in extremely quickly and cheerfully.

"Come on, it's lovely!" he shouted encouragingly to his brother and sisters.

"Don't splash," said Charlotte crossly. "I'm not coming in at all unless you go away."

"Come on, David, I'll race you," shouted Ben. So David lowered himself gingerly into the cold water and stepped forward until it came over his waist—always the hardest bit.

"OK—ready, steady, go!" he cried and the two boys set off downriver. Now all was peaceful in the pool, Charlotte sat on a handy rock, dangling her toes in the water.

"It's not **too** cold," she admitted. She had changed into her swimming costume, but she still wasn't sure. Nor was Hannah, who had got changed too and put her armbands on, just in case.

And then, there was a whirl and a ripple and there, splashing towards them with an excited grin, came little Tut. He had heard the putter putter of the boat's engine and was very pleased to see her.

"Come and swim with me!" he cried. "I'll race you. See who can get to the bank first."

So Charlotte and Hannah carefully lowered themselves off the rock and into the freezing water and followed the little turtle. He won easily! By the time the two girls had reached the bank, he was happily running around in circles to dry himself.

"You are slow," he turtled.

"I'm not slow really," explained Charlotte, "I was waiting for Hannah."

"Arm bands make you slow," admitted Hannah, "but I can't swim without them. I wish I could swim like you. You're even faster than Ben!"

And then Tut the Turtle had a very good idea.

"I know," he turtled. "I'll go and get my Great Granny—she's a very good swimmer and she could easily manage to carry you on her back. Then we could explore downriver."

"O yes, please!" said Hannah. "Can Charlotte come too?"

"As long as she can swim by herself," said Tut, surveying the long brown legs of Hannah's older sister. "She couldn't manage both of you."

"I don't need managing," said Charlotte, "I'm just as good a swimmer as Ben. But I *would* like to come too."

So the two girls waited on the sunny grass; there was no sign of the boys—they must have gone far away downstream. It wasn't too long before they saw a great whirling and a rippling and there, deep underwater and swimming towards them with slow steady strokes of her flippers, came a very large and aged turtle: the Great Granny. She surfaced with a swoosh and scrambled heavily up onto the grassy bank. Little Tut looked tiny beside her. She had two twinkling eyes, covered in a mass of wrinkles, a stiff, wrinkly neck and a great round diamond patterned shell, which looked cracked and battered. She must be very old!

Her voice was slow and deep, quite unlike the excited turtlings of her great grandson.

"My name is Grot," she said. "How do you do?"

"How do you do?" echoed Charlotte and Hannah politely.

"My great grandson says that you would like a lift," she continued. "But the big one will have to swim by itself."

"I know!" said Charlotte. "Can we go downriver? Then we can find the boys."

"Certainly we can," agreed Grot obligingly. "Swimming downstream is always best."

So, very excited, Hannah scrambled up onto Grot's great round shell; it felt a bit slippery, but she clung on tight with her legs and hands as the aged Great Granny lurched awkwardly down the bank into the cold water. Once she was afloat, it was much easier. Turtles can be quite clumsy on land, but in the water they are beautifully smooth swimmers. Hannah thought it was just lovely, sitting there, with the top half of her body warm in the sunlight and the lower half creaming smoothly through the water. She had an excellent view of the overhanging trees and grassy banks of Turtle River. Charlotte had to work hard to keep up, but the current helped and little Tut kindly waited for her, swimming round and round her in circles, whenever he got too far ahead.

And then, there, standing up on a little gravelly beach and seeing who could throw stones the furthest, were David and Ben.

Chapter 17
Picnic Time

"Good shot," cried David, as Ben's stone landed with a whumph on the far side of the river. "Now, watch this!"

"Not bad," admitted Ben, as his older brother hurled his stone right across the river, where it landed with a splat on the faraway grassy bank. "OK, my turn."

Ben stooped down to pick up a smooth round stone—very good for throwing. He had just raised his arm in order to hurl it with all his might when…

"Look out!" shouted David, as the most extraordinary sight came into view from round a bend in the river: their younger sister, sitting atop a great round shell, wearing her armbands and waving cheerfully.

"Golly!" gulped Ben and froze in mid-throw.

"There you are," cried Hannah joyfully. "Look at me—isn't it brilliant?" And then round the bend, came a very small and excited turtle zooming round and round their older sister who was swimming elegantly towards them, helped by the river's fast flowing current.

"Wow!" said David, as the swimming creatures splashed their way up onto the gravelly beach. "Can I have a go?"

"No, you're too big," explained Hannah. "Grot says she can carry me, but no one else." By now, she was safely on land and she slithered down from the mighty turtle.

"Thank you very much," she said politely. "These are my brothers. And this is Tut, my school friend and this is Grot, his Great Granny."

"Wow!" said David and Ben in unison, very impressed.

"How do you do?" said the aged turtle. "And now, it is surely time for some refreshments."

Well, everyone was hungry, especially after all that swimming, but while the turtles could find their own refreshments quite easily, the children's picnic was miles away upstream. Bother.

"Watch me!" exclaimed Tut proudly, as his little tongue flickered out and he caught a buzzing fly and swallowed it with a greedy gulp—delicious. Meanwhile, Grot paddled back into the water; only a few seconds later, her mouth opened wide to catch a silvery fish. She crunched it, grinding its bones between her chomping jaws and swallowed it, licking her black lips. Then both turtles, being omnivores, took delicious mouthfuls of soft green grass, chewing cheerfully in the hot sunlight.

Watching them made the children feel even hungrier, but their picnic was miles away, sitting on a rock—always supposing Mummy and Daddy hadn't eaten it all—**and** it was an upstream swim, which is always harder.

"I'm going to walk back," announced Charlotte. "I'm sure it will be quicker."

"I'll come with you," said David who was feeling exceptionally hungry. "What about you, Ben?"

"I'll swim," said Ben, "and I bet I get there first. Ready? Steady? Go!"

And he was off, without even having said goodbye properly.

But David and Charlotte had remembered their manners.

"It was lovely to meet you," said David to the turtles. "Can you manage Hannah going upstream? Otherwise, she can walk with us."

"Of course I can; there's life in the old turtle yet!" said the aged Great Granny, in her deep voice.

"What about you, Tut?" asked Charlotte. "Shall I carry you back?" Secretly, she would just love to carry the tiny turtle in her arms and she was very pleased when he accepted her offer enthusiastically.

Hannah was very pleased too. She just loved her stately progress through the water. Grot was very lumbery on land, but in the river she was as smooth as silk.

And so, in their different ways, the four children and the two turtles made their way back to picnic rock. Amazingly, Ben **did** get their first, but only just. Hard on his heels came Grot and Hannah—and indeed they might have been first back, had Grot not stopped to catch some more silvery fishes on the way. David, Charlotte and Tut arrived soon afterwards; they had got on very well, swapping interesting stories about Grannies and Great Grannies as they went.

The parents were soon awoken from their snoozle—a few cold splashes from their younger son worked wonders—and the picnic basket was unpacked. There were cheese rolls with tomatoes, cucumber and lettuce, followed by large slices of specially made Apple Cake. The turtles turned up their wrinkled noses at everything except the tomatoes, but they devoured those greedily. None of the humans really minded going without tomatoes—and thankfully, neither turtle was partial to Apple Cake. Instead, they caught more flies for some extra pudding.

After lunch, everyone stretched out on the rocks, enjoying the early spring sunshine. As she lay there, her eyes closed against the bright light, Hannah wondered if Alona was sunbathing on her rocky ledge, far away above Flower Meadow. Perhaps the yellow eyed cat would be missing her?

But by the time they had said goodbye to the turtles, packed up the picnic, set off down the river, it was almost dark. And it was completely dark by the time everyone had changed into dry clothes and Daddy had lit the wood burner. Too late to see if the wildcat was there—for by now, she might be out hunting, either alone or with the Owl. And Hannah didn't want to see that. Supposing the little mice forgot about the warning, or one of the baby birds fell out of the nest? No, it was much better to be safe in her little bed, with a hot bottle to curl her feet around and a bedtime story from her lovely mummy!

Chapter 18
Sunday

On Sunday morning, Mummy insisted that the children do their homework—even Ben. Hannah didn't have any, so instead she practised drawing the letters A to D in the sandpit. As soon as even the slowest homeworker (Ben) had finished, Mummy said there would be snacks (ginger biscuits, apples and orange juice) and then they could play what they liked.

Well, the boys wanted to play football and Charlotte obligingly said she didn't mind being in goal; and Hannah supposed she could help her. Daddy was busy cooking a Sunday roast and Mummy was busy pruning the geraniums, which had grown very long and straggly. So no one noticed the unexpected visitor. Ever since he had spotted the football from his perch on the rooftop of the house, the young stork (whose name was Kaka, if you remember, as he was a very good Kicker) had been dying to come back. And that morning, being Sunday, the church bells underneath his home on the church roof had donged so loudly and persistently, that the mother Stork declared she had a headache and needed the nest all to herself and she really couldn't be bothered with squabbling storklets anymore. This was Kaka's chance. Leaving his older brothers and sisters fighting over who should have which telegraph pole to sit on, he flew eagerly over to the house. Now where was that ball? There it was—and—yippee!—people were playing football with it! He watched while David headed a spectacular goal, which gave the goalkeeper and her small assistant goalie no chance and Ben put his fingers in his mouth to whistle.

"Five, four!" Ben announced and placed the football in the centre spot for a kick-off.

Down flew Kaka. Without waiting for introductions, he dribbled the ball down the field with his enormous feet, finishing with a mighty kick which would have landed the ball in the top corner of the goal, if there had been a netting; as it was, the ball lodged itself in the upper branches of the old apple tree.

"One!" he chortled proudly. The stork didn't know how to count properly, but he was clever and had picked up the basics from the piglet. Then he flew up and shook the branch until the ball rolled down onto the ground.

Everyone was impressed. David decided that they should play in teams, now they had an extra player: he and Charlotte would take on Ben and the Stork.

"What about me?" demanded Hannah. That stork was a ferocious kicker and she didn't want to get knocked over by a hurtling ball.

Then she remembered: Hurtle! She hadn't seen her for ages (not since Friday) and she wanted to find out what she had been doing.

She probably missed me, Hannah thought. So, with a quick "See you later!" she was off, running happily down the little path.

The players decided that it didn't matter not having any goalies, as they hadn't been much use anyway.

When Hannah reached the burrow, she lay down and peered through the big round entrance. Hopefully, the family would be inside.

"Hurtle!" she shouted. "It's me, Hannah. Are you there?"

But there was no answer.

"Hop! Scotch?" she queried. Still nothing. Bother! O well, never mind. It would probably be lunch time soon anyway: she wouldn't want to miss one of Daddy's roast lunches.

But while Hannah was making her way slowly back down the little path, she heard excited noises coming from the vegetable patch. Of course! The rabbit family would be inspecting their vegetables.

And so they were. Except that there wasn't anything to inspect, yet. After all, the seeds had only been planted a few days ago. Disappointed, the rabbits were staring at the empty patch of neatly raked brown earth. Where was their great green bean stalk—and where were the scrumptious orange carrots?

Hannah decided she had better explain.

"It's Ok," she said. "Vegetables take ages to grow, you see. You'll have to wait at least another week, I should think. I know, why don't you have some weeds instead?"

The rabbits thought that was a good idea and Hannah kept a careful eye on them, in case anyone mistook strawberry plants for nettles.

"And I'm sure you can stay for lunch," Hannah went on. "Daddy always makes loads of vegetables. Come and see."

Off they all went, chattering excitedly, down the path to the football field. They were just in time to watch Kaka scoring a spectacular long distance goal. And then, of course, all the small rabbits wanted to play too. So they divided them up between the two teams, Hurtle and Hannah in David's team and Hop and Scotch in the Stork's team. Meanwhile, the rabbit parents helped Mummy with the geraniums—they were delicious!

Finally, when the score was twenty to seventeen (according to David) Daddy came out to announce that lunch would be served in five minutes exactly and please could everyone get ready **now**. They decided to have the meal outside, as it was such a lovely day and they had so many visitors. So Charlotte and Hannah quickly laid the old wooden table while David and Ben collected all the wobbly green and white chairs they could find.

It was an excellent lunch. The Rabbits decided that they did **quite** like cooked carrots and cabbages, even though raw ones were much nicer; the Stork decided that he just loved roast potatoes. Sadly for him, so did all the humans, so he wasn't allowed just to help himself. Ben helpfully turned on the hose pipe for all the creatures to drink from and the younger ones (both humans and animals) definitely enjoyed getting wet too. Pudding was ice cream and bananas, which everyone loved! Then Ben turned on the hosepipe again to wash off all the sticky bits. Ice cream can be very annoying on fur and feathers—not to mention hair.

While Mummy and the children helped clear up, Daddy decided that the weather really was good enough to put up the hammock! He explained the principles of weight distribution and non-slip knots to the intelligent Stork, while the rabbits watched eagerly.

Now, how many creatures can you fit inside a hammock? David counted them as they all clambered in: four Children, five rabbits and one stork make…ten! Crikey! But then there was no one to swing the heavy load. So the older children kindly got out again, taking it in turns to swing the rope.

After a very long time, everyone had had enough. Anyway, the light was now fading fast and it was feeling distinctly colder. The rabbits said goodbye and thank you very politely. The Stork didn't (storks hardly ever do) but it was clear to everyone that he had had a brilliant time.

"I expect Ma's got over her headache by now," he said to himself as he flapped downstream to the untidy nest on the top of the church.

Hannah was going to sneak off to see if Alona was all right but Mummy spotted her and said it was really too late—and anyway, all the children simply had to have a bath as it was school the next day. So they did. Hannah had hers first and then she got straight into her pyjamas for supper and bed. It had been a lovely weekend.

I simply must go and see Alona tomorrow, she thought as she snuggled up under her soft white duvet. In no time at all, she was fast asleep.

Chapter 19
Rain

Next morning was Monday—and it was horribly wet! Outside, the poor hammock was all soaked and droopy. Everyone had to put on oilskins and sou'westers and wellies—bither bother. It was a cold and muddy walk to Human School. And when you got to school, you couldn't play out and sports had to be cancelled. It was a long morning for Hannah. The children learned how to write E, F, G and H; but as Hannah already knew H and I, she was allowed to learn K instead. (She was particularly interested in K, as she knew it began and middled the stork's name—Kaka). At long last, the lesson was over and it was time to go.

But it hadn't stopped raining. Mummy and Hannah had a cold, wet walk back and they had to have their lunch indoors. Still, Mummy had made nice hot vegetable soup, which was delicious. Then Hannah had to put on her wet oilskins again for Animal School. Bither bother!

The schoolroom was crowded and hot. It was also quite muddy round the edges, as all the animals had arrived with dripping fur and hair. Only Hannah was nice and dry under her oilskins. It was sometimes very useful being a human and having clothes which you could take on and off. The poor Sheep had caught a cold and kept sneezing as she struggled to keep her noisy class under control.

"Shhhh. Sit still. Behave yourself! Ashoo! Shhh," she admonished the goat, who was going round waggling his wet beard at the smaller animals, scattering spray everywhere. Only the frogs seemed happy, leaping around, their bright eyes shining. Frogs like wetness.

"O dear, O dear," bleated the Teacher. "It really is too wet to go outside. And we were going to have a running lesson, but there simply isn't enough room in here. Ashoo!"

Hannah put up her hand.

"Please, Miss," she said, "I can teach the animals their letters. Well, up to K, anyway. Would you like me to?"

"That's a very good idea, my dear. Ashoo!" said the poor Sheep. "Now everyone, sit still and listen to Hannah."

Hannah felt very important. She didn't have a pencil, but of course none of the animals would be able to hold one anyway, not having hands. Anyway, she could use her fingers and they could use their hooves or paws. And she didn't have paper, but the earth floor in the middle of the circle of animals was nice and soft, so that would be fine. She didn't know anyone whose name began with an A, so she decided to start with B.

"B for Bubble-and-Squeak!" she announced importantly. She drew a big B in the middle of the circle. "Now you try," she encouraged the mice. Hannah showed them how to start with a big straight line, which they could easily manage, using their front paw; the curly bits were trickier, but in the end they did it, Bubble drawing the top half and Squeak the bottom bit.

But then she thought that Squeak really ought to have his own letter, so she explained that S looked and sounded like a snake—sssss. The mice were alarmed but Hannah kindly explained that letters were quite different from creatures and could begin lots of names. Actually, S is really just like the curly bit of B, only backwards and Squeak mastered it in no time.

"Now, does anyone else's name begin with a B?" asked Hannah, after the mice had finished and scampered proudly off to the edge of the circle.

And, to her surprise, the four frogs started leaping up and down excitedly.

"Brekekekex Korax Korax!" they croaked in unison.

"I'm Breka!" said one of them.

"I'm Kex," croaked a second.

"I'm Kor!" said the third.

"I'm Krax," exclaimed the fourth.

"I see," said Hannah. "But only one of those names begins with a B. Still, I can do K too, I learned it today. I'll show you."

Actually, frogs are quite clever. The first one soon got the hang of B for Breka and then Hannah showed the other three how to do a nice big K: one long straight line and two shorter ones, sticking out like sideways ears.

"That's my letter too," announced the intelligent stork As Hannah could also do As like anything, she was able to show Kaka how to write out his **whole** name.

He was the only one (apart from Hannah herself) who could do this and he was very pleased and proud.

Now, who else could she do? Hurtle, of course! H was her favourite letter. And it wasn't too difficult—Hurtle managed it really well, apart from a bit of lopsidedness.

"And I can teach Hop when I get home," squeaked Hurtle.

"You can. And you can try doing a nice S for Scotch too," said Hannah proudly. That reminded her. S for Sheep.

"S stands for Sheep too," she explained to the teacher, who was interested in the writing lesson, although she found it all rather muddling. But the Sheep decided not to have a go at writing, just in case she couldn't manage it.

Then Hannah remembered the Head who was, of course, a B for Bull as well as an H for Head. Well, he never came inside the schoolroom, but she explained the spelling to the animals who were very impressed: fancy Hannah being able to write the fierce Head's letters!

"And you can choose one more name to learn, my dear," said the Sheep. "Who would you like?"

"Um…the Deer," said Hannah. She liked the look of the shy little deer, who hardly ever said anything but who had beautiful dark brown eyes (just like her own!).

"What's your name?" she asked.

"Dora," said the Deer timidly.

"O that's easy!" said Hannah "I can do Ds because of David," she added.

Carefully, she drew a beautiful big D on the floor. By now, it was almost covered over with letters! Shyly, the Deer came forward and with her front right paw she neatly copied Hannah's lovely D.

"I'm afraid that's all I know," Hannah explained to the little turtle. "We haven't done T yet." She hadn't learned the goat and the piglet's names either; they would just have to wait. And then she thought: *Of course, I can do the Chicky Bird too. C and B. Hurrah!*

But the little bird really couldn't manage it at all; he needed both claws for standing on and when he tried to stand on one leg, he kept wobbling. Never mind—at least he knew what his letters looked like.

Then the piglet announced the end of school and the goat bonged his bell three times. It was still raining, but animals are used to wet.

"Thank you, my dear," said the Sheep as she waddled towards the back entrance. Really, she was getting bigger every day; she could only just squeeze through. "That was an excellent lesson."

Hannah felt pleased and proud. Perhaps she would be a teacher one day, when she grew up. She was sure she would be a good one. She put on her oilskins and said goodbye to Hurtle.

"I'd better run," said Hurtle, "I hate wet fur! Thanks for teaching me." And off she scampered, through the front tunnel, over the stream, up the steep slope and into her nice dry burrow. She was looking forward to teaching her younger siblings their letters.

Hannah thought she should go and see if Alona was waiting for her. So she went through the back tunnel into Flower Meadow, which was looking very bedraggled, with the flowers and grasses all drooping their heads under the heavy rain. The little stream had grown and was rushing noisily by. Hannah looked up through the raindrops. There was no sign of the yellow eyed cat on the rocky ledge. But of course, there wouldn't be. Like Hurtle, she wouldn't want to get her fur wet. Would she be inside her cave? And would she let Hannah in?

Well, she would try and see.

Chapter 20
Flapjacks and Friends

Hannah splashed her way across Flower Meadow and up to the foot of the rocky crag. Good job she had her wellies on—there were some huge puddles that even David wouldn't have been able to jump across. She looked upwards again. As she had expected, there was still no sign of the yellow eyed cat on the rocky ledge. The rain was absolutely pouring down—no cat would want to be outside in this, not even a wild one. For a moment, Hannah thought she would go home, where it would be nice and warm and maybe there would be flapjacks for tea. Then she remembered—she hadn't bought a flapjack with her, bither bother. Perhaps she should just go home and come back tomorrow, when the weather might be better. But then she thought that she hadn't seen Alona since last Friday, which was ages ago. She really should go and see if she was OK. Maybe the grey cat had missed her?

So Hannah slowly scrambled her way up the rocky slope. It was really hard in the rain, because everything was so slithery and she couldn't see her way properly. Also, welly boots are really not designed for rock climbing. But Hannah was a determined little girl and she kept going, despite the rain and general slitheriness. At last, she reached the rocky ledge, which was also exceedingly wet and slippery. Still no sign of the cat. Hannah knelt down and peered into the darkness of the cave.

"Alona?" she called. "It's me, Hannah. Are you OK?"

From the back of the cave, two yellow eyes peered back at her. But the cat said nothing.

"Please can I come in?" asked Hannah. "It's really wet out here."

Nothing. Just the gleam of yellow eyes.

"I'm sorry I couldn't come before. I was busy," explained Hannah.

"Sssssss," came the angry sound from the back of the cave. O dear! Was Alona really cross with her? She tried again.

"Don't be angry," she said. "Wouldn't you like me to come and sing again? I forgot about the flapjack, but I could stroke you. You'd like that, wouldn't you?"

But Alona wouldn't. Suddenly she darted forward, her eyes gleaming, her claws extended, her back arched. She looked really wild!

"Sorry," said Hannah, quickly. "I'll go now, shall I?"

Almost in tears, the little girl, still kneeling, shuffled away. She was sure Alona wouldn't really scratch her, but she certainly hadn't looked friendly. O dear. But worse was to come. Hannah lost her grip on the slippery rocky ledge. Backwards she tumbled, head over heels down the slippery slope. Luckily, she didn't fall far, as a prickly bramble bush stopped her. She put out her hand to steady herself—and then realised, to her dismay, that her hand was touching something soft and slithery! It wriggled angrily. A snake? O no!

Well, it wasn't really the snake's fault. Snakes hate rain and it had just taken shelter, burying itself deep under the fallen leaves of a handy bramble bush, when suddenly a great hand had descended from above and almost squashed it flat!

"Ssssss," went the snake. It reared up and opened its jaws. Out came its long, flickering tongue…

Hannah shrieked, but at that same moment, there was a great caterwaul from high above and, with a massive leap through the air, down came the yellow eyed cat! She landed right on top of the snake, clamping her claws on its tail and giving Hannah just enough time to back hastily out of reach of the flickering tongue.

"Ssssss," went the cat!

"Sssssss," went the snake. Then with one furious wriggle, it freed its tail and slunk back into the safety of the bramble bush.

"O, Alona!" cried the little girl. "You rescued me." And, without even thinking about it, she picked the grey cat up in her arms and hugged her.

And do you know what? Alona didn't mind at all! She purred and purred. You see, Alona **did** really like Hannah and she wanted to be her friend. But she was too proud to say so. And when Hannah hadn't come to see her for two whole days, she had been really upset and had decided never to make friends with anyone ever again, but just to be the cat who always walks by herself. But when she saw the snake getting ready to strike Hannah, she just **pounced,** without even thinking about it. Of course she wouldn't have let the snake hurt her! Of course Hannah was her friend!

The two just sat there on the rocky slope, hugging each other, never mind the pouring rain. At last, Hannah spoke:

"Alona, come home with me. You can be a secret. I can smuggle you into my bed—it's lovely and warm and dry. And I'll get you a flapjack, I promise. And then you can go home again to your cave. It isn't far. You'll easily be back before the others get home from school. Will you come?" The yellow eyed cat looked at her.

"Will," she said.

So Hannah led the way and the cat followed silently in her footsteps: down the rocky crag, across Flower Meadow, past Frog Pond and the vegetable patches and into the House. It was very quiet, except for the gentle crackling of a lovely wood fire which someone—Daddy probably—had thoughtfully lit to warm up the room. Hannah smuggled Alona into her bed.

"I won't be a minute," she said and ran downstairs. Mummy and Daddy were fast asleep on the sofa—(wet weather was always a great excuse for an unscheduled snoozle). Quietly, Hannah sneaked into the kitchen, took the two biggest flapjacks from the tin and crept back upstairs. There was the grey cat curled up on the pillow. Hannah took off her soaking oilskins and snuggled up beside her. Together, the two friends shared the flapjacks—never mind the crumbs on the bedclothes, Hannah was used to those.

Afterwards, Alona sat on Hannah's lap to be stroked and Hannah sang:

Wildycat, Wildycat, where have you been?

Following Hannah through mud and through rain.

Wildycat, Wildycat, will you be my friend?

Always and ever, right up to the end!

When Hannah had finished, Alona licked her hand lovingly and jumped out of bed.

"I'm going now. I know the way—cats never get lost."
"I'll come and see you tomorrow," Hannah promised.
And so she did. But that's another story.

Chapter 21
The Running Lesson

Next day was lovely and sunny—thank goodness! Hannah had a happy morning in Human School doing colouring in. The children went outside for their break and had great fun playing tag. Hannah was one of the fastest runners and hardly ever got caught. Then there was Daddy, coming through the school gate with all the other parents and ready to walk her home.

"Are you going to Animal School this afternoon?" asked Daddy, as they walked along the path.

"Yes, of course," said Hannah. "I think we've got running, now that the weather's better—and I love running. And then I want to go and see…"

But then she remembered that, although her parents knew all about Animal School, the wildcat was a secret. Only she and her siblings knew about Alona.

"Go and see what?" asked Daddy.

"Nothing," said Hannah.

She decided to wear trainers which were better than sandals for running and miles better than welly boots. So after a nice lunch of last night's warmed up pasta, she set off happily down the path to Flower Meadow. She called at Hurtle's burrow on the way to pick her up. All three little rabbits were waiting for her outside the burrow.

"Come and see!" said Hurtle. And she showed Hannah a lovely new patch of soft earth, just in front of the round entrance to the burrow. "My daddy dug it for me—it's for writing," she explained proudly. "And I did all the letters—look!"

"Yes, there on the soft earth were two Hs and an S: for Hurtle, Hop and Scotch."

"Very good," said Hannah encouragingly.

Then, not wanting to be late, the two friends hurtled down the steep slope, jumped over the stream and made their way through the green tunnel to the schoolroom. They weren't late, not quite and they weren't the last, either: neither the goat not the piglet were there yet. They arrived together, a few minutes later, giggling:

"Listen to this, everybody," announced the Goat.

"Knock, knock, who's there?" giggled the Piglet.

"Teacher," laughed the Goat.

"Teacher who?" asked the Piglet.

"Teach-A-shoo!" chortled the Goat who thought he was very funny.

But the Sheep was not amused.

"You're late," she said. "You've kept everyone waiting. Today we're going outside for our running lesson. In twos please and quietly!"

"O good," whispered Hannah, as she and Hurtle walked side by side through the back tunnel. "I'm good at running!"

Well, as it turned out, she wasn't that good after all. You see, although having two arms and hands instead of four legs is brilliant for lots of things, it doesn't make you a particularly fast runner. The Sheep tried to get everyone to stand in a line so she could say *ready, steady, go* before they set off together to race over to the big oak tree and back. But the piglet and the goat were in a silly mood and they just wouldn't line up properly. The goat kept starting before the word *go* and the piglet fell about laughing at him, so it was all very difficult.

"You two, stop fooling around," said the Sheep. But they wouldn't.

Then Kaka the clever stork had a good idea.

"I know," he said. "They should stand on top of that rocky crag up there; and then the rest of us will line up properly and start running. And the piglet can count up to five and then the goat should ring the bell and everyone freezes when they hear it; and the creature who has run the furthest is the winner! And they can be the judges, because they'll be able to see everyone from up there."

The Sheep was a bit puzzled by this, but after the stork had gone over it several times, she could see that it would be a good idea after all. At least it would keep the silly goat and pig busy, so they couldn't fool around.

"You'll have to count slowly," continued the Stork, "otherwise there won't be time to run far."

And so it was agreed. Off went the piglet and goat to scramble up the rocky crag. Hannah watched them anxiously. She hoped they wouldn't see the wild cat or her cave—she knew Alona wouldn't like that at all. But she couldn't really say anything, otherwise she might give away the secret. Luckily, the two silly animals were much too busy making up jokes to notice anything.

"Where do sheep get their hair cut?" asked the goat.

"I don't know," replied the pig.

"At a baa-baa's!" chortled the Goat. And by now they were standing right on top of the crag and hadn't noticed a thing!

Once again, the Sheep lined up the animals. This time it was much better, as everyone stood nice and still.

"Ready…steady…GO!" baaed the sheep. And they were off. But the silly piglet counted too fast. You really can't get far when you've only got a rapid 1 2 3 4 5 and then you have to stop at the sound of the bell. Hannah had only managed a few steps across Flower Meadow before she heard the bell and froze. Even so, she'd run further than Tut the turtle and the little mice Bubble and Squeak, whose legs were just too tiny for fast running. Donk the Donkey had long legs, but he was a bit confused about the rules, so hadn't really got going at all. As for the Chicky Bird, she had used her wings to fly to the nearest tree, so she had to be disqualified—it can't be a running race if you use wings. The Stork had done really well, for all that football practice meant that he was a good runner, despite only having two legs; he had got twice as far as Hannah. The frogs had managed three gigantic leaps, which meant that they were *runners up.* But the winner, according to the piglet, was Hurtle! She had bounded across Flower Meadow and was almost at the big oak tree before the bell had sounded. Everyone clapped and cheered as she made her way back to the starting point and she felt pleased and proud. Down scrambled the piglet and goat from the rocky crag—and again, they didn't notice the dark entrance of Alona's cave. Thank goodness. Then they all went over to the stream and had a nice cool drink, because running (even for only five seconds) is thirsty work.

And it was only when they came back again and sat down in a nice big circle, that Hannah noticed.

"But where," she cried anxiously, "is Dora the Deer?"

O dear. Everyone looked around. She definitely wasn't there. What could have happened?

"Perhaps she never even heard the bell," suggested Kaka, "so she didn't know when to stop."

You see, deer are exceptionally fast runners. Probably she was out of earshot before the five seconds were up. So she would have just gone on running. She might still be running! Goodness knows how far her long legs would have carried her by now.

"Suppose she got lost?" asked Hannah anxiously.

"O dear, O dear," said Hurtle. "She was really the winner, not me."

"We should send out a search party," said the Stork importantly. "I'll fly over in that direction and see if I can spot her."

Storks are good flyers, with their great wings, but even they can't go as fast as running deer. When he returned, after about ten minutes, he said that he had seen no sign of a fleet-footed, brown-eyed little deer.

Now what should they do? It was three o'clock, according to the piglet and time for the animals to go home.

"I expect she'll be all right," said the Sheep. "Deer can look after themselves; I expect she'll know how to get home. The rest of you go home safely, back to your parents." She certainly didn't want to lose any more animals.

So off they all went, all except Hannah. She had promised the cat that she would go and see her after school; and besides, she was a good hunter and might be able to help.

Chapter 22
Hunting

Alona was waiting for her on the rocky ledge.

"Did you see what happened?" asked Hannah. "Everyone ran their fastest and then stopped when they heard the bell; except that the Deer didn't hear the bell, so she never stopped!"

"I watched," said Alona. "From my cave. No one saw me but I saw her."

"Where did she go?" asked Hannah anxiously.

"Over the hills and far away," said the wild cat. "Look, there are her hoof marks." Hannah looked. The little deer must have bounded up the rocky crag and onwards, for there were her hoofmarks on the ground, leading away from the crag and towards the distant hills.

"Shall we go and look for her?" said Hannah. "She might be lost. Do you think you could find her?"

"Of course," said the cat. "I'm a good hunter."

"Can I come too?" asked Hannah.

But Alona said she was much better hunting on her own. Hannah would get tired and make too much noise—and the one thing cats need for hunting is silence. They have excellent ears and can hear the slightest sound; and they also have a brilliant sense of smell, much better than humans. And besides, Alona might not be back until after dark and while cats can see extremely well in the dark, people can't.

"I shall go by myself," said Alona.

"O dear," said Hannah. She would never get to sleep worrying about poor Dora. "Will you come and tell me when you've found her?" she asked. "There's an apple tree just outside my window. You could climb up it and call me and then I'd open the window and you could tell me. Will you?"

Alona looked at her with her great yellow eyes.

"Will," she said.

And then off she went, her nose to the ground, her ears twitching, following the footsteps of the running deer.

Hannah decided to go and ask the teacher if she knew where Dora's deer family lived. She wanted to explain that help was on its way, otherwise the deer family would be worried. Hannah knew that **her** family would be worried if she didn't come back when she was supposed to. She mustn't tell them about Alona, of course, because the wild cat was a secret. She set off in the direction of the field.

When she got there, there was no sign of the Sheep. But just then Donk came trotting up; he had spotted Hannah in the field and was always pleased to see her.

"Hello, Donk," said Hannah. "Where is the Sheep, do you know?"

"She's gone to find the deer family and explain what happened," said the Donkey. "She asked me if I knew where they lived."

"*Do* you know?" asked Hannah excitedly. "Can you show me? I want to tell them something."

"Climb up on my back," said the helpful donkey. "I'll take you." He knelt down so Hannah could easily get onto his hairy back. Then they set off.

It wasn't far. There was a little wood on the far side of the farmer's field, where the deer family had their home among the trees. And yes, there was the Sheep, explaining all about it to the anxious Deer family.

Hannah scrambled down from Donk's back.

"You mustn't worry," she said earnestly. "She's going to be found! I have a very good friend who knows all about hunting and she's promised to find her and then come and tell me. Only it might take a long time."

"Hunting!" said the father Deer anxiously. "With guns?"

"O no, no, it's not a human hunter," said Hannah. "No guns! Just eyes and ears and smell. Only it's a secret so I can't tell you exactly who. But Dora will be safe, I'm sure."

"Thank you for telling us," said the mother Deer. She knew that deer's only enemies were humans, so she believed the little girl. "That was very kind."

"She is a very good pupil," said the Sheep. "Always so helpful!"

And Hannah felt pleased and proud!

She said goodbye and scrambled back up on Donk's back. When she got to the stream, Hannah gave him a kiss on his hairy nose and ran back home. She had done what she could and now she would just have to wait…

That night, she lay awake in her little bed, waiting for the tap tap on the window which would mean that Alona had safely returned. She listened while first Ben and then David and Charlotte climbed upstairs, scrambled into their beds and finally—after a lot of reading—put out their lights with a click. Hannah didn't feel sleepy; she was too busy wondering what might have happened. Would the little deer be frightened when she realised that she was lost? Would Alona be able to find her, without getting lost herself? She imagined the little deer huddled up by a tree in the dark, not knowing which way to go and then seeing the gleaming yellow eyes of the cat coming to rescue her!

Was that a tap on the window? No, just a branch of the apple tree in the wind.

She imagined the wild cat leading the deer home, in the silvery moonlight, over the dark hills. How glad Dora would be when she got back to Flower Meadow and knew where her home was—just round the corner in the nearby wood. And how happy her deer family would be to see her safe and sound. Hannah smiled to herself as she imagined it all.

And then—yes! Tap tap tap on the window!

Quietly, she crept out of bed and reached up to the handle. There, staring at her from the other side, were the gleaming eyes of the wild cat. She opened the window and Alona leaped silently inside and padded over to Hannah's pillow.

"Was it all right?" asked Hannah. "Did you find her? Did you show her the way home?"

Alona looked at her—and smiled!

"Did. Knew I would."

"O thank you, dear Alona," whispered Hannah. She stroked the cat. How lovely it was to have her as a friend at last! She couldn't really sing out loud, because of not waking up the others, but she whispered the words of the song into her friend's soft grey ear:

I love my Alona, her hearing's so good;
And she showed little Dora the way to her wood.
And her eyes burned so bright in the darkness of night
And she's safely back home now and it's all a-all right!

And then, with a whisk of her tail, Alona leaped up onto the window sill and out into the darkness of night.

Chapter 23
The Exam

Next morning was foggy again, but Daddy said that the sun would probably be out by lunch time. It was a cold walk to Human School. Hannah had her pink woolly hat on and her stripy scarf. She remembered what the Sheep had said about black sheep and not having ever seen one. Could there possibly be a pink sheep, making pink wool? Or even a stripy sheep! She asked David and he said that you only got black or white sheep and that their wool was always dyed to make the different colours. Hannah didn't quite understand.

"What's dye?" she asked.

"A bit like painting, except the colours don't come off, even if you wash them," explained David.

Hannah wanted to know more but now the Human School was in sight and it was time to concentrate on lessons.

As it happened, they did wool that very morning. The human teacher had brought a whole load of different coloured balls of wool and some knitting needles. She showed the children a long scarf that she was making—a bright blue colour (just imagine a bright blue sheep!) and then said that everyone could choose a different coloured ball of wool and knitting needles and have a go themselves. What fun! Hannah chose a little pink ball of wool (like her hat) and some silver needles—great long things, not at all like the sharp needles that Mummy used for getting out splinters. Knitting was quite difficult, but she managed a bit, with some help from the teacher. Anyway, the children were allowed to take their knitting home with them and Hannah was confident that Mummy would be able to help her. Perhaps she could knit a present for the Sheep? She explained her plans to Mummy as they made their way back home and Mummy said it was an excellent idea, but maybe later, as she and the parent rabbits had agreed to meet and do a lot of nettling that afternoon.

"And Hop and Scotch?" asked Hannah.

"Well, they are coming too, but I don't know if they'll get much done," explained Mummy.

For a moment, Hannah wanted to stay behind and help, but then she remembered. She really wanted to get to school early because she needed a private word with Dora the deer. So she didn't even stay to eat her p-but sandwich and flapjack, but rushed off with them so she could eat while she waited. This time, she didn't go her usual way, down the steep slope and over the stream, but followed the path down to Flower Meadow, where the back tunnel came out. She sat there and waited, munching her delicious sandwich.

The first to arrive was the Sheep looking rounder than ever, but Hannah explained that she couldn't come in yet, as she was waiting for Dora.

"O dear," said the Sheep. "I do hope she got back all right last night."

"She did!" exclaimed Hannah proudly. "Only I can't tell you how I know, because it's a secret."

The Teacher looked puzzled, but luckily she didn't ask any more questions. She wasn't a very inquisitive sheep.

"All right, my dear; I'll go inside and leave you in peace," she said amiably. She waddled through the tunnel entrance and Hannah was left alone.

And the next animal that came along was indeed Dora the Deer: Hurray!

"Dora," said Hannah urgently, "you mustn't tell anyone about Alona. She's really a secret, you see. So, if anyone asks, just say you managed to find your way home and it was fine."

"OK," agreed Dora. Then she said. "Will you come home with me after school? My parents want to thank you. And will you ask the wildcat if she'll come too?"

"I will," said Hannah. "But I don't know if she'll want to. She likes walking alone, you see." And she peered upwards. Yes, there was the gleam of yellow eyes from the rocky ledge high above them.

And then along came the goat and the piglet, giggling together as usual.

"How do you start a teddy bear race?" asked the goat.

"No idea," said the piglet. "How **do** you start a teddy bear race?"

"Ready, teddy, go!" chortled the goat.

And the two of them fell about laughing.

"And how do you finish a deer race?" the goat asked Dora.

"I don't know," she answered, mystified.

"You don't finish it at all! You just go on running. O deer, O deer!"

"Take no notice," whispered Hannah. "They're just being stupid."

By now, all the other animals had arrived; it was time to go inside. The Sheep welcomed Dora back, but luckily she wanted to get on with her lesson, so there was no time for any more questions.

"This is an **exam** about **products**," she announced importantly. "Paws or hooves up if you know the answers. What can you get from a sheep?"

Hannah's hand went shooting up:

"Yes, my dear?" beamed the teacher.

"Wool!" exclaimed Hannah. "White wool or black wool. And if you want pink or blue or stripy wool, you have to dye it."

"Die?" quivered the Sheep.

"It's a bit like painting, only better," explained Hannah.

"O, I see," said the Teacher, except she didn't really. Hastily, she got on with her next question.

"And what can you get from a bird?"

This time, the Stork's enormous foot waved in the air. He knew all about birds.

"Eggs!" he said importantly. "And if you are a hen, you can give the eggs to humans and they look after you and feed you in return. But we storks keep our own eggs. No humans could reach them anyway, as storks build their nests far too high up."

"Good answer," said the Sheep. She always said that to the Stork, even if she didn't quite understand; she knew that he was probably cleverer than she was!

"And what can you get from a Donkey?"

Again, the Stork knew the answer. No one else did, not even Hannah. And not even the Donkey himself.

"Hair," cried Kaka, waving his foot. "Thick grey hair—very good for lining nests with!"

Donk looked pleased and proud. Yes, he did sometimes lose a tuft of hair, here and there, as he went about his daily business; he was glad to think that the tufts would be lining a stork's nest for the baby storklets to be nice and warm.

"Now," said the Sheep importantly. "This is the last question. Paws and hooves up! What can you get from humans?"

This time, little Hurtle waved her paw in the air. "Vegetables!" she shouted with glee. "You can sow the seeds and then you get beautiful carrots and onions and leeks and cabbages! Only you have to wait."

"A very good answer," said the Sheep. "Well done, everyone. Now we will go outside."

Out they all went, through the back tunnel and into Flower Meadow.

"Now," she said, when they had all finally settled in a circle on the ground. "This is the second part of the exam. I want everyone to go exploring and find a useful **product** from a tree! And bring it back here. Off you go!"

Well, that should be fun. Hannah wondered, *what she could get.* Then she thought of the wood burning stove at home—however would the family manage without it? She knew that wood came from trees, as she had watched Daddy chopping up fallen branches into logs for the fires. She couldn't find any fallen branches, though, so she asked Donk to help her and he managed to chew a hazel tree branch off with his big yellow teeth. Hannah was delighted.

"I can have nuts as well as wood for my useful product!" she exclaimed. The nuts were too small to eat yet but she knew they would grow by Autumn.

"But what can I have?" asked the Donkey mournfully. "I don't like nuts."

"Never mind," said Hannah, "you like thistles don't you? Let's go and pick some. They aren't really trees but I don't suppose the Sheep will notice."

So that is what they did. The thistles were just beginning to grow up from the ground and weren't too prickly yet, Hannah was pleased to see. Donk ate most of them up but managed to save one for the lesson.

Nearly everyone had found something from a tree. Hurtle had found some early apple blossom, which she thought was just lovely for decorating the burrow; the mice had found a fallen leaf and carried it back between them in their tiny paws.

"Leaves are good for hiding under," explained Bubble. "Only you have to watch out for snakes because they like them too," added Squeak.

"Very good, my dears," said the Teacher. "Who is next?"

The Chicky Bird had brought a beakful of twigs, which she said were brilliant for nest building. Kaka, the Stork, had found a bees' nest in an old oak tree and had caught and eaten a bee, which he said counted, as it was a **by-product** of the tree. Bees, he assured them, were surprisingly good to eat. The piglet and the goat had gone off together and come back with a mouthful each of acorns which had been lying on the ground under an old oak tree. And the Deer had torn a strip of tree-bark off with her sharp teeth—which she explained was really good for eating too.

It was harder for the water creatures, though. Tut the Turtle hadn't been able to think of anything; but the Stork explained that flies often perched on trees and he liked flies, didn't he? So that was all right. And just then a nice juicy fly settled on a nearby hazel tree and Tut showed them how good he was at catching it with his long black tongue. The frogs said they liked eating water weeds, which were a bit like underwater trees and would they count? Happily, the Sheep said they would—so that was all right too. Everyone had passed their exam—hurray!

And then it was three o'clock and time to ring the bell and go home.

But Hannah and Dora waited quietly, until the other animals had disappeared.

Chapter 24
Antlers

"Please can you wait for me by your wood?" asked Hannah. She didn't want Dora to see her climbing up the rocky crag. Alona's house must be kept secret. "Then I would love to come to tea. And I **will** ask Alona, only I expect she will say no."

So the little girl scrambled up the steep rocky cliff—and there was the wild cat waiting for her on her rocky ledge. Hannah sat down and stroked her.

"It was so lovely seeing you last night," she said. "And don't worry, no one else knows how Dora got home. Except the Deer family, of course, but they won't say anything. Dora says would you like to come with me so they can say thank you?" Alona stared at her with her yellow eyes.

"Won't," she said.

"OK," agreed Hannah. She thought it was a pity to have only one friend, but if that's what Alona wanted, it was fine.

"I brought you a flapjack." And she held out her hand nice and flat so that the cat could lick all the crumbles with her tickly tongue.

"I'll come and see you tomorrow and tell you what they said."

"If you want to," said Alona—which was certainly an improvement on "If you must!"

So Hannah slithered down the slope and found Dora patiently waiting for her in front of her wood.

"I'm afraid Alona didn't want to come," explained Hannah. "I thought she probably wouldn't."

"Never mind," replied Dora. "Would you like to ride on my back?" she continued. "It's quite a long way through the woods."

"Yes, please," said Hannah excitedly, "if you're sure you can manage."

So Dora the Deer knelt down and Hannah scrambled up. Then Dora stood up. Her back felt very different from Donk's, much knobbier and thinner and somehow more dangerous. But Hannah was a brave little girl and she trusted Dora. She leaned forward and held on to the little deer's neck and clung on tight with her legs. Well, Dora was **much** faster than the donkey and it was an exciting ride. Deer are very fleet-footed and Dora simply bounded under the trees in her wood. It was exciting. When they arrived, Dora knelt down again so that Hannah could easily slither off her back. It was good to feel the firm ground under her feet.

There were the mother and father Deer, lifting up their beautiful heads to greet her.

"Hello," said Hannah shyly. "Alona can't come and please can you keep her a secret?"

"Of course we will," agreed the mother Deer. "Most animals want their homes to be a secret. We quite understand."

Hannah was puzzled. She certainly didn't want **her** home to be a secret; it was nice when visitors came to tea—or even to stay. Still, humans are different from animals in many ways, as she was discovering at Animal School.

"We wanted to say thank you to you as well," explained the father Deer. "It was very good of you to help us last night."

"And we've got you a present," added the mother Deer. Proudly, the father Deer presented Hannah with a pair of splendid antlers. Hannah was thrilled.

"They're beautiful," she said. But she was puzzled. "Don't you want them?" she asked. The father Deer already had a pair of great antlers growing out of his head, it was true, but why did he have spare ones?

"Each year we grow new ones," he explained. "These are from last year. I used them for fighting with, but now I have a new pair."

"Goodness!" exclaimed Hannah. She could see that they would be good for fighting; they were big and strong, with very sharp points. Then she remembered her manners.

"Thank you very much," she said. But how was she to get them home? She probably couldn't manage to carry them as well as cling on tight to Dora's back.

She explained the problem.

"That's all right," said the father Deer. "I will give you a lift home. If you are sure, you don't mind me knowing where your home is. And you can wedge the old antlers in with the new ones. And then you can hold both pairs of antlers with both hands."

It sounded confusing, but it worked. The father Deer knelt down and Hannah managed to wedge the old antlers in tight, twisting them carefully among the new ones—how useful it was to have hands with fingers and thumbs! Then up she got—and up got the father Deer. Hannah found that it was much easier to have antlers to hold tight to than a slithery neck, which was just as well, as the father Deer was an amazing runner! He leaped a fallen tree trunk in one great bound and then almost at once they were home. How proud Hannah felt as she arrived triumphantly on the father Deer's back!

Ben and David were swinging in the hammock as they arrived and Charlotte was sitting on the sofa outside, reading.

"Wow!" said David.

"Look at those antlers!" said Ben.

But Charlotte was too busy reading to say anything!

The Deer knelt down and Hannah slithered down. Carefully, she untangled the present; David helped her carry it over to the sofa. By now, Charlotte had noticed.

"Goodness!" she said, letting her book fall onto the floor. "A Deer!"

And father Deer stood quite still as she stroked his beautiful nose and ears.

Everyone said goodbye and off the father Deer bounded, back to his woodland home. Only Hannah knew where it was and she decided to keep it a secret, because that's what most animals liked.

As for the antlers, well they were magnificent. Everyone admired them. Ben and David wanted to use them for fighting, but Daddy said they were really too sharp and dangerous.

"Have you ever seen male deer fight?" he asked. "Those antlers can hurt!"

Then Mummy said they would make a beautiful clothes hanger; so Daddy fixed them up in Hannah's bedroom and she spent a happy half hour hanging up all her best coats and dresses, where she could admire them from her bed.

That evening, after supper (a yummy fish pie and peas), Hannah asked Mummy if she knew about knitting.

"I do a bit," said Mummy.

"I do a bit too," said Hannah. And she showed Mummy the blue wool and needles from her Human School.

"I want to knit the Sheep a surprise present," she said. "Because I really like her. Will you help me?"

"I will," agreed Mummy, "but it may take some time."

"That's all right," said Hannah.

So together they managed three whole rows of what might turn out to be a pink scarf, before it was time for story and bed.

Chapter 25
Ben Goes to Animal School

Next day was a holiday at Human School. That meant the family could have a nice lie-in and then spend a lazy morning at home, not doing much at all. Hannah wondered if there would be a holiday at Animal School too. She decided to ask Donk. Ben said he would come with her, as he had nothing better to do. He couldn't wait to eat his proper breakfast so he snatched a whole new packet of ginger biscuits from the cupboard and put it in his rucksack, along with some lonely-looking flapjacks and two oranges. The children crossed the field to find the donkey. There he was, peacefully chewing the grass and swishing his tail.

"Donk," said Hannah. "Do you know if we've got Animal School this afternoon? Because there isn't any Human School today and I was wondering."

"Er," said the donkey. "I don't know. Why don't you ask the Sheep? That's her field, just over there."

So Hannah and Ben set off. There was a whole flock of sheep in the next field, all looking very big and wobbly: which one was Hannah's teacher?

"It's difficult to tell," she explained to Ben. "They all look alike."

And so they did: a whole flock of wobbly white sheep, with not a black or pink or blue one to be seen.

But then, Hannah heard a familiar voice.

"Hannah, my dear! How nice to see you. Who is that?"

And up waddled Hannah's Sheep.

"This is Ben," she explained. "He's my brother and he was bored so he came with me."

"Teacher," continued Hannah, "is there any Animal School today? Because there isn't any Human School."

"It's because it's an inset day," explained Ben. But the Sheep didn't know about insets.

"Yes, my dear," she said, "school will start after lunch, as usual. I will see you then. And if he likes, your brother can come too."

"O good!" said Ben. He thought Hannah's afternoon school sounded interesting and it would definitely make a change from his ordinary one.

Well, Ben couldn't wait to see the Animal School. So he and Hannah had an early lunch and dashed down the path together.

"We'll go through the back tunnel," explained Hannah, "as that's the way the really big animals go inside. You're much bigger than me."

So the two of them made their way past Frog Pool and into Flower Meadow.

"The back tunnel is just over there," she explained. "And over here is where we have our outside lessons, sitting on the grass. The others aren't here yet, because we're really early."

But then she stopped suddenly.

"O no," she said. "Look!"

Instead of a lovely circle of smooth green grass, there was a great patch of churned up brown earth. It looked as if someone had been digging, only not nice neat digging with a spade, but horrible rough slashing with something pointed and sharp.

"What's happened?" cried Hannah.

Ben bent down to look. He saw trotter prints in the muddy bits.

"It looks like pigs," he said. "They've got footprints like this. Is there a pig in your school?"

"There is," admitted Hannah, "but I'm sure he wouldn't do this. He's a bit silly sometimes but he's nice—and he's the only one who can count!"

Then she had a good idea. She would climb up and ask Alona if she had seen anything last night. Except that Ben couldn't come with her.

"Ben," said Hannah, "I've just got to ask someone something. You go through the big tunnel and then you can see our lovely schoolroom. And don't come out until I find you, OK? And don't look behind you."

Obligingly, Ben made his way over to the back tunnel which led to the schoolroom. As soon as he was out of sight, Hannah scrambled up the steep crag. There was Alona, waiting for her on her rocky ledge.

"Alona!" cried Hannah excitedly. "Something's been digging in our outside place and it's a horrible mess. Did you see anything last night?"

"Did. A beast with tusks and bristles. Big. Heard too. Grunting and snorting and gnashing."

"O dear," exclaimed Hannah. It sounded horrible. "Did it see you?"

"No," said the Cat. "No one sees me. No one hears me. Shut my eyes. Lay still. Not afraid."

"O good," said Hannah. "Where did it go?"

"Through tunnel," said the Wild Cat.

"O, no," said Hannah. Perhaps the beast would have slashed the schoolroom too. Perhaps, instead of a nice circle of smooth soft earth, it would be all jagged and horrible now. Then she remembered.

"Ben!" she cried. "He's gone inside by himself. Will he be all right? I must go and see."

Chapter 26
The Wild Boar

Quickly saying goodbye to Alona, she scrambled down the rocky crag and ran to the tunnel entrance; there she paused. She couldn't see anything because there was a bend in the tunnel and you can't see round bends. But she could hear snorting and grunting and stamping. Then the whole tunnel started to shake!

"Ben," she shouted, "are you OK? Come outside!"

"I'm coming," came the voice of her brother and there was the sound of running feet. Thank goodness—he must be all right. And so he was.

"There's a wild boar in there," he said. "It looks really angry. It's got all tangled up in the brambles and it can't get out. And it's making a horrible mess of the floor."

"O dear," said Hannah. She didn't really know much about wild boar, except that Daddy had once said they were bad for the grass.

"Is it big?" she asked. It certainly sounded big! Well, you would have to be big to make the tunnel shake like that.

"Massive," said Ben cheerfully. "But it can't move because its tusks are caught up in the brambles. So it's not dangerous. Unless it manages to break free, of course."

"I hope it won't," said Hannah nervously. "What shall we do? Perhaps we should go and tell the Sheep. Or find Daddy?" she added, thinking he would probably be much more useful in an emergency.

But before Ben could answer, along came the goat and the piglet, laughing as usual. They stopped when they saw Ben. Of course, they had never met him before.

"It's another human!" exclaimed the piglet.

"Is it a girl or a boy?" asked the goat. "I **think** it's a boy."

"What's your name?" the piglet asked Ben. Then, without waiting for an answer, he turned to Hannah.

"That reminds me," he went on. "You didn't ask anyone their names yesterday. So you can ask **two** names today. And it's definitely our turn."

"Never mind all that now," said Hannah impatiently. "Listen: there's a beast inside our schoolroom and he's making a horrible mess and he might be dangerous."

"A beast!" cried the goat. "What sort of beast?"

"A wild boar," explained Ben. "I went inside and saw it. It's got tusks and trotters and lots of black bristles."

"Tusks!" exclaimed the piglet. "I bet I know who it is—my great uncle Tusker—it must be. He's always getting lost and stuck. My ma says he's a real nuisance these days. But he won't hurt **me**. Come on!"

The piglet led the way through the tunnel. After him came Ben, then Hannah, with the goat following nervously behind. The wild boar might not hurt his great nephew, but supposing he didn't like goats? Lots of creatures didn't, much. Then he might charge. And tusks were sharper than horns. He was going to keep well back.

As soon as she rounded the corner, Hannah could see the boar. Yes, it was really big and bristly—much bigger than the piglet. It was tearing at the bramble walls with its great sharp tusks—but the more it tore, the more it got tangled up. A bit like Hurtle and the geraniums, she thought, only scarier. And it was still making a terrific din.

But the piglet wasn't at all alarmed.

"Hello, Great Uncle Tusker," he said. "It's me."

"Eh? What? Who?" exclaimed the boar, peering at the piglet with its beady black eyes. "Good Lord—Augustus!"

So that was the piglet's name! Augustus.

"What are you doing here?" asked Augustus, the piglet.

"Trying to get out," grunted Great Uncle Tusker. "What are **you** doing in this infernal place? Eh?"

"Going to school," answered the piglet promptly.

"School!" exclaimed Great Uncle Tusker. "Is this a school? What? I don't want to go to school, not at my age."

He stamped on the ground with his trotters. "Get me out!"

"If you keep still," said Ben sensibly, "I can probably help. I've got hands, you see."

"Mind the tusks, Ben," warned Hannah. "You will keep still, won't you?" she asked the boar. "You mustn't jab at Ben."

"Confound it," said the angry Great Uncle. He really felt like lowering his tusks and charging. But of course, he couldn't. Botheration!

"Lie down," said Ben, "then I can reach better." Ben was used to brambles. Then he had a good idea. "I'll give you some biscuits," he offered, "if you keep still. It will take your mind off things."

"Biscuits, eh, what?" said the boar. "Ah!"

You see, boars are omnivorous, which means they like eating almost everything. Especially sweet things.

So Great Uncle Tusker lay down on his hairy tummy and Hannah unpacked Ben's rucksack and gave him three biscuits and both oranges for luck. She didn't hold them out on her hand, because she didn't want to get too close, but she put them on the floor where he could reach. He made a horrible mess of eating them, with lots of slurping and grunting, but at least it kept him busy. Hannah was interested to see that he ate all the orange skins up as well as the soft bits inside.

Ben took off his stripy top and wrapped it round his right hand, so the prickly bits wouldn't get at him. (Daddy always used thick gloves when he was brambling in the garden.) He managed to untangle quite a thick wad of brambles, but it was hard work.

Now that he could see that the danger was over, the goat came forward.

"I'll help," he offered. "With my horns."

"Thanks," said Ben. "That would be useful. My name's Ben, by the way."

"And my name's Griff," replied the Goat. He got a particularly prickly branch of bramble between his two horns and pulled with all his might. There was a tearing sound and then a whole mass of brambles came up by the roots. Great Uncle Tusker was free at last. He got to his feet. He looked rather lost and old, standing there in the middle of the schoolroom. Suddenly, he didn't feel like charging at all.

"Come on Great Uncle Tusker," said Augustus the Piglet. "I'll take you *all the way home*."

"Ah. Good lad," said the Great Uncle.

So the little pink piglet led the great black boar out of the back tunnel, through the crowd of startled animals who had been gathering outside and up the river valley.

Into the schoolroom waddled the Sheep, followed by all the other animals.

"Are you all right?" she asked anxiously. "Boars can be fierce."

"Well at least they aren't **boring**," giggled Griff the Goat. "Not like lessons," he added, but luckily the Sheep didn't hear.

"O dear, O dear," she bleated. "What a terrible mess. My nice earth floor!"

"I know," said Hannah. "But he did eat all the skins. Shall we help tidy up?"

"That's a very good idea, my dear," said the Sheep.

So they did. Soon all the prickly bits of leaves and branches had been swept away—tails are very useful for this and Donk was especially helpful; even Griff the goat did a bit. Hurtle was very good at jumping up and down on all the bumpy bits of earth to make them lovely and smooth again and Ben and Hannah used their useful hands to pat it down firmly. Then they all went outside and did the same to the earth there. Ben said the grass would soon grow back—it always did, only it would be helpful to water it. So the frogs and Tut the turtle organised a watering session, leaping (or crawling) from the river to the ground and scattering drips where needed. It was fun and everyone got pretty wet in the process.

And then, trotting back down the valley came Augustus the piglet.

"I took him home," he said. "And Ma said she'd keep an eye on him. He gets a bit confused, now he's so old and he doesn't always remember where he lives."

So that was all right.

By now, everyone was tired after their busy afternoon. There was just time for a quick lie down in the warm sun, before Augustus counted up to three on his trotters and Griff rang the bell. Time to go home.

That night, curled up on her little bed, Hannah heard rain pattering on the window. Good—that would mean the circle of earth would get a nice watering to help the green grass grow.

Chapter 27
Hurtle Goes to Human School

Next morning was bright and sunny. But when Hannah opened the door of the house, she noticed that the ground was looking quite damp. It must have rained a lot in the night. After breakfast, she would just have time to run down to inspect the circle of earth and see how the grass was getting on after its uprooting by the boar. But, as it happened, she didn't get that far. She was just skipping down the path to Flower Meadow when she bumped into the whole rabbit family coming in the opposite direction.

"Hello!" she said. "How nice to see you. Where are you going?"

"We're going to inspect our vegetable patch," said the father Rabbit. "It rained a lot last night and rain is good for vegetables. We want to see if anything's growing."

"Come with us," said Hurtle. So Hannah did. She would see the earth circle that afternoon, anyway.

"OK," she agreed. "But I mustn't be long."

When they got to the rabbits' patch, they all peered down excitedly. And yes—there in the soft smooth earth were some beautiful green leaves. Hurrah!

"I expect there'll be carrots and onions under there," she said. "The vegetable bits grow underground, you see and then you have to dig them up to eat them."

"We want to, we want to!" squeaked the two small rabbits, Hop and Scotch.

"I don't think you should yet," said Hannah doubtfully. "They might need a bit longer to grow properly."

"O," squeaked Hop and Scotch. "Just one! Please."

"Go on then," agreed the mother Rabbit. "Just one—and you'll have to share."

So with their tiny paws, Hop and Scotch dug and dug and then Hurtle pulled on the leaves with her sharp teeth—and out came a beautiful orange carrot! It really was very small, but just enough for all three small rabbits to have a bite each. Delicious. They didn't mind at all about it not being washed or peeled first.

"I really will have to go now," said Hannah. "We've got Human School this morning and I mustn't keep the others waiting."

"Human School?" echoed Hurtle. "Can I come with you? Please!"

Hannah thought that would be a lovely idea and the Rabbit parents agreed. Then, of course, Hop and Scotch wanted to come too, but mother Rabbit said that they really were too little.

"I had to wait ages until I went to school," explained Hannah. "Not till I was three and a bit! But I'm sure Hurtle's old enough. It's going to be such fun!"

So the two of them said goodbye to the other rabbits and set off back to the house. As Hurtle had only had the tiniest breakfast, Hannah found her a big onion to eat from the vegetable basket. She told the others that Hurtle was going to school with her and that her parents had agreed.

"Right then," said Mummy. It was her turn to do the school run as Daddy had set off at crack of dawn for a peaceful canoe trip up the river. Hannah held hands with Mummy and Hurtle trotted close behind as they walked to school along the wet path. Soon they had arrived.

"Hallo, Miss!" said Hannah, as soon as she saw her human teacher coming down the corridor,

"This is my good friend Hurtle. She's coming to school! Is that ok? Please, Miss, she won't be any bother, I promise."

Chapter 28
The Rabbit Lesson

Miss was a bit surprised to have a rabbit in her class, but when she found out that Hurtle could talk, she became very excited.

"We're doing animals today, Hannah," she told the little girl. "And I'm sure your rabbit will be very useful."

"O good," said Hannah happily. She carried Hurtle into her class room and sat her down on the table. All the other children were delighted to see a real live rabbit in their midst!

"Now children," said Miss when everyone was settled. "We are doing animals today and Hannah's rabbit is kindly going to help us. Can you see how long her ears are? Much bigger than ours. That means she has excellent hearing, isn't that right?"

"Yes!" said Hurtle proudly. "I can hear for miles. All rabbits can. It's so we can listen out for danger."

"Good!" said Miss. "Now we are going to do an experiment. Everyone, close your eyes and open your ears. Listen as hard as you can. And then we'll see if rabbits' ears really are better."

"I'm good at hearing too," whispered Hannah, as she shut her eyes. She was remembering that time in Flower Meadow, when the Sheep had given them all a listening lesson.

The classroom became very quiet. Hannah opened her ears and listened (can you open your ears?). Inside the room, she could hear the gentle breathing of the other children and the drowsy buzz of a stray fly. From down the corridor, came the sound of the older children laughing and she was almost certain she could make out Charlotte's high giggle above the others. From outside in the playground, she could hear the shouts of another class playing football; someone had just scored a goal and there was cheering and shouting. Then she heard the raucous squawk of Kaka the Stork; perhaps he had flown down from his church steeple down to join in the game? Perhaps he had scored the goal! Or it might have been Ben—she couldn't tell. She could hear wind blowing the trees outside and the hum of a lorry going past on the road and then the squeal of its brakes. And far, far away and very faint, came the sound of an outboard engine on the River. She thought that might be Daddy until she remembered he had set off in the canoe that morning. Canoes don't make much noise at all. Last of all, she heard the sound of distant goats' bells, blown on the wind.

"Now open your eyes!" came the voice of the teacher, loud and near. Hannah blinked in the bright sunlight. One by one the children told Miss what they had heard. Then it was Hurtle's turn. And it was true—her ears heard much more than the children's ever could.

"I heard the waves of the river lapping on the shore," she said. "And I heard an ant running over the floor," she continued, "it went over there somewhere—O look, there it is!" And so it was—a tiny, tiny ant, scurrying along the tiled floor. None of the children could hear its footsteps, but Hurtle could.

"I heard the patter of rain over the faraway hills and the swish of the turning windmills. And I heard an acorn falling from its tree and the crack of an egg hatching in the storks' nest on the church steeple," the little rabbit went on, "and the wingbeats of a kingfisher on the river. I know all the different wing sounds, because of listening out for owls at night."

"Excellent!" said Miss. "And did you know, children, that rabbits can see in the dark?" The children didn't (except for Hannah, of course) so the teacher said they would do another experiment.

"We'll all go inside the book cupboard," she said. "And when I shut the door it will be completely dark. And we'll see what we can see."

So in they all squeezed and Miss shut the door behind them. It was very dark! The children kept bumping into each other and tripping over things, so Miss told them to stand very still, open their eyes as wide as they could—and look as hard as they could.

Hannah could easily make out the green eyes of her rabbit friend, but that was about it. She caught glimpses of shining white, which must have been the children's eyes, but she couldn't make out the coloured bits in the middle. And was that someone's teeth, shining faintly in the darkness?

But Hurtle could see masses of things!

"I can see all of you," she said, "only I can't count how many. And I can see some cobwebs on top of the cupboard and a spider hanging down." At this, some of the girls squealed; no one wanted an invisible spider crawling in their hair!

"Shhh, don't be silly," said Miss, sounding really rather like the Sheep. "Anything else, Hurtle?"

"Lots and lots of books," said Hurtle, "all piled on top of each other." (She had learned about books when she had visited Hannah's bedroom, if you remember). "And they're different colours and sizes and shapes. And some of them have got pictures."

"Very good," beamed the teacher. "Anything else?"

"And coloured sticks like the ones Hannah uses for drawing," said Hurtle. "They're lovely. I like the green ones best."

"Excellent!" said the teacher. "Crayons!" She opened the cupboard door and everyone blinked in the sudden dazzle of light.

"And now we will have a drawing lesson. Back to your seats, everyone."

The children loved drawing lessons. They were given a big piece of paper and lots of coloured crayons. But of course, Hurtle couldn't draw as she didn't have any hands. Luckily, Miss had thought of that.

"Today, we shall draw the rabbit!" said the teacher. "Hurtle, you jump up and sit on my big table where everyone can see you. Keep as still as you can while the children draw you."

What fun! Hannah drew her friend's great ears, with pink bits in the middle and beautiful green eyes. Then she chose a grey crayon to draw her soft fur and a white crayon for her little round tail and a silver crayon to draw her whiskers.

"What are whiskers for?" asked Hannah. She had never been quite sure.

"A very good question," smiled Miss. "You can all guess and then after break, Hurtle will tell you the right answer. Now finish your drawings, please. It's time for your snacks."

Out ran the children, into the lovely sunny warmth of the playground. Hannah unpacked her snack.

"A biscuit for me and an onion for you," she explained. Hurtle asked if Hannah wanted to share her onion, but Hannah said no thank you, she much preferred biscuit. Hurtle said she much preferred onion, so that was all right. Then they played a quick game of tag with the other children and Hurtle proved an excellent player with her four strong legs. No one could escape her—and no one could catch her either! Hannah felt very proud of her furry friend.

Then it was time to go back into the classroom for the last part of the Rabbit lesson.

"So, who knows what whiskers are for?" asked the Teacher. "Hands up!"

"For looking beautiful?" asked Hannah, who had greatly enjoyed drawing Hurtle's silver whiskers. She rather wished she had some of her own!

"Well, they do look beautiful," agreed the Teacher, "but that's not what they're **for**."

"For tickling people!" said Jonny. He liked tickling people and making them squeal with laughter and he thought Hurtle's whiskers would be brilliant at tickling.

"Certainly not," said the Teacher. "Keep still, Jonny. We all know what tickling is, you don't have to demonstrate. Anyone else?"

"For drinking with, like a straw?" asked Gertrude.

"No," said the Teacher. "They drink with their mouths, just like humans. Anyone else?"

But no one else had any ideas.

"Tell the children, please, Hurtle," said the Teacher.

"Well," said Hurtle, jumping on to the teacher's table again, where everyone could see her. "I live with my family in a burrow—that's a hole under the ground. And there are lots and lots of different rooms in the house, so it's called a warren. And some of the rooms are quite small. So your sticking-out whiskers tell you if the rest of you will fit, because otherwise your body might get stuck. So if you can feel the edges with your whiskers, you know not to go into that bit of the warren, until it's been made bigger."

"Very good," said the Teacher again. "And how do you make the rooms bigger?"

"We dig," said Hurtle. "Rabbits are really good diggers."

"It's lovely inside the burrow," said Hannah. "I had tea there once, but I didn't really like the onions. Rabbits don't have biscuits, you see. But the rooms are beautiful and Hurtle's got leaves and pictures in her room."

"That reminds me," said the Teacher, "Hurtle can choose the best picture to take home with her. Whose shall it be?"

"Mine! Mine!" shouted all the children. Hurtle looked carefully at all the pictures of herself. Some of them had rather lopsided ears and some of them hadn't got any tails. But Hannah's picture was brilliant: Hannah had drawn her friend smiling with all her teeth gleaming white!

"Can I take yours?" she asked.

"Of course you can," said Hannah proudly. "And we'll show Mummy on the way."

And then it was time to go home. There was Mummy waiting for them on the steps. Hannah held tightly onto her friend so she wouldn't get lost and Hurtle held tightly onto her picture, so it didn't blow away in the wind. She couldn't wait to show her family and to tell them all about her lovely morning in Human School.

Chapter 29
The Human Lesson

That afternoon, the Sheep took all her pupils outside as it was a lovely day and all the pink blossoms on the apple trees were trembling in the Spring wind. They couldn't sit in their usual circle, because the grass was still growing back after the Wild Boar attack, so they settled down under the shade of the tree.

"Today, we're going to have a lesson about Humans," explained the Sheep. "And I expect Hannah will be a great help."

"I will," agreed Hannah, who liked being helpful.

"Thank you, my dear," said the kindly Sheep. "But don't be **too** helpful just yet. I want the other animals to say what they know first. And then you can tell them if they're right or wrong."

"OK," agreed Hannah. This was going to be interesting.

"Now," said the Sheep, "what are the main differences between humans and other animals?"

"They can't fly," cheeped the Chicky Bird. "That is certainly true," agreed the Sheep. "But lots of other animals can't fly either."

"O," said the little Chicky Bird, looking rather disappointed. She hadn't thought of that.

"You need wings to fly," explained Kaka, the clever stork. "And only two legs. Humans can play football," he added, "but so can storks!" He puffed out his feathers proudly. "So that isn't a proper difference. I think the real difference is that they build such huge houses. Far too big, really. Birds' nests are much smaller and we manage perfectly well. There are six of us in our nest. The last one hatched this morning!"

"I heard it!" squeaked Hurtle, very excitedly. "I heard the egg crack!"

"Is it true about houses?" asked the Sheep. She hadn't actually been inside a human's house, although she had seen the outside of the farmer's house from her field.

"I suppose it is," replied Hannah, who had never thought about it before. "There's a bit for cooking and another part for eating and then another one for sitting; and then you climb some stairs and that's where we sleep. And we have our own bedrooms. And there's a kitchen for cooking and washing up."

"I've been inside it!" squealed Hurtle. "And there was a piano and lots of toys for playing and a wood fire."

Hannah wondered what it would be like for her whole family to live in a nest. Or a burrow underground, or in a cave, like Alona. Hmmm. She liked having lots of rooms.

"That's another difference," said Kaka. "Humans have fires; animals can't make fires."

"And we can cook," agreed Hannah. "We don't eat much raw food—except oranges and apples and things."

"I know! I know!" piped up little Bubble. "We've only got one coat; Hannah has loads of different ones."

"They're lovely," agreed Squeak. "I wish I had lots of coats too."

"She means clothes," explained Griff the goat. "Every day, she comes in a different clothe. Animals always have the same one. *I'm a goat with only one coat!"* he joked.

"It's true," said Hannah. "I like having different coloured clothes and being able to take them on and off. Isn't it a bit boring wearing the same coat each day? And what happens when you get too hot? Or too cold? Or too wet?"

She was thinking about her pink knitting present for the Sheep, which would be good if it got cold suddenly, but it was still a secret so she didn't say anything.

"Animals can run faster," said Dora the Deer. Well, that was certainly true. Or, even if they weren't great runners, they could swim faster, like Tut's great grandmother, or jump faster, like the frogs.

"Humans are quite slow," Hannah admitted, "even fast ones like David."

"What do **you** think is the most important difference, my dear?" the Sheep asked Hannah.

That was a difficult question. Hannah had to think hard before she gave her answer.

"I think having hands, instead of trotters or hooves or paws and claws," said Hannah. "It means we can do lots of useful things like knitting, or untangling, or sowing seeds, or cooking, or drawing. It would be hard to hold things without fingers and thumbs."

"Or playing the piano," added Hurtle who had just loved it when David had played for her.

"Well, my dears," said the Sheep, "that was a very good lesson. Well done. I think we have all learned something useful."

"It's not exactly useful if we can't do anything about it," argued Kaka the Stork. "But it was interesting. I'm glad I'm a stork, though. Flying is best!"

"It is, it is!" cheeped the Chicky Bird. And to show everyone how lovely it was, he flew up to the apple tree and perched on the topmost branch.

Then Hannah remembered. She now knew everyone's names—except the Chicky Bird's.

"Chicky Bird, fly down here and tell me your name," she cried.

So down he flew; "My name's Chicharito," he said. "It means Little Pea in Spanish. We fly to Spain when it gets cold and my mummy likes the name."

"It's lovely," agreed Hannah. "You look a bit like a little pea—all sweet and round!"

Just then, there was an unexpected whumph, followed by a frantic chirping. One of the tiny blackbird fledglings had fallen out of its nest and landed on the grass underneath. It wasn't quite strong enough yet to fly back, although it kept trying, hopping up and down and flapping its stubby wings furiously in an attempt to lift off. From the nest above, the mother Blackbird peered out anxiously. And she couldn't fly down and pick it up, because she didn't have any hands. You can hold twigs and worms and flies in your beak, but not eggs or baby birds.

"It's all right," said Hannah. "I'll get it."

She glanced anxiously up at Alona's rocky ledge. Yes, there was a gleam of fierce yellow eyes watching her. Would the Wild Cat be cross if she rescued the bird? O well, it couldn't be helped. With her useful hands, she gently picked up the little fledgling. Its whole body was quivering with fear and it cheeped anxiously.

"Don't be frightened," said Hannah. "I won't hurt you."

But she was too small to reach up to the nest; and she couldn't climb up the tree trunk with only one hand. Luckily, Donk the Donkey came to the rescue. He knelt down and Hannah carefully scrambled up on his back, holding on to his hairy coat with one useful hand, while she cradled the baby bird in the other one. And when Donk got up onto his hooves, she was able to reach up and gently pop the baby back inside its snug little nest. Hurrah! Safe again. Perhaps it would be more careful now until its wings grew stronger.

"Well done, Hannah," said the Sheep. "That was a very good example of the usefulness of hands!"

After three o'clock, when everyone else had gone home again, Hannah stayed behind. She wanted to see Alona. But when she got to the rocky ledge, there was no sign of the Wild Cat. Hannah knelt down and peered into the darkness of the cave. Two yellow eyes gleamed back at her.

"Alona," said Hannah, "don't be cross."

"Spoiled my hunting," hissed Alona. "Eat baby birds. Told you. Can't now. Hungry."

"O dear," said Hannah. "I **had** to rescue it. I'm sorry, Alona, but I really had to. Please come and be stroked. And I brought you a flapjack, so you won't be hungry. Please come."

"Sssss," hissed the Wild Cat. But in the end she did come out onto the ledge. She poked out her rough pink tongue and Hannah held out her useful hand with all the crumbs neatly spread out. She loved the tickling feeling of Alona's tongue. It reminded her of what Johnny had said that morning.

"What do you use your whiskers for, Alona?" she asked.

"Hunting," said Alona. "Sneaking up. Eyes shut. Whiskers show me. Then pounce."

"O," said Hannah, "I see."

She started to stroke the cat's soft grey fur. And after a while, Alona curled up on Hannah's lap and shut her yellow eyes—and purred like anything! Hannah started to sing:

Rock-a-bye blackbirds, on the tree top,
When the wind blows the blackbirds will rock;
When the bough breaks, the blackbirds will fall—
Down will come blackbirds, babies and all.

Alona opened her yellow eyes, stopped purring and stared at her balefully. Quickly, Hannah started on her second verse:

Hush a bye, Wild Cat, on her high ledge;
Safe in my lap, not too close to the edge;
When the wind blows she won't come to harm,
She'll sleep in her cave, all snuggly and warm.

That was better; Alona had shut her eyes again and the purring grew louder. Just to be sure that they really were friends again, Hannah quickly made up one more verse:

Alona has bright eyes and lovely grey fur,
And whenever I stroke her, then she starts to purr.
The Wild Cat's a hunter, but she can be kind;
I rescued a fledgling, but she didn't mind.

"You didn't really mind, did you?" the little girl asked.

"Purrr," said Alona.

Which Hannah supposed was her way of saying she didn't really mind, after all. Thank goodness!

Chapter 30
Poems

"Today we are going to learn a poem," explained Hannah's human teacher. "And then all you children are going to recite it together."

O good, thought Hannah. She liked poems and was good at reciting them. She wondered which poem Miss would choose.

"This is a poem that I made up myself," said the teacher proudly. "It's about going to school! Listen carefully." She stood up in front of the class, put on her special voice and recited her poem:

In our little village, by the river cool,
Near the old church steeple, there's a little school;
All the children go there, nearly every day,
And they learn all their lessons and after that they play.

"Is that it?" said Hannah. She thought it would be much longer; it would be easy to learn that!

"It certainly is," said the teacher, very pleased with herself. "It's a beautiful poem and a perfect length."

She was a bit surprised when all the children learned it in about five minutes, as she had been expecting it to last all morning. So she gave them an extra-long play time. The children played tag and hide and seek. And then they watched the big ones play football. Hannah was particularly pleased to see that Kaka the Stork was now a regular member of David's team. David and Kaka each scored two goals and everyone cheered.

After break, they went back into class to see if they could remember the poem. They could. So they said it about twenty more times, before school finally ended.

All the way back home, Hannah was thinking, *Wouldn't it be fun to have a poetry recital at her Animal School? And she could make up a really good poem for all the animals, much longer than the teacher's one.* As she made her way upriver, Hannah started to create the words in her mind…

That afternoon, when everyone had assembled in the bramble school room, the Sheep, who was looking fatter than ever, started to yawn.

"O dear, O dear," she yawned. "I just couldn't get to sleep last night, the owls were making such a horrible racket. So I didn't plan anything for today's lesson. Does anyone have a good idea?"

"I do!" shouted Hannah, getting in quickly, before Kaka could open his bill. He was probably only going to suggest football, anyway and not all the animals shared his love of the game.

"I thought we could make up poems and then recite them to each other."

"Um," bleated the Sheep. She wasn't very good at poems. "What sort of poems?"

"Nice long ones," said Hannah. "I've already done mine."

The Sheep really wasn't sure about poems, but as she was feeling so sleepy, she decided to let Hannah take the lesson. Then she might be able to have a quiet snoozle.

"Right, my dear," she agreed. "You explain to the animals and I'll just pop outside and you can come and get me when you're ready."

And with a mighty yawn, she waddled through the back tunnel and out into Flower Meadow.

Hannah felt proud and pleased. She was going to enjoy this! She had always liked giving orders to other people. Perhaps she would be a teacher when she grew up.

"Now," she announced importantly, "this is my poem. I'll tell it to you so you can see what I mean. And then every animal has to make up its own special poem to say. OK?"

Even Kaka thought it sounded interesting. So everyone became very quiet and listened as Hannah recited her poem.

Animal School
Underneath the brambles, beside the little river,
Where no one else can see it, there's an Animal School!
When the wind blows, the bramble leaves all quiver

And inside the schoolroom it's very green and cool.
Our teacher is a sheep and the Head is a black bull,
*And he's a bit scary, but the teacher is **not**;*
She is very big and wobbly and has lots of white wool,
And she gets a bit forgetful when the weather gets too hot.
And when the sun is shining, then we go outside

"We aren't outside today," protested the Stork. "And it's really sunny!"

"Shhh!" said Hannah, sounding more like a teacher than ever, "I haven't finished yet."

She started her third verse again:

And when the sun is shining, then we go outside;
But we have to stay dry inside when it gets too wet—
We play lots of games, like how to Seek and Hide,
And we learn lots of lessons. But I haven't finished yet:
And all kinds of animals come along together,
There's a Donkey and a Chicky Bird and that isn't all;
And we come every day, never mind about the weather,
And some of us are big and some of us are small.

"That's as far as I got," explained Hannah, "but it's nice and long already and you can add your bits to it. Now, get into twos," she told them firmly (she really was an excellent teacher) "and you can each make up a poem about yourselves. OK?"

"We'll have to go outside," protested Kaka. "There isn't room in here."

Well, that was true.

"All right," agreed Hannah. "But find somewhere private, because I don't want the Sheep to hear until we're ready."

But when they got outside, they saw that the Sheep was fast asleep, snoring gently under the hazel tree. So they tiptoed past and found nice private places and she didn't wake up at all!

Chapter 31
More Poems

Griff the Goat and Augustus the pig set off together. They found a big flat rock in the middle of the stream and settled down to work. This wasn't going to be easy.

"It has to be funny," said Griff. "We need jokes."

"OK," agreed the Piglet. "And it has to have numbers in it. Because I'm the only one who can count."

"All right," said Griff. "And bells!"

After a great deal of thinking and some fooling around—the goat kept pushing the piglet off the rock into the water and then the piglet made a great fuss about getting back up again—the two friends finally managed their verse. This is it:

I'm Augustus the Piglet and this is me,
And every day I count up to three;
And I'm Griff the Goat and I ring my bell,
And I tell lots of excellent jokes as well.
What do you put on a pig's sore trotter?
I don't know, what do you put on a pig's sore trotter?
Oinkment!

Griff and Augustus were very pleased with their poem. Once they had learned it properly, they had a very good game in the river. Griff leaped nimbly from rock to rock while Augustus scrambled about in the water and tried to catch him by his beard. This went on for ages and by the time they got back, most of the other animals had finished their poems.

The two little mice, Bubble and Squeak, had scampered back to their lovely round home in the cornfield to work on theirs. No one would bother them here and they wanted it to be really good! This is what they made up:

We're two little mice
And we're very, very nice;
We live in a house
Just right for a mouse!
It's lovely and gold
And it keeps out the cold.
It's in the field of corn
And it's where we both were born.

But when they got back, they were too shy to tell everyone, so they whispered it into Hannah's ear instead. She said it was excellent!

The frogs went off together, all four of them and sat on a rock beside their pool. After a lot of croaking and burping, they came up with this:

Brekekekex Korax Korax!
When frogs are around, you should mind your backs!
We *like leap-frogging, up, up and over,*
*So if **you** don't like it, then take cover!*
We're slimy and green with bulging eyes
So you just might think it's a nasty surprise
When you feel our frog flippers on your backs—
Brekekekex Korax Korax!

Proudly, the frogs leaped back to the grass and recited their poem in unison, with a lot of extra burping to make it sound particularly fierce. Next were the flying creatures—Kaka the Stork and Chicharito the Chicky Bird. Kaka did most of the inventing, because he was clever, but Chicharito added his own bit on the end.

Birds are very superior creatures,
Feathery wings are their best features;
If you have wings, nothing can catch you—

But if you don't, then a wild cat could snatch you.
Free and fast, you fly in the sky,
Surveying the ground as you spiral up high;
When your glorious feathery wings are unfurled,
You're the undisputed Kings of the world.
I can fly too,
Though not as well as you.
I'm called after a pea,
And that is me!

"Very good," exclaimed Hannah. And everyone was impressed. "Tut and Hurtle," she continued, "please may we hear your poem now?"

"You can!" squeaked Hurtle proudly. She had found an excellent rhyme to begin it with!

A rabbit called Hurtle,
Has a friend who's a Turtle!
The rabbit's house is under the ground,
It's hidden away and it's never been found,
By an owl or a fox or a fierce wild cat,
So we're safe and sound,
And that is that!
The Turtle is called Tut,
And he lives with Granny Grot.
They have each got a shell,
And they get on really well.

Everyone clapped and Hurtle and Tut felt pleased and proud. Just then, along came Augustus and Griff. They wanted to show off their poem, but Hannah said they were **late** and they would just have to **wait** (which was a poem, although it wasn't meant to be!).

So next came Donk's and Dora's turn. As the two biggest animals, they thought they really ought to make up a long poem, but it had proved more difficult than expected. Donk couldn't think of anything to say, so Dora had to do all the work. Luckily, she was a gentle, kind deer and didn't mind at all. This is what she made up—and it was a very small poem indeed (rather like Hannah's human teacher's poem!):

My best friend is Donk and he is a Donkey;
His back is hairy and his ears are wonky.
My name is Dora and I am a Deer;
I live over there and Donk lives near here.

"Call yourself a Deer?" joked Griff. "You don't have much **idea!**"

But the other animals didn't really understand the joke; only Augustus laughed—but then, he always did!

"And now it's our turn," Griff continued, but just at that moment, the Sheep gave a great sigh and woke up. For a moment, she couldn't think where she was; then she scrambled up as quickly as she could—which wasn't very quick at all—to her feet. It would never do for a teacher to be found napping on duty. And goodness knows how long she had been asleep in the hot sun.

"What's the time?" she asked.

The piglet considered.

"Four o'clock!" he confessed. "I forgot to ring the bell at three."

"O dear, O dear," bleated the Sheep. "You must all run back to your homes," she said. "Your parents will be wondering where you are."

Off they all scampered, even Hannah. She knew she ought to go and see if Alona was all right, but she didn't want her parents to be worried. Perhaps she would come back later and see. Anyway, it had been a lovely day—she had really enjoyed being a teacher.

Chapter 32
Sore Paw

Luckily, Hannah's parents hadn't been wondering at all. Daddy had already set off to the village to pick up the others and Mummy was busy making a carrot cake. The new carrots on the vegetable patch were still too small to pick, but there were a lot of juicy orange ones left over from Daddy's shopping trip. Hannah settled down in the rocking chair to do some more knitting with her lovely pink wool while she watched. And then it was time to lick the bowl—yum! And then she remembered Alona.

"Mummy," said Hannah, "can I go and see a friend?"

"No, Small, you can't," explained Mummy. "There really isn't time before supper and it will be getting dark afterwards."

Oh dear. Hannah remembered the words of her song:

Wildycat, wildycat, will you be my friend?

Always and ever, right up to the end.

Surely Alona wouldn't stop being her friend, just because she missed one day? Anyway, there was nothing she could do about it. And tomorrow, she would take her a huge slice of carrot cake to make up for it.

There was the sound of scurrying feet and zooming down the grassy slope came Ben, followed by David, Charlotte and Daddy. They were all tired and hungry and looking forward to their supper. So Hannah helped lay the table and by the time the others had washed their hands, the supper was ready: sausages and mashed potatoes and gravy—yum. Then Mummy opened the oven and took out her beautiful carrot cake—all warm and steamy. Charlotte helped with the icing and it made an excellent pudding. Hannah watched anxiously as everyone devoured their slices in no time and asked for more. She really did want to give Alona some tomorrow, to make up for having missed a day. Luckily, Mummy was firm:

"You've had quite enough," she proclaimed. "It took ages to make and I want it to last."

And then there was washing and toothing and pyjama-ing—and time for a bed-time story. Mummy read Hannah a Pooh Bear story about honey pots, which was lovely. Hannah liked Pooh and was proud of being a Bear herself! Well, sort of. She had had a busy day—it was hard work being a teacher—and in no time at all, she fell fast asleep.

Suddenly she woke up. What was that scratching noise? Something was scratching at the blue door of the house. It was very dark and the only other noise to be heard was the gentle snoring of her parents down the corridor and the fierce screech of an owl in the middle distance. Hannah shivered—but she expected that Hurtle would be safe and sound in her burrow where the owl couldn't get at her. What had Hurtle's poem said?

The rabbit's house is under the ground,
It's hidden away and it's never been found...

But what was that scratching at the door? Could it be the wild boar come back again? She listened with all her might. But wild boars make grunting and oinking sounds and Hannah couldn't hear any of those. Just the faint *scritch scratch scritch* at the door. And then she heard a sound that she did recognise and that set her heart beating wildly! It was the sound of a **caterwaul!**

"Alona!" gasped Hannah. She scrambled out of bed, tiptoed down the stairs, ran over to the door and opened it wide. Yes, there on the doorstep was the Wild Cat, her yellow eyes glaring at her in the darkness.

"Alona!" whispered Hannah. "Are you all right? I'm sorry I couldn't come and see you after school but the piglet forgot the time and the Sheep was asleep and I had to run and then Mummy said it was too late and I couldn't."

The wild cat glared at her.

"Hurt," she said, bitterly. "Hurt paw. Hurts."

And she lifted up her front right paw. Hannah bent down to inspect it. O dear—there was a nasty wound, with real red blood trickling out.

"O, Alona," whispered the little girl. "I am sorry! How did you do it?"

"Fight!" said Alona. "Fight with rats. Biting rats. Wanted to get into my cave."

"O dear," said Hannah. She didn't know much about rats, except they were probably fierce. She wondered how many there had been and whether Alona had won. But now was not the time to ask questions. She thought hard. If she turned the light on she might wake everyone and that would never do. Alona must be kept secret.

"Wait here," she said, "I won't be a second." Quickly and quietly, she crept upstairs into David's bedroom. Yes, there was his head torch, on the floor beside the bed. David was fast asleep—and, though he did turn over and sigh as the door squeaked open, he didn't wake up. Hannah snatched the torch and ran back to Alona.

Shining David's torch in front of her, she led the way to the kitchen, Alona limping slowly behind. The kitchen door squeaked too, but it was probably too far away for anyone to hear. Standing on tiptoe, she could just reach the light switch. Surely no one upstairs would see it? In a moment, everything was flooded with light, which made it all much easier. Hannah removed a pile of clean washing from the table, gently lifted up the cat and settled her down on the table top.

"Blood needs washing," she explained. "Then it will get better soon. And it will hurt, but only a bit."

She found a pink washing-up cloth and ran the tap to moisten it. Then, ever so carefully, she washed the sore paw. Quite a lot of blood came off onto the cloth, but as it was pink it didn't show too much. Soon, the wound was lovely and clean. Alona was very brave; she made hardly any sound, just a faint Ssss, even when Hannah had to scrape out the bits of dirt from the wound. Then she wrapped the poor paw up with a tea towel.

"How does it feel?" she asked.

"Better," admitted Alona. She shivered. "Cold."

"O dear," said Hannah again. "Why don't you come to bed with me? It's lovely and warm and you can't go hunting with a sore paw, can you? And besides, the rats might come back again."

"Won't," she said. "Bit them. Ran away."

"O good," said Hannah. "But do stay the night anyway. Will you?"

Alona stared at her with her gleaming yellow eyes.

"Hungry," she said.

"I'll get you some food," promised Hannah. She did want her friend to stay; it would be lovely to snuggle up together under her soft white duvet.

"Mummy's made a brilliant carrot cake and we weren't allowed to eat it all up, so there's plenty left. And it's even nicer than flapjacks."

She scampered over to the kitchen cupboard. She had to open the door really slowly, because it was a bit squeaky unless you were careful but she managed it. So far, so good. There was the cake, on the top shelf but luckily within her reach. And there was the knife, right next to it. Hannah climbed up onto one of the chairs and managed to cut a huge slice. It was a bit of a wobbly cut and Mummy would be sure to notice it next morning and she might notice the flannels too and the missing tea towel, but never mind. She got down off the chair.

"Here you are!" she said proudly. "It's delicious!"

And so it was. Hannah held out her hand and Alona ate it all up, every little bit, licking her lips and purring with pleasure.

"Will you stay the night with me?" asked Hannah again. She was thinking how much nicer her warm bed was than Alona's bare cave. And surely the hurt paw should be rested?

Alona stared at her with her yellow eyes.

"Will," she said.

Delighted, Hannah scooped her up in her arms. She turned off the kitchen light, put David's torch on her head and by its dim light she found her way back up the stairs and into her own dear bed. David wouldn't need the torch now and she could explain tomorrow. She didn't have a spare hand to shut the door with—but it didn't really matter. There was no wind to bang it and the bed was snug and warm.

Alona didn't want to get under the duvet, so she settled down in a soft, warm heap on Hannah's tummy. It was so lovely lying in bed and feeling the weight of the wild cat on top of her. Hannah lay awake in the darkness, listening to the gentle snoring of her parents and the soft purring of her dear friend…

But when she woke up next morning, Alona was gone.

Chapter 33
Goats and Jokes

Griff had gone home from school feeling very disgruntled. He just loved showing off, you see and there had been no time to recite his excellent poem to the others. And no one (except Augustus) had laughed at his **i-dea** joke, which he thought had been very funny. His home was in a rocky pasture a long way away from school, but goats are fast runners and his mother wasn't at all worried that he was back later than usual. Griff felt better after he had had supper (nice juicy green grass) but he still wanted to show off his poem. So he decided to recite it to his younger brother, Whiff. Although Whiff wasn't at all interested in poetry, Griff was considerably bigger so he usually got his own way. Whiff thought the poem was OK, but he wasn't nearly as enthusiastic as Griff had expected. And when Griff tried out his **deer with no idea** joke, Whiff just didn't get it. By the time Griff had explained it, it didn't seem that funny after all and Whiff still didn't laugh. By now, Griff's bad mood was back—he needed something to really impress his annoying small brother with. Then he had an idea.

"There's a Bear at my school," he announced importantly. He had remembered that one of Hannah's names was Bear, so it was sort of true. "And she's not little either; she's really big!"

Now Whiff really **was** impressed; he stopped scratching his front left leg on a handy rock and stood quite still, staring open mouthed at his big brother.

"A real Bear?" he asked. "Aren't you frightened?"

"I'm never frightened," Griff boasted. "I can **bear** anything!"

But Whiff was too worried to get the joke. (He hardly ever laughed at his brother's jokes, anyway.)

"Has the Bear got teeth?" he quavered. "And horrible claws?"

"It has!" replied Griff, emphatically. After all, Hannah certainly had got teeth, which she often showed when she smiled and there were sort of claw things on the ends of her fingers.

"And if you try to hide, it's really good at finding you," he went on, remembering the hide and seek game.

"Crikey!" said Whiff. He was **really** worried now. Next term, he would be old enough to go to Animal School and he didn't want to go there with a Bear!

"And it's really fierce," continued Griff, enjoying his little brother's frightened expression. "It gives orders and you have to obey…or else!"

He was remembering Hannah being a teacher—she had been fierce, he thought; she hadn't let him and Augustus recite their excellent poem.

"And it's mean," he said. He knew that Hannah wasn't actually mean at all and he was secretly very fond of her, but he was having such fun scaring his little brother that he didn't want to stop.

"And it's got huge brown eyes that stare right at you," he went on. (That was true, anyway).

Suddenly, Whiff had had enough. "Mummy!" he cried, running over the field towards the mother Goat. "I don't want to go to school next term."

"Don't be ridiculous," she said firmly. "Of course you're going. Anyway, bed time now—and you too Griff. Get a move on."

It doesn't take long for animals to go to bed—because there aren't any. Goats sleep outside—and there isn't any toothing or washing to be done either. But poor Whiff couldn't get to sleep. He lay awake, thinking about the horrible Bear at Animal School. And when he did **finally** get to sleep, he had a nasty dream about a huge Bear with enormous brown eyes and white teeth and claws chasing after him. He woke up with a start! Thank goodness, it was only a dream.

But the Bear was real enough, he thought. It was quite late by now and Griff had already set off. (It was too early for school, but he wanted to call in on his friend Augustus the piglet and boast about how he had fooled his baby brother). Now, although Whiff often found his older brother annoying, he certainly wouldn't want him to get hurt. He scampered over to find his mother.

"Mummy!" said Whiff. "You have to help. There's a Bear coming to Animal School and it's huge and fierce with teeth and claws. And Griff might get caught, because it's very good at finding!"

"Goodness," said the mother Goat. "A Bear! How do you know?"

"Griff told me," whimpered little Whiff. "But now he's gone and I'm afraid he might get eaten!"

"O no!" said the mother Goat. What should she do? She herself was much too small to fight a Bear! She needed help.

"I know," she cried. "You stay here and I'll go and find the Bull. He's supposed to be in charge of the school and he's much bigger than us. He'll know what to do." And it was then that, in spite of all the upset and worry, little Whiff made his first ever joke!

"If he's in **charge**, he can **charge** at the Bear!" he announced proudly—and suddenly felt much better.

"Hmmm," said his mother, without laughing at all. (I think she found jokes rather trying!) "Wait here."

And off she bounded—to find the Bull.

Chapter 34
The Bull and the Bear

The Bull lived on his own in a faraway field. As I have said, goats are fast runners, but even so, it took ages for the mother Goat to reach his home. She got a bit lost on the way and had to ask directions from a passing Hare. Finally, tired and hot, she spotted his huge black shape, peacefully grazing at the far end of a large field. She hesitated. Usually, other animals leave bulls alone, as they can be quite fierce—but then this was an emergency. Annoying as her oldest son often was, she didn't want him to be eaten by a Bear. She approached the Bull cautiously.

"Excuse me, Sir Bull," she said.

The Bull lifted up his great black head and stared at her.

"What is it?" he asked, gruffly. He didn't like being bothered. That was one reason why he let the Sheep do all the hard work in his school, which he only visited occasionally, just to make sure things were in good order.

"Well, I think you should know that there's a Bear coming to the school," said the mother Goat. "My son told me that his brother told him that it's a particularly dangerous Bear and it's coming to get the pupils. Please can you help?"

"I can!" bellowed the Bull. No one should be allowed to interfere with his school. And Bears are dangerous. He had better be quick. Bulls are extremely fast runners when aroused—and they can be dangerous too, with their sharp horns. He would find that Bear and stop it. At once!

Without waiting to hear any more details, he lowered his horns and charged. Over the hills and fields he went, along the river valley, his four great hooves making a noise like thunder. All the other animals leaped hurriedly backwards as he passed them; no one would dare to get in the way of a charging Bull. Even

Alona, nursing her sore paw high on her rocky ledge, shuffled back into the safety of her cave.

As for the pupils—well, they were in the middle of a very peaceful lesson inside their brambly schoolroom. The Teacher was still feeling rather snoozly; she too had had a dream but rather a nice one, about meeting a rather handsome sheep with soft black wool, so she decided that the lesson that afternoon would be about dreams. Kaka was just in the middle of telling the others about his brilliant football dream where he had scored six goals in a cup final, when everyone was startled by the noise of thundering hooves coming towards them and making the whole room shake. The hooves skidded to a halt, just outside the back tunnel and a great bellow resounded through the room.

"**Come out, wherever you are! Come outside! Now**!" bellowed the Bull.

Everyone looked at each other in amazement.

"It's the Head," squeaked Hurtle, huddling up close to Hannah. "O dear, O dear, he sounds really cross."

"We must do as he says, my dears," bleated the Sheep. "Two by two, please, in silence!"

And even Kaka stopped his dream story without making a fuss. Heads have to be obeyed, especially Bull Heads!

So, two by two, out filed the animals, the small ones at the front and the bigger ones at the back. Hannah cuddled Hurtle in her arms as she walked through the tunnel, following the goat, who was the next one down in size to her. And there, his huge horned head lowered, his great front hooves pawing the ground, his black eyes glittering angrily, stood the Head.

"**Where is that Bear?**" he bellowed in a terrible voice. "**Come out, Bear!**"

O dear! What Bear? What could he mean? No one knew. Except…Griff the Goat. He could guess what must have happened. Bother that brother! He shuffled his hooves uneasily; then he gave Hannah a nudge with his head.

"I think he means you," he muttered, feeling a bit ashamed of himself.

"Me?" gasped Hannah. Well, she supposed she was a Bear, sort of—but it was only a pet name for her family—and why would that make the Bull so angry? Still, she was a brave little girl and she almost always did as she was told.

"**Come out, Bear,**" repeated the Bull, with another angry bellow, "**wherever you are.**"

And Hannah stepped forward.

"Please, Sir," she said bravely, "I'm a Bear. It's one of my names."

"What? What? You?" stuttered the Bull. "But…you're not a Bear. You're a girl."

"Yes, Sir," said Hannah. "I am. And my name is Hannah. But sometimes my family call me Bear. I don't know why—they just do. Or Small. Because I am the smallest in my family, you see, although I'm not the smallest here. And I'm not really a Bear at all."

The Head raised his head. He stared at her out of his sharp black eyes. Then he gave a huge bellow, the loudest noise Hannah had ever heard! And then Hannah realised that it was a bellow, not of anger but of laughter!

"**You**…**a bear!**" he roared. "**I've come all this way to fight you! O my giddy aunt**!" And his great black sides heaved and shook with laughter. "**What a joke!**"

At this, Griff perked up. He hadn't meant it to be a joke at all, but it felt brilliant to see someone laughing so much—and all because of him! Even so, he didn't think he would own up to the Head; he would keep *his* head well down for the moment. He shuffled cautiously backwards.

Luckily, the Bull was in such a good mood after all that laughing, he decided not to ask any awkward questions. It was a lovely day and his school was safe and sound.

"Well, Bear," he said to Hannah, without bellowing at all. "I'm not going to fight you, because you are a bit Small for me—ho ho ho—but I will show you how fast we Bulls can charge when we want to. Up you get, girl."

He knelt down. Hannah scrambled up on his huge black neck and leaned forward, clinging tight to his two huge horns and he stood up and ran, as fast as the wind, his great hooves thundering, over the hills and far away and then round in a massive great loop until there they were, back in Flower Meadow again. It was the most exciting ride Hannah had ever had. Even riding on the father Deer seemed ordinary in comparison—and it was a million times wilder and faster than riding Donk! The Bull's thundering hooves and wild bellows of joy only added to the excitement. How envious her siblings would be if they could only see her—especially Ben. It was just brilliant.

When she scrambled down again, her hair was wild from all the blowing of the wind and her eyes were sparkling bright. Greatly daring, she stroked the Bull on his huge black nose.

"Thank you, it was wonderful," she said.

After everyone had gone home, Hannah climbed up the rocky crag to see how Alona was. The yellow-eyed cat was waiting for her on the rocky ledge.

"Did you see me riding the Bull?" she asked. "It was brilliant!"

"Did," said Alona. "Saw. Wild!"

"How is your poor paw?" asked Hannah.

"Better," replied Alona. She showed Hannah her front right paw. The ointment must have worked, because there was no blood and only a tiny sore place where once the wound had been.

"Did you kill the rats?" asked Hannah. "How many were there?"

"Not kill," replied the wild cat. "Bite. Three rats' tails. Won't come back."

"O good," said Hannah. "Would you like me to stroke you?" she asked.

Alona didn't say anything, but she snuggled up on the little girl's lap—and purred like anything as Hannah stroked her, from the top of her head right down to the tip of her lustrous grey tail. As she stroked, she sang the first tune that came into her head.

Three wild rats
Three wild rats;
See how they run
See how they run.
They all ran after the wildycat
But she bit off their tails and that was that!
Alona won and they won't come back
Those three wild rats.

Chapter 35
Tails

As Hannah ran home, she just couldn't get the tune of *Three Blind Mice* (or *Three Wild Rats*) out of her head. Indeed, she was still singing it when the others came home. Then the children and their parents all joined in and sang it as a round, which they were very good at. Of course, they had to use the proper Nursery Rhyme words, as Alona was still really a secret, but never mind. Anyway, Hannah managed the round very well, singing together with Charlotte, who showed her where to come in.

That night, tucked up in bed, Hannah asked Mummy a question. There was something that she had been wondering about:

"Mummy," said Hannah. "Why do mice have tails? And rats? And why are their tails so thin and not furry?" She was thinking of Alona's lovely furry tail, but she didn't say that out loud.

"That's a good question," said Mummy. "I don't really know."

Just then David came in, looking for his head torch.

"What don't you know?" he asked.

"Why mice and rats have hairless tails," answered Mummy. "Do you know, David?"

"Actually, I do," said David. (David always knew loads of things!) "Mice need tails to help them climb and to keep their balance. But a thick, furry tail would get in the way because they live in very small places. There just wouldn't be room."

"O yes," said Hannah. She had never seen a rats' home but she remembered the little mice's lovely round home, woven out of golden wheat stems. There probably wouldn't be room for a great furry tail inside—let alone two tails. And also, if you were good at dancing but very tiny, like the mice, a heavy tail would just be a bother—it was difficult enough standing up on tiptoes without having to worry about a great hairy tail as well. She wondered what it would be like to have a furry tail herself. Lovely and warm in bed, she reckoned (you wouldn't need a hot bot) but perhaps a bit too warm in the summer.

She said goodnight to her mother and brother and settled down happily to sleep, her little toes feeling the lovely soft hot bot, which she still had in bed, even though it was nearly Easter now and the weather was definitely getting warmer at night.

Next morning, in Human School, Miss said they should start drawing Easter cards. She explained that they should draw chocolate eggs and rabbits and chicky birds as these were all to do with Easter. Well, these were some of Hannah's favourite things, so she had a lovely time painting them all. She drew a yellow and blue chicky bird with an unexpected green tail (because by the time she got there, the paints had got mixed up and yellow and blue make sludgy green, as I expect you know) and then she drew a grey rabbit. This time she made sure to wash her brush carefully before she painted in a pretty white fluffy tail. The Teacher said the paintings were lovely and the children should keep them at school until they had decided who they were for—then they could write the names on.

Lunch was gloopy egg and toast—yum—with apple pie for pudding. And then it was time for Animal School. The Sheep said they could have the lesson outside, as it was such a nice day and all the Spring flowers were springing up in the meadow—red and blue and pink and white and yellow. They would make a lovely painting too, Hannah thought. But of course, you can't do painting in Animal School, because of animals not having hands and fingers for holding brushes.

The Sheep didn't seem to have any ideas about a lesson (she really was getting lazier and lazier) so Hannah decided to ask if they could learn about tails. Humans managed perfectly well without tails, so what exactly were animals' tails for? "Please, Sheep," she said, waving her hand in the air, "what are tails for?"

"Um," answered the Sheep. "That's a very difficult question. I've never really understood why lambs have such long tails and we grown-up sheep have such short ones."

Everyone stared at the teacher. Her long white woolly coat almost trailed to the ground and you wouldn't guess that there was a little tail hidden underneath. Whereas lambs, as Hannah knew, had really long tails! How funny.

"*Birds'* tails are for flying," announced Kaka the Stork. "They help us balance as we soar through the air and they're really good for steering too."

"It's true, it's true," cheeped little Chicharito. "If I want to fly one way, I just wiggle my tail around in the right direction. It's easy!" And to show them, he flew in a zigzag, left, right, left, right, over Flower Meadow, before turning round and zigzagging back.

"My tail's for steering too," said Tut the Turtle. "Only for swimming, not flying. I'll show you!" And he dived into the little stream and did a brilliant underwater zigzag. He had to stop suddenly when he bumped into an unexpected rock, but luckily his tough shell meant he didn't get hurt. He climbed out again, dripping.

"But why don't frogs have tails?" she asked. "They swim too, don't they?"

"Ah," answered Brekka, the slimiest of the four frogs. "Tails would get in the way of leapfrogging. But we used to have tails when we were tadpoles; and even when we were froglets. Then they just fell off. Come and see."

"Come where?" asked Hannah.

"To our pool!" cried Korax. "We'll show you our younger brothers and sisters. They've still got tails."

So everyone, except the Sheep who was only too glad to enjoy an unscheduled snoozle, followed the leaping frogs a little way downstream to Frog Pool. And there were the tadpoles, millions of them, with lively black tails, wiggling like anything. And on the muddy bank, tiny green froglets were jumping around; everyone could see that they still had little tails, even though otherwise they looked just like baby frogs.

"Their tails will fall off soon," explained Krex, "and then they'll be old enough to come to Animal School."

"What, all of them?" exclaimed Hannah. If all those tadpoles turned into frogs, goodness knows how many there would be at Animal School!

Poor Sheep, she thought, *however is she going to manage all those pupils?*

She tried to count but it was hopeless—they kept wriggling around and, as everyone knows, you can really only count things that stay still.

She had just got up to *thirty-nine*, when she saw a long, smooth ripple in the water; the ripple came nearer and nearer and then up came the sleek head of a water snake, its mouth wide open, its beady eyes gleaming hungrily.

"Gulp!" A dollop of squirming tadpoles disappeared into its mouth. O no! But the frogs didn't seem to mind.

"That always happens," said Brekka, "water snakes love eating tadpoles and there are so many of them it's a good thing they do; otherwise there just wouldn't be room for us all."

Hannah was very surprised. She would certainly mind if anyone ate her brothers and sister in a great gulp! But then there were only three of them, not millions, so she supposed it was different. Anyway, time to go back to Flower Meadow. As the animals splashed or swam back upstream, Hannah thought about the water snake. He was really just one long tail, except for the head on the end. You couldn't even tell where the neck ended and the tail began. That would explain why he was such a good swimmer with excellent steering skills.

The animals made such a clatter and kerfuffle sitting down again in their circle, that the Sheep woke up with a start.

"Now, where were we?" she asked, blearily. "What were we talking about?"

"Tails!" joked Griff the Goat. "Telling tales about tails! I bet you can't guess what my tail is for."

Griff, like all goats, had only a short, stubby and rather manky sort of tail. It didn't look as if it were much use for anything. No one could guess.

"It's for spreading my poo around!" he laughed. "I swish it to get the poo out of the way, so it doesn't make a mess when I want to sit down."

And, although no one believed him and only Augustus the Piglet laughed, what Griff said about goats' tails was actually true! As for Augustus' small curly tail, well, Hannah couldn't see how it could be useful for anything. It didn't swish—it didn't even reach the ground—and you couldn't use it for steering as it was far too curly; you would just go round and round in circles if you tried!

"It's for looking beautiful," explained Augustus. And, although it did look rather sweet in its way, no one believed him either!

Then up spoke Donk, who for once knew the answer to the question.

"My tail is used for swishing away the flies," he explained. "Look."

A particularly large and buzzy fly had just settled down on Donk's behind. With an elegant swish of the tail, he swept it away. He didn't hurt the fly—Donk was much too gentle an animal to hurt anything—and it didn't really put the fly off landing there again, as flies are very persistent creatures. But you could see that Donk was proud of his tail, as he swished it back and forth, back and forth.

Then Hannah remembered her lovely rabbit drawing, with the rabbit's fluffy white tail. Yes, Hurtle had a little round white bobtail, just the same. Whatever could it be for? And why was it white, when the rest of the rabbit was grey? "It's for signalling danger," explained Hurtle, when Hannah asked her. "It shows up white, even in the dark. So if you see something dangerous, like an owl coming near, you flick up your tail to warn the others."

"That's what my tail is for too," said Dora the Deer, shyly. "It's the same shape and it's a warning; if you smell anything dangerous coming you just flick, flick, flick, up goes your tail to warn everyone."

"That really is useful," agreed Hannah.

It had been a long but interesting lesson. Everyone was glad when Augustus announced that it was finally three o'clock and Griff bonged his bell three times. Time to go home.

Except that Hannah wasn't going home just yet. First, she would climb up the rocky crag and ask about Alona's beautiful furry tail.

Chapter 36
Cat Tails

Alona was waiting for her on the rocky ledge. Hannah gave her a biscuit, which she had put in her pocket after lunch; Mummy had said that they had run out of flapjacks and she was just too busy to make any more just yet. They did seem to be getting through them surprisingly quickly! Anyway, the biscuit was excellent—chocolate on each side with a white creamy middle. When the wild cat had finished licking her paws and whiskers clean and settled down beside her, Hannah asked her question.

"Alona," she said, "why do cats have tails?"

Alona stared at her out of her great yellow eyes.

"Hunting," she said. "Crawling along branches. Balance. Getting at nests."

"O," said Hannah. She didn't really like the idea of Alona sneaking along a high branch, her great thick tail swishing from side to side to keep her balance. But she didn't say this out loud. Instead she said, "What else?"

"Jumping," said Alona. "Through the air. Soaring."

"Ah!" said Hannah. This she could understand. She remembered when Alona had made a great leap through the air to save her from the snake; her thick tail had been spread wide—a bit like a bird soaring—and it would have slowed her fall, so she could make a nice soft landing, without hurting herself.

"Anything else?" she asked (sounding a bit like a teacher!)

"Cross," said Alona. She stood up and swished her fluffy tail from side to side, arching her back and extending her claws. "Cross."

She certainly looked very cross and very fierce.

"But you aren't really cross, are you?" Hannah asked anxiously. "What does your tail do if you're happy?"

Alona looked at the little girl. She really did love her, even though she found it difficult to say so. Perhaps she could show Hannah her tail-talk.

"Lift up," she said. "When you come, lift up. Happy!"

"O, Alona, how lovely," said Hannah. "I wish I had a tail so I could lift mine up too. I am always so happy to see you!" And she smiled her biggest smile—which is of course how humans show when they are happy.

"And I know what else it's for!" she exclaimed triumphantly. "It's for stroking."

She reached over and pulled the wild cat onto her lap. And she stroked her friend from the top of her head to the tip of her tail. And as she stroked she sang her favourite song, making the words up as she went along:

I love my Alona, her tail is so long;
And I love cuddling he-er and singing my song.
A-and while I am stroking her soft silky fur,
Then Alona will lift up her tail and she'll purr.

Chapter 37
Chocolate Eggs

Next morning at Human School, Miss said they should paint some more Easter cards. Hannah was pleased—she wanted to give the cards to her cousins, who were coming to stay. She had only done one—the blue, yellow and green chicky bird and so she needed two more. She decided to paint a gigantic Easter Egg, all wrapped up in sparkly paper and tied with a ribbon. She needed lots of colours for this: red and blue and green and purple and pink. Miss said it was beautiful and would she like to use her special gold paint for extra loveliness? Hannah definitely would! By the time she had finished, it looked just amazing. But she still needed one more card. She remembered the flowers in Flower Meadow and decided they would make a lovely card, especially now that she had all the different colour paints ready and waiting. She drew some lovely flowers—a dandelion, a daisy, a poppy, some apple blossom and a beautiful bluebell. Then she grew some lovely long green grass.

"Finished!" she shouted triumphantly. Miss said she could take them home and write the names on later.

She showed them to Mummy, as they walked up the steep street to the village shop. Mummy said she would put them away somewhere safe until it was Easter Day and time for the cousins. And do you know what Mummy wanted to buy at the shop? Chocolate Cream Eggs! You see, she was going to make a treasure hunt for all the children. She counted carefully—three cousins and four of her own made…seven! That gave Hannah a very good idea: she would make a chocolate egg treasure hunt for the animals. They would love that! But she couldn't be bothered to wait for Easter day—she would do it as soon as she got back, so it would be all ready for when the animals arrived for afternoon school.

But there was a problem. She would have to buy the eggs now—and her pocket money was in her bedroom. Bother. But Mummy said she would kindly lend Hannah some money, so that was all right. Only then she thought of another problem. How would the animals manage to unwrap the paper, not having hands and fingers? Um.

"Have you got any Easter eggs without wrapping paper?" she asked the friendly shopkeeper. He said he hadn't, but he showed Hannah a packet of chocolate drops, which were like flat little chocolate eggs, only without the wrapping. Hannah thought they would do perfectly. She tried to count up how many animals were in the school, but she kept getting lost; never mind, it looked as if there were loads of chocolate drops in the packet and Hannah was sure there would be enough. She said goodbye and thank you; she couldn't wait to surprise all the animals with her treasure hunt!

There was just enough time before lunch to get the treasure hunt ready. Hannah quickly found her pocket money to pay Mummy back and Mummy helpfully cut open the top of the packet. Then Hannah zoomed down to Flower Meadow, with the packet of chocolate drops held tight in her hand: she didn't want to drop them (even if they were called **drops**!) Now—where to hide them? She walked through the meadow, stooping down to hide the eggs under flowers and on top of rocks in the stream and under pebbles and in the crook of an old hazel tree. She lost count after seven, but there were masses more, plenty for all the animals. She took care not to hide them too near Alona's rocky ledge—she didn't want any of the animals climbing up there. She still had a few left, so she went through the back tunnel and hid some inside the schoolroom, minding the prickly bits as she poked them on the bramble stems. There—it was done! Time for lunch. Hannah was now so hungry that she almost ate one of the chocolate drops there and then. But no—she must wait for the hunt.

Back she ran to the house. Mummy made her a toasted cheese sandwich with a poached egg on top, which she ate outside on the patio; then she was allowed to choose a yogurt from the fridge. She chose a blackberry yogurt which was delicious and finished her meal with a drink of orange. Yum.

And then it was finally time to go to Animal School and organise the Treasure Hunt.

Chapter 38
The Treasure Hunt

Augustus the piglet was also having an excellent lunch: his mother didn't cook, of course, as only humans know how to do that; instead she led her piglets on foraging expeditions, digging in the earth with their snouts for roots and snuffling up the odd leaf or flower that might be lying nearby. Augustus was feeling very full—pigs are greedy creatures and don't always know when to stop—and had just decided to have a quick lie down before afternoon school, when suddenly he smelt the most delicious smell he had ever come across! Did you know that pigs are particularly good at smelling? That's why their snouts are so moist and snuffly! Anyway, Augustus sniffed and sniffed. He had never smelled anything quite like it before, so sweet and rich and glorious a smell it was. It was definitely coming from the direction of Flower Meadow. He decided to investigate.

Augustus' sensitive snout quickly led him to a beautiful blue flower, blowing gently in the soft wind that ruffled Flower Meadow. With his long snout, he snuffled at the bottom of the stem, where the delicious smell was coming from. Goodness—what was that? With his little twinkly eyes, he peered down at a little round brown shape—a bit like a small egg, only flatter. What could it be? He had never seen anything like it before—but that didn't matter—the important thing was the smell! It was sure to taste delicious. And so it did. O how sweet and slurpery and smooth it felt, as it slipped down into his tummy. He didn't even need to chew on it—not like the tough roots and leaves which he was used to—it just slithered softly down. Heaven! He lifted his snout into the air and sniffed greedily; yes, just over there, among the pebbles, there must be another of the glorious things—and over there, another…and another. Augustus waddled from hiding place to hiding place, his snout scenting out each one of poor Hannah's twenty odd chocolate drops. He just couldn't stop himself. To be fair, he didn't know that Hannah had hidden them specially for a treasure hunt—he probably thought that a mysterious new vegetable had suddenly appeared in the night—but still, he was definitely being greedy! By the time he had eaten the last one, which Hannah had hidden near the stream under a large rock, he was feeling extremely full and sleepy. He settled down under the shade of an old oak tree and in no time at all was fast asleep, snoring loudly and dreaming of deliciousness.

When the Sheep took the register to see if everyone had arrived safely to Animal School, she was surprised to find that Augustus the piglet was absent.

"Have you seen him, Griff?" she asked.

"No," said Griff the Goat. "He usually waits for me in his field, but he wasn't there today. The mother Pig said he had gone off much earlier, but she didn't know why."

"O dear," baaed the Sheep. "We had better go and find him. He might have hurt a trotter and need help. This will have to be a hunting lesson: hunt the pig! Now, how are you going to find him? Paws up!"

"Use your listening skills," said Kaka the Stork, standing on one leg and waving an enormous foot in the air. "Augustus makes loads of noise: listen out for snuffles and grunts and oinks."

"Good," agreed the Sheep. "Anyone else?"

"Use your eyes," said Hurtle. As you know, she had very sharp eyes. "He's a bright pink colour, well unless he's got particularly muddy, so you should easily spot him."

"Very good, Hurtle," said the Sheep. "Anyone else?"

"Use your noses!" exclaimed Griff the Goat. "He can be smelly—a bit like my brother!"

"Good," agreed the Sheep. "Now off you all go and I'll wait just outside."

O bother, thought Hannah. She had really wanted a Hunt the Treasure lesson not a boring Hunt the Pig. Still, she was a kind little girl and if Augustus really had hurt one of his trotters, he should be found as soon as possible.

So off they all went. And, as you might expect, it took hardly any time at all before he was found. Eyes, ears and noses all clearly showed the animals where he was: lying on his back under an oak tree, smelling faintly of a strange sweet deliciousness, looking exceedingly pink (except for his snout which was a strangely smeary dark brown colour) and snoring away like anything. It was quite difficult to wake him, he was so fast asleep. In the end, the frogs dived into the stream to get particularly wet and slippery and then leapfrogged onto his fat pink tummy. That did the trick. Augustus gave one last grunt, opened his piggy eyes and scrambled up, as fast as his considerable weight allowed, onto all four trotters. He clearly hadn't hurt himself at all.

"You're a lazy pig," chortled Griff, as the animals and Hannah made their way back down the valley. Poor Augustus was still feeling very full—and even slightly sick, which was most unusual for a pig. But then, he had just eaten up at least twenty chocolate drops!

When they reached the circle of grass, they saw that Augustus was not the only lazy animal in the school. There, fast asleep, snoring gently in the hot sunlight, lay the Sheep.

"Shall we wake her up?" asked the frogs eagerly. But Hannah decided that this was her chance.

"Not yet," she said. "I can be the teacher for a bit. She does look very tired. Listen everyone: we can play Hunt the Treasure. I've hidden lots of chocolate drops all around the meadow—and they haven't got paper on so you don't need hands. See how many you can find and then bring them back here and we can have a feast! They are delicious!"

"What is chocolate?" asked Donk. Indeed, none of the animals knew so they all listened quietly as Hannah explained.

"It's the best food in the world," she said. "It's brown and quite sticky and if you're not careful it goes all over you, but it smells gorgeous and it tastes of sweetness and smoothness and soft deliciousness. And the chocolate drops are quite small, but if you look carefully, you should spot them—and those of you with good noses might even be able to smell them!"

And at that moment, Augustus realised what he had just gone and done. He had eaten up all Hannah's treasure. O dear, O dear. Augustus was not a bad pig and he decided at once that he would just have to own up.

"Er...stop!" he grunted, as the animals were just rushing off. "Stop, all of you. I...I...um...there isn't any treasure. Not now. I've just eaten it."

"O **Augustus!**" cried all the animals and Hannah in unison. **"You greedy Pig!"**

"Sorry," said Augustus. "I didn't know. I thought it was a new kind of vegetable, you see. Some vegetables are brown, after all," he added. "How was I to know?"

And a very small tear ran down his long snout, making a nice pink channel in his smeary brown skin.

"Never mind," said Hannah, who was a very kind little girl and who didn't like to see her friends upset. "It was supposed to be a Treasure Hunt—and you did hunt the treasure, didn't you?"

The other animals grumbled a bit, but when Hannah said she would save up her pocket money and try to buy some more treasure, they decided to forgive the poor piglet. By this time, it was three o'clock. Griff rang his bell three times and all the animals set off for home—very hungry (except one) and ready for their tea! But the Sheep was still asleep! Hannah stayed behind to wake up her Teacher. She did this very considerately—not at all like a frog—by tugging gently on her thick white coat and singing:

Golden slumbers kiss your eyes (she didn't kiss the Sheep's eyes though, as she thought that might startle her)

Smiles awake you when you rise (there was no difficulty about that bit: Hannah was always smiling)

Wake up dear Tea-teacher, do-o not cry-y
Then I'll stop singing this lullaby.

When the Sheep finally opened her eyes and stood up blearily on her four feet, Hannah stopped singing. She explained that she had organised the afternoon's lesson and it was past three o'clock now and everyone had gone safely home. She explained that the Hunt for the Pig lesson had gone really well and that Augustus hadn't been hurt at all.

"He was just a bit sleepy," she said. "I expect he had too much to eat for his lunch."

But she didn't say anything about the Treasure.

Then she clambered up the rocky crag to see Alona. Hannah explained all about the missing Treasure. She said she would definitely bring Alona some chocolate tomorrow, as it was extremely delicious, even better than flapjacks. Then she rushed home—she wanted to do some more knitting, as the pink scarf was nearly ready. She had decided that she would give it to the Sheep as a present. How amazed her Animal Teacher would be to see bright pink wool! She couldn't wait to give it to her!

Chapter 39
Late for School

At Human School next morning, Miss said it was the last day of term, as the Easter holidays started tomorrow! She had brought in some hard-boiled eggs which she said the children could paint and then eat for breakfast on Easter day. Hannah decided to paint a baby lamb on her egg. She hadn't done a lamb yet and Miss had said it was an Eastery sort of thing. She remembered to give it a lovely long tail as well as soft white wool—beautiful!

After school, she told Daddy, who had come to meet her as Mummy was busy cooking, that she had to go to the village shop. She had found some more pocket money and really wanted to buy another packet of chocolate drops for her animal friends. The shopkeeper was surprised that Hannah needed more chocolate drops, but luckily there was just one packet left in the shop. They walked home especially fast so there was plenty of time before lunch. Just as well: Hannah wanted to finish her knitting. She ran straight upstairs to fetch it, after saying a quick hello to Mummy.

She finished another row and looked at it critically—surely it was long enough now? The Sheep could easily wrap it round her neck. It was the most beautiful pink and she was sure it would make a lovely present to say thank you for having her in Animal School. But she would need Mummy to help finish it. Hopefully, she wouldn't be too busy. Down Hannah skipped, into the kitchen. Mummy was icing a beautiful Easter cake: it was lemon yellow icing and Hannah was just in time to share the licking of the icing bowl with Daddy—yum. Then she helped Mummy put some tiny silver balls and sweet little chocolate eggs, all wrapped in sparkly paper, round the edges. Mummy showed her how to write HAPPY EASTER in icing sugar. It was tricky, but Hannah was good at Hs and As, so she managed to do the first two letters before Mummy finished the rest.

"It's not for today," Mummy said firmly. "We'll have it on Easter day when the cousins are here."

"OK," agreed Hannah. But all that lettering had reminded her. "Mummy," she said, "Please can I write on my Easter cards now? I've done two more, which makes three altogether and I want to give them to the cousins, because there are three of them."

"Good idea," agreed Mummy. "We'll do it now, only mind your sticky fingers. Where are the cards?"

"In my bedroom," said Hannah. So off she rushed again, first to the sink to get rid of all the stickiness and then upstairs to find the three cards: the chicky bird, the sparkling egg and the flowers. She decided that Sam could have the egg and Harry the chicky bird—while the flowers would be just lovely for little Holly!

Mummy was very impressed. She had found a nice thick red crayon and together they wrote out the names. Hannah was very good at H for Harry and Holly and also expert at drawing a wiggly snake S for Sam. Then Mummy found some envelopes and they had to do the names again, so they would know which one was which. She hid them on top of the cupboard, where no one would find them too early by mistake.

Once that was finished, Hannah showed Mummy the scarf.

"Mummy, please can you finish my knitting for me? I want it to be a scarf and to give it to the Sheep as a thank-you-for-having-me present."

"What a lovely idea," said Mummy. And she *cast off* the stitches—which is another way of saying she finished it off nicely, setting the scarf free from the needles. Then Hannah showed Mummy her hard-boiled egg with the picture of the lamb on it and Mummy said it was lovely too and she should keep it in the fridge, ready for Easter breakfast.

Now all this busy-ness took some time.

"O my Goodness," cried Mummy, looking at the kitchen clock, "it's nearly one already. You'll have to hurry, or you'll be late. Quick, what do you want in your sandwich?"

"O, anything, Mummy," said Hannah. "But quickly—I don't want to be late."

But by the time she had gobbled down her sandwich (a honey one, because that was the quickest) and then remembered to pack the chocolate drops as well as the pink scarf into her rucksack, it was nearly ten past one. She simply hurtled down the path. She had just got to the steep bit, when there was Hurtle, slithering down the steep slope from her burrow.

"O dear, O no," the little rabbit was muttering to herself. "I'm going to be late."

She didn't even notice Hannah until she bumped into her on the little path.

"Hannah!" she gasped. "You're late too."

"I know," said Hannah. "There was so much to do. Did you know it's the last day of school today? My Human Teacher said so."

"O goodness," gasped the little rabbit, "is it? I was late because Hop and Scotch had eaten all the lunch up and then I had to dig up some nettles really quickly and I got my paws all dirty and my mother said I couldn't go to school with dirty paws so I had to lick them clean."

"I had sticky hands too," said Hannah. "Anyway, come on. We don't want to be even more late, do we?"

Chapter 40
Last Day of School

Together, Hannah and Hurtle bounded through the front tunnel. But when they got to the brambly school room, they found that it was empty.

"O dear, O dear," exclaimed Hurtle, "we are late; they must have gone outside already."

"Listen," said Hannah.

Faintly through the big back tunnel came the sounds of excited animals.

"Come on," cried Hannah. "Quick!"

The two friends ran as fast as they could through the dim green tunnel and out into the dazzling sunlight of Flower Meadow. There were all the animals, sitting in a circle under the shade of the almond tree—and there, standing on three hooves and waving its front hoof in the air was…not the Sheep but the Bull.

"**You're late,**" bellowed the Head. "**Why are you late, hey?**"

"Sorry," said Hannah. "It was the cake, you see—and the cards and…"

But then she remembered that she wanted the knitting to be a surprise present for the Sheep. Only, where was the Sheep?

"Sorry," said Hurtle. "I got my paws muddy, only it wasn't really my fault."

"**Not your fault, hey?**" said the Bull, "**Lateness is always a fault. Remember that, all of you.**"

"But the Sheep's late!" whispered Griff the goat to his friend Augustus the piglet. Unfortunately for him, the Bull heard!

"**What's that you said, hey? Little animals do not make cheeky comments about their teachers! Do you understand?**" "Yes, Sir," mumbled Griff. "Sorry, Sir."

"Now listen carefully, all of you," bellowed the Bull. **"I have two important announcements to make."**

The animals stared up at him eagerly. What could the announcements be? And where **was** their kindly Sheep Teacher? Was she really late or had she hurt herself?

"My first announcement," said the Bull still in a very loud voice, though not quite as loud as a bellow, "is that today is the last day of the term. Tomorrow, the Easter holiday starts. Is that clear, hey? So none of you come here for school tomorrow, because there won't be any! I shall close the schoolroom. And my second announcement is that **I** am taking the class today," the Bull went on, "because your Sheep teacher is…indisposed."

Indisposed? Whatever did he mean? Even Hannah didn't understand the word.

"Isn't she well?" she asked anxiously.

"She's probably still as-sheep," chortled Griff the goat. "She's always sheeping these days."

"What did I just tell you?" thundered the Bull, who was not amused. "She is not asleep," he continued, looking severely at Griff. "I will show you. Follow me, all of you. Two by two, smallest at the front and **no talking**."

Mystified, the animals sprang to their feet and formed a long line. Hannah was near the back, with little Hurtle in her arms.

"Where are we going?" whispered the little rabbit. The Bull's back was turned and he wouldn't see them whispering. Anyway, whispering isn't really talking, is it?

"What do you think has happened to the Sheep?"

"I don't know," whispered Hannah. "I hope she's all right."

They followed the Bull over the stream, up the other side and along the track, until they reached the farmer's field. There, the flock of sheep (all white ones) was grazing peacefully in the golden sunlight. The Bull led them over to a corner of the field on the far side—and there, curled up on the soft grass was their own dear Teacher; and there, curled up just beside her were two baby lambs!

"Hello, my dears," she beamed up at them. "My two darling babies were born last night! Their names are Blossom and Daisy—two dear little girls!"

She heaved herself up onto her four hooves.

Then the baby lambs scrambled up too; they were very wobbly, but they managed to stand upright—and everyone could see their lovely long tails.

"Hallo, Blossom; hallo, Daisy," said Hannah. What pretty flower names. So all this time, the Sheep had had the two little lambs inside her tummy—no wonder she had been so round and sleepy.

"They were born just in time for Easter!" Hannah exclaimed, thinking of the little lamb which she had painted on her hard-boiled egg.

"So they were, my dear," beamed the Sheep. Everyone watched, as the little lambs had a lovely warm milk drink, tugging at their mother's tummy (which wasn't quite so wobbly now!) their long tails wriggling in delight.

It must taste delicious, thought Hannah. She liked warm milk, even though she preferred hers out of cartons. That reminded her: the chocolate drops.

"Please, Sir Bull," she said, putting her hand in the air. "Please may I give everyone a chocolate drop? They're a bit like Easter eggs and it is nearly Easter and the animals haven't tasted chocolate yet. Except Augustus has, but he didn't know they were really treasure. And I've got enough for everyone, I think. And they are delicious!"

Well, the Head hadn't heard of chocolate, but he did like delicious things—and after all, it was the last day of school—and ever since the misunderstanding about the Bear, he had really liked Hannah.

"Possibly," he said. "But I shall taste the first one," he added, "to make sure that they are suitable for my pupils."

So everyone, including the Bull and the new lambs and the Sheep, sat down in a big circle on the grassy field. Hannah rummaged in her bag and took out the packet, opening it carefully with her useful fingers, so as not to spill any. She put a drop on the palm of her hand and held it out to the Bull; he licked it up with his enormous black tongue. Everyone watched anxiously as he sucked it and swallowed it. Then:

"Delicious!" he pronounced. "Hannah, you may give everyone a chocolate drop."

"And don't **drop** them," chortled Griff and this time everyone laughed!

Hannah was a bit anxious that there wouldn't be enough to go round—but in the end there were—just! She even gave Augustus one, although you could say that he didn't really deserve it. But when she got to the lambs, the Teacher said they were too little for anything except milk, but she would kindly eat theirs instead.

And then, running clumsily across the field, their tummies swaying from side to side, bleating at the tops of their voices, came the whole flock of sheep. O no!

Hannah had just eaten the last chocolate drop herself—there weren't any left. And sheep can be very pushy and bothersome when they want something. And you wouldn't believe the noise they made, all bleating at once! Luckily, however, the Bull took charge: he didn't *charge* them, but he got to his hooves and bellowed in his deepest bass voice: **"Be off with you!"**

And, with startled baaaas, the whole flock turned tail (except you couldn't see their tails beneath their long white coats) and fled.

Then Hannah rummaged again in her rucksack and got out the lovely pink scarf.

"It's for you," she said to the Sheep. "It's a thank-you-for-having-me present, as it's the end of term. I chose pink wool, because I don't expect you've ever seen a pink sheep before. And I hope it fits."

"Why, thank you, my dear," said the kindly Sheep. "It's just the thing for a new mother! Please will you put it on for me?"

"Of course," said Hannah proudly. She stood up and wove the scarf carefully round the Sheep's fat neck. And it did fit—there was just enough scarf left for Hannah to tie a knot with her useful hands, so it wouldn't slip off. Perfect!

And then it was time to go home. The piglet counted three and the goat bonged his bell and off scampered all the little animals.

"Goodbye, goodbye, see you next term," they cried cheerfully, as they made their way homewards.

"Goodbye, Hannah," said the Bull. "And thank you for my chocolate."

And off he bounded, over the hills and far away.

Hannah decided that the best way home would be to walk back with Donk and over the little stream to her house.

"Good bye, Donk. Happy Easter," she cried happily as she waved goodbye.

And it was because she took the quickest way home that Hannah forgot all about going to see Alona on her rocky ledge…

Chapter 41
Spring Greens

David, Charlotte and Ben came bounding down the little path in a very good mood. School was finished for the term—hurray! That meant that homework was finished too—so there was that lovely feeling you get, part lazy and part excited, when you have the whole of the holidays to look forward to. And everyone was excited about Easter eggs and the Treasure Hunt.

"What's for supper?" asked Ben hungrily.

"O dear," said Mummy, "I was so busy making the Easter cake that I forgot all about supper. I expect there might be some bread left over from yesterday which hasn't gone too stale; and there's always tuna and corn mix."

This was clearly not up to Mummy's usual excellent standard, but they supposed they would just have to put up with it. No doubt the cake would be delicious, when the time came.

Mummy was just rummaging inside the cupboard for tins, when there came an excited squeaking at the door. Hannah ran to open it—and there, jumping up and down on the patio was the whole rabbit family, all five of them.

"Come and see! Come and see!" squeaked Hurtle.

"It's the vebe-ga-tables!" squeaked Scotch.

"They've come!" squeaked Hop. "Come on!"

The rabbits bounded full tilt down to the vegetable patch and the whole human family chased after them (even David, who was a very fast runner couldn't catch up). And when they got there, what a glorious sight met their eyes!

Hannah could see, poking up from the earth, exciting round onion shapes and lovely long, orange carrot tops under their green feathery leaves. And what was this? In the rabbits' patch was a whole row of green bean stalks—not as high as the ones in the Jack-and-the-Beanstalk story, but definitely looking tall and important. And there were masses of cabbages and broccoli and spinach, not to mention nettles.

"Spring greens," said Mummy. "Brilliant!"

How thrilled those rabbits were with their very own vegetables! They would have dug the whole lot up at once, if Father Rabbit hadn't stopped them. He explained that if they had just two onions and two carrots and two beans each, it would make an excellent supper and then they could keep the rest of the vegetables for another day.

"What about the strawberries?" asked little Scotch. He went over to look at the neat row of strawberry plants. Well, there weren't any red berries, not yet—but there were lots of little white strawberry flowers where the berries would be—perhaps in a few more weeks' time. They would just have to wait.

But they couldn't wait for supper. The human family watched as the rabbit family used their furry paws to dig up their supper—Hannah helped them count, so they didn't take more than two each of everything. What a feast! The rabbits ate it there and then, speedily nibbling and crunching the raw vegetables and not bothering at all about the earthy bits that came with them—or the odd slug or two.

"Thank you very much," said Mother Rabbit politely, when they had finished. "There's nothing like really fresh vegetables, is there?"

"No indeed," replied Mummy. Then she had a good idea. "I know; let's have stir fry vegetables for supper!" Everyone agreed, so now it was the rabbits' turn to watch the human family dig up their supper, using handy trowels and forks and shaking the earth off. Ben turned on the hose, so that he could wash the vegetables—and most of the children (both human and rabbit) got quite wet in the process. It was fun. But of course, humans do like their vegetables cooked, so the two families said goodbye and went their separate ways.

After her delicious spring green supper, Hannah settled down happily on the swing, swinging her legs and watching the red sun sink slowly down over the horizon. It was a beautiful Spring evening. She could hear the buzz and hum of a few late insects, making their way home before dark; and the sweet singing of blackbirds coming from the trees.

But then she heard a sound, so sad and so haunting that it made the hair on the back of her neck tingle. What was it? She stood up and listened with all her might. There it came again…the long wailing cry of a distant caterwaul.

"Alona!" gasped Hannah. "O no; I forgot!"

And the next moment, she was off, running as fast as she had ever run in her whole life, back down the little path towards Flower Meadow.

Chapter 42
Always and Ever

As she ran along the path, her breath coming in great gasps, Hannah could hear the desolate caterwauling getting louder and louder. On and on, it went. By the time Hannah had reached the foot of the rocky crag, it was almost dark—the great red sun was sinking fast and a cool evening wind had sprung up. Hannah looked upwards: there on the ledge, she could just make out the dim grey shape of the wild cat; but the yellow eyes must have been closed, for she couldn't see their gleam. And still the noise went on.

Breathlessly, Hannah scrambled up the dark crag until she reached the rocky ledge. There stood Alona, her back arched, her eyes shut, her mouth wide open as she cried and cried.

"Alona!" gasped Hannah. "It's me; don't cry—it's me!" And she picked the wild cat up in her arms and just stood there, perched high above the world, holding her friend as tightly as she could.

"It's me; I'm here; don't cry."

At last, the terrible wailing died down—and there was a great quietness. Then Alona spoke:

"Not coming. Never again. All alone. Lonely."

"I'm sorry, I'm sorry," said Hannah. "It's just that there were the baby lambs, you see, so I went to see and then there were all the vegetables and…" It was hard to explain.

"Bull said," interrupted Alona. "Said, no more. Not to come back. Never."

"No, not never," explained Hannah, still hugging the wild cat. "Just for the holidays. And he only meant the Animal School, not Flower Meadow. I can still come here every day. Even more, because I'll have the whole time free to come and see you."

And gradually, as she held Alona tight, the wild cat became calm; her heart stopped pounding, her claws went in and her tail lifted up in happiness. She stared at Hannah out of her beautiful yellow eyes.

"Promise?" she asked. For, although Alona was still the proud wild cat who walked by herself, she had learned to love Hannah.

"I promise," said Hannah solemnly.

She sat down on the ledge, cuddling the wild cat on her lap; she began to stroke her, very gently, from the top of her head to the tip of her tail. And as she stroked, she sang their special song,

Wildycat, Wildycat, where have you been,
So grey in the darkness, you couldn't be seen?
Wildycat, Wildycat, will you be my friend?

Always and ever, right up to the end!

And Alona purred like anything.

By now, it was nearly dark; as Hannah watched from the high rocky ledge, she could see the sun sink below the horizon in a glorious blaze of red and gold and purple; the night wind blew cold, ruffling Alona's fur. Hannah shivered. It was time to say goodnight. The others would be wondering where she was.

So she gave her friend one last stroke and scrambled back down the rocky crag to make her way across Flower Meadow, past Frog Pool and along the little path to home.

Epilogue

One day in the garden, Hannah and Ben were playing in the sandpit when along hopped a rabbit!

"Would you like to come to tea?" asked the rabbit.

"O yes, please!" said Hannah and Ben together. They were feeling **hungry**. So off they all went.

Poor rabbit! He had tried so hard to get a great feast ready for his guests. But he forgot that children don't tend to like raw vegetables.

O dear…

Broccoli?
Too smelly!
Aubergine?
Not keen…
Cauliflower?
No fear!
Asparagus?
Worse and worse!
Avocado?
Urgh! O! Waaa! No!
Courgette?
Too…wet…
Brussel Sprout?
Take it out!
Cabbage?
Rubbish!
Artichoke?
It's a joke!
Spinach?

Not much…
Potato?
No, no, no, no!
D' you like swede?
Haven't tried…
Coriander?
Can't remember…
Raw carrot?
Not a lot!
Onion?
O, come on!
Garlic?
Feel sick!
Parsnip?
O…flip!
Parsley?
Ghastly!
Celery?
Too scrunchy!
Mushroom?
Hmmmm…
Chilli?
Don't be silly!
Corn?
Yawn!
Beetroot?

No…PROPER food:
Not horrible
Raw vegetables!
Silly bunny—
Toast and honey!
Silly rabbit—
Chocolate biscuit!

O dear! But then
Hannah and Ben
Suddenly knew
What to do.

Rabbit, look,
Let's cook!
Over here
On the fire,
On the grass.
Mummy, pass
Pots and cans,
And frying pans.

Boiled and mashed,
Steamed and smashed,
Fried and roasted,
Baked and toasted,
Add some spice—
Very nice!
Salt and pepper,
Lovely supper—
Very good
HUMAN food!

Rabbit, come,
Do you want some?
Don't be shy,
Have a try,
Have a smell…
Don't feel well?

Rabbit sneezes,
Rabbit wheezes,
Whiskers twitch,
Ears itch;

Wrinkles nose—
And off he goes!
And Hannah and Ben?
Well, yum, yum, yum.
Very scrummy
In their tummy—
BEAUTIFUL
Cooked Vegetables!

THE END